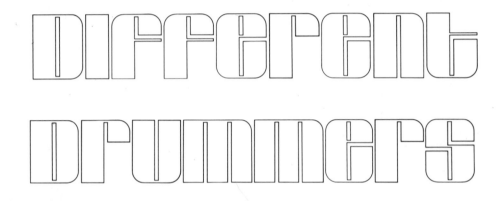

Different Drummers

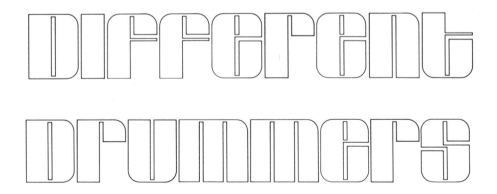

Different Drummers

Consulting Editor:

CHRISTOPHER R. REASKE
University of Michigan

Different Drummers

READINGS FOR COMPOSITION

EDITED BY CECILE ROCHON VYE AND ELIZABETH CANAR

RANDOM HOUSE
NEW YORK

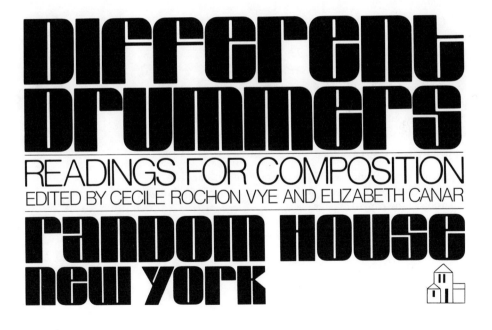

First Edition

987654321

Copyright ©1973 by Random House, Inc.

Library of Congress Cataloging in Publication Data

Vye, Cecile Rochon, 1935–   comp.
    Different drummers.

    1. College readers. I. Canar, Elizabeth, 1919–
joint comp.   II. Title.
PE1122.V93   808'.04275   72–10102
ISBN 0–394–31304–6

Manufactured in the United States of America. Composed by Volt Information Sciences, Inc., New York, N.Y. Printed and bound by Halliday Lithograph, West Hanover, Mass.

Design by James McGuire

permissions
acknowledgments

Acme Boot Company, advertisement, "The Dingo Man."
Reprinted by permission.

John W. Aldridge, excerpt from *In the Country of the Young.* Copyright © 1969 by John W. Aldridge. Reprinted by permission of Harper & Row, Publishers, Inc.

Saul Alinsky, "Gumming up the Campus" from *The Professional Radical: Conversations with Saul Alinsky* by Marion K. Sanders. Copyright © 1965, 1969, 1970 by Marion K. Sanders and Saul Alinsky. Reprinted by permission of Harper & Row, Publishers, Inc.

W. H. Auden, "The Unknown Citizen" from *Collected Shorter Poems 1927–1957.* Copyright 1950 and renewed 1968 by W. H. Auden. "Under Which Lyre? A Reactionary Tract for the Times" from *Collected Shorter Poems 1927–1957.* Copyright 1946 by W. H. Auden. Reprinted by permission of Random House, Inc. and Faber and Faber Ltd.

Hal Bennett, "Dotson Gerber Resurrected" from *Playboy Magazine* (November 1970). Copyright © 1970 by George H. Bennett. Reprinted by permission of William Morris Agency, Inc., on behalf of the author.

Bennett M. Berger, "The New Stage of American Man—Almost Endless Adolescence" from *The New York Times Magazine* (November 2, 1969). Copyright © 1969 by The New York Times Company. Reprinted by permission of the New York Times Company.

Franz Boaz, "Prayer to the Young Cedar" from *Ethnology of the Kwakiutal, 35th Annual Report of the Bureau of American Ethnology, Part I.* Copyright 1921 by Smithsonian Institution Press. Reprinted by permission of Smithsonian Institution Press.

Ray Bradbury, excerpt from *Dandelion Wine.* Copyright © 1957 by Ray Bradbury. Reprinted by permission of Harold Matson Company, Inc.

"Bridging the Generation Gap" from *The New Republic* (November 28, 1970). Copyright © 1970 by Harrison-Blaine of New Jersey, Inc. Reprinted by permission of *The New Republic.*

Richard Cavendish, frontispiece drawing and excerpts from "Astrology" and "The Black Mass" from *The Black Arts.* Copyright © 1967 by Richard Cavendish. Reprinted by permission of G. P. Putnam's Sons and Collins-Knowlton-Wing, Inc.

Stuart Chase, excerpt from "Gobbledygook" in *Power of Words.* Copyright 1953, 1954 by Stuart Chase. Reprinted by permission of Harcourt Brace Jovanovich, Inc.

John Cheever, "The Season of Divorce" from *The Enormous Radio and Other Stories.* Copyright 1953 by John Cheever. Reprinted by permission of the publisher, Funk & Wagnalls Publishing Company, Inc.

Daniel Cohen, "Witches in our Midst" from *Science Digest* (June 1971). Copyright © 1971 by The Hearst Corporation. Reprinted by permission of Science Digest.

Harvey Cox, excerpt from "Mystics and Militants" from *The Feast of Fools.* Reprinted by permission of Harvard University Press. "Sex and Secularization" from *The Secular City,* Revised Edition. Copyright © 1965, 1966 by Harvey Cox. Reprinted by permission of The Macmillan Company.

Victor Hernandez Cruz, "Megalopolis" from *Snaps.* Copyright © 1969 by Victor Hernandez Cruz. Reprinted by permission of Random House, Inc.

Joe Darion, lyrics from "The Impossible Dream" from the musical play *Man of La Mancha,* words by Joe Darion and music by Mitch Leigh. Copyright by Andrew Scott, Inc., Helena Music Corporation, Sam Fox Publishing Company, Inc. Used by special permission.

Frank Marshall Davis, "Roosevelt Smith" from *Black Insights,* edited by Nick Aaron Ford. Copyright © 1971 by Frank Marshall Davis. Reprinted by permission of the author.

John Diebold, excerpt from *Man and the Computer.*

Copyright © 1968 by Frederick A. Praeger, Publishers. Reprinted by permission of Frederick A. Praeger, Publishers.

Peter Drucker, "Man Moves into a Man-made Environment" from *Technology in Western Civilization,* Vol. II, edited by Melvin Kranzberg and Carroll W. Pursell, Jr. Copyright © 1967 by The Regents of The University of Wisconsin. Reprinted by permission of Oxford University Press, Inc.

Bob Dylan, lyrics from "The Times They Are A-Changin'." Copyright © 1968 by M. Witmark & Sons. Reprinted by permission of the author and Warner Bros. Music.

Paul R. Ehrlich and Richard L. Harriman, "Spaceship in Trouble" from *How to Be a Survivor.* Copyright © 1971 by Dr. Paul R. Ehrlich and Richard L. Harriman. Reprinted by permission of Ballantine Books, Inc.

Loren Eiseley, excerpts from "The World Eaters" and "The Last Magician" from *The Invisible Pyramid.* Copyright © 1970 by Loren Eiseley. Reprinted by permission of Charles Scribner's Sons.

Jacques Ellul, "A Look at the Year 2000" from *The Technological Society.* Copyright © 1964 by Alfred A. Knopf, Inc. Reprinted by permission of Alfred A. Knopf, Inc.

Don Fabun, illustration from *Communications: The Transfer of Meaning.* Copyright © 1968 by Kaiser Aluminum & Chemical Corporation. Reprinted by permission of Benziger Bruce & Glencoe, Inc., a division of The Macmillan Company.

Julius Fast, "Three Clues to Family Behavior" from *Body Language.* Copyright © 1970 by Julius Fast. Reprinted by permission of the publisher, M. Evans and Company.

F. Scott Fitzgerald, "Letter to Scottie" from *The Letters of F. Scott Fitzgerald,* edited by Andrew Turnbull. Copyright © 1963 by Frances Scott Fitzgerald Lanahan. Reprinted by permission of Charles Scribner's Sons.

George Frazier, "The Masculine Mystique" from *Mademoiselle* (July, 1970). Reprinted by permission of the author.

Betty Friedan, "The Crisis in Woman's Identity" from *The Feminine Mystique.* Copyright © 1963 by Betty

Friedan. Reprinted by permission of W. W. Norton & Company, Inc.

Allen Ginsberg, "America" from *Howl and Other Poems.* Copyright © 1956, 1959 by Allen Ginsberg. Reprinted by permission of City Lights Books.

Nikki Giovanni, "The Weather as a Cultural Determiner" from *Gemini.* Copyright © 1971 by Nikki Giovanni. Reprinted by permission of the publisher, The Bobbs-Merrill Company, Inc.

Marilyn Goldstein, excerpt from "The Case for Symbols" from *Midwest Magazine: Magazine of the Chicago Sun-Times* (March 19, 1972). Copyright © 1972 by *Newsday.* Reprinted by permission of the Los Angeles Times/Washington Post News Service.

Robert Graves, "The Cool Web" from *Collected Poems 1955.* Copyright © 1955 by Robert Graves. Reprinted by permission of Collins-Knowlton-Wing, Inc.

John Haines, "The Legend of Paper Plates" from *The Stone Harp.* Copyright © 1969 by John Haines. Reprinted by permission of Wesleyan University Press.

Edward and Mildred Hall, "The Sounds of Silence" from *Playboy Magazine* (June, 1971). Copyright © 1971 by Playboy. Reprinted by permission of Playboy.

Philip Handler, "In Man's View of Himself" from *Biology and the Future of Man,* edited by Philip Handler. Copyright © 1970 by Oxford University Press, Inc. Reprinted by permission of Oxford University Press, Inc.

Sheldon Harnick, words from "Sunrise, Sunset" by Sheldon Harnick and Jerry Bock from the production *Fiddler on the Roof.* Copyright © 1964 by Sunbeam Music, Inc. (A Metromedia Company). Used by permission of Sunbeam Music, Inc. All rights reserved.

Ernest Hemingway, "Hills Like White Elephants" from *Men Without Women.* Copyright 1927 by Charles Scribner's Sons, renewal copyright © 1955 by Ernest Hemingway. Reprinted by permission of Charles Scribner's Sons.

Nicholas Johnson, "The Myth of Lack of Impact" from *How to Talk Back to Your Television Set.* Copyright © 1967, 1968, 1969, 1970 by Little, Brown and Company. Reprinted by permission of Atlantic-Little, Brown and Co.

LeRoi Jones, "In Memory of Radio" from *Preface to a Twenty-Volume Suicide Note.* Copyright © 1961 by LeRoi Jones. Reprinted by permission of Totem Press/Corinth Books.

Gerald Leach, "Runaway Biology?" from *Chicago Sun-Times Viewpoint* (October 25, 1970), reprinted from *The Observer* (London). Copyright © 1970 by Gerald Leach. Used by permission of the author.

John Logan, "The Picnic" from *Ghosts of the Heart.* Copyright © 1960 by University of Chicago Press. Reprinted by permission of the author.

Charlotte Leon Mayerson, "Neighborhood," "Juan Gonzales," and "Peter Quinn" from *Two Blocks Apart,* edited by Charlotte Leon Mayerson. Copyright © 1965 by Holt, Rinehart and Winston, Inc. Reprinted by permission of Holt, Rinehart and Winston, Inc.

Carson McCullers, "The Sojourner" from *The Ballad of the Sad Cafe.* Copyright © 1955 by Carson McCullers. Reprinted by permission of the publisher, Houghton Mifflin Company.

Frank O'Connor, "First Confession" from *The Stories of Frank O'Connor.* Copyright 1951 by Frank O'Connor. Reprinted by permission of Alfred A. Knopf, Inc. and A. D. Peters and Company.

Natalie Petesch, "Ericka." Copyright © 1972 by Natalie Petesch. Reprinted by permission of Harold Matson Company, Inc.

James Rado and Gerome Ragni, lyrics from "Aquarius." Copyright © 1966, 1967, 1968 by James Rado, Gerome Ragni, Galt MacDermot, Nat Shapiro, and United Artists Music Co., Inc. All rights controlled and administered by United Artists Music Co., Inc. Used by permission.

Gene Raskin, words from "Those Were the Days", words & music by Gene Raskin. TRO-Copyright © 1962, 1968 by Essex Music, Inc. Used by permission of Essex Music, Inc.

Malvina Reynolds, words from "Little Boxes," words and music by Malvina Reynolds. Copyright © 1962 by Schroder Music Co. (ASCAP) Reprinted by permission of Schroder Music Co.

Leo Rosten, "Mr. K*A*P*L*A*N the Magnificent" from *The Many Worlds of L*E*O R*O*S*T*E*N.* Copyright © 1964 by Leo Rosten. Reprinted by permission of Harper & Row, Publishers, Inc.

Acknowledgments vii

Philip Roth, "The Conversion of the Jews" from *Goodbye, Columbus*. Copyright © 1959 by Philip Roth. Reprinted by permission of the publisher, Houghton Mifflin Company.

Mike Royko, "Neighborhood-Towns" from *BOSS: Richard J. Daley of Chicago*. Copyright © 1971 by Mike Royko. Reprinted by permission of the publisher, E. P. Dutton & Co., Inc.

Louis B. Salomon, "Univac to Univac" from *Harper's Magazine* (March 1958). Copyright © 1958 by Minneapolis Star and Tribune Co., Inc. Reprinted by permission of the author.

James V. Schall, "Ecology—an American Heresy?" from *America* (March 27, 1971). Copyright © 1971 by *America*. All rights reserved. Reprinted by permission of the publisher.

Anthony Schillaci, "Film As Environment" from *Saturday Review* (December 28, 1968). Copyright © 1968 Saturday Review, Inc. Reprinted by permission of the author and publisher.

Peter Schrag, "Growing Up on Mechanic Street" from *Out of Place in America*. Copyright © 1970 by Peter Schrag. Reprinted by permission of Random House, Inc.

W. B. Seabrook, "The Witch's Vengeance" from *The Evil People,* edited by Peter Hauning. Reprinted by permission of Leslie Frewin Publishers, Ltd.

Anne Sexton, "Cinderella" from *Transformations*. Copyright © 1971 by Anne Sexton. Reprinted by permission of the publisher, Houghton Mifflin Company.

Robert Somerlott, excerpt from *Here, Mr. Splitfoot*. Copyright © 1971 by Robert Somerlott. Reprinted by permission of The Viking Press, Inc.

Alvin Toffler, excerpts from "The 800th Lifetime," "The Accelerative Thrust," and "A Diversity of Life Styles" from *Future Shock*. Copyright © 1970 by Alvin Toffler. Reprinted by permission of Random House, Inc.

John Updike, "A & P" from *Pigeon Feathers and Other Stories*. Copyright © 1962 by John Updike. Reprinted by permission of Alfred A. Knopf, Inc. Originally appeared in the *The New Yorker*. "Ex-Basketball Player" from *The Carpentered Hen and Other Tame Creatures*. Copyright © 1957 by John Updike. Reprinted by permission of Harper & Row, Publishers, Inc. Originally appeared in *The New Yorker*.

Judith Viorst, "A Women's Liberation Movement Woman" from *People and Other Aggravations*. Copyright © 1970, 1971 by Judith Viorst. Reprinted by permission of The World Publishing Company.

Kurt Vonnegut, Jr., "Epicac" from *Welcome to the Monkey House*. Copyright 1950 by Kurt Vonnegut, Jr. A Seymour Lawrence Book / Delacorte Press. Reprinted by permission of the publisher. Originally appeared in *Collier's*.

John Anthony West and Jan Gerhard Toonder, "Free Will or No Free Will? The Eternal Question" from *The Case for Astrology*. Copyright © 1970 by John Anthony West and Jan Gerhard Toonder. Reprinted by permission of Coward, McCann & Geoghegan, Inc. and Robert P. Mills Ltd.

Lynn White, Jr., excerpt from "The Historical Roots of Our Ecologic Crisis" from *Science* (March 10, 1967). Copyright © 1967 by the American Association for the Advancement of Science. Reprinted by permission of the author and publisher.

Tom Wicker, "Arcadia and Aquarius," Introduction from *The New York Times Great Songs of the Sixties,* edited by Milton Okun. Copyright © 1970 by Quadrangle Books, Inc. Reprinted by permission of Quadrangle Books, Inc.

Norbert Wiener, from "Introduction" to *Cybernetics*. Copyright © 1948, 1961 by Massachusetts Institute of Technology. Excerpt from *God and Golem, Inc.* Copyright © 1964 by Massachusetts Institute of Technology. Reprinted by permission of the M.I.T. Press.

Elie Wiesel, excerpts from *Night*. Copyright © 1958 by Les Editions de Minuit. English translation copyright © 1960 by MacGibbon & Kee. Reprinted by permission of Hill and Wang, a division of Farrar, Straus & Giroux, Inc.

John A. Williams, "Son in the Afternoon" from *The Angry Black*. Reprinted by permission of the author.

Keith Wilson, "Growing Up" from *Sketches for a New Mexico Hill Town*. Copyright © 1966, 1967 by Keith Wilson. Reprinted by permission of the author.

If a man does not keep pace with
his companions, perhaps it is
because he hears a different drummer.
Let him step to the music which he
hears, however measured or far
away.

Henry David Thoreau   *Walden* XVIII

preface

Different Drummers will appeal to students and teachers who enjoy reading, investigating and thinking. Its purpose is to examine contemporary issues which are broadly based and command more than passing attention. We emphasize human values, sex roles, the supernatural—both holy and unholy, man's relationship to his environment and his creations, and the complex nature of communication.

Because an "issue" is a matter in dispute, we present a diversity of viewpoints and a wide range of genres, authors and ideas. We juxtapose Bennett Berger's study of college students in "Endless Adolescence" with Peter Schrag's description of blue-collar youth in "Growing Up on Mechanic Street." W.H. Auden's "The Unknown Citizen" is a foil to Alvin Toffler's "A Diversity of Life Styles." Opposing John Haines' poem "The Legend of Paper Plates" with the Kwakiutl "Prayer to the Young Cedar" succinctly illustrates a major difference between two cultures. In Chapter 2, "Hers and His," we move away from the polemical rhetoric of women's liberation to seek a middle ground by examining the sex roles of both men and women. Elsewhere the writings of Nikki Giovanni, John A. Williams, and Victor Hernandez Cruz provide a racial and ethnic balance.

Chapter 3, "Religion and the Occult," is especially provocative because one does not expect to explore the shared characteristics of two such dissimilar topics. Yet both require belief and neither submits to rational analysis.

Whenever possible we have included humor to encourage students to develop this important perspective on the human condition. It would be a worthwhile project to find additional comic pieces and to share them in the classroom.

The authors represented are free-lance writers, educators, scientists, poets, journalists, and fiction writers. Some selections are familiar—Harvey Cox's "Sex and Secularization," John Updike's "A & P," and Philip Roth's "The Conversion of the Jews." Others are fresh and engaging. Natalie Petesch's fine short story "Ericka" appears here in print for the first time. Hal Bennett's "Dotson Gerber Resurrected" was chosen as one of the best short stories of 1970. Elie Wiesel's "Night," a chilling account of the suffering of the Jews in World War II, provides new perspectives for those who are familiar with *The Diary of Anne Frank*.

In using *Different Drummers* we hope you will discover and enjoy its unusual characteristics. Each chapter is thematically integrated, and all the chapters are linked by the search for values. While we provide introductions to the chapters, headnotes and study questions for each selection, as well as general questions at the end of each chapter, we have by no means exhausted all the possibilities for discussion. We encourage you to use the text creatively and to investigate its variety and interrelationships, which we feel are the strongest features of the book.

ACKNOWLEDGMENTS

We would like to express our appreciation to all our friends and colleagues who aided us in compiling this anthology, especially to Malcolm Vye whose assistance made Chapter 4 possible. We are also indebted to Rev. Raymond Tillrock, Marilyn Jacobson, Mary Seale, Jim Smith, Helen Litton, Christopher Reaske, and the librarians of Kendall College and the Wilmette Public Library. Finally, we wish to thank the administration of Kendall College who created the atmosphere that made our collaboration possible.

C.R.V.
E.C.

Evanston, Illinois
1972

Contents

xvi   Contents

3 Religion and the Occult / 161

4 Fill the Earth and Subdue It / 239

Contents **xvii**

xviii   Contents

Contents   **xix**

different
drummers

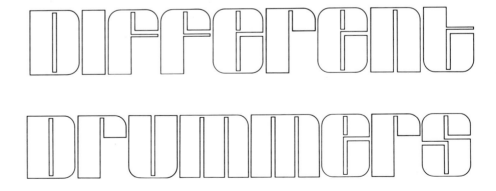

1

VALUES

Although the generation gap is generally believed to be a lack of communication and understanding between two age groups, it is really a gap between the values of those who cherish the past and those who seek to establish a new order. In "Values" we examine the nature of this gap: the *awakening* to the problem, the *turmoil* of defining the issues, the *milieu* of different groups, and the *challenge* of creating new values and life styles.

The values of the "good old days," or, to use Tom Wicker's term, "Arcadia," were challenged by militants who claimed that the democratic procedures which seemed to represent the "American way" had failed to solve the problems created by Vietnam, minorities, technology, and the preservation of the environment. Many longed for the "Age of Aquarius," when peace and understanding would rule the world. But such an age is not born effortlessly by a particular conjunction of the planets. As Wicker suggests, it comes, if at all, through painful self-examination and an honest commitment to establishing a world based on a sense of values and not on material standards.

As hostility between the Arcadians and Aquarians grew, the kind of disillusionment that Allen Ginsberg expresses in "America"—disenchantment with militarism, institutions, materialism, and the Puritan ethic—came to be identified with the New Left and eventually with college students. The Arcadians, who felt their way of life threatened, reacted very much like John Aldridge. They grew weary of the youth cult and the extraordinary attention given to the Now Generation. Upholding traditional American values, they harshly criticized the dissenters.

Sometimes the more reasonable voices were lost in the shouting. The students in "Bridging the Generation Gap" explain their position. They appreciate the benefits they derive from American affluence, yet they are disturbed by pollution, war, and the deprivation suffered by minorities. They dislike the hostility that exists between generations. In discussing the difficulty of reconciling the factions in American society, Representative Udall pinpoints the problem when he says, "Isn't it likely . . . that we are all captives to a certain degree of our own backgrounds, needs, and experiences?"

In order to understand the complexity of the value gap, it is helpful to delve into the milieu of different groups in American society—the college students, the blue-

4 Values

collar youth, and the blacks—to learn more about the forces which shape their beliefs and allegiances. As Bennett M. Berger tells us, many young Americans who spend long years preparing for careers and professions must adapt to "Endless Adolescence." For some this postponement of adult responsibility is intolerable. We learn from Peter Schrag that "Growing Up on Mechanic Street" creates different problems for blue-collar youth, who experience the boredom of unimaginative high school training and later routine employment. In "Son in the Afternoon," John A. Williams writes of the hostility that still exists between the races despite the success of many talented blacks.

As we look to the future, we find that the legacy of the Sixties is the challenge of creating new identities and new life styles. Will we become as faceless as "The Unknown Citizen" of Auden's poem? Will we submit to social and psychological pressures to belong and choose a life style out of need rather than conviction? Or like Sammy in John Updike's "A & P," will we buck the system and find ourselves adrift without the comforting yet stifling perimeters of convention? If, as Alvin Toffler tells us, the choice of a life style is a superdecision, we must recognize its repercussions in all areas of our lives, especially the role it plays in determining our values.

AWAKENING

ARCADIA AND AQUARIUS
TOM WICKER

The divergent values that emerged in the Sixties were frequently embodied in the clichés, the "good old days" and the "Age of Aquarius." In this essay, which was written as an introduction to a songbook of the Sixties, Tom Wicker discusses the idyllic nature of these two views of American society, claiming that the one never existed and that the other is not viable. Emphasizing the importance of change, he calls for the establishment of new values.

Some believe it really was the dawning of the Age of Aquarius, the beginning of an era of

> . . . harmony and understanding,
> sympathy and trust abounding,
> no more falsehoods or derisions,
> golden living dreams of visions,
> mystic crystal revelation
> and the mind's true liberation. . .

and thus they said the decade of the Sixties heralded a time when

> . . . peace will guide the planets
> and love will steer the stars.

Tom Wicker (1926–), author and journalist, is an associate editor of *The New York Times*.

This idyllic view could be made momentarily plausible to even the most jaded audience (despite some reservations as to how the mind should be liberated) by the frenetic young cast of "Hair," the American Tribal Love-Rock Musical, a Broadway show that my daughter informed me "everyone ought to be required to see" and which stands with Woodstock as symbols of the flower-child experience of the Sixties.

But the older you were, and the more weary, the shorter the hold the Aquarius notion was likely to have. Less mindblowing but still optimistic was the view of Senator Eugene McCarthy, the Pied Piper of Political Participation. With many others, he saw the decade as a sort of solemn national revival in which youthful evangelists equipped with "intelligence, a deep sense of moral responsibility, an openness of spirit and hope" made "deep, even dangerous commitments." And that meant that "in retrospect the Sixties will be distinguished as the decade in which the spirit of America, largely through its young people, was renewed and revitalized."

Others were not so sanguine, as they watched President Richard M. Nixon usher in the Seventies. Not a few mothers, before and after seeing "Hair," looked at their offspring and wondered with Tevye and Golde of Anatevka:

> Is this the little girl I carried?
> Is this the little boy at play?
> I don't remember growing older,
> When did they?

And there were also those who found champions in Governor Ronald Reagan or Vice President Spiro T. Agnew—who saw the "revolution" of the Sixties as a menace to American traditions, democratic ideals, and property values. Some spoke darkly of parallels to the conditions that spawned Nazi Germany; the national commission on civil disorders warned of "two nations, separate, and unequal"—black and white. And why not, voices kept asking plaintively throughout a decade of marching and alarm, talk about what's right with America?

So those were the days, my friend, we thought they'd never end, but what did they really mean, if anything? What *were* the Sixties all about, other than the age-old phenomena of man, tears and laughter and love and hate and the melancholy of time passing . . . *oh my friends we're older but no wiser.* After all, for many, life in the Sixties was, as always, a cabaret, even if we *were* waist deep in the Big Muddy; and if still others had to live in the profound faith that we shall overcome, for want of anything better to believe, they at least had John Kennedy to remind them that life is inherently unfair.

I am not sure you can find the meaning of a time, if it had one, in its music, and this book on songs from *Up, Up and Away* through *(I Can't Get No) Satisfaction* to *Alice's Restaurant* makes the point. Let us suppose that The Beatles, some of whose work is, authorities say, "as carefully constructed as a Mozart quartet," made the authentic sound of the Sixties. One might draw a conclusion from that; but what would he then do with *Where Have all the Flowers Gone?* or Nashville or Aretha Franklin or *My Way* bellowed by a travesty of what used to be Frank Sinatra when I was learning to jitterbug at the high school gym thirty years ago? The Beatles were probably the best we had in the Sixties, but the musical expression of the decade? One could as accurately say that in politics it was L.B.J.'s Voting Rights Act, which might also have been the best we had, but didn't begin to symbolize the Sixties. There is just too much of a decade—politically, musically, socially, in every way—to pin down.

But surely it can be said that certain music inevitably reflects certain aspects of a certain time. It interests me that much of the music of the Sixties—including most of the songs I've mentioned—hangs on some aspect of *change*, even when they don't seem to. The mystery of what the girl and Billy Joe threw off the Tallahatchee Bridge means less to me than the revelation in the last verse that it was all in the past, time has gone by—sad reflections, new circumstances, brother's off to Tupelo with a bride—*change*. And the reason that

> . . . one man, scorned and covered with scars,
> still strove with his last ounce of courage
> to reach the unreachable stars. . .

was that "the world will be better for this." Again, *change*. I am willing to link that word to the Sixties, but not many others, and it seems to me that Bob Dylan may have described the decade best:

> There's a battle
> Outside and it's ragin'
> It'll soon shake your windows
> And rattle your walls.

Dylan was not referring to Vietnam, at least not exclusively. Vietnam was not so much the battle itself as the distant artillery rumble that finally woke some of us to what Dylan had been trying to convey. The times, they were a-changin'—more swiftly and more profoundly than ever before,

and *that* was the battle, that was the central experience of the Sixties, whether one urged it on and welcomed it, or resisted and lamented. And it came to us all.

Change arrived in so many guises in the Sixties that it was difficult to tell what mattered and what was superficial or faddish. When American young men opted more widely than at any time since the Civil War for long hair and beards, no doubt the basic impulse was rebellion against the crew-cut, gray-flannel, surburban-house conformity of post-war America

> And the children go to school,
> and the children go to summer camp,
> and then to the university
> where they are put in boxes
> and they all come out the same . . .
> and they're all made out of ticky-tacky
> and they all look just the same.

Yet, the hairy look itself soon came to be a kind of orthodoxy, as did all those denim pants, Indian beads and sandals. The sudden immense popularity of pro football on television probably had some psychological derivation from the violence of the times, as often argued, but pro boxing went virtually off the air, and what about the sudden immense popularity of pro golf? What probably mattered most, in each case, was that the pace of pro football was naturally swift, and the networks cut out most of the preliminaries and also-rans in the big golf tournaments and focused on the closing holes and contending players for a fast, dramatic show; thus, these sports, like the games, *moved*. Most of the boxers we saw in the Fifties on Fight of the Week seldom did.

Minor change sometimes suggested deeper

Tom Wicker   11

change. When the Supreme Court outlawed prayer in the public schools, that was not intrinsically so great a matter; religion in America had never been dependent on the schools and many denominations actively supported the strict separation of church and state. Yet, the Court's action came at a time of precipitous decline for church influences in American life, and seemed to symbolize the emergence of a new way of life—rationalist and enlightened to some, hedonist and decadent to others—*change* to both.

Other movement was ambiguous. The miniskirt, perhaps, was only part of the long-established ability of the master salesmen of the *couture* to put hemlines down or up at will; yet, the ladies were showing more of themselves than ever before in other ways, too—bikinis, see-through blouses, discarded underwear—even while the strongest feminist movement since Susan B. Anthony was emerging at the end of the decade. Development of The Pill, as well as the national movement towards more easily available abortions, obviously had profound implications, but which was most important—that they tended to set women free to enjoy sex as never before, or that they tended to set women free from the dominance of children and the men who fathered them? Or was that the same thing? In the Sixties, it was only possible to be sure that the world of the female was undergoing metamorphosis perhaps even more than that of the male.

Other changes really were developments from a familiar past. In music, the rise of rock was phenomenal, as was the popularization of country music—primarily, I think, by Johnny Cash and Glen Campbell; yet . . . relatively traditional ballads continued to attain great popularity, and anyway rock and the Nashville sound had deep roots in the musical past. Film became the hot new art form, as Hollywood died and the choking grip of studios, the star system and the money-making moguls was relaxed; but almost everybody alive today grew up with the movies, and now artists instinctively work in cinematic terms, even as audiences (readers, for instance) instinctively react to cinematic devices and influences. It is possible, nowadays, to see a movie exactly like the book it was made from, because the book was written in the first place by someone who did his learning at the movies and constructed his work out of that experience.

But far more traumatic forms of change were experienced in the Sixties, the most shaking of which may have been that many Americans—some of the most patriotic—came to believe that the national power somehow was out of control. The vast American war machine, which in the Eisenhower era they had learned to think of as a defense machine, and which they knew from a heritage aptly confirmed in World War II and Korea was *good* and even beneficial to oppressed mankind—the war machine became a menace, and not just to Cuba, the Dominican Republic, North Vietnam and the N.L.F., but to Americans and American society. The draft to man the machine, the funds to sustain it, the urge to use it, the controversy evoked among supporters and critics, the political power "defense" wielded over resources and priorities needed for other things, the corruption it fostered (the C.I.A. financing students, unions, foundations; the armed forces bribing Congressmen and reporters with junkets and preferment; contractors profiting from astronomical cost overruns on contracts politically awarded; universities on the take)—all these brought power itself into disrepute, and the uses of power under sweeping challenge. And this happened even though, throughout the decade, the threat of world war seemed to rise steadily in the Middle East; and even though, in Czechoslovakia, the Soviet Union bluntly demonstrated its own power, its own brutal willingness to wield it.

The liberal faith also was shaken to its roots—not the political ideals, if any, of the so-called liberals of the two major parties, but the deep-seated American belief in man's ability to "get together and work things out." That sort of ingrained rationalism had been seen in American institutions from the town meeting through the P.T.A. to collective bargaining. But in the Sixties—first—blacks lost whatever faith they had had in white intention to "work things out"; they began sitting in and burning down. Then white students, many of whom had gone to Mississippi in the early Sixties to teach illiterates and rebuild burned churches, and then had voted in 1964 for L.B.J. and against the war in Vietnam, discovered in action that "working within the system" was a slow and often fruitless task; they turned to mass demonstrations, draft resistance, campus strikes, building seizures. These "radical" actions, however the end seemed to justify the means, alarmed and outraged many other Americans—who abandoned *their* liberal faith in "working things out" by condoning or encouraging the sort of police violence loosed on white demonstrators at the Chicago national convention of the Democrats in 1968, or by acquiescing in various forms of "backlash" against black militants—electing reactionary officials, approving repressive action against the Black Panthers and others, opposing school integration, moving to the suburbs.

"What else could we do?" cried leaders on all sides, in the death rattle of liberal confidence, and in 1970, the whole action-reaction cycle of the Sixties came to a dreadful climax when the National Guard shot and killed four white demonstrators at Kent State, and Mississippi state police fired into a crowd of black students at Jackson State, killing two and wounding eleven. Another commission was appointed.

The loss of faith in "working things out" changed the spirit of accommodation in American life—which had always had its exceptions, particularly racial—to one of hostility; no wonder that at the end of the decade Mr. Nixon felt it necessary to pledge he would "bring us together." Roughly, the division was the young, the black, and the poor—the welfare poor, not the low-income poor—against everyone else. But the lines were not really that rigid—some young people, like the "Okie from Muskogee," were more hostile than anyone to draft resistance, long hair, militant blacks, campus unrest; some older persons like Senator McCarthy saw in the student movement the salvation of "the spirit of America," and some whites of every class and age continued to support the newly militant black cause. A better line of demarcation lay, perhaps, between those who believed *on faith* in the beneficence of American life and attitudes, and those who believed *on the evidence they saw* that the American idea was being perverted by "manipulators" such as Lyndon Johnson and Dean Rusk, later Richard Nixon, by the white power structure, the military-industrial complex, and corrupted institutions such as universities doing "defense" research or labor unions excluding blacks from good jobs.

But the division went deeper than that, too, sprang more directly from *change* itself—from loss and growth and pain, sorrow and remembrance, bewilderment and anger, dreams gone wrong and myths demolished. Here is a cry from the American heart, clipped from the letters column of a Texas newspaper:

Dear Mr. Editor:

A few ideas, as we travel back down through memory lane:

If you are a native American, and you are old enough, you will probably remember when you never dreamed our country could ever lose; when you took for granted that women and the elderly and the clergy were to be respected; when you went to church and found spiritual food; when the clergy talked about religion; when a girl was a girl; when a boy was a boy, and when they liked each other.

You will probably remember when taxes were only a nuisance; when you knew your creditors and paid your debts; when the poor were too proud to take charity; when the words "care," "concern," "poverty" and "ghetto" were ordinary words and not overworked; when there was no bonus on bastards; when you knew that the law meant justice, and you had a feeling of protection and appreciation at the sight of a policeman; when young fellows tried to join the Army and Navy, when songs had a tune; when you bragged about your home state and your home town, and when politicians proclaimed their patriotism.

You will remember when clerks in stores tried to please you; when our government stood up for Americans anywhere in the world; when a man who went wrong was blamed, not his mother's nursing habits or his father's income; when everyone knew the difference between right and wrong; when you considered yourself lucky to have a good job, when you were proud to have one.

You may remember when people expected less and valued what they had more; when riots were unthinkable, when you took it for granted that the law would be enforced and your safety protected; when our flag was a sacred symbol; when America was the land of the free and home of the brave.

Do you remember when—or do you?

Of course, there never really was such an America as that, but the poignant final question may be the one that mattered most in the Sixties. No matter what your age or party or color, if you longed for that kind of Arcadian America, what was actually happening frightened and repelled you, and so you were likely to be ranged against those who were in the thick of the "movement"— whether it was a movement of blacks, students, peacelovers, "hippies" or feminists. George Wallace even created a kind of reverse "movement" out of all those who were against the other movements. Surely, The Beatles touched a profound truth when they sang

> . . . yesterday, love was such an easy game to
>   play,
> now I need a place to hide away—
> Oh I believe in yesterday.

In particular, the yesterday many Americans believed in—the shaping time of the older generations, who came to maturity with different desperations, born of Depression and World War II—*that* yesterday was not infused with the peculiar apocalypses of today, the contrapuntal horrors of nuclear annihilation, the "population bomb," environmental destruction. This fact alone was change of incalculable import. Marching in the streets of the Sixties was the first generation to grow up entirely in the knowledge that if man's life was threatened with extinction, the fault lay not as much in his stars as in his habits and achievements—the first generation to

14   **Awakening**

place highest importance on man's survival against himself, rather than on the expansion of his domain, and the first generation that had had to. Hence, the singular fact that young people generally—particularly black young people—were not nearly so moved or enthralled as their elders by the landing on the moon; it was not the giant step for mankind that many of them thought most needed.

And what was to give them hope? Wherever they—and many others—saw bright promise in the decade, it was cut down. John Kennedy, the triumph of the test-ban treaty in his hand, the Bay of Pigs far behind, the tragedy of Vietnam in the unimaginable future—his brain shattered on a sunlit day in Dallas. John XXIII, the interim Pope whose generosity of spirit lit the world—how brief *his* time of inspiration. From the blacks, one by one, gunmen and the fates took Malcolm X, Medgar Evers, the great Martin King, so different, so alike in their steadiness of purpose, *free at last, free at last*—but not the people for whom they spoke and died. Robert Kennedy, the inheritor of a legend, torn between political instinct and a suffering heart—downed at a moment of hope, the victim of a strange up-rooted boy who stood witness to a displaced, distraught world of tortured dreams and frightened men. In this progression of death and violence was the most discouraging change—as if heroes could no longer survive nor hope live in such a world.

But somewhere, there had to be the *roots* of change, on the strength of which it could flourish so wildly in such a strange, wounding decade. Some sought the reasons in permissive parents, Supreme Court decisions, liberal politics, failing patriotism, black movement "too far too fast."

But the search for such scapegoat sources of trouble never made more convincing progress than the most doctrinaire young radicals did in their attempts to isolate the "manipulators" and conspirators they believed to be blocking the world from its ordained path to the Age of Aquarius. Certain black advances, notably in the use of public accommodations in the South and the opening of housing patterns elsewhere, may have led to more black agitation for even further social gains, for instance, but this was a minor cause of racial conflict in the Sixties, compared to the urban aftermath of that all but unnoticed phenomenon of the Fifties—the great black migration from the Southern countryside into the black ghettos of the North and California.

For my part, I trace the Sixties' tidal wave of change, the decade's pervasive impression of disaster impending, its twilight sense of eras dying, as well as its suggestion—Aquarius again—of a new and brilliant dawn, to even deeper and more profound change here in America. At the heart of the decade, it seems to me, were two forces:

Technological accomplishment so far-reaching as actually to alter the means by which man perceived and learned, actually to extend his environment to new planets while threatening his extinction on his own.

Economic development so sweeping as to render all but obsolete the material standards by which American society had been able to gauge itself—making poverty, for instance, an interest-group problem like farm prices, shifting the basic issue of politics from the standard of living to the quality of life, and raising for millions of young Americans the unprecedented problem of finding something useful to do with their lives.

Tom Wicker 15

It is not yet clear what technology has in store for us, but it seems to bear the seeds of a mass and unhuman sort of life, no matter what our wealth. Already Americans are jammed into huge urban masses, in which they live stacked upon one another in numbered cells in beehive apartment buildings, or in endlessly sprawling suburbs whose houses have the same deadly sameness as units from the production line. Already these modern Americans submit to being sealed into gigantic toothpaste tubes and hurled through the skies at incredible speeds, literally peas in a pod, and already, for reasons no one can explain, the speed is being whipped up to supersonic levels. Already creatures of shrinking dimensions drive to work on swarming eight-lane highways, where metal monsters reduce human drivers to dollsize; and someday, if electronics prosper as predicted, the highway itself will drive the cars. Everywhere man turns, from the classroom to the supermarket to Mission Control, he is being dwarfed by his own handiwork—hapless and driven in his zip-code world, among his reactors and data banks, breathing his canned or polluted air and eating his frozen foods, even his physical security dependent—he is assured—upon the reaction time and judgment of an IBM computer. How typical and pathetic it was that when the great power failure of 1965 deprived urban Americans for a night of their greatest technological prop, human nature instinctively asserted itself in the darkness, and more children were conceived in and out of wedlock than on any other single occasion of which we have records on our ubiquitous punch cards.

Yet, the great impact of technology and affluence in the Sixties derived not only from what they did to American life but from what they did

not do. When men were put on the moon by the aerospace industry and the "systems engineer," financed by a government bemused by political rivalry with the Soviet Union, the question was also raised in many an American mind why the same quality of effort and organization, the same level of financing, could not be brought to bear on, say, the housing problem or the transportation crisis. If technology could bounce the image of Richard Nixon off Telstar to Afghanistan, why could it not dispose of industrial waste without turning rivers purple and skies black? Why were superhighways easier to build for middle-class drivers than mass transit systems for the urban poor?

Somewhat similarly, it has to be supposed that if wealth is suddenly commonplace, after having been spread more widely than in any society in history, that fact will at some point make insistent the question why wealth can't be spread further—why, for instance, in the richest nation ever dreamed of, children still go hungry by the miserable thousands, and politicians can find nothing more to do about it than distribute surplus potatoes and food stamps designed mostly to make certain the poor can't buy TV sets or bottles of cheap wine or otherwise undermine their own moral fiber?

Almost subversively, in the Sixties, technology and affluence thus betrayed institutions and ethics based on an older, different order of things. They helped produce, for instance, the issue of "relevance" or lack of it in American education. A generation reared before the TV set, blasé about computer technology, unimpressed by the glories and dangers of the past (as compared to those of the Sixties in America), and with little if any concern about money, found the university not only a stuffy place but its wares unexciting and seemingly not very useful in the social cause. Billions of dollars annually, technically augmented firepower, and computer-run pacification programs could neither win the war in Vietnam nor convince Americans it was necessary, much less an exercise of benevolent power.

Before the possibilities raised by technology and affluence, moreover, it became apparent that the home political system had all but broken down. Organized fundamentally for the needs of the Nineteenth Century, divided into fifty historical accidents, each of *them* subdivided with stultifying effect into outmoded, inefficient, underfinanced, overlapping, jealous and innumerable smaller jurisdictions, this antiquated system channeled the lion's share of tax revenues to its swollen central government, which was therefore expected to provide an impossible variety and scope of activities, for most of which it has small understanding or aptitude; but the population was concentrated in cities that had no appreciable powers of government and no revenue sources but the most unproductive and unfair.

And what kind of political, economic and technological society was it that could spawn the monstrous Rayburn Building on Capitol Hill and the F-111 in Fort Worth and the whiz-kid systems analysts of Robert McNamara (the spoiled priest of a technological god that failed) and still not be able to collect the garbage in New York City or protect old ladies walking their dogs or place any useful restriction on the nation's ninety million privately owned firearms?

By the end of the Sixties, it was thus becoming reasonably clear that the United States of America, rich and ingenious as it might be, simply was not organized to cope with the Twentieth Century or to do the things its affluence and technology made possible; and those born too far along in this breakdown of the American system to defend it blindly and on faith seemed more and more justified in their mistrust of its workings and claims.

Failing institutions, moreover, mean failing ethical standards. When government, local or national, cannot restrain the violence of its own agents, preaching non-violence to radicals and blacks will not have much effect. Veneration for the Presidency cannot long be sustained if the occupants of that office too often are caught misleading or mistrusting the people. Political rhetoric about the glories of the nation's history will sound the more hollow as it is used to respond to those who point out present deficiencies.

And where affluence and technology are so pervasive, what is—for example—the sense of continuing to emphasize the old values of primitive, pioneer America—hard work, iron self-discipline, personal material success, the primacy of productivity? Particularly if conformity to those values is made the only norm of respectability and social acceptability, the ethic itself can only seem the more irrelevant, the conformity the more choking.

Recently, a man of some distinction told me that he was glad he had grown to manhood years ago, at a time when it not only was possible but probably was necessary for him to erect a material standard by which to measure his life. It had been possible for him to judge the worth of his labors, over the years, by asking how much he had been able to ease the physical difficulties of his family, increase the prosperity of his society, conquer the technical obstacles to abundance for all. But in the age of affluence and technology, he said, no such simple material standard could suffice. Wealth had become the general rule and the gross national product dwarfed the wildest dreams; miracles were commonplace, and men could survive even with other men's hearts pumping their blood, at the bottom of the sea and in the great void of space, by the mere technological expedient of carrying their environment with them. Every day, another of man's limitations fell away.

As for affluence, then, what is to be its net worth? What kind of lives shall we live and what values shall we profess and what rich rewards of the mind and spirit are we to seek, with means and leisure and the advantages they afford? Accumulation itself, as a goal and certainly as a value, is satisfying, if at all, only to those who accumulate from need, and material overachievement can have no more utility than nuclear overkill. What value can be erected in its stead?

And as for technology, are we going to use it in a reasoned way to improve the lot of man, materially, spiritually, intellectually, in his environment, or are we going to become technology's slaves—as seems dreadfully possible—mounting each new scientific Everest not because it serves man's purpose but merely because it is there?

On how we come to use our affluence and technology and the things they afford us, it is not too much to say, depends the question whether Americans of today and tomorrow, born in a new world and reared in its influences, can find something that *they will regard as useful to do with their lives in their times.* Building a better mousetrap lost its essential appeal once it ceased to mean a more craftsmanlike piece of work and

suggested, instead, trickier packaging and louder advertising; and the extension of built-in obsolescence (not excluding that of human beings who become progressively less employable after 40) throughout the gross national product marks the extent to which the old material standard defrauds rather than measures honest value. Social involvement, personal, intellectual or esthetic development, environmental preservation, back-to-nature communes, public services, the constructive use of leisure—all these and other callings plainly offer more nearly a pioneer challenge today than the business successes, industrial feats and financial wizardries that once sang their siren songs to young Americans.

So I believe we have now to turn away from the gods of production that for so long comforted us, as we measured ourselves against their demands; I think the Sixties—*change*—taught, if we would learn, that we have before us the task of making a tolerable life in a new and difficult world no less than did those who came centuries ago to the wild shores of America in search of freedom and opportunity. But that task will demand of us primarily a sense of value, not the material standard that served them; it will require us to believe, with Thoreau, that the world is more to be admired than used; that our lives are more to be cultivated and contemplated than driven and exploited; that the only true progress is within ourselves, toward the only true value—the old enduring values of the human heart, courage and pity and joy and the generosities of love.

Oh when will you ever learn? sang the young people of the Sixties, in their innocence, their green ignorance of the small daily deaths of the spirit that life itself—not some political or economic system—deals to the great and the small. *When will we ever learn?* It was hard to live in the music and clangor of the Sixties without asking that question. In their echoes, in an America changing from a lusty boomer's youth to maturity or decline, it is even harder to believe in Arcadia or Aquarius. *When will we ever learn?* After the Sixties, perhaps as never before, the answer, my friend, is blowin' in the wind; the answer is blowin' in the wind.

Discussion Questions

1. Explain the meaning of the words "Arcadia" and "Aquarius." What conflict exists between these views? What similarity?

2. Wicker finds that the major characteristic of the decade is change. List a few of the changes and events of the Sixties. Discuss one in detail.

3. Wicker says that the two major forces which influenced the decade were technological accomplishment and economic development. How did these forces affect individuals? How did they produce confusion in the country?

4. Wicker finds fault with both the Aquarians and the Arcadians. What alternative does he offer?

5. Wicker quotes liberally from songs of the Sixties. Discuss the effectiveness of these quotes in the essay.

6. Bring some song lyrics to class and discuss their social or political implications.

GROWING UP
KEITH WILSON

A big Jack, cutting outward toward blue,
little puffs of my bullets hurrying him.
Sage crushed underfoot, crisp & clean—

My father, a big Irishman, redfaced & watching,
he who could hit anything within range,
who brought a 150-lb buck three miles
out of the high mountains when he was 57

—a man who counted misses as weaknesses,
he whipped up his own rifle, stopped the Jack
folding him in midair, glanced at me, stood
silent

My father who never knew I shot pips from
   cards
candleflames out (his own eye) who would've
been shamed by a son who couldn't kill. Riding
beside him.

Keith Wilson (1927–) is an educator and a poet of his native
Southwest.

Discussion Questions

1. In what way is the son "growing up"? Is the father immature?

2. What is the value gap between the father and the son?

3. Generally speaking, what differences over sexual mores, economic aspirations, and apparel commonly occur between parents and offspring?

AMERICA

ALLEN GINSBERG

America I've given you all and now I'm nothing.
America two dollars and twentyseven cents
    January 17,1956.
I can't stand my own mind.
America when will we end the human war?
Go fuck yourself with your atom bomb.
I don't feel good don't bother me.
I won't write my poem till I'm in my right
    mind.
America when will you be angelic?
When will you take off your clothes?
When will you look at yourself through the
    grave?
When will you be worthy of your million
    Trotskyites?
America why are your libraries full of tears?
America when will you send your eggs to India?
I'm sick of your insane demands.
When can I go into the supermarket and buy
    what I need with my good looks?
America after all it is you and I who are perfect
    not the next world.
Your machinery is too much for me.
You made me want to be a saint.
There must be some other way to settle this
    argument.

Allen Ginsberg (1926–), a contemporary American poet, is one of the major voices of the counterculture.

Burroughs is in Tangiers I don't think he'll come
back it's sinister.
Are you being sinister or is this some form of
practical joke?
I'm trying to come to the point.
I refuse to give up my obsession.
America stop pushing I know what I'm doing.
America the plum blossoms are falling.
I haven't read the newspapers for months,
everyday somebody goes on trial for murder.
America I feel sentimental about the Wobblies.
America I used to be a communist when I was a
kid I'm not sorry.
I smoke marijuana every chance I get.
I sit in my house for days on end and stare at
the roses in the closet.
When I go to Chinatown I get drunk and never
get laid.
My mind is made up there's going to be trouble.
You should have seen me reading Marx.
My psychoanalyst thinks I'm perfectly right.
I won't say the Lord's Prayer.
I have mystical visions and cosmic vibrations.
America I still haven't told you what you did to
Uncle Max after he came over from Russia.

I'm addressing you.
Are you going to let your emotional life be run
by Time Magazine?
I'm obsessed by Time Magazine.
I read it every week.
Its cover stares at me every time I slink past the
corner candystore.
I read it in the basement of the Berkeley Public
Library.
It's always telling me about responsibility.
Businessmen are serious. Movie producers are
serious. Everybody's serious but me.
It occurs to me that I am America.
I am talking to myself again.

Asia is rising against me.

I haven't got a chinaman's chance.
I'd better consider my national resources.
My national resources consist of two joints of
marijuana millions of genitals an
unpublishable private literature that goes 1400
miles an hour and twentyfive-thousand mental
institutions.
I say nothing about my prisons nor the millions
of underprivileged who live in my flowerpots
under the light of five hundred suns.
I have abolished the whorehouses of France,
Tangiers is the next to go.
My ambition is to be President despite the fact
that I'm a Catholic.

America how can I write a holy litany in your
silly mood?
I will continue like Henry Ford my strophes are
as individual as his automobiles more so
they're all different sexes.

America I will sell you strophes $2500 apiece
$500 down on your old strophe
America free Tom Mooney
America save the Spanish Loyalists
America Sacco & Vanzetti must not die
America I am the Scottsboro boys.

America when I was seven momma took me to
Communist Cell meetings they sold us
garbanzos a handful per ticket a ticket costs a
nickel and the speeches were free everybody
was angelic and sentimental about the workers
it was all so sincere you have no idea what a
good thing the party was in 1935 Scott
Nearing was a grand old man a real mensch
Mother Bloor made me cry I once saw Israel
Amter plain. Everybody must have been a spy.
America you don't really want to go to war.
America it's them bad Russians.

26   Turmoil

Them Russians them Russians and them
    Chinamen. And them Russians.
The Russia wants to eat us alive. The Russia's
    power mad. She wants to take our cars from
    out our garages.
Her wants to grab Chicago. Her needs a Red
    Readers' Digest. Her wants our auto plants in
    Siberia. Him big bureaucracy running our
    fillingstations.
That no good. Ugh. Him make Indians learn
    read. Him need big black niggers. Hah. Her
    make us all work sixteen hours a day. Help.
America this is quite serious.
America this is the impression I get from looking
    in the television set.

America is this correct?
I'd better get right down to the job.
It's true I don't want to join the Army or turn
    lathes in precision parts factories, I'm
    nearsighted and psychopathic anyway.
America I'm putting my queer shoulder to the
    wheel.

Discussion Questions

1. What is Ginsberg's vision of America? What are
   the implications of his views?
2. In what ways are his views current?
3. Isolate one of Ginsberg's complaints against
   American society and discuss it in detail.

IN THE COUNTRY OF THE YOUNG
JOHN ALDRIDGE

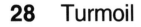

In the following excerpt from *In the Country of the Young*, John Aldridge argues that student unrest stems from sending to college a mediocre majority lacking in cultural interest and intellectual incentive. Understandably bored, these students find escape in political activism.

One cannot observe the student activist drama for very long without beginning to feel, with Marianne Moore, that "there are things that are important beyond all this fiddle." At one time, we would not have needed to be reminded what those things are. But after nearly a decade of activist fiddle and at least two decades of being brainwashed by the doctrine that whatever is young is right, we have become ashamed to admit a truth we once thought too self-evident to need stating: that universities are not primarily rebel encampments, forums of political debate, or media for the distribution of pamphlets, but institutions whose first function is to train intelligence and preserve cultural standards.

It is perfectly true that historical precedent

John Aldridge (1922–) is a professor of English at the University of Michigan. He is a leading critic and essayist who analyzes the connection between social experience and literary achievement.

exists, particularly in Europe and South America, for both the activist and the educational roles of the universities. Very often in the past, students have served as indispensable agents of public conscience, using their relative freedom from the pressures of expediency and compromise to impress upon the adult world the reality of moral issues on which there must be no compromise. But almost always in the past the two roles have existed in some sort of balanced relation to each other, and except in times of the most extreme ideological crisis, the one did not usurp, eclipse, or threaten to vitiate the authority of the other. Today, however, the activist role has become so inflated in our universities, and the educational role so diminished where not downright subverted, that we now accept it as customary to find students whose function on the campus is primarily that of agitation and only marginally that of becoming educated. Obviously, there are serious and intelligent students who are dedicated to activism. But since we can hardly assume that the many thousands or even millions of young people now engaged to one degree or another in campus agitation are *all* serious or intelligent enough to be dedicated political idealists, we must presumably seek elsewhere for an explanation of their behavior.

In addition to . . . the rather complicated psychological motives for confrontation, the need, among other things, to oppose, and be opposed by, adult authority in order to define personal identity, one might suggest that the present college population is so constituted that many of its members are bound to be drawn to activism simply because they are suited to no other role. This is, after all, the first student generation to be admitted to the universities on the principle that higher education is a right that should be available to all and, at the same time, a necessity for anyone who hopes to achieve some measure of success in middle-class society. The result is that for the first time in our history the universities have had to accept large masses of students who may have proper credentials from the secondary schools—because those schools have themselves been obliged to lower their standards to accommodate the mediocre majority—but who possess neither the cultural interest nor the intellectual incentive to benefit from higher education. Such students, when confronted with complex ideas or stringent academic requirements, tend to sink into a protective lethargy or to become resentful because demands are being made on them which they are not equipped to meet and have no particular desire to meet. Most of them did not want to come to the universities in the first place but did so for reasons of practical expediency: parental pressure, fear of the draft, or the promise of a better job after graduation. But these motives, since they are imposed from without rather than generated from within, are not sufficient to sustain them through the rigors of their course work or give them a sense of purpose inside the structure of the university. Hence their natural impulse is to try to compensate for their failure of ability or interest by involving themselves in some extracurricular activity, which happens today to be political activism.

This kind of involvement has at least one important advantage over involvement in football and fraternity life: popular opinion has sanctified it as a worthy, even a heroic, cause. Students with only marginal interests in anything else can therefore give themselves up to it not only without feeling guilty or frivolous but with the

John Aldridge   29

pious conviction that they are doing something far more valuable—and certainly far more "relevant"—than training their minds, and something also which requires no special talent or mental capacity beyond a certain talent for indignation and the power to be vigorously inarticulate while trying to express it. Thus they are afforded moral justification for not doing what they do not want to do and, at the same time, an approved outlet for hostilities resulting from the pressures that are exerted upon them to do what they are not readily able to do. Besides, engaging in attacks on the universities is the surest strategy for deflecting criticism from themselves. Whatever failure they may be charged with they can blame on the institution and thereby convert their sense of individual inadequacy into a far more comfortable sense of collective self-righteousness. Finally, of course, activist participation has the advantage of guaranteeing students the approval of their peers—a measurable status within a university community as a rule so large that a person would normally be lost in it—and the privilege of feeling socially effective, which is a rare privilege for the socially ineffective.

But perhaps the most crucial factor of all is simply the boredom of the vast majority of students, a boredom which must be at least equal to, if not considerably worse than, that of the population as a whole. Without strongly internalized ambitions and interests that are satisfiable within the university system, average students, like average people everywhere, are entirely dependent upon outside stimuli to provide them with the distractions needed to make life bearable. The greater the intellectual vacuum, the greater the need for distraction, a vacuum in

people being presumably even more abhorrent than it is in nature. Thus run-of-the-mill students are especially vulnerable to the enticements of activism as well as to those of its soul-brother philosophy of hippyism. Activism supplies them not only with abundant opportunity to be active without having to think but with a sense of concrete physical involvement in a kind of experience from which normally they feel rather tragically excluded. Here, after all, they are: young, vigorous, hairy, horny, not terribly bright, and aching for murder, and all the great occasions for challenge and adventure seem to have passed them by. They were born twenty years too late to have a part in that knightly crusade against tyranny which World War II now seems sentimentally to symbolize for their fathers. They did not even have the small but appealing satisfaction of going hungry in the Depression. And, to make matters worse, the only available war is one they cannot morally accept and which they would consent to fight in only under the gravest duress. Obviously, there is a vacuum here more insidious than an intellectual vacuum, an absence of the opportunity for therapeutic bloodshed, and for the really imperative confrontation between man and his fear of death.

The virtue of activism is that it provides a fair substitute for this lost opportunity. It restores the primitive connection between belligerent virility and a hostile environment, and, in so doing, makes it possible for the young to get a little of their own back from history. It allows them to fight their own morally acceptable war, carry on their own knightly crusade against tyranny, in brick-throwing street battles with the police and in stalwart confrontations of nerve with authorities old enough to be as enviably favored by history as Dad. They can taste blood in these encounters, and they can taste fear, and with a little luck they can contrive to become martyrs and spend a night or two in jail. The police may not be entirely satisfactory replacements for the Nazis (although there are differences of opinion on this score), but they can be as easily charged with brutality as the universities can be charged with corruption, and so can be conveniently transformed into enemies one can hate with a clear conscience and attack whenever one needs proof of one's courage or relief from one's boredom. Through activism, in short, life can become once again a frontier and a battlefield. The bland abstractedness of university life is canceled by violence and melodrama, and those who cannot function effectively on the frontier of ideas are brought back into touch with a reality they can understand.

•   •   •

Discussion Questions

1. Aldridge says that the first function of a university is to train intelligence and preserve cultural standards. Do you agree with this premise?
2. According to Aldridge, why are so many students attracted to activism? Do you agree with him? State your own reasons.
3. Discuss the relationship between Ginsberg's complaints in "America" and the activists' moral stance.

John Aldridge   **31**

BRIDGING THE GENERATION GAP
from *The New Republic*

Every summer Representative Morris K. Udall (D., Ariz.) selects two or three college students to work as "interns" in his Washington office. During the course of the summer, these young people perform routine office duties, work on major legislation, and chat with Udall. The following conversation is an edited summary of many discussions on the Vietnam war, student activists, dropouts, and the attitudes of the older generation.

UDALL: As I read my mail, I find in some cases what amounts to a sense of betrayal being felt by many adults. They can't understand why so many young people are so "turned off" by the very system which has made it possible for them to have advantages of financial security, access to education, and a range of opportunities far beyond those available to any past generation.

INTERN 1: You have to define who are the young people who are being turned off. When you look, you will find that they are white, mid-to-upper-class students. That constitutes a very small portion of the total population of what you call the young. These people are totally rejecting the life styles they see as favoring one socio-economic group. These students want to change the very society that creates these inequities. The consequence is that they develop what scholars refer to as an "identification with the lowly."

What I mean by this is that these people feel guilty that they have had the highest standard of living ever. They feel guilty because while they are enjoying this highest standard of living, American Indians are starving and black ghettos are overrun by rats. What they see is that in America, home of that "glorious dream," all sorts of people are *starving*. This goes on while they eat steak every day. Their sense of moral indignation can't stand this; and they realize that the blame rests on the shoulders of their class. But then this strange identification with the lowly occurs. Their "heroes" are oppressed so they want to be oppressed. Their "heroes" are poor so they want to live a nonmaterial life.

INTERN 2: None of us would deny that living in America has made possible the extraordinary education and material advantages we've been favored with. But that does not mean that everything is right with this country, or that because we personally have been treated so well we should mute our dissatisfaction with some of the things going on around us. The anger and concern of youth is not merely directed at the war, although most students believe that what we are doing in Vietnam in support of what amounts to a petty dictatorship is an absurd waste of lives and an orgy of destruction. . . . Advantages and all, I still can't tolerate the richest country on earth allowing migrant children to grow up thinking they are "bums," and letting slum children be bitten by rats in their sleep, while the government gives money to farmers *not* to grow crops, and appropriates funds for a supersonic transport which could damage our environment, and an anti-ballistic missile system which may be obsolete by the time it's installed. I should think that would be enough to turn *anybody* off!

INTERN 3: All that I would like to add is that students are not the only segment of youth which is questioning the country's progress. There are 40 million young people between 14 and 24. Some have been disenchanted from the American dream since birth.

UDALL: But why is it, do you think, that some of our young people, particularly students who are the best educated, feel that their only recourse in the face of such problems is to riot or to engage in other forms of mindless violence?

INTERN 3: On my campus, I don't think more than 50 out of 12,000 students participated in violence, and that's less than 1/2 of 1 percent. But it *is* time that we start making a distinction between violent protestors, nonviolent protestors, and innocent bystanders. This distinction should be made both in speech and in action. And I think it is time that we realize that innocent bystanders do exist—they may be your children. When I walk from my dormitory to the library, I have the right to do that. I am an innocent bystander of any action which goes on during the course of my walk. When I walk in a national park, I do not want to be stopped, questioned, treated rudely—just because I am 22 and someone else is 45. If a person participates in a nonviolent protest which is illegal, he is subject to arrest or fine. But I don't want to see him beaten over the head and perhaps have his brain scrambled for the rest of his life.

Concepts of overkill just encourage the violent dissidents and force nonviolent dissidents into another realm. Overkill is what is happening in this country. I am getting tired of the paranoia and hate reflected by policemen, students, parents. No one is the sole possessor of right. Let's face it—just because a man is a policeman does not mean he is automatically good or that he is automatically bad. All youth aren't sweet and innocent. Fine. But we'd better start making the distinction, and we'd better listen when there are grievances on both sides.

INTERN 2: We ought to start asking why violence occurs instead of merely condemning rioters out of hand. If we can make our social and political institutions more responsive to human needs, the causes of violence will be uprooted.

UDALL: Isn't there some validity to the charge that the complaints of youth are often presented in a very moralistic way, which makes it appear that they believe that their elders don't judge actions by any moral standard? If so, isn't this a bit arrogant?

INTERN 1: I definitely don't think so. I think the basic arrogance lies with the people who can only relate events to the money in their pockets. People criticize the antiwar student for saying the war is immoral because the US napalms children, and so forth. This doesn't affect the older generation. The only thing that will make them indignant is when the war starts costing them more in taxes. That's arrogance!

INTERN 3: Sometimes I feel that youth doesn't express its beliefs in the most effective manner for sympathetic understanding. However, I don't think that the term "arrogance" can be applied to most of the young. Most have simply been taught two things in America. One, that independent thinking is good. Two, that the independent thinking should follow certain ideals. For example, we have been taught that killing is wrong, that all men are entitled to the same rights, that somehow we have a responsibility to our neighbors, that the laws should apply equally. In a recent CBS poll 76 percent of the adults quest-

ioned—three out of four—said that citizens should *not* be allowed to organize protests against the government, even if there appears to be no danger of violence. Yet our constitution guarantees the right of the people peaceably to assemble. Perhaps we have been too carefully taught that in a very selfish way we must preserve the right of the minority to speak—if only because some day we may be in the minority. In our independent thinking we have determined that America has not lived up to its ideals. And further, I suppose, many believe that if those ideals do not become a workable reality, the world will come apart. Literalness, not arrogance, may be the fault of youth.

UDALL: Young people can force us to take another look at things to see if changes can't be made. But it's been my observation that many young people expected to end the war in Southeast Asia by a single moratorium or to save the environment between Earth Day and commencement. I've found, to my dismay at times, that the work of social renewal is tougher than that. I wonder if we can take the efforts of young activists seriously when much of what they do seems to show a transient interest rather than a continuing willingness to expend the effort necessary for real change.

INTERN 2: I think your criticism is largely justified. When the time has come for hard work and research, and the enthusiasm has died down, a lot of students involved in the initial protest seem to have disappeared. And that is unfortunate. But students were the first to start the civil rights "sit-ins" and similar protests as far back as *ten* years ago—and yet even today they are often almost alone when they march against the war or fight pollution, and that's enough to disillusion anybody. I can recall public hearings on air pollution where hardly anyone in the room was over 30. The apathy and unconcern of many adults is not exactly the thing that encourages their children to keep trying. Students are often criticized for not taking responsibility, but when they seek to influence changes in areas where they are affected, whether on the campuses or in the political system, they are often ignored. I find it very difficult to understand, for instance, why there is so much reluctance to allow students to participate in meetings of college boards of trustees or regents, or to let them be involved in the choosing of new university presidents. Young people, simply because they are fresh upon the scene, are bound to contribute something new to a discussion, or notice something that would never have occurred to their elders. Students at the University of Arizona have already done marvelous work in helping make curriculum improvements, in developing new programs to orient freshmen, and in establishing procedures for handling disciplinary cases. And they've added something to every university-wide committee they've been on. Yet the state's Board of Regents doesn't want the student body presidents to have a dialogue with the board for a mere half hour at their monthly meeting! It's true that a lot of students have "copped out" when their particular cause was no longer glamorous, but by the same token a lot of adults have turned a deaf ear to students even when they have made intelligent proposals and were begging to be heard.

UDALL: But aren't the bitterness, anger, resentment, and desperation of many young people counter-productive? I mean, not only because they have a negative effect on others whose help will be needed, but because they are in some cases a substitute for hard work to correct these wrongs?

INTERN 3: To say that sometimes these emotions are counter-productive does not eliminate the fact that they exist. We are the first generation to be taught of the possibility that this world could be blown up for the sake of one man's conception of honor. We are the first generation that has been told that world famine is a real possibility within a decade. We are the first generation to be told that the earth cannot sustain unlimited life. And we've got the privilege of probably seeing it all in living color on our TV sets! We are the first generation that has been told that man has the ability to make it impossible for his species to breathe.

Yes, I get angry. I got angry when I went to New York and found the air stifling. I'm lucky, though! I could leave. Most of the people in New York cannot ever go away on the weekend to escape the choking air. They can't afford it. I get angry when people talk only about the *American* deaths in Vietnam. Some of those Americans were my friends. Yet in that war we may have made the place safe against attack only to leave behind thousands of Vietnamese civilian graves—and a land so destroyed by bombing and defoliant activity that it may not be able to support the survivors. Have we destroyed Vietnam in order to save it? I wonder. I get angry when people talk as if we could afford to have a "next war."

I'm sorry to say that most of your optimism is not shared by young people. Many feel that they have neither the time nor the power to determine whether our world is going to be here. To be sure, many of our generation will limit the size of our families to two children. But other people of my age, getting married now, have seriously considered not having any children at all—and not for reasons of overpopulation. Rather, they think there won't be a world suitable for any limited pursuit of happiness. A child is the greatest and most beautiful commitment to the future that exists. Yet some young people are willing to deny themselves children—and their parents grandchildren, I might add. Why? Many of my generation don't believe there is much of a future left.

UDALL: This kind of pessimism is very distressing to me. I think this human race still has a great untapped potential, and you people are proof of this. One of the things that troubles me most is the current lack of understanding between young and old. Isn't it likely that there are no absolute answers, and that we are all captives to a certain degree of our own backgrounds, needs, and experiences? How do we bridge the gap?

INTERN 2: I agree we'd better do something about the growing mistrust and misunderstanding between the generations, and do it in a hurry. One sign that went up after the Kent State tragedy read, "National Guard 4, Kent State Students 0." The same people who have always yelled "Communist" at anything they didn't understand are now blaming students for all the world's ills. We've got to do something about that kind of ignorance and hatred before it tears the country apart. The young and old should be teaching each other, because each generation has a level of experience that the other has not had and should benefit from. But instead we seem to be condemning one another out of hand, staring at each other as if we were enemies and forgetting that it's our parents or our children that we're talking about.

Young people can do their share to bridge the gap, by curbing their self-righteousness and remembering that they are certainly not going to be always right. I still find myself learning things from my parents, just as I hope I teach them something once in a while. We ought to speak in a language our elders can understand, and lower our voices so they can hear us. And when we are particularly impatient and perceive our elders as slow to catch on, we ought to temper that impatience by asking ourselves what *our* kids will think of us when *we're* fifty.

A lot of people have the mistaken idea that young people want everything done just their way. That's just not true. What students *do* want is the opportunity to be listened to, the right to participate. That's why it's so urgent for my parents' generation to treat young people as intelligent and valuable members of our society, whether in the home or on the college campus, or in a governmental agency. I might add that older people do a great deal of damage when they ridicule students who are merely exercising their right of dissent or peaceful protest.

UDALL: I suppose, too, that differing life styles add to the problem. As I travel around Southern Arizona, talking to all kinds of people, I find that many of them have no sympathy for the ideas and reforms suggested by the young, simply because they say that it's hard to believe that young people are idealistic or serious when they insist on trying to shock older people. They look at young people's long hair, different styles of dress, use of language. And they wonder if all these things aren't better indications of young people's attitudes toward society than all their demands for improvement.

INTERN 1: Adults make a false assumption that

long hair and unconventional dress are designed to shock older people. You talked about arrogance earlier; there is nothing more arrogant to me than someone who discriminates against other persons because of the length of their hair or style of dress. Just because a kid smokes marijuana doesn't mean that he is a revolutionary. What is important is that a growing number of students are becoming totally dissatisfied with the entire social and political functions of this society. They are looking for something new, they are experimenting with new modes of life. The hair, the clothes, they are all part of the investigation.

INTERN 3: I don't think it is right to say that all young people dress the way they do, or act the way they do, to shock older people. Older people don't wear crew-cuts to shock me.

We are all victims of generalizations—generalizations gone wild. One young person may have long hair because he just likes it—and he may be more conservative politically than his parents. But if long hair *is* a way of identifying with change today, I see nothing wrong with this. Symbolic identifications of this kind *can* be divisive, of course, but I don't think they have to be.

I *am* concerned by the utter hate, distrust, lack of most basic civilities on all sides. Foul language, many young people feel, is far more honest than the language of the deceptive diplomat who may say "equality"—and mean the exact opposite. We are dealing with people, not pigs, not bums. I cannot ask anyone to abandon symbols, but I can ask him to abandon the symbols which convey inaccurate messages—like "I'm somehow better than you are."

Discussion Questions

1. Are the interns activists, radicals, or hippies? Explain. How do they justify their moral indignation? How do they feel about adult disapproval of young people? Do the interns seem arrogant?
2. How does Udall suggest that the generation gap is a value gap?
3. How can the generation gap be bridged?
4. Compare Aldridge's view of the activists and hippies to the observations of the interns. Which view seems most accurate?
5. "America" is a poem, "In the Country of the Young" an essay, and "Bridging the Generation Gap" a rap session. How does the form of each piece contribute to its effect? Discuss the objectivity and subjectivity of each.

GUMMING UP THE CAMPUS
SAUL ALINSKY

I was lecturing at a college which is run by a very conservative, almost fundamentalist Protestant denomination. Afterward some of the students came to my motel to talk to me. Their problem was that they couldn't have any fun on campus. They weren't permitted to dance or smoke or have a can of beer. I had been talking about the strategy of effecting change in a society and they wanted to know what tactics they could use to change their situation. I reminded them that a tactic is doing what you can with what you've got. "Now what have you got?" I asked. "What do they permit you to do?" "Practically nothing," they said, "except—you know—we can chew gum." I said, "Fine. Gum becomes the weapon. You get two or three hundred students to get two packs of gum each, which is quite a wad. Then you have them drop it on the campus walks. This will cause absolute chaos. Why, with five hundred wads of gum I could paralyze Chicago, stop all the traffic in the Loop." They looked at me as though I was some kind of a nut. But about two weeks later I got an ecstatic letter saying, "It worked: It worked. Now we can do

Saul Alinsky (1909–1972) was a Chicago-born sociologist and criminologist who organized community-action groups.

just about anything so long as we don't chew gum.''

Discussion Questions

1. One of the aims of student activists was to bring the Vietnam war to a halt. In other words, the students were demonstrating on college campuses in order to change a national policy that had been adopted in Washington. What can students learn from Saul Alinsky's anecdote?

2. How can young people influence national policy?

"You think you're the only one around here with an identity crisis?"

ENDLESS ADOLESCENCE
BENNETT M. BERGER

The true vocation of man is to find his way to himself.
—*Hermann Hesse*

In this study, Bennett M. Berger relates student restlessness and activism to "endless adolescence," the artificial postponement of maturity required of students who engage in extensive preparation for professions and careers. This prolongment creates tensions for the students as well as the institutions which house them.

When I was an undergraduate 20 years ago, I was chairman of one of the radical student groups at my college and an active official in the regional intercollegiate association of that group. I marched in my share of picket lines, published an article attacking my college president for anti-Semitism, was sung to by the sirens of the local Communist party and even, in a burst of creativity, wrote what in this age of instant classics I suppose qualifies as a classic militant's love song. I called it, "You and I and the Mimeograph Machine" and dedicated it to all the youthful romances born amidst the technology of moral protest.

Later, when I got older and became a sociologist, I resisted becoming a "political sociol-

Bennett M. Berger (1926–) is a professor of sociology at the University of California, Davis.

ogist," by which in this context I mean what a lot of the militants mean: a former activist who traded his credentials as a conscious moral and political agent in exchange for the rewards of expertise about political behavior. Though the remarks about student militance which follow may be analytic, I yield nothing to the young in the way of moral credentials.

In trying to throw some sociological light on the nature and character of student unrest, I am not going to comfort the militants by saying that students protest because this is a racist, plastic society or because the curriculum is irrelevant or because the university has sold its soul to the military-industrial complex or because the university is a machine in which students are treated as raw material—when, indeed, their up-tight teachers take time from their research to treat them as anything at all. On the other hand, I am not going to comfort their critics by saying that students rebel for kicks or because their upbringing was too permissive or because they are filled with a seething self-hatred or because they are symbolically murdering their fathers in a recurrent ritual melodrama of generational conflict.

What I will try to do is show how certain conditions generic to the direction of our present societal development have helped to bring about the present situation among youth and in the universities. I will also hazard a prediction as to the effects of these conditions during the next decade. An understanding of the problem will not make the solution any easier, for knowledge is not power, but it can at least arm us against panaceas.

The problem of student unrest is rooted in the prolongation of adolescence in industrialized countries. But it should be understood that "adolescence" is only minimally a biological category; there are only a very few years between the onset of puberty and the achievement of the growth and strength it takes to do a man's or woman's work. As we know, however, culture has a habit of violating nature. Proto-adolescent behavior now begins even before puberty (which itself is occurring earlier) with the action—and the orientation—we call "preadolescent," while at the other end, technological, economic and social developments conspire to prolong the dependence of the young, to exclude them from many of the privileges and responsibilities of adult life, and therefore to *juvenilize*[1] them.

The casual evidence in support of this deep institutionalization of adolescence is diffuse and quite remarkable. It includes such spectacles as 6-foot, 200-pound "boys" who in another time and place might be founders of dynasties and world-conquerors (like Alexander of Macedon) cavorting on the fraternity house lawn hurling orange peels and bags of water at each other, while tolerant local police, who chucklingly *approve*, direct traffic around the battlefield. It includes the preservation of childlike cadence and intonation in voices otherwise physically mature. It includes the common—and growing—practice (even in official university documents) of opposing the word "student" to the word "adult"—as if students were by definition not adults, even as

---

[1]"Juvenilize": a verb I have devised to describe a process through which "childish" behavior is induced or prolonged in persons who, in terms of their organic development, are capable of participating in adult affairs. If the process exists, there ought to be a verb to describe it.

the median age of university students rises with the increase of the graduate student population.

Adolescence, then, is not the relatively fleeting "transitional stage" of textbook and popular lore but a substantial segment of life which may last 15 or 20 years, and if the meaning of adolescence is extended only slightly, it can last longer than that. I have in mind the age-graded norms and restrictions in those professions which require long years of advanced training, and in which the system of sponsorship makes the advancement of one's career dependent upon being somebody's "boy" perhaps well on toward one's middle-age—a fact not uncharacteristic of university faculties.

Much of the discussion of "youth culture" in recent years reflects the prolongation of adolescence, since it is not surprising that a period of life which may last from age 12 to age 35 might develop its own cultural style, its own traditions and its own sources of motivation, satisfaction—and dissatisfaction. There is thus an enormous stratum of persons caught in the tension between their experience of peak physical strength and sexual energy on the one hand, and their public definition as culturally "immature" on the other.

This tension is exacerbated by a contradictory tendency: while modern industrial conditions promote juvenilization and the prolongation of dependence, they also create an "older," more experienced youthful cohort. They have more and earlier experience with sex and drugs; they are far better educated than their parents were; urban life sophisticates them more quickly; television brings into their homes worlds of experience that would otherwise remain alien to them. Young people, then, are faced not only with the ambiguity of the adolescent role itself and its prolon-

gation but with forces and conditions that, at least in some ways, make for *earlier* maturity. The youthful population is a potentially explosive stratum because this society is ill-equipped to accommodate it within the status system.

Erik Erikson's well-known theory of the "psycho-social moratorium" of adolescence takes the facts of adolescent prolongation and transforms them into a triumph of civilization. By emphasizing the increased time provided for young persons to postpone commitments, to try on social roles and to play the game called "the search for identity," Erikson suggests that the moratorium on lasting adult responsibilities contributes to the development and elaboration of personal individuality. I have no wish to quarrel with Erikson's general thesis here; I have done so elsewhere. Instead, I want to emphasize a fact that is seemingly contradictory to Erikson's observations about the moratorium on adult commitments. Namely, there have actually been increasing and clearly documented pressures on young people for earlier and earlier occupational planning and choice. "Benjamin," ask that famous Graduate's parents repeatedly, "what are you going to *do*?" And the question is echoed by millions of prosperous American parents who, despite their affluence, cannot assure the future economic position of their heirs.

Logically, of course, prolonged identity play and early occupational choice cannot be encouraged at the same time; the fact is, they are. And like other ambiguous values (and most moral values are ambiguous, or can be made so), this pair permit different groups of youngsters to rationalize or justify the kinds of adaptations that differing circumstances in fact constrain them to make. The public attention generated by protest-

Bennett M. Berger 45

ing youth in recent years (hippies, the New York Left, black militants) obscures the fact that the majority of young people are still apparently able to tolerate the tensions of prolonged adolescence, to adjust to the adolescent role (primarily, student), to take some satisfaction from the gains it provides in irresponsibility (i.e., "freedom") and to sail smoothly through high school into college where they choose the majors, get the grades and eventually the certifications for the occupations which they want, which want them and which higher education is equipped to provide them—degrees in education, business, engineering, dentistry and so on.

For others, however, the search for identity (quote, unquote) functions as a substitute for an occupational orientation; it gives them something "serious" to do while coping with their problems of sex, education, family and career. In college most of these people tend to major in the humanities or social sciences (particularly sociology) where they may take 10 years or more between the time they enter as freshmen, drop out, return, graduate and go on to pursue graduate degrees or give up on them entirely. I will return to this matter, but for the moment I want to make two general points: (1) that the contradictions create understandable tensions in the young and feed their appetite to discover "hypocrisy" in their elders; (2) that this condition is largely beyond the control of the universities; it is generated by the exigencies of a "post-industrial" society which uses institutions of higher education as warehouses for the temporary storage of a population it knows not what else to do with.

The situation has become critical over the past 10 years because the enormous numbers of the young (even small percentages of which yield formidable numbers of troops for worthy causes) and their concentration (in schools and cities) have promoted easy communication and a sense of group solidarity among them. Numbers, concentration and communication regarding common grievances have made increasingly viable, in almost precisely the way in which Karl Marx described the development of class consciousness among workers, the creation and maintenance of "deviant subcultures" of youth.

This youthful population is "available" for recruitment to moral causes because their marginal, ambiguous position in the social structure renders them sensitive to moral inconsistencies (note their talent for perceiving "hypocrisy"), because the major framework of their experience ("education") emphasizes "ideal" aspects of the culture and because their exclusion from adult responsibilities means that they are generally unrestrained by the institutional ties and commitments which normally function as a brake upon purely moral feeling; they also have the time for it.

The two great public issues of the decade (the Vietnam war and the rights of despised minorities) have been especially suited to enlist the militant predispositions of the young precisely because these issues are clearly moral issues. To take a strong "position" on these issues requires no great *expertise* or familiarity with arcane facts. And the moral fervor involved in taking such a position nicely reflects our traditional age-graded culture to the extent that it identifies virtue with "idealism," unspoiledness and innocence, precisely the qualities adults like to associate with the young.

It is almost as if the young, in the unconscious division of labor which occurs in all societies, were delegated the role of "moral organ" of society—what with all the grown-ups being too busy running the bureaucracies of the world (with their inevitable compromises, deals, gives and takes) to concern themselves with "ideals." This even makes a sort of good structural sense because the unanchored character of the young (that is, their relative unfetteredness to family, community and career) fits them to perform their "ideal" functions—in the same sense and for the same reason that Plato denied normal family life to his philosopher-kings and the Roman Catholic Church denies it to their priests.

It is the combination of moral sensitivity and alienation that accounts both for the extreme juvenophile postures of moral critics like Edgar Friedenberg, Paul Goodman and John Seeley (which sometimes reach the belief that the young are simply better people than the old or middle-aged, and hence even a belief in juvenocracy) and the fear of and hostility toward militant youth by writers epitomized by Lewis Feuer in his new book on student movements. In the latter view, the idealism of the young becomes corrupt, violent, terroristic and destructive precisely because, alienated, detached from institutions, youth are not "responsible"—that is, not accountable for the consequences of their moral zealotry upon the groups and organizations affected by it.

So one is tempted to say that society may just have to accept youth's irresponsibility if it values their moral contributions. But evidence suggests that adult society is in general sympathetic neither to their moral proddings nor toward granting the young any greater responsibility in public affairs. Research by English sociologist Frank Musgrove clearly documents that adults are unwilling to grant real responsibilities any earlier to the young, and there is good reason to believe the same is true in the United States, as is suggested by the repeated failures of the movement to lower the voting age to 18. And as for the "idealism" of youth, when it goes beyond the innocent virtues of praising honesty, being loyal, true and brave and helping old ladies across the street, to serious moral involvements promoting their own group interests ("student power") or those of the domestic or "third world" dispossessed, the shine of their "idealism" is likely to tarnish rather quickly.

Moreover, the moral activism of youth *is* sometimes vulnerable to attack on several counts. The "morality" of a political action, for example, is weakened when it has a self-congratulatory character (and the tendency to produce a holier-than-thou vanity in the actor). It also loses something when it does not involve substantial risk of personal interests or freedom (as it unambiguously *does* with the young only in the case of draft resisters). In the end, along with the society's prolongation of adolescence and encouragement of "the search for identity," continuing praise of the young for their "idealism" (except when it becomes serious) and continuing appeals to them to behave "responsibly"—in the face of repeated refusal to grant them real responsibilities (except in war)—are understandable as parts of the cultural armory supporting the process of juvenilization.

Colleges, universities and their environs are the places apparently designated by society as the primary locations where this armory is to be expended. It is clear that the schools, particularly institutions of higher learning, are increasingly being asked by society to perform a kind of holding operation for it. The major propaganda

Bennett M. Berger   47

campaign to encourage students not to drop out of high school is significant less for the jobs which staying that last year or two in high school will qualify one for than it is for the reduced pressure it creates on labor markets unable to absorb unskilled 16- and 17-year-olds. The military institutions, through the draft, help store (and train) much of the working-class young, and the colleges and universities prepare many of the heirs of the middle classes for careers in business, the professions and the semiprofessions. But higher education also gets the lion's share of the identity seekers: those sensitive children of the affluent, less interested in preparing themselves for occupations which the universities are competent to prepare them for than in transcending or trading in the stigmata of their bourgeois backgrounds (work ethic, money-grubbing, status-seeking) for a more "meaningful" life.

It is these students who are heavily represented among the student activists and among whom the cry for "relevance" is heard most insistently. Does it seem odd that this cry should be coming from those students who are *least* interested in the curricula whose relevance is palpable, at least with respect to occupations? Not if one observes that many of these students are, in a sense, classically "intellectuals"—that is, oriented toward statuses or positions for which the universities (as well as other major institutions) have seldom been able or competent to provide certification.

The statuses such students want are those to which one appoints oneself or which one drifts into: artist, critic, writer, intellectual, journalist, revolutionist, philosopher. And these statuses have been undermined for two generations or more by technical and bureaucratic élites whose training has become increasingly specialized and "scientific." In this context the cry for relevance is a protest against technical, value-neutral education whose product (salable skills or the posture of uncommitment) contributes nothing to the search by these students for "identity" and "meaningful experience."

Adding final insult to the injury of the threatened replacement of traditional humanistic intellectuals by technical élites is the ironic transformation of some of their traditional curricula (social sciences particularly) into instruments useful to the "power structure" or "the establishment" in pursuing its own ends. It makes no sense to call a curriculum "irrelevant" and then to turn right around and accuse its chief practitioners of "selling out"; the powerful do not squander their money so easily. The ironic point, then, is not that these curricula are "irrelevant" but that they are far *too* relevant to the support of interests to which the left is opposed.

The villains here are the methodological orthodoxies of the social sciences: their commitment to objectivity, detachment and the "separation" between facts and values. In the view of radical students, these orthodoxies rationalize the official diffidence of social scientists regarding the social consequences of their research, a diffidence which (conveniently—and profitably—for social scientists, goes the argument) promotes the interests of the established and the powerful. This is far from the whole truth, of course. There is plenty of research, supported by establishments, whose results offer the establishment little comfort. But like other "nonpartisan" or value-neutral practices and procedures, the methodological orthodoxies of the social sciences do tend in general to support established interests, simply because the powerful, in command of greater resources and facilities, are better able to make use of "facts" than the weak, and because avoidance of ideological controversy tends to perpetuate the inequities of the status quo.

But the demands for a more activist and "committed" social science and for social scientists to function as advocates for oppressed and subordinated groups may not be the best way of correcting the inequities. A thorough *doctrinal* politicization of social science in the university is likely to mean the total loss of whatever little insulation remains against the ideological controversies rending the larger society; and the probable result would be that the university, instead of being more liberal than the society as a whole, would more accurately reflect the still-burgeoning reactionary mood of the country.

For students who tend to be "around" a university for a long time—the 10-year period mentioned earlier is not uncommon—the university tends to become a kind of "home territory," the place where they really live. They experience the university less as an élite training institution than as a political community in which "members" have a kind of quasi-"citizenship" which, if one believes in democratic process, means a right to a legitimate political voice in its government.[2]

This conception of the university is quite discrepant with the conception held by most faculty members and administrators. To most faculty members the university is the élite training institution to which students who are both willing and able come to absorb intellectual disciplines—"ologies"—taught by skilled and certified professionals whose competences are defined by and limited to those certifications. But which way one sees the university—as a political community or as an élite training institution—is not purely a matter of ideological preference.

The fact seems to be that where training and certification and performance in politically neutral skills are clearest, the more conservative view is virtually unchallenged. This is true not only for dentistry and mathematics but for athletics, too. Presumably many militant blacks are not for any kind of a quota system with respect to varsity teams, and presumably football players in the huddle do not demand a voice in the decisions that shape their lives. But where what one's education confers upon one is a smattering of "high culture" or "civilized manners" or the detached sensibility and ethics of a science whose benefits, like other wealth, are not equitably distributed—in short, where the main result of liberal education is *Weltanschauung*—it indeed has "political" consequences.

These consequences were not controversial so long as the culture of the university was fairly homogeneous and so long as the "aliens" it admitted were eager to absorb that culture. They have become controversial in recent years because the democratization of higher education has revealed the "class" character of academic culture and because of the appearance on the campus of students who do not share and/or do not aspire to that culture. These newcomers have arrived in sufficiently large numbers to mount a

[2]Much remains to be clarified about the nature of "membership" in academic communities. So much cant has gone down in the name of "community" that I often feel about this word much like that Nazi who has gone down in history as having said, "When I hear the word 'culture,' I reach for my revolver."

serious challenge to the hegemony of traditional academic culture.

Discussion Questions

1. Distinguish between the majority of students, who tolerate the tensions of prolonged adolescence, and the identity seekers.

2. How has endless adolescence contributed to the role of students as the "moral organ" of society?

3. Berger claims that post-industrial society "uses institutions of higher education as warehouses for the temporary storage of a population it knows not what else to do with." How do you as students see your position and role in a university?

4. How do you define relevancy in education?

5. Compare Berger's views of student activists and hippies to those of Aldridge. To those of the interns.

EX-BASKETBALL PLAYER
JOHN UPDIKE

The most prestigious activities of high school have no lasting value; next year, or the year after that, there will be no band, no football, no pep club. Too often, life reaches its highest point at seventeen.

—Peter Schrag

Pearl Avenue runs past the high school lot,
Bends with the trolley tracks, and stops, cut off
Before it has a chance to go two blocks,
At Colonel McComsky Plaza. Berth's Garage
Is on the corner facing west, and there,
Most days, you'll find Flick Webb, who helps
   Berth out.

Flick stands tall among the idiot pumps—
Five on a side, the old bubble-head style,
Their rubber elbows hanging loose and low.
One's nostrils are two S's, and his eyes
An E and O. And one is squat, without
A head at all—more of a football type.

Once, Flick played for the high school team, the
   Wizards.
He was good: In fact, the best. In '46,
He bucketed three hundred ninety points,
A county record still. The ball loved Flick.
I saw him rack up thirty-eight or forty

John Updike (1932–) is an award-winning writer who publishes poetry, short stories, novels, and magazine articles.

In one home game. His hands were like wild
  birds.

He never learned a trade; he just sells gas,
Checks oil, and changes flats. Once in a while,
As a gag, he dribbles an inner tube,
But most of us remember anyway.
His hands are fine and nervous on the lug
  wrench.
It makes no difference to the lug wrench,
  though.

Off work, he hangs around Mae's Luncheonette.
Grease-grey and kind of coiled, he plays pinball.
Sips lemon cokes, and smokes those thin cigars;
Flick seldom speaks to Mae, just sits and nods
Beyond her face towards bright applauding tiers
Of Necco Wafers, Nibs, and Juju Beads.

Discussion Question

1. What is the social criticism in this poem?

GROWING UP ON MECHANIC STREET
PETER SCHRAG

Most men lead lives of quiet desperation.
—Henry David Thoreau

"Growing Up on Mechanic Street" portrays youth of a social group, the sons and daughters of blue-collar workers. Unlike the college students who are pursuing goals, careers, and new lives, these young people do not visualize a life very much different from that of their parents; they grow up without a sense of the future. Saul Alinsky has suggested the working class may be the next group in America to be radicalized.

It is impossible to think of those adolescents without a strange mixture of affection, apprehension and fear. To imagine them at all it becomes necessary to shoulder aside the black/white clichés of youth talk—about middle-class revolt and ghetto rebellion—and to perceive a grayer reality. I am not writing here of affluent suburbs or what others have called blacktown, but about the children of those whom Americans once celebrated as workingmen. (Again sociology fails us; there are no definitions or statistics. If there were, the matter would be better understood.) They exist everywhere, but convention has almost wiped them from sight. They are not

German-born Peter Schrag (1931–) has been a newspaper reporter, a college administrator, and a magazine editor.

supposed to be there, are perhaps not really supposed to believe even in their own existence. Thus they function not for themselves but to define and affirm the position of others: those who are very poor or those who are affluent, those who go to college. In visiting the schools they attend, one must constantly define them not by what they are, but by what they are not, and sometimes, in talking to teachers and administrators, one begins to doubt whether they exist at all.

Phrases like "the forgotten man" and "the silent majority" are too political to use as normative descriptions, but there is no doubt that there are forgotten kids who are indeed genuine victims: children of factory workers and truck drivers, of shop foremen and salesclerks, kids who live in row houses above steel mills and in tacky developments at the edge of town, children who will not go to college, who will not become affluent, who will not march the streets, who will do no more, nor less, than relive the lives of their parents.

We have all seen them: the kids on the corner with their duck-tail haircuts; the canvas-bag-toting types, lonely and lost, lining up at the induction centers; kids in knocked-down cars which seem to have no springs in back—whose wedding announcements appear daily in the newspapers of small towns (Mr. Jones works for the New York Central Railroad—no particular job worth mentioning—Miss Smith is a senior at Washington High), and whose deaths are recorded in the weekly reports from Saigon—name, rank, hometown. On the south side of Bethlehem, Pennsylvania, just above the mills, there is an alley called Mechanic Street; once, it was the heart of the old immigrant district, the first residence of thousands of Hungarians, Russians, Poles, Mexicans, Germans, Czechs and Croats. Most of them have now moved on to materially better things, but they regard this as their ancestral home. Think of the children of Mechanic Street; think of places called Liberty High and South Boston High, of Central High and Charlestown High, and of hundreds of others where defeat does not enjoy the ironic distinction or the acknowledged injustice of racial oppression.

The fact that defeat is not universal makes the matter all the more ugly. The record of college placement and vocational success which schools so love to celebrate, and the occasional moments of triumphant self-realization which they do not, obscure—seem, in fact, to legitimize—the unexpressed vacancy, the accepted defeat, and the unspoken frustration around and beyond the fringe. We have a pernicious habit of confusing the beginning of a trend with its ultimate accomplishment: when we see a growing number of students from blue-collar families going to college we begin to assume that they will all be happy and successful when they get there. Yet it is still a fact, as it always was, that the lower ranks of the economic order have the smallest chance of sending their children on, and that those who fall below the academic middle in high school tend to represent a disproportionate percentage of poor and working-class families. It seems somehow redundant and unnecessary to say all this again; but if it isn't said, there will be no stopping the stories of blissful academic success.

The social order of most white high schools—the attitudes that teachers and students have about other students—is based (in proper democratic fashion) on what people do in school, on their interests, their clubs, their personalities, their accomplishments. (Students from blue-collar families with serious college ambitions associate with the children of white-collar professionals, and share their attitudes, styles, and beliefs, which tend to be more liberal—politically and personally—than those of their parents. A few participated in the Vietnam moratorium last fall, and a handful, unknown to their fathers, have gone to the local draft counselors if any were available. But they represent a minority.) It is possible to leave Mechanic Street through school achievement—to community and state colleges, to technical schools, to better jobs—yet it is unlikely. Fewer than half actually go. What kids do in school tends, as always, to be predetermined. The honors class is filled with the children of professionals, kids whose parents have gone to college. The general course (meaning the dead end) and the vocational track are composed of the sons and daughters of blue-collar workers. The more "opportunity," the more justified the destiny of those who are tagged for failure. The world accepts the legitimacy of their position. And so do they. Their tragedy and the accompanying threat lie precisely in their acceptance of the low esteem in which school, society, and often their parents regard them and their inability to learn a language to express what they feel but dare not trust.

Imagine, says a school counselor, that you could become an animal, any animal. What species would you choose? The secret heart would choose freedom: eagles soaring over mountains, mustangs running across the plain, greyhounds loping through fields. Freedom.

Dreams are to be denied. The imagined future is like the present without parents. Jobs, domesticity, children—with little joy—seen in shades of gray. Coming out of school in the afternoon the boys already resemble their fathers when the shifts change—rows of dark, tufted mail-order-house jackets, rows of winter hats with the earflaps laced above the head, crossing the road from the plant to the parking lot, from the high school to the waiting buses and the bare-wheeled Chevvies. The girls, not yet stretched by pregnancy, often trim in short skirts and bright sweaters, will catch up with their mothers, will be married at eighteen or twenty, will often be engaged before the tedium of school is at an end. "Unwanted kids," says a school administrator, "kids of guys who got girls in trouble, kids of Korean War veterans and veterans of World War II, who didn't want the first child, and before they knew it they had two or three. All their lives their kids have been told to get out of the way, to go watch television. They don't have anybody to talk to. There was a recent survey that indicated that seventy-two percent of the first children of this generation were unwanted. These are the kids."

They sit in rows of five, five by five, in the classroom, existing from bell to bell, regurgitating answers, waiting for the next relief. The mindless lessons, the memory and boredom, and the stultifying order of cafeterias and study halls—no talking, sit straight, get a pass—these things need not be described again. From bell to bell: English, mathematics, history, science, and, for some, release to the more purposeful and engaging activities of the shop: auto mechanics, data processing, welding, wiring, carpentry and all the rest—some relevant, some obsolete, but all direct. There is an integrity, even joy, in material results—a sharp tool, an engine repaired, a solid joint—that the artificial world of the conventional academic course rarely allows. Material things respond, theory is applicable and comprehensible—either this thing works or it doesn't; it never prevaricates or qualifies, while words and social behavior, metaphors and politics, remain cloudy, elusive, and distant. You see them wiring an electric motor, or turning a machine part, a lathe, or fixing a car: pleasure, engagement or, better, a moment of truth. The Big Lie, if there is one, will be revealed later. ("No," says the director of a vocational school in an industrial city, "We don't tell the students that the construction unions are hard to join; it would discourage them in their work. They'll find out soon enough that it helps to know someone, to have a father or an uncle in the union. . . But after a kid manages to break in, he's proud of what he learned in the school of hard knocks, and he'll do the same thing to the new guys.")

From class to class, from school to home and back, there is a sort of passing-through. What is learned is to defer—to time, to authority, to events. One keeps asking, "What do they want, what do they do, what do they dream about?" and the answer is almost always institutional, as if the questions no longer applied: they go to school, they have jobs—in the candy factory, at the gas station, in a little repair shop, in a diner—and they ride and repair their cars. Many of them live in a moonlight culture, a world where people have second jobs, where mothers work, where one comes home and watches whatever happens to be on television, and where one no longer bothers to flip channels in search of something better.

Some distinctions are easy and obvious. Schooling certifies place; it selects people not only for social class but also for geographic mobility. The college-bound students speak about moving somewhere else—to the cities, to the West Coast, wherever events still permit the fantasy of a better future, or at least of change; the more national the college, the more likely they are to move. Among those who don't go to college there is little talk (except in depressed towns) of moving on. Academic losers stay put. "I know this is a dreary place," said a high school senior in Bethlehem. "But I like dreary places." It wasn't meant to be a joke. Big cities, they tell you again and again, are dangerous. (And in the cities they talk about protecting the neighborhood, or about how *they* still live in a good neighborhood.) Some places, they say, you can't walk the streets without getting knifed—by you know who. You hear it from sixteen-year-olds.

The instrument of oppression is the book. It is still the embodiment of the Great Mystery; learn to understand its secrets and great things will follow. Submit to your instinctive and natural boredom (lacking either the skills to play the game or the security to revolt), and we will use it to persuade you of your benighted incompetence: "I didn't want to write a term paper but the teacher said it would be good if I did; when I handed it in she made fun of it, so I quit school." The family knows that you should stay in school, that you should go to college and "get an education," but it does not know that often the school doesn't work, or that it works principally at the expense of its own kids.

One of the tragedies of the black revolt is that it frequently confused the general incompetence and boorishness of schools with racism, thus helping to persuade much of the blue-collar community that its children were in fine shape, that the educational system was basically sound, and that complaints came either from effete intellectuals or ungrateful, shiftless blacks. Teachers who purported to represent genuine intellectual achievement were thus allowed to continue to conceal their contempt for both kids and brains behind their unwavering passion for conformity and order, and to reaffirm the idea, already favored among working-class parents, that schooling was tough, boring, vicious, and mindless.

The school is an extension of the home: in the suburbs it is rated on college admissions, on National Merit winners, and similar distinctions; in the working-class neighborhood of the city it tends to be judged on order and discipline. Either way, the more talk there was nationally about the need for technologically trained people, the more the school was able to resist challenges to its own authority. "Technological complexity" replaced naked authority as the club of conformity in the school.

What the school did (and is doing) was to sell its clients, young and old, on the legitimacy of the system which abused them. Of course there are exceptions—students, teachers, schools—and even the drearier institutions are sufficiently equipped with the paraphernalia of *fun*—sports, bands, clubs—to mitigate the severity and enlist community support. It is hard to find schools which do not arrogate to themselves some sort of distinction: the state-championship marching band, league leadership in football or track, a squad of belles who twirl, hop, bounce, or step better than any other in the country. A girl makes her way from junior pom-pom girl to cheerleader or majorette, a boy comes from the obscurity of an ethnic neighborhood to be chosen an all-state tackle. There is vitality and engagement and, for the moment, the welding of new common-interest groups, new friendships, new forms of integration. It is the only community adolescents have, and even the dropouts sometimes sneak back to see their friends. And yet, many of these things come to a swift and brutal end: a note in the yearbook, some clippings, a temporary sense of value and distinction convertible into an early marriage, a secretarial job, an occasional scholarship, or into permanent fat. The most prestigious activities of high school have no lasting value; next year, or the year after that, there will be no band, no football, no pep club. Too often, life reaches its highest point at seventeen.

Discussion Questions

1. Compare the future prospects of the youth on Mechanic Street with the prospects of college students.
2. Discuss this essay in relation to "Ex-Basketball Player."
3. Describe a typical day of a blue-collar youth.
4. How does Schrag criticize high school education?
5. Generally speaking, do college students have a different attitude toward blacks than do blue-collar youth?
6. What values of college students and blue-collar youth conflict?
7. If blue-collar workers are radicalized or become politically active, how will they assert themselves? What demands will they make of the government?

Peter Schrag   **57**

ROOSEVELT SMITH

FRANK MARSHALL DAVIS

You ask what happened to Roosevelt Smith

Well . . .

Conscience and the critics got him

Roosevelt Smith was the only dusky child born
    and bred in the village of Pine City, Nebraska

At college they worshipped the novelty of a
    black poet and predicted fame

At twenty-three he published his first book . . . .
    the critics said he imitated Carl Sandburg,
    Edgar Lee Masters and Vachel Lindsay . . .
    they raved about a wealth of racial material
    and the charm of darky dialect

So for two years Roosevelt worked and observed
    in Dixie

At twenty-five a second book . . . Negroes
    complained about plantation scenes and said
    he dragged Aframerica's good name in the
    mire for gold . . . "Europe," they said,
    "honors Dunbar for his 'Ships That Pass in
    the Night' and not for his dialect which they
    don't understand"

Frank Marshall Davis (1905–) is a journalist and poet who
was the first editor of the *Atlanta Daily World*, the first
successful black daily newspaper in America. Since 1948 he
has lived in Honolulu, Hawaii where he operates a wholesale
paper firm and works in the advertising field.

For another two years Roosevelt strove for a
different medium of expression

At twenty-seven a third book . . . The critics
said the density of Gertrude Stein or T.S. Eliot
hardly fitted the simple material to which a
Negro had access

For another two years Roosevelt worked

At twenty-nine his fourth book . . . the critics
said a Negro had no business initiating the
classic forms of Keats, Browning and
Shakespeare . . . "Roosevelt Smith," they
announced, "has nothing original and is
merely a blackface white. His African heritage
is a rich source should he use it"

So for another two years Roosevelt went into the
interior of Africa

At thirty-one his fifth book . . . interesting
enough, the critics said, but since it followed
nothing done by any white poet it was
probably just a new kind of prose

Day after the reviews came out Roosevelt traded
conscience and critics for the leather pouch
and bunions of a mail carrier and read in the
papers until his death how little the American
Negro had contributed to his nation's
literature . . .

Discussion Questions

1. How does being black restrict Roosevelt Smith?
   Any black creative artist?
2. What values govern Roosevelt Smith's actions?
   What advice would you give him?

Frank Marshall Davis   59

SON IN THE AFTERNOON
JOHN A. WILLIAMS

In the 1960s the terms "black power" and "black rage" rose from the smoldering flames of Watts, Detroit, Chicago, and Hough. In "Son in the Afternoon" we learn that reprisals for injustice and humiliation can find a more subtle expression.

It was hot. I tend to be a bitch when it's hot. I goosed the little Ford over Sepulveda Boulevard toward Santa Monica until I got stuck in the traffic that pours from L.A. into the surrounding towns. I'd had a very lousy day at the studio.

I was—still am—a writer and this studio had hired me to check scripts and films with Negroes in them to make sure the Negro moviegoer wouldn't be offended. The signs were already clear one day the whole of American industry would be racing pell-mell to get a Negro, showcase a spade. I was kind of a pioneer. I'm a *Negro* writer, you see. The day had been tough because of a couple of verbs—slink and walk. One of those Hollywood hippies had done a script calling for a Negro waiter to slink away from the table where a dinner party was glaring at him. I said the waiter should walk, not slink, because later on he becomes a hero. The Hollywood hippie, who

John A. Williams (1925–) is a contemporary black short-story writer and novelist.

understood it all because he had some colored friends, said that it was essential to the plot that the waiter slink. I said you don't slink one minute and become a hero the next; there has to be some consistency. The Negro actor I was standing up for said nothing either way. He had played Uncle Tom roles so long that he had become Uncle Tom. But the director agreed with me.

Anyway . . . hear me out now. I was on my way to Santa Monica to pick up my mother, Nora. It was a long haul for such a hot day. I had planned a quiet evening: a nice shower, fresh clothes, and then I would have dinner at the Watkins and talk with some of the musicians on the scene for a quick taste before they cut to their gigs. After, I was going to the Pigalle down on Figueroa and catch Earl Grant at the organ, and still later, if nothing exciting happened, I'd pick up Scottie and make it to the Lighthouse on the Beach or to the Strollers and listen to some of the white boys play. I liked the long drive, especially while listening to Sleepy Stein's show on the radio. Later, much later of course, it would be home, back to Watts.

So you see, this picking up Nora was a little inconvenient. My mother was a maid for the Couchmans. Ronald Couchman was an architect, a good one I understood from Nora who has a fine sense for this sort of thing; you don't work in some hundred-odd houses during your life without getting some idea of the way a house should be laid out. Couchman's wife, Kay, was a playgirl who drove a white Jaguar from one party to another. My mother didn't like her too much; she didn't seem to care much for her son, Ronald, junior. There's something wrong with a parent who can't really love her own child, Nora thought. The Couchmans lived in a real fine residential section, of course. A number of actors lived nearby, character actors, not really big stars.

Somehow it is very funny. I mean that the maids and butlers knew everything about these people, and these people knew nothing at all about the help. Through Nora and her friends I knew who was laying whose wife; who had money and who *really* had money; I knew about the wild parties hours before the police, and who smoked marijuana, when, and where they got it.

To get to Couchman's driveway I had to go three blocks up one side of a palm-planted center strip and back down the other. The driveway bent gently, then swept back out of sight of the main road. The house, sheltered by slim palms, looked like a transplanted New England Colonial. I parked and walked to the kitchen door, skirting the growling Great Dane who was tied to a tree. That was the route to the kitchen door.

I don't like kitchen doors. Entering people's houses by them, I mean. I'd done this thing most of my life when I called at places where Nora worked to pick up the patched or worn sheets or the half-eaten roasts, the battered, tarnished silver—the fringe benefits of a housemaid. As a teen-ager I'd told Nora I was through with that crap; I was not going through anyone's kitchen door. She only laughed and said I'd learn. One day soon after, I called for her and without knocking walked right through the front door of this house and right on through the living room. I was almost out of the room when I saw feet behind the couch. I leaned over and there was Mr. Jorgensen and his wife making out like crazy. I guess they thought Nora had gone and it must have hit them sort of suddenly and they went at it like the hell-bomb was due to drop any minute. I've been that way too, mostly in the spring. Of course, when Mr. Jorgensen looked over his shoulder and saw me, you know what happened. I was thrown out and Nora right behind me. It was the middle of winter, the old man was sick and the coal bill three months overdue. Nora was right about those kitchen doors: I learned.

My mother saw me before I could ring the bell. She opened the door. "Hello," she said. She was breathing hard, like she'd been running or something. "Come in and sit down. I don't know *where* that Kay is. Little Ronald is sick and she's probably out gettin' drunk again." She left me then and trotted back through the house, I guess to be with Ronnie. I hated the combination of her white nylon uniform, her dark brown face and the wide streaks of gray in her hair. Nora had married this guy from Texas a few years after the old man had died. He was all right. He made out okay. Nora didn't have to work, but she just couldn't be still; she always had to be doing something. I suggested she quit work, but I had as much luck as her husband. I used to tease her about liking to be around those white folks. It would have been good for her to take an extended trip around the country visiting my brothers and sisters. Once she got to Philadelphia, she could go right out to the cemetery and sit awhile with the old man.

I walked through the Couchman home. I liked the library. I thought if I knew Couchman I'd like him. The room made me feel like that. I left it and went into the big living room. You could tell that Couchman had let his wife do that. Everything in it was fast, dart-like, with no sense of ease. But on the walls were several of Couchman's conceptions of buildings and homes. I guess he was a disciple of Wright. My mother walked rapidly through the room without looking

at me and said, "Just be patient, Wendell. She should be here real soon."

"Yeah," I said, "with a snootful." I had turned back to the drawings when Ronnie scampered into the room, his face twisted with rage.

"Nora!" he tried to roar, perhaps the way he'd seen the parents of some of his friends roar at their maids. I'm quite sure Kay didn't shout at Nora, and I don't think Couchman would. But then no one shouts at Nora. "Nora, you come right back here this minute!" the little bastard shouted and stamped and pointed to a spot on the floor where Nora was supposed to come to roost. I have a nasty temper. Sometimes it lies dormant for ages and at other times, like when the weather is hot and nothing seems to be going right, it's bubbling and ready to explode. "Don't talk to *my* mother like that, you little—!" I said sharply, breaking off just before I cursed. I wanted him to be large enough for me to strike. "How'd you like for me to talk to *your* mother like that?"

The nine-year-old looked up at me in surprise and confusion. He hadn't expected me to say anything. I was just another piece of furniture. Tears rose in his eyes and spilled out onto his pale cheeks. He put his hands behind him, twisted them. He moved backwards, away from me. He looked at my mother with a "Nora, come help me" look. And sure enough, there was Nora, speeding back across the room, gathering the kid in her arms, tucking his robe together. I was too angry to feel hatred for myself.

Ronnie was the Couchman's only kid. Nora loved him. I suppose that was the trouble. Couchman was gone ten, twelve hours a day. Kay didn't stay around the house any longer than she had to. So Ronnie had only my mother. I think kids should have someone to love, and Nora wasn't a bad sort. But somehow when the six of us, her own children, were growing up we never had her. She was gone, out scuffling to get those crumbs to put into our mouths and shoes for our feet and praying for something to happen so that all the space in between would be taken care of. Nora's affection for us took the form of rushing out into the morning's five o'clock blackness to wake some silly bitch and get her coffee; took form in her trudging five miles home every night instead of taking the streetcar to save money to buy tablets for us, to use at school, we said. But the truth was that all of us liked to draw and we went through a writing tablet in a couple of hours every day. Can you imagine? There's not a goddamn artist among us. We never had the physical affection, the pat on the head, the quick, smiling kiss, the "gimmee a hug" routine. All of this Ronnie was getting.

Now he buried his little blond head in Nora's breast and sobbed. "There, there now," Nora said. "Don't you cry, Ronnie. Ol' Wendell is just jealous, and he hasn't much sense either. He didn't mean nuthin'."

I left the room. Nora had hit it of course, hit it and passed on. I looked back. It didn't look so incongruous, the white and black together, I mean. Ronnie was still sobbing. His head bobbed gently on Nora's shoulder. The only time I ever got that close to her was when she trapped me with a bearhug so she could whale the daylights out of me after I put a snowball through Mrs. Grant's window. I walked outside and lit a cigarette. When Ronnie was in the hospital the month before, Nora got me to run her way over to Hollywood every night to see him. I didn't like that worth a damn. All right, I'll admit it: it did

upset me. All that affection I didn't get nor my brothers and sisters going to that little white boy, who, without a doubt, when away from her called her the names he'd learned from adults. Can you imagine a nine-year-old kid calling Nora a "girl," "our girl?" I spat at the Great Dane. He snarled and then I bounced a rock off his fanny. "Lay down, you bastard," I muttered. It was a good thing he was tied up.

I heard the low cough of the Jaguar slapping against the road. The car was throttled down, and with a muted roar it swung into the driveway. The woman aimed it for me. I was evil enough not to move. I was tired of playing with these people. At the last moment, grinning, she swung the wheel over and braked. She bounded out of the car like a tennis player vaulting over a net.

"Hi," she said, tugging at her shorts. "Hello."

"You're Nora's boy?"

"I'm Nora's son." Hell, I was as old as she was; besides, I can't stand "boy."

"Nora tells us you're working in Hollywood. Like it?"

"It's all right."

"You must be pretty talented."

We stood looking at each other while the dog whined for her attention. Kay had a nice body and it was well tanned. She was high, boy, was she high. Looking at her, I could feel myself going into my sexy bastard routine; sometimes I can swing it great. Maybe it all had to do with the business inside. Kay took off her sunglasses and took a good look at me. "Do you have a cigarette?"

I gave her one and lit it. "Nice tan," I said. Most white people I know think it's a great big deal if a Negro compliments them on their tans. It's a large laugh. You have all this volleyball about color and come summer you can't hold the white folks back from the beaches anyplace where they can get some sun. And of course the blacker they get, the more pleased they are. Crazy. If there is ever a Negro revolt, it will come during the summer and Negroes will descend upon the beaches around the nation and paralyze the country. You can't conceal cattle prods and bombs and pistols and police dogs when you're showing your birthday suit to the sun.

"You like it?" she asked. She was pleased. She placed her arm next to mine. "Almost the same color," she said.

"Ronnie isn't feeling well," I said.

"Oh, the poor kid. I'm so glad we have Nora. She's such a charm. I'll run right in and look at him. Do have a drink in the bar. Fix me one too, will you?" Kay skipped inside and I went to the bar and poured out two strong drinks. I made hers stronger than mine. She was back soon. "Nora was trying to put him to sleep and she made me stay out." She giggled. She quickly tossed off her drink. "Another, please?" While I was fixing her drink she was saying how amazing it was for Nora to have such a talented son. What she was really saying was that it was amazing for a servant to have a son who was not also a servant. "Anything can happen in a democracy," I said. "Servants' sons drink with madames and so on."

"Oh, Nora isn't a servant," Kay said. "She's part of the family."

Yeah, I thought. Where and how many times had I heard *that* before?

In the ensuing silence, she started to admire her tan again. "You think it's pretty good, do you? You don't know how hard I worked to get it." I moved close to her and held her arm. I placed my other arm around her. She pretended not to see or feel it, but she wasn't trying to get away either. In fact she was pressing closer and the register in my brain that tells me at the precise moment when I'm in, went off. Kay was very high. I put both arms around her and she put both hers around me. When I kissed her, she responded completely.

"Mom!"

"Ronnie, come back to bed," I heard Nora shout from the other room. We could hear Ronnie running over the rug in the outer room. Kay tried to get away from me, push me to one side, because we could tell that Ronnie knew where to look for his Mom: he was running right for the bar, where we were. "Oh, please," she said, "don't let him see us." I wouldn't let her push me away. "Stop!" she hissed. "He'll *see* us!" We stopped struggling just for an instant, and we listened to the echoes of the word *see*. She gritted her teeth and renewed her efforts to get away.

Me? I had the scene laid right out. The kid breaks into the room, see, and sees his mother in this real wriggly clinch with this colored guy who's just shouted at him, see, and no matter how his mother explains it away, the kid has the image—the colored guy and his mother—for the rest of his life, see?

That's the way it happened. The kid's mother hissed under her breath, *"You're crazy!"* and she looked at me as though she were seeing me or something about me for the very first time. I'd released her as soon as Ronnie, romping into the bar, saw us and came to a full, open-mouthed halt. Kay went to him. He looked first at me, then at his mother. Kay turned to me, but she couldn't speak.

Outside in the living room my mother called, "Wendell, where are you? We can go now."

I started to move past Kay and Ronnie. I felt many things, but I made myself think mostly, *There you little bastard, there.*

My mother thrust her face inside the door and said, "Good-bye, Mrs. Couchman. See you tomorrow. 'Bye, Ronnie."

"Yes," Kay said, sort of stunned. "Tomorrow." She was reaching for Ronnie's left hand as we left, but the kid was slapping her hand away. I hurried quickly after Nora, hating the long drive back to Watts.

Discussion Questions

1. What are the motives of Wendell? Was his action justified?
2. Generally speaking, do most blacks harbor hostile feelings toward whites?
3. How does Wendell differ from Roosevelt Smith?

John A. Williams **65**

CHALLENGE

THE UNKNOWN CITIZEN
W.H. AUDEN

To JS/07/M/378
This Marble Monument is Erected by the State

He was found by the Bureau of Statistics to be
One against whom there was no official
   complaint,
And all the reports on his conduct agree
That, in the modern sense of an old-fashioned
   word, he was a saint,
For in everything he did he served the Greater
   Community.
Except for the War till the day he retired
He worked in a factory and never got fired,
But satisfied his employers, Fudge Motors Inc.
Yet he wasn't a scab or odd in his views,
For his Union reports that he paid his dues,
(Our report on his Union shows it was sound)
And our Social Psychology workers found
That he was popular with his mates and liked a
   drink.
The Press are convinced that he bought a paper
   every day

Born in 1907 and educated in England, W.H. Auden is an educator, poet, and dramatist who recently returned to England after living and working in the United States for many years.

W. H. Auden   **69**

And that his reactions to advertisements were normal in every way.
Policies taken out in his name prove that he was fully insured,
And his Health-card shows he was once in hospital but left it cured.
Both Producers Research and High-Grade Living declare
He was fully sensible to the advantages of the Installment Plan
And had everything necessary to the Modern Man,
A gramophone, a radio, a car and a frigidaire.
Our researchers into Public Opinion are content
That he held the proper opinions for the time of year;
When there was peace, he was for peace; when there was war, he went.
He was married and added five children to the population,
Which our Eugenist says was the right number for a parent of his generation,
And our teachers report that he never interfered with their education.
Was he free? Was he happy? The question is absurd:
Had anything been wrong, we should certainly have heard.

Discussion Questions

1. How would you answer the questions that Auden raises at the end of the poem: "Was he free? Was he happy?"
2. How would you relate "The Unknown Citizen" to blue-collar workers?

A DIVERSITY OF LIFE STYLES
ALVIN TOFFLER

The search for a life style may be each person's greatest challenge, for it will provide him with his psychological, intellectual, and cultural anchors.

In San Francisco, executives lunch at restaurants where they are served by bare-breasted waitresses. In New York, however, a kooky girl cellist is arrested for performing avant garde music in a topless costume. In St. Louis, scientists hire prostitutes and others to copulate under a camera as part of a study of the physiology of the orgasm. But in Columbus, Ohio, civic controversy erupts over the sale of so-called "Little Brother" dolls that come from the factory equipped with male genitalia. In Kansas City, a conference of homosexual organizations announces a campaign to lift a Pentagon ban on homosexuals in the armed forces and, in fact, the Pentagon discreetly does so. Yet American jails are well populated with men arrested for the crime of homosexuality.

Seldom has a single nation evinced greater confusion over its sexual values. Yet the same might be said for other kinds of values as well.

Alvin Toffler (1928–), former news correspondent and associate editor of *Fortune* magazine, is the author of *Future Shock,* from which this excerpt is taken.

America is tortured by uncertainty with respect to money, property, law and order, race, religion, God, family and self. Nor is the United States alone in suffering from a kind of value vertigo. All the techno-societies are caught up in the same massive upheaval. This collapse of the values of the past has hardly gone unnoticed. Every priest, politician and parent is reduced to head-shaking anxiety by it. Yet most discussions of value change are barren for they miss two essential points. The first of these is acceleration.

Value turnover is now faster than ever before in history. While in the past a man growing up in a society could expect that its public value system would remain largely unchanged in his lifetime, no such assumption is warranted today, except perhaps in the most isolated of pre-technological communities.

This implies temporariness in the structure of both public and personal value systems, and it suggests that *whatever* the content of values that arise to replace those of the industrial age, they will be shorter-lived, more ephemeral than the values of the past. There is no evidence whatsoever that the value systems of the techno-societies are likely to return to a "steady state" condition. For the foreseeable future, we must anticipate still more rapid value change.

Within this context, however, a second powerful trend is unfolding. For the fragmentation of societies brings with it a diversification of values. We are witnessing the crack-up of consensus.

Most previous societies have operated with a broad central core of commonly shared values. This core is now contracting, and there is little reason to anticipate the formation of a new broad consensus within the decades ahead. The pressures are outward toward diversity, not inward toward unity.

This accounts for the fantastically discordant propaganda that assails the mind in the techno-societies. Home, school, corporation, church, peer group, mass media—and myriad subcults—all advertise varying sets of values. The result for many is an "anything goes" attitude—which is, itself, still another value position. We are, declares *Newsweek* magazine, "a society that has lost its consensus . . . a society that cannot agree on standards of conduct, language and manners, on what can be seen and heard."

This picture of a cracked consensus is confirmed by the findings of Walter Gruen, social science research coordinator at Rhode Island Hospital, who has conducted a series of statistical studies of what he terms "the American core culture." Rather than the monolithic system of beliefs attributed to the middle class by earlier investigators, Gruen found—to his own surprise—that "diversity in beliefs was more striking than the statistically supported uniformities. It is," he concluded, "perhaps already misleading to talk of an 'American' culture complex."

Gruen suggests that particularly among the affluent, educated group, consensus is giving way to what he calls "pockets" of values. We can expect that, as the number and variety of subcults continues to expand, these pockets will proliferate, too.

Faced with colliding value systems, confronted with a blinding array of new consumer goods, services, educational, occupational and recreational options, the people of the future are driven to make choices in a new way. They begin to "consume" life styles the way people of an earlier, less choice-choked time consumed ordinary products.

MOTORCYCLISTS AND INTELLECTUALS

During Elizabethan times, the term "gentleman" referred to a whole way of life, not simply an accident of birth. Appropriate lineage may have been a prerequisite, but to be a gentleman one had also to live in a certain style: to be better educated, have better manners, wear better clothes than the masses; to engage in certain recreations (and not others); to live in a large, well-furnished house; to maintain a certain aloofness with subordinates; in short, never to lose sight of his class "superiority."

The merchant class had its own preferred life style and the peasantry still another. These life styles, like that of the gentleman, were pieced together out of many different components, ranging from residence, occupation and dress to jargon, gesture and religion.

Today we still create our life styles by forming a mosaic of components. But much has changed. Life style is no longer simply a manifestation of class position. Classes themselves are breaking up into smaller units. Economic factors are declining in importance. Thus today it is not so much one's class base as one's ties with a subcult that determine the individual's style of life. The working-class hippie and the hippie who dropped out of Exeter or Eton share a common style of life but no common class.

Since life style has become the way in which the individual expresses his identification with this or that subcult, the explosive multiplication of subcults in society has brought with it an equally explosive multiplication of life styles. Thus the stranger launched into American or English or Japanese or Swedish society today must choose not among four or five class-based styles of life, but among literally hundreds of diverse possibilities. Tomorrow, as subcults proliferate, this number will be even larger.

How we choose a life style, and what it means to us, therefore, looms as one of the central issues of the psychology of tomorrow. For the selection of a life style, whether consciously done or not, powerfully shapes the individual's future. It does this by imposing order, a set of principles or criteria on the choices he makes in his daily life.

This becomes clear if we examine how such choices are actually made. The young couple setting out to furnish their apartment may look at literally hundreds of different lamps—Scandinavian, Japanese, French Provincial, Tiffany lamps, hurricane lamps, American colonial lamps—dozens, scores of different sizes, models and styles before selecting, say, the Tiffany lamp. Having surveyed a "universe" of possibilities, they zero in on one. In the furniture department, they again scan an array of alternatives, then settle on a Victorian end table. This scan-and-select procedure is repeated with respect to rugs, sofa, drapes, dining room chairs, etc. In fact, something like this same procedure is followed not merely in furnishing their home, but also in their adoption of ideas, friends, even the vocabulary they use and the values they espouse.

While the society bombards the individual with a swirling, seemingly patternless set of alternatives, the selections made are anything but random. The consumer (whether of end tables or ideas) comes armed with a pre-established set of tastes and preferences. Moreover, no choice is

Alvin Toffler 73

wholly independent. Each is conditioned by those made earlier. The couple's selection of an end table has been conditioned by their previous choice of a lamp. In short, there is a certain consistency, an attempt at personal style, in all our actions—whether consciously recognized or not.

The American male who wears a button-down collar and garter-length socks probably also wears wing-tip shoes and carries an attaché case. If we look closely, chances are we shall find a facial expression and brisk manner intended to approximate those of the stereotypical executive. The odds are astronomical that he will not let his hair grow wild in the manner of rock musician Jimi Hendrix. He knows, as we do, that certain clothes, manners, forms of speech, opinions and gestures hang together, while others do not. He may know this only by "feel," or "intuition," having picked it up by observing others in the society, but the knowledge shapes his actions.

The black-jacketed motorcyclist who wears steel-studded gauntlets and an obscene swastika dangling from his throat completes his costume with rugged boots, not loafers or wing-tips. He is likely to swagger as he walks and to grunt as he mouths his anti-authoritarian platitudes. For he, too, values consistency. He knows that any trace of gentility or articulateness would destroy the integrity of his style. Why do the motorcyclists wear black jackets? Why not brown or blue? Why do executives in America prefer attaché cases, rather than the traditional briefcase? It is as though they were following some model, trying to attain some ideal laid down from above.

We know little about the origin of life style models. We do know, however, that popular heroes and celebrities, including fictional charac-ters (James Bond, for example), have something to do with it.

Marlon Brando, swaggering in a black jacket as a motorcyclist, perhaps originated, and certainly publicized a life style model. Timothy Leary, robed, beaded, and muttering mystic pseudo profundities about love and LSD, provided a model for thousands of youths. Such heroes, as the sociologist Orrin Klapp puts it, help to "crystallize a social type." He cites the late James Dean who depicted the alienated adolescent in the movie *Rebel Without a Cause* or Elvis Presley who initially fixed the image of the guitar-twanging rock-'n'-roller. Later came the Beatles with their (at that time) outrageous hair and exotic costumes. "One of the prime functions of popular favorites," says Klapp, "is to make types visible, which in turn make new life styles and new tastes visible."

Yet the style-setter need not be a mass media idol. He may be almost unknown outside a particular subcult. Thus for years Lionel Trilling, an English professor at Columbia, was the father figure for the West Side Intellectuals, a New York subcult well known in literary and academic circles in the United States. The mother figure was Mary McCarthy, long before she achieved popular fame.

An acute article by John Speicher in a youth magazine called *Cheetah* listed some of the better-known life style models to which young people were responding in the late sixties. They ranged from Ché Guevara to William Buckley, from Bob Dylan and Joan Baez to Robert Kennedy. "The American youth bag," wrote Speicher, lapsing into hippie jargon, "is overcrowded with heroes." And, he adds, "where heroes are, there are followers, cultists."

74   Challenge

To the subcult member, its heroes provide what Speicher calls the "crucial existential necessity of psychological identity." This is, of course, hardly new. Earlier generations identified with Charles Lindbergh or Theda Bara. What is new and highly significant, however, is the fabulous proliferation of such heroes and mini-heroes. As subcults multiply and values diversify, we find, in Speicher's words, "a national sense of identity hopelessly fragmented." For the individual, he says, this means greater choice: "There is a wide range of cults available, a wide range of heroes. You can do comparison shopping."

LIFE STYLE FACTORIES

While charismatic figures may become style-setters, styles are fleshed out and marketed to the public by the sub-societies or tribe-lets we have termed subcults. Taking in raw symbolic matter from the mass media, they somehow piece together odd bits of dress, opinion, and expression and form them into a coherent package: a life style model. Once they have assembled a particular model, they proceed, like any good corporation, to merchandise it. They find customers for it.

Anyone doubting this is advised to read the letters of Allen Ginsberg to Timothy Leary, the two men most responsible for creating the hippie life style, with its heavy accent on drug use.

Says poet Ginsberg: "Yesterday got on TV with N. Mailer and Ashley Montagu and gave big speech . . . recommending everybody get high . . . Got in touch with all the liberal pro-dope people I know to have [a certain pro-drug report] publicized and circulated . . . I wrote a five-page summary of the situation to this friend Kenny Love on *The New York Times* and he said he'd perhaps do a story (newswise) . . . which could then be picked up by U.P. friend on national wire. Also gave copy to Al Aronowitz on New York *Post* and Rosalind Constable at *Time* and Bob Silvers on *Harper's* . . ."

No wonder LSD and the whole hippie phenomenon received the immense mass media publicity it did. This partial account of Ginsberg's energetic press agentry, complete with the Madison Avenue suffix "wise" (as in newswise), reads precisely like an internal memo from Hill and Knowlton or any of the other giant public relations corporations whom hippies love to flagellate for manipulating public opinion. The successful "sale" of the hippie life style model to young people all over the techno-societies, is one of the classic merchandising stories of our time.

Not all subcults are so aggressive and talented at flackery, yet their cumulative power in the society is enormous. This power stems from our almost universal desperation to "belong." The primitive tribesman feels a strong attachment to his tribe. He knows that he "belongs" to it, and may even have difficulty imagining himself apart from it. The techno-societies are so large, however, and their complexities so far beyond the comprehension of any individual, that it is only by plugging in to one or more of their subcults, that we maintain some sense of identity and contact with the whole. Failure to identify with some such group or groups condemns us to feelings of loneliness, alienation and ineffectuality. We begin to wonder "who we are."

In contrast, the sense of belonging, of being part of a social cell larger than ourselves (yet small enough to be comprehensible) is often so rewarding that we feel deeply drawn, sometimes even against our own better judgment, to the values, attitudes and most-favored life style of the group.

However, we pay for the benefits we receive. For once we psychologically affiliate with a subcult, it begins to exert pressures on us. We find that it pays to "go along" with the group. It rewards us with warmth, friendship and approval when we conform to its life style model. But it punishes us ruthlessly with ridicule, ostracism or other tactics when we deviate from it.

Hawking their preferred life style models, subcults clamor for our attention. In so doing, they act directly on our most vulnerable psychological property, our self-image. "Join us," they whisper, "and you become a bigger, better, more effective, more respected and less lonely person." In choosing among the fast-proliferating subcults we may only vaguely sense that our identity will be shaped by our decision, but we feel the hot urgency of their appeals and counter-appeals. We are buffeted back and forth by their psychological promises.

At the moment of choice among them, we resemble the tourist walking down Bourbon Street in New Orleans. As he strolls past the honky-tonks and clip joints, doormen grab him by the arm, spin him around, and open a door so he can catch a titillating glimpse of the naked flesh of the strippers on the platform behind the bar. Subcults reach out to capture us and appeal to our most private fantasies in ways far more powerful and subtle than any yet devised by Madison Avenue.

What they offer is not simply a skin show or a new soap or detergent. They offer not a product, but a super-product. It is true they hold out the promise of human warmth, companionship, respect, a sense of community. But so do the advertisers of deodorants and beer. The "miracle ingredient," the exclusive component, the one thing that subcults offer that other hawkers cannot, is a respite from the strain of overchoice. For they offer not a single product or idea, but a way of organizing all products and ideas, not a single commodity but a whole style, a set of guidelines that help the individual reduce the increasing complexity of choice to manageable proportions.

Most of us are desperately eager to find precisely such guidelines. In the welter of conflicting moralities, in the confusion occasioned by overchoice, the most powerful, most useful "super-product" of all is an organizing principle for one's life. This is what a life style offers.

THE POWER OF STYLE

Of course, not just any life style will do. We live in a Cairo bazaar of competing models. In this psychological phantasmagoria we search for a style, a way of ordering our existence, that will fit our particular temperament and circumstances. We look for heroes or mini-heroes to emulate. The style-seeker is like the lady who flips through the pages of a fashion magazine to find a suitable dress pattern. She studies one after another, settles on one that appeals to her, and decides to create a dress based on it. Next she begins to collect the necessary materials—cloth, thread, piping, buttons, etc. In precisely the same way, the life style creator acquires the necessary props. He lets his hair grow. He buys art nouveau posters and a paperback of Guevara's writings. He learns to discuss Marcuse and Frantz Fanon.

He picks up a particular jargon, using words like "relevance" and "establishment."

None of this means that his political actions are insignificant, or that his opinions are unjust or foolish. He may (or may not) be accurate in his views of society. Yet the particular way in which he chooses to express them is inescapably part of his search for personal style.

The lady, in constructing her dress, alters it here and there, deviating from the pattern in minor ways to make it fit her more perfectly. The end product is truly custom-made; yet it bears a striking resemblance to others sewn from the same design. In quite the same way we individualize our style of living, yet it usually winds up bearing a distinct resemblance to some life style model previously packaged and marketed by a subcult.

Often we are unaware of the moment when we commit ourselves to one life style model over all others. The decision to "be" an Executive or a Black Militant or a West Side Intellectual is seldom the result of purely logical analysis. Nor is the decision always made cleanly, all at once. The research scientist who switches from cigarettes to a pipe may do so for health reasons without recognizing that the pipe is part of a whole life style toward which he finds himself drawn. The couple who choose the Tiffany lamp think they are furnishing an apartment; they do not necessarily see their actions as an attempt to flesh out an overall style of life.

Most of us, in fact, do not think of our own lives in terms of life style, and we often have difficulty in talking about it objectively. We have even more trouble when we try to articulate the structure of values implicit in our style. The task is doubly hard because many of us do not adopt a single integrated style, but a composite of elements drawn from several different models. We may emulate both Hippie and Surfer. We may choose a cross between West Side Intellectual and Executive—a fusion that is, in fact, chosen by many publishing officials in New York. When one's personal style is a hybrid, it is frequently difficult to disentangle the multiple models on which it is based.

Once we commit ourselves to a particular model, however, we fight energetically to build it, and perhaps even more so to preserve it against challenge. For the style becomes extremely important to us. This is doubly true of the people of the future, among whom concern for style is downright passionate. This intense concern for style is not, however, what literary critics mean by formalism. It is not simply an interest in outward appearances. For style of life involves not merely the external forms of behavior, but the values implicit in that behavior, and one cannot change one's life style without working some change in one's self-image. The people of the future are not "style conscious" but "life style conscious."

Discussion Questions

1. Toffler quotes a *Newsweek* statement that says we are "a society that cannot agree on standards of conduct, language and manners." Support or refute this contention.
2. In your opinion, do people consciously choose a life style or do circumstances compel them to accept one?
3. Toffler says that some people become models for

a life style. Discuss an individual whose life style has influenced others.

4. Why is the choice of a life style a superdecision? Discuss the advantages and disadvantages of belonging to a subcult.

5. If belonging to a subcult provides a person with psychological identity, why do young men and women no longer emulate their parents as they did several generations ago? Would you adopt the life style of your parents?

A & P
JOHN UPDIKE

To know oneself, one should assert oneself.

—Albert Camus

The revolt against society or "the establishment" is not limited to college students. In John Updike's "A & P" Sammy rebels against conventions which regiment people.

In walks these three girls in nothing but bathing suits. I'm in the third checkout slot, with my back to the door, so I don't see them until they're over by the bread. The one that caught my eye first was the one in the plaid green two-piece. She was a chunky kid, with a good tan and a sweet broad soft-looking can with those two crescents of white just under it, where the sun never seems to hit, at the top of the backs of her legs. I stood there with my hand on a box of HiHo crackers trying to remember if I rang it up or not. I ring it up again and the customer starts giving me hell. She's one of these cash-register-watchers, a witch about fifty with rouge on her cheekbones and no eyebrows, and I know it made her day to trip me up. She'd been watching cash registers for fifty years and probably never seen a mistake before.

By the time I got her feathers smoothed and

"A & P" was originally published in *Pigeon Feathers and Other Stories* in 1962.

her goodies into a bag—she gives me a little snort in passing, if she'd been born at the right time they would have burned her over in Salem—by the time I get her on her way the girls had circled around the bread and were coming back, without a pushcart, back my way along the counters, in the aisle between the checkouts and the Special bins. They didn't even have shoes on. There was this chunky one, with the two-piece—it was bright green and the seams on the bra were still sharp and her belly was still pretty pale so I guessed she just got it (the suit)—there was this one, with one of those chubby berryfaces, the lips all bunched together under her nose, this one, and a tall one, with black hair that hadn't quite frizzed right, and one of these sunburns right across under the eyes, and a chin that was too long—you know, the kind of girl other girls think is very "striking" and "attractive" but never quite makes it, as they very well know, which is why they like her so much—and then the third one, that wasn't quite so tall. She was the queen. She kind of led them, the other two peeking around and making their shoulders round. She didn't look around, not this queen, she just walked straight on slowly, on these long white prima-donna legs. She came down a little hard on her heels, as if she didn't walk in her bare feet that much, putting down her heels and then letting the weight move along to her toes as if she was testing the floor with every step, putting a little deliberate extra action into it. You never know for sure how girls' minds work (do you really think it's a mind in there or just a little buzz like a bee in a glass jar?) but you got the idea she had talked the other two into coming in here with her, and now she was showing them how to do it, walk slow and hold yourself straight.

She had on a kind of dirty-pink—beige maybe, I don't know—bathing suit with a little nubble all over it, and what got me, the straps were down. They were off her shoulders looped loose around the cool tops of her arms, and I guess as a result the suit had slipped a little on her, so all around the top of the cloth there was this shining rim. If it hadn't been there you wouldn't have known there could have been anything whiter than those shoulders. With the straps pushed off, there was nothing between the top of the suit and the top of her head except just *her*, this clean bare plane of the top of her chest down from the shoulder bones like a dented sheet of metal tilted in the light. I mean, it was more than pretty.

She had sort of oaky hair that the sun and salt had bleached, done up in a bun that was unravelling, and a kind of prim face. Walking into the A & P with your straps down, I suppose it's the only kind of face you *can* have. She held her head so high her neck, coming up out of those white shoulders, looked kind of stretched, but I didn't mind. The longer her neck was, the more of her there was.

She must have felt in the corner of her eye me and over my shoulder Stokesie in the second slot watching, but she didn't tip. Not this queen. She kept her eyes moving across the racks, and stopped, and turned so slow it made my stomach rub the inside of my apron, and buzzed to the other two, who kind of huddled against her for relief, and then they all three of them went up the cat-and-dog-food-breakfast-cereal-macaroni-rice-raisins-seasonings-spreads-spaghetti-soft drinks-crackers and cookies aisle. From the third slot I look straight up this aisle to the meat counter, and I watched them all the way. The fat one with the tan sort of fumbled with the cookies, but on second thought she put the package back. The sheep pushing their carts down the aisle—the girls were walking against the usual traffic (not that we have one-way signs or anything)—were pretty hilarious. You could see them, when Queenie's white shoulders dawned on them, kind of jerk, or hop, or hiccup, but their eyes snapped back to their own baskets and on they pushed. I bet you could set off dynamite in an A & P and the people would by and large keep reaching and checking oatmeal off their lists and muttering "Let me see, there was a third thing, began with A, asparagus, no, ah, yes, applesauce!" or whatever it is they do mutter. But there was no doubt, this jiggled them. A few houseslaves in pin curlers even looked around after pushing their carts past to make sure what they had seen was correct.

You know, it's one thing to have a girl in a bathing suit down on the beach, where what with the glare nobody can look at each other much anyway, and another thing in the cool of the A & P, under the fluorescent lights, against all those stacked packages, with her feet paddling along naked over our checkerboard green-and-cream rubber-tile floor.

"Oh Daddy," Stokesie said beside me. "I feel so faint."

"Darling," I said. "Hold me tight." Stokesie's married, with two babies chalked up on his fuselage already, but as far as I can tell that's the only difference. He's twenty-two, and I was nineteen this April.

"Is it done?" he asks, the responsible married man finding his voice. I forgot to say he thinks he's going to be manager some sunny day, maybe in 1990 when it's called the Great Alexandrov and Petrooshki Tea Company or something.

What he meant was, our town is five miles from a beach, with a big summer colony out on the Point, but we're right in the middle of town, and the women generally put on a shirt or shorts or something before they get out of the car into the street. And anyway these are usually women with six children and varicose veins mapping their legs and nobody, including them, could care less. As I say, we're right in the middle of town, and if you stand at our front doors you can see two banks and the Congregational church and the newspaper store and three real-estate offices and about twenty-seven old freeloaders tearing up Central Street because the sewer broke again. It's not as if we're on the Cape; we're north of Boston and there's people in this town haven't seen the ocean for twenty years.

The girls had reached the meat counter and were asking McMahon something. He pointed, they pointed, and they shuffled out of sight behind a pyramid of Diet Delight peaches. All that was left for us to see was old McMahon patting his mouth and looking after them sizing up their joints. Poor kids, I began to feel sorry for them, they couldn't help it.

Now here comes the sad part of the story, at least my family says it's sad, but I don't think it's so sad myself. The store's pretty empty, it being Thursday afternoon, so there was nothing much to do except lean on the register and wait for the girls to show up again. The whole store was like a pinball machine and I didn't know which tunnel they'd come out of. After a while they come around out of the far aisle, around the light bulbs, records at discount of the Caribbean Six or Tony Martin Sings or some such gunk you wonder they waste wax on, sixpacks of candy bars, and plastic toys done up in cellophane that fall apart when a kid looks at them anyway. Around they come, Queenie still leading the way, and holding a little gray jar in her hand. Slots Three through Seven are unmanned and I could see her wondering between Stokes and me, but Stokesie with his usual luck draws an old party in baggy gray pants who stumbles up with four giant cans of pineapple juice (what do these bums *do* with all that pineapple juice? I've often asked myself) so the girls come to me. Queenie puts down the jar and I take it into my fingers icy cold. Kingfish Fancy Herring Snacks in Pure Sour Cream: 49¢. Now her hands are empty, not a ring or a bracelet, bare as God made them, and I wonder where the money's coming from. Still with that prim look she lifts a folded dollar bill out of the hollow at the center of her nubbled pink top. The jar went heavy in my hand. Really, I thought that was so cute.

Then everybody's luck begins to run out. Lengel comes in from haggling with a truck full of cabbages on the lot and is about to scuttle into that door marked *manager* behind which he hides all day when the girls touch his eye. Lengel's pretty dreary, teaches Sunday school and the rest, but he doesn't miss that much. He comes over and says, "Girls, this isn't the beach."

Queenie blushes, though maybe it's just a brush of sunburn I was noticing for the first time, now that she was so close. "My mother asked me to pick up a jar of herring snacks." Her voice kind of startled me, the way voices do when you see the people first, coming out so flat and dumb yet kind of tony, too, the way it ticked over "pick up" and "snacks." All of a sudden I slid right down her voice into her living room. Her father and the other men were standing around in ice-cream coats and bow ties and the women were in sandals picking up herring snacks on toothpicks off a big glass plate and they were all holding drinks the color of water with olives and sprigs of mint in them. When my parents have somebody over they get lemonade and if it's a real racy affair Schlitz in tall glasses with "They'll Do It Every Time" cartoons stenciled on.

"That's all right," Lengel said. "But this isn't the beach." His repeating this struck me as funny, as if it had just occurred to him, and he had been thinking all these years the A & P was a great big sand dune and he was the head lifeguard. He didn't like my smiling—as I say he doesn't miss much—but he concentrates on giving the girls that sad Sunday-school-superintendent stare.

Queenie's blush is no sunburn now, and the plump one in plaid, that I like better from the back—a really sweet can—pipes up, "We weren't doing any shopping. We just came in for the one thing."

"That makes no difference," Lengel tells her, and I could see from the way his eyes went that he hadn't noticed she was wearing a two-piece before. "We want you decently dressed when you come in here."

"We *are* decent," Queenie says suddenly, her lower lip pushing, getting sore now that she remembers her place, a place from which the crowd that runs the A & P must look pretty crummy. Fancy Herring Snacks flashed in her very blue eyes.

"Girls, I don't want to argue with you. After this come in here with your shoulders covered. It's our policy." He turns his back. That's policy for you. Policy is what the kingpins want. What the others want is juvenile delinquency.

All this while, the customers had been showing

up with their carts but, you know, sheep, seeing a scene, they had all bunched up on Stokesie, who shook open a paper bag as gently as peeling a peach, not wanting to miss a word. I could feel in the silence everybody getting nervous, most of all Lengel, who asks me, "Sammy, have you rung up their purchase?"

I thought and said "No" but it wasn't about that I was thinking. I go through the punches, 4, 9, *groc, tot*—it's more complicated than you think, and after you do it often enough, it begins to make a little song, that you hear words to, in my case "Hello(*bing*) there, you (*gung*) happy *pee-pul (splat)!*"—the *splat* being the drawer flying out. I uncrease the bill, tenderly as you may imagine, it just having come from between the two smoothest scoops of vanilla I had ever known were there, and pass a half and a penny into her narrow pink palm, and nestle the herrings in a bag and twist its neck and hand it over, all the time thinking.

The girls, and who'd blame them, are in a hurry to get out, so I say "I quit" to Lengel quick enough for them to hear, hoping they'll stop and watch me, their unsuspected hero. They keep right on going, into the electric eye; the door flies open and they flicker across the lot to their car, Queenie and Plaid and Big Tall Goony-Goony (not that as raw material she was so bad), leaving me with Lengel and a kink in his eyebrow.

"Did you say something, Sammy?"

"I said I quit."

"I thought you did."

"You didn't have to embarrass them."

"It was they who were embarrassing us."

I started to say something that came out "Fiddle-de-doo." It's a saying of my grandmother's, and I know she would have been pleased.

"I don't think you know what you're saying," Lengel said.

"I know you don't," I said. "But I do." I pull the bow at the back of my apron and start shrugging it off my shoulders. A couple customers that had been heading for my slot begin to knock against each other, like scared pigs in a chute.

Lengel sighs and begins to look very patient and old and gray. He's been a friend of my parents for years. "Sammy, you don't want to do this to your Mom and Dad," he tells me. It's true, I don't. But it seems to me that once you begin a gesture it's fatal not to go through with it. I fold the apron, "Sammy" stitched in red on the pocket, and put it on the counter, and drop the bow tie on top of it. The bow tie is theirs, if you've ever wondered. "You'll feel this for the rest of your life," Lengel says, and I know that's true, too, but remembering how he made that pretty girl blush makes me so scrunchy inside I punch the No Sale tab and the machine whirs "pee-pul" and the drawer splats out. One advantage to this scene taking place in summer, I can follow this up with a clean exit, there's no fumbling around getting your coat and galoshes, I just saunter into the electric eye in my white shirt that my mother ironed the night before, and the door heaves itself open, and outside the sunshine is skating around on the asphalt.

I look around for my girls, but they're gone, of course. There wasn't anybody but some young married screaming with her children about some candy they didn't get by the door of a powder-blue Falcon station wagon. Looking back in the big windows, over the bags of peat moss and aluminum lawn furniture stacked on the pavement, I could see Lengel in my place in the slot, checking the sheep through. His face was

John Updike 83

dark gray and his back stiff, as if he'd just had an injection of iron, and my stomach kind of fell as I felt how hard the world was going to be to me hereafter.

Discussion Questions

1. How do Sammy and the girls defy convention or accepted value systems?
2. Was Sammy's action a mere gesture or has he begun to explore the possibilities of his personality?
3. What does Sammy mean when he says that life will be harder for him in the future?

Reflections

1. In the section titled "Turmoil," Aldridge and the interns represent different sides in the debate over changing values. What are the values which influence them?
2. The young have not agreed on one set of values. Discuss the different values that are represented in the section titled "Milieu."
3. How do the values expressed in the "Milieu" section reflect Udall's statement that "we are all captives to a certain degree of our own backgrounds, needs, and experiences"?
4. Does Udall's statement contradict Toffler's theory that each individual has almost unlimited possibilities to choose from when selecting a life style? Explain.
5. Is Sammy's action in "A & P" representative of the response of the majority to stifling conventions? Compare Sammy to Stokesie. To "The Unknown Citizen."

HERS AND HIS

The current debate over women's liberation has sparked a discussion of the roles that society prescribes for the sexes. Too often these roles are so narrowly conceived that they hamper both men and women from achieving a sense of dignity and worth. In this chapter we explore some of the problems of sexual identity. Incidentally, we have chosen to ignore the traditional secondary position of women by placing the "Hers" portion of this chapter before the "His."

When young girls are raised on fairy tales, they dream of being snatched away from drab existences by handsome, rich young men to lead glamorous lives. Anne Sexton satirizes this unrealistic expectation in "Cinderella." In "The Crisis in Woman's Identity," Betty Friedan is concerned with cultural conditioning. Because society expects less of women than of men, many women seek fulfillment in marriage and child rearing only to discover that they are dissatisfied with their lives. Certainly Ethel in John Cheever's "The Season of Divorce" suffers from the limitations of her life and regrets that she cannot use her education.

While the feminists demand freedom from household drudgery and greater opportunities to contribute to society, some women feel like the speaker in Judith Viorst's poem, "A Women's Liberation Movement Woman." Despite the tediousness of their domestic responsibilities, they enjoy the comforts and security of marriage. However, not all women wish to conform. Ericka in Natalie L. M. Petesch's story rejects the roles of "sexpot, mother symbol, husband catcher." She struggles to work and educate herself, realizing that when her two-year-old son is twenty her life will continue. Although Ericka experiences difficulties, she differs from other women because she is creating her own identity rather than following a traditional social role. On the other hand, Gertrude, Dr. Ascher's wife, who devotes herself to her family, depends on her husband for her status. Her position is greatly diminished when he pursues other women.

In "The Picnic" John Logan describes two young people who discover and enjoy each other. However, not all male-female relationships are uncomplicated. In exploring sexual identity we learn that men experience problems just as women do. In "Sex and Secularization" Harvey Cox claims that *Playboy* provides a masculine model for young men—a life style frequently categorized by the feminists as male chauvinism.

86   Hers and His

Just as society expects women to be homemakers, men are expected to be breadwinners. If a man is unable to provide for his family, he may feel inadequate. Ethel's husband in "The Season of Divorce" fights to preserve his marriage knowing that his wife's suitor, Dr. Trencher, offers her greater financial security than he is able to provide. Because some men are unable to find pleasant and rewarding employment, they become frustrated and resent what they consider to be the easier lot of women. Finding the male world full of drudgery and onerous responsibility, George Frazier IV is impatient with the feminists. In "The Masculine Mystique" he declares that he is only too willing to exchange his male prerogatives for the simpler world of housework and soap operas.

Despite the problems of married life, a happy marriage is rewarding. In Carson McCullers' "The Sojourner" we witness a warm domestic scene. The happiness of the Baileys reaffirms the traditional value of woman as homemaker. John Ferris' rootless existence seems barren by comparison.

The importance of respect in marriage is examined in Hal Bennett's unusual short story, "Dotson Gerber Resurrected." Although conditioned by a white society to be self-effacing, Walter Beaufort unexpectedly asserts himself, gaining the admiration and respect of his wife and children. This new feeling improves the Beaufort family life.

In a changing age when life styles are in flux and men and women are experimenting with new roles, tolerance, mutual understanding, and respect will promote harmonious relations between the sexes.

Riddle:

A father and son are driving down a highway. There is a terrrible accident in which the father is killed, and the son, critically injured, is rushed to the hospital. There the surgeon approaches the patient and suddenly cries, "My God, that's my son!" How can this be true?

CINDERELLA

ANNE SEXTON

You always read about it:
the plumber with twelve children
who wins the Irish Sweepstakes.
From toilets to riches.
That story.

Or the nursemaid,
some luscious sweet from Denmark
who captures the oldest son's heart.
From diapers to Dior.
That story.

Or a milkman who serves the wealthy,
eggs, cream, butter, yogurt, milk,
the white truck like an ambulance
who goes into real estate
and makes a pile.
From homogenized to martinis at lunch.

Or the charwoman
who is on the bus when it cracks up
and collects enough from the insurance.
From mops to Bonwit Teller.
That story.

Once
the wife of a rich man was on her deathbed
and she said to her daugher Cinderella:
Be devout. Be good. Then I will smile
down from heaven in the seam of a cloud.
The man took another wife who had
two daughters, pretty enough

Anne Sexton (1928–) is an educator and Pulitzer Prize-
winning poet.

but with hearts like blackjacks.
Cinderella was their maid.
She slept on the sooty hearth each night
and walked around looking like Al Jolson.
Her father brought presents home from town,
jewels and gowns for the other women
but the twig of a tree for Cinderella.

She planted that twig on her mother's grave
and it grew to a tree where a white dove sat.
Whenever she wished for anything the dove
would drop it like an egg upon the ground.
The bird is important, my dears, so heed him.

Next came the ball, as you all know.
It was a marriage market.
The prince was looking for a wife.
All but Cinderella were preparing
and gussying up for the big event.
Cinderella begged to go too.
Her stepmother threw a dish of lentils
into the cinders and said: Pick them
up in an hour and you shall go.
The white dove brought all his friends;
all the warm wings of the fatherland came,
and picked up the lentils in a jiffy.
No, Cinderella, said the stepmother,
you have no clothes and cannot dance.
That's the way with stepmothers.

Cinderella went to the tree at the grave
and cried forth like a gospel singer:
Mama! Mama! My turtledove,
send me to the prince's ball!
The bird dropped down a golden dress
and delicate little gold slippers.
Rather a large package for a simple bird.
So she went. Which is no surprise.
Her stepmother and sisters didn't
recognize her without her cinder face
and the prince took her hand on the spot
and danced with no other the whole day.

As nightfall came she thought she'd better
get home. The prince walked her home
and she disappeared into the pigeon house
and although the prince took an axe and broke
it open she was gone. Back to her cinders.
These events repeated themselves for three days.
However on the third day the prince
covered the palace steps with cobbler's wax
and Cinderella's gold shoe stuck upon it.

Now he would find whom the shoe fit
and find his strange dancing girl for keeps.
He went to their house and the two sisters
were delighted because they had lovely feet.
The eldest went into a room to try the slipper
    on
but her big toe got in the way so she simply
sliced it off and put on the slipper.
The prince rode away with her until the white
    dove
told him to look at the blood pouring forth.
That is the way with amputations.
They don't just heal up like a wish.
The other sister cut off her heel
but the blood told as blood will.
The prince was getting tired.
He began to feel like a shoe salesman.
But he gave it one last try.
This time Cinderella fit into the shoe
like a love letter into its envelope.

At the wedding ceremony
the two sisters came to curry favor
and the white dove pecked their eyes out.
Two hollow spots were left
like soup spoons.

Cinderella and the prince
lived, they say, happily ever after,
like two dolls in a museum case
never bothered by diapers or dust,
never arguing over the timing of an egg,

never telling the same story twice,
never getting a middle-aged spread,
their darling smiles pasted on for eternity.
Regular Bobbsey Twins.
That story.

Discussion Questions

1. From earliest childhood, girls hear stories of
   princes and princesses who fall in love and live
   happily ever after in a magic fairyland. Do you
   feel that such false expectations can influence
   future marital happiness?
2. How can young adults prepare themselves to meet
   the realities of married life?

THE CRISIS IN WOMAN'S IDENTITY
BETTY FRIEDAN

The whole education of women ought to be relative to men. To please them, to be useful to them, to make themselves loved and honored by them, to educate them when young, to care for them when grown, to counsel them, to console them, and to make life sweet and agreeable to them—these are the duties of women at all times and what should be taught them from their infancy.

—Jean Jacques Rousseau

Probably no book has contributed as much to contemporary feminism as Betty Friedan's *The Feminine Mystique,* from which this excerpt is taken. Although her study of the social pressures which encourage women to become wives and mothers despite temperament, training, and talent seems tame by comparison to more recent publications, Ms. Friedan had difficulty finding a publisher in 1963.

I discovered a strange thing, interviewing women of my own generation over the past ten years. When we were growing up, many of us could not see ourselves beyond the age of twenty-one. We had no image of our own future, of ourselves as women.

I remember the stillness of a spring afternoon

Betty Friedan (1921–) is an author, feminist, and lecturer who founded the National Organization of Women.

on the Smith campus in 1942, when I came to a frightening dead end in my own vision of the future. A few days earlier, I had received a notice that I had won a graduate fellowship. During the congratulations, underneath my excitement, I felt a strange uneasiness; there was a question that I did not want to think about.

"Is this really what I want to be?" The question shut me off, cold and alone, from the girls talking and studying on the sunny hillside behind the college house. I thought I was going to be a psychologist. But if I wasn't sure, what did I want to be? I felt the future closing in—and I could not see myself in it at all. I had no image of myself, stretching beyond college. I had come at seventeen from a Midwestern town, an unsure girl; the wide horizons of the world and the life of the mind had been opened to me. I had begun to know who I was and what I wanted to do. I could not go back now. I could not go home again, to the life of my mother and the women of our town, bound to home, bridge, shopping, children, husband, charity, clothes. But now that the time had come to make my own future, to take the deciding step, I suddenly did not know what I wanted to be.

I took the fellowship, but the next spring, under the alien California sun of another campus, the question came again, and I could not put it out of my mind. I had won another fellowship that would have committed me to research for my doctorate, to a career as professional psychologist. "Is this really what I want to be?" The decision now truly terrified me. I lived in a terror of indecision for days, unable to think of anything else.

The question was not important, I told myself. No question was important to me that year but love. We walked in the Berkeley hills and a boy said: "Nothing can come of this, between us. I'll never win a fellowship like yours." Did I think I would be choosing, irrevocably, the cold loneliness of that afternoon if I went on? I gave up the fellowship, in relief. But for years afterward, I could not read a word of the science that once I had thought of as my future life's work; the reminder of its loss was too painful.

I never could explain, hardly knew myself, why I gave up this career. I lived in the present, working on newspapers with no particular plan. I married, had children, lived according to the feminine mystique as a suburban housewife. But still the question haunted me. I could sense no purpose in my life, I could find no peace, until I finally faced it and worked out my own answer.

I discovered, talking to Smith seniors in 1959, that the question is no less terrifying to girls today. Only they answer it now in a way that my generation found, after half a lifetime, not to be an answer at all. These girls, mostly seniors, were sitting in the living room of the college house, having coffee. It was not too different from such an evening when I was a senior, except that many more of the girls wore rings on their left hands. I asked the ones around me what they planned to be. The engaged ones spoke of weddings, apartments, getting a job as a secretary while husband finished school. The others, after a hostile silence, gave vague answers about this job or that, graduate study, but no one had any real plans. A blonde with a ponytail asked me the next day if I had believed the things they had said. "None of it was true," she told me. "We don't like to be asked what we want to do. None of us know. None of us even like to think about it. The ones who are going to be married right away are the lucky ones. They don't have to think about it."

But I noticed that night that many of the engaged girls, sitting silently around the fire while I asked the others about jobs, had also seemed angry about something. "They don't want to think about not going on," my ponytailed informant said. "They know they're not going to use their education. They'll be wives and mothers. You can say you're going to keep on reading and be interested in the community. But that's not the same. You won't really go on. It's a disappointment to know you're going to stop now, and not go on and use it."

In counterpoint, I heard the words of a woman, fifteen years after she left college, a doctor's wife, mother of three, who said over coffee in her New England kitchen:

The tragedy was, nobody ever looked us in the eye and said you have to decide what you want to do with your life, besides being your husband's wife and children's mother. I never thought it through until I was thirty-six, and my husband was so busy with his practice that he couldn't entertain me every night. The three boys were in school all day. I kept on trying to have babies despite an Rh discrepancy. After two miscarriages, they said I must stop. I thought that my own growth and evolution were over. I always knew as a child that I was going to grow up and go to college, and then get married, and that's as far as a girl has to think. After that, your husband determines and fills your life. It wasn't until I got so lonely as the doctor's wife and kept screaming at the kids because they didn't fill my life that I realized I had to make my own life. I still had to decide what I wanted to be. I hadn't finished evolving at all. But it took me ten years to think it through.

The feminine mystique permits, even encourages, women to ignore the question of their identity. The mystique says they can answer the question "Who am I?" by saying "Tom's wife . . . Mary's mother." But I don't think the mystique would have such power over American women if they did not fear to face this terrifying blank which makes them unable to see themselves after twenty-one. The truth is—and how long it has been true, I'm not sure, but it was true in my generation and it is true of girls growing up today—an American woman no longer has the private image to tell her who she is, or can be, or wants to be.

The public image, in the magazines and television commercials, is designed to sell washing machines, cake mixes, deodorants, detergents, rejuvenating face creams, hair tints. But the power of that image, on which companies spend millions of dollars for television time and ad space, comes from this: American women no longer know who they are. They are sorely in need of a new image to help them find their identity. As the motivational researchers keep telling the advertisers, American women are so unsure of who they should be that they look to this glossy public image to decide every detail of their lives. They look for the image they will no longer take from their mothers.

In my generation, many of us knew that we did not want to be like our mothers, even when we loved them. We could not help but see their disappointment. Did we understand, or only resent, the sadness, the emptiness, that made them hold too fast to us, try to live our lives, run our fathers' lives, spend their days shopping or yearning for things that never seemed to satisfy them, no matter how much money they cost?

Strangely, many mothers who loved their daughters—and mine was one—did not want their daughters to grow up like them either. They knew we needed something more.

But even if they urged, insisted, fought to help us educate ourselves, even if they talked with yearning of careers that were not open to them, they could not give us an image of what we could be. They could only tell us that their lives were too empty, tied to home; that children, cooking, clothes, bridge, and charities were not enough. A mother might tell her daughter, spell it out, "Don't be just a housewife like me." But that daughter, sensing that her mother was too frustrated to savor the love of her husband and children, might feel: "I will succeed where my mother failed, I will fulfill myself as a woman," and never read the lesson of her mother's life.

Recently, interviewing . . . girls who had started out full of promise and talent, but suddenly stopped their education, I began to see new dimensions to the problem of feminine conformity. These girls, it seemed at first, were merely following the typical curve of feminine adjustment. Earlier interested in geology or poetry, they now were interested only in being popular; to get boys to like them, they had concluded, it was better to be like all the other girls. On closer examination, I found that these girls were so terrified of becoming like their mothers that they could not see themselves at all. They were afraid to grow up. They had to copy in identical detail the composite image of the popular girl—denying what was best in themselves out of fear of femininity as they saw it in their mothers. . .

[One] girl, a college junior from South Carolina told me:

I don't want to be interested in a career I'll have to give up.

My mother wanted to be a newspaper reporter from the time she was twelve, and I've seen her frustration for twenty years. I don't want to be interested in world affairs. I don't want to be interested in anything beside my home and being a wonderful wife and mother. Maybe education is a liability. Even the brightest boys at home want just a sweet, pretty girl. Only sometimes I wonder how it would feel to be able to stretch and stretch and stretch, and learn all you want, and not have to hold yourself back.

Her mother, almost all our mothers, were housewives, though many had started or yearned for or regretted giving up careers. Whatever they told us, we, having eyes and ears and mind and heart, knew that their lives were somehow empty. We did not want to be like them, and yet what other model did we have?

The only other kind of women I knew, growing up, were the old-maid high-school teachers; the librarian; the one woman doctor in our town, who cut her hair like a man; and a few of my college professors. None of these women lived in the warm center of life as I had known it at home. Many had not married or had children. I dreaded being like them, even the ones who taught me truly to respect my own mind and use it, to feel that I had a part in the world. I never knew a woman, when I was growing up, who used her mind, played her own part in the world, and also loved, and had children.

I think that this has been the unknown heart of woman's problem in America for a long time, this lack of a private image. Public images that defy reason and have very little to do with women themselves have had the power to shape too much of their lives. These images would not have such power, if women were not suffering a crisis of identity.

The strange, terrifying jumping-off point that American women reach—at eighteen, twenty-one, twenty-five, forty-one—has been noticed for many years by sociologists, psychologists, analysts, educators. But I think it has not been understood for what it is. It has been called a "discontinuity" in cultural conditioning; it has been called woman's "role crisis." It has been blamed on the education which made American girls grow up feeling free and equal to boys—playing baseball, riding bicycles, conquering geometry and college boards, going away to college, going out in the world to get a job, living alone in an apartment in New York or Chicago or San Francisco, testing and discovering their own powers in the world. All this gave girls the feeling they could be and do whatever they wanted to, with the same freedom as boys, the critics said. It did not prepare them for their role as women. The crisis comes when they are forced to adjust to this role. Today's high rate of emotional distress and breakdown among women in their twenties and thirties is usually attributed to this "role crisis." If girls were educated for their role as women, they would not suffer this crisis, the adjusters say.

But I think they have seen only half the truth.

What if the terror a girl faces at twenty-one, when she must decide who she will be, is simply the terror of growing up—growing up, as women were not permitted to grow before? What if the terror a girl faces at twenty-one is the terror of freedom to decide her own life, with no one to order which path she will take, the freedom and the necessity to take paths women before were not able to take? What if those who choose the path of "feminine adjustment"—evading this terror by marrying at eighteen, losing themselves in having babies and the details of house-keeping—are simply refusing to grow up, to face the question of their own identity?

Mine was the first college generation to run head-on into the new mystique of feminine fulfillment. Before then, while most women did indeed end up as housewives and mothers, the point of education was to discover the life of the mind, to pursue truth and to take a place in the world. There was a sense, already dulling when I went to college, that we would be New Women. Our world would be much larger than home. Forty per cent of my college class at Smith had career plans. But I remember how, even then, some of the seniors, suffering the pangs of that bleak fear of the future, envied the few who escaped it by getting married right away.

The ones we envied then are suffering that terror now at forty. "Never have decided what kind of woman I am. Too much personal life in college. Wish I'd studied more science, history, government, gone deeper into philosophy," one wrote on an alumnae questionnaire, fifteen years later. "Still trying to find the rock to build on. Wish I had finished college. I got married instead." "Wish I'd developed a deeper and more creative life of my own and that I hadn't become engaged and married at nineteen. Having expected the ideal in marriage, including a hundred-per-cent devoted husband, it was a shock to find this isn't the way it is," wrote a mother of six.

Many of the younger generation of wives who marry early have never suffered this lonely terror. They thought they did not have to choose, to look into the future and plan what they wanted to do with their lives. They had only to wait to be chosen, marking time passively until the husband, the babies, the new house decided what the rest of their lives would be. They slid easily into their sexual role as women before they knew who they were themselves. It is these women who suffer most the problem that has no name.

It is my thesis that the core of the problem for women today is not sexual but a problem of identity—a stunting or evasion of growth that is perpetuated by the feminine mystique. It is my thesis that as the Victorian culture did not permit women to accept or gratify their basic sexual needs, our culture does not permit women to accept or gratify their basic need to grow and fulfill their potentialities as human beings, a need which is not solely defined by their sexual role.

Biologists have recently discovered a "youth serum" which, if fed to young caterpillars in the larva state, will keep them from ever maturing into moths; they will live out their lives as caterpillars. The expectations of feminine fulfillment that are fed to women by magazines, television, movies, and books that popularize psychological half-truths, and by parents, teachers and counselors who accept the feminine mystique, operate as a kind of youth serum, keeping most women in the state of sexual larvae, preventing them from achieving the maturity of which they are capable. And there is increasing evidence that woman's failure to grow to complete identity has hampered rather than enriched her sexual fulfillment, virtually doomed her to be castrative to her husband and sons, and caused neuroses, or problems as yet unnamed as neuroses, equal to those caused by sexual repression.

There have been identity crises for man at all the crucial turning points in human history, though those who lived through them did not give them that name. It is only in recent years that the theorists of psychology, sociology and theology have isolated this problem, and given it a name. But it is considered a man's problem. It is defined, for man, as the crisis of growing up, of choosing his identity, "the decision as to what one is and is going to be," in the words of the brilliant psychoanalyst Erik H. Erikson:

I have called the major crisis of adolescence the identity crisis; it occurs in that period of the life cycle when each youth must forge for himself some central perspective and direction, some working unity, out of the effective remnants of his childhood and the hopes of his anticipated adulthood; he must detect some meaningful resemblance between what he has come to see in himself and what his sharpened awareness tells him others judge and expect him to be. . . In some people, in some classes, at some periods in history, the crisis will be minimal; in other people, classes and periods, the crisis will be clearly marked off as a critical period, a kind of "second birth," apt to be aggravated either by widespread neuroticisms or by pervasive ideological unrest.[1]

In this sense, the identity crisis of one man's life may reflect, or set off, a rebirth, or new stage, in the growing up of mankind. "In some periods of his history, and in some phases of his life cycle, man needs a new ideological orientation as surely and sorely as he must have air and food," said Erikson, focusing new light on the crisis of the young Martin Luther, who left a Catholic monas-

---

[1] Erik H. Erikson, *Young Man Luther, A Study in Psychoanalysis and History* (New York: Norton, 1958), p. 15. See also Erikson, *Childhood and Society* (New York: Norton, 1950), and Erikson, "The Problem of Ego Identity," *Journal of the American Psychoanalytical Association* 4 (1956):56–121.

tery at the end of the Middle Ages to forge a new identity for himself and Western man.

The search for identity is not new, however, in American thought—though in every generation, each man who writes about it discovers it anew. In America, from the beginning, it has somehow been understood that men must thrust into the future; the pace has always been too rapid for man's identity to stand still. In every generation, many men have suffered misery, unhappiness, and uncertainty because they could not take the image of the man they wanted to be from their fathers. The search for identity of the young man who can't go home again has always been a major theme of American writers. And it has always been considered right in America, good, for men to suffer these agonies of growth, to search for and find their own identities. The farm boy went to the city, the garment-maker's son became a doctor, Abraham Lincoln taught himself to read—these were more than rags-to-riches stories. They were an integral part of the American dream. The problem for many was money, race, color, class, which barred them from choice—not what they would be if they were free to choose.

Even today a young man learns soon enough that he must decide who he wants to be. If he does not decide in junior high, in high school, in college, he must somehow come to terms with it by twenty-five or thirty, or he is lost. But this search for identity is seen as a greater problem now because more and more boys cannot find images in our culture—from their fathers or other men—to help them in their search. The old frontiers have been conquered, and the boundaries of the new are not so clearly marked. More and more young men in America today suffer an identity crisis for want of any image of man worth pursuing, for want of a purpose that truly realizes their human abilities.

But why have theorists not recognized this same identity crisis in women? In terms of the old conventions and the new feminine mystique women are not expected to grow up to find out who they are, to choose their human identity. Anatomy is woman's destiny, say the theorists of femininity; the identity of women is determined by her biology.

But is it? More and more women are asking themselves this question. As if they were waking from a coma, they ask, "Where am I . . . what am I doing here?" For the first time in their history, women are becoming aware of an identity crisis in their own lives, a crisis which began many generations ago, has grown worse with each succeeding generation, and will not end until they, or their daughters, turn an unknown corner and make of themselves and their lives the new image that so many women now so desperately need.

In a sense that goes beyond any one woman's life, I think this is the crisis of women growing up—a turning point from an immaturity that has been called femininity to full human identity. I think women had to suffer this crisis of identity, which began a hundred years ago, and have to suffer it still today, simply to become fully human.

Discussion Questions

1. According to Friedan, what forces encourage young women to seek marriage, home, and family rather than a career?
2. Discuss the male identity crisis described by Erik H. Erickson. How do women avoid experiencing such a crisis?
3. Bring several women's magazines to class. What image of women do these magazines project?
4. Watch five or ten television commercials directed at women. Why do the feminists say that these ads insult women?
5. Bring a television guide to class. What kinds of programs are offered for daytime viewing? What is your opinion of these programs?
6. Think about the novels and short stories you have read and the movies and television programs you have watched. Are the male characters more interesting than the female? Explain your answer.
7. How do media images influence young girls and married women?

"He loves me for myself, he loves me for my body . . ."

102   Hers

THE SEASON OF DIVORCE
JOHN CHEEVER

Nature intended women to be our slaves . . . they are our property; we are not theirs. They belong to us, just as a tree that bears fruit belongs to a gardener. What a mad idea to demand equality for women! . . . Women are nothing but machines for producing children.
—Napoleon Bonaparte
The frustrations of the educated woman who devotes herself to her husband and children are experienced by Ethel in this story.

My wife has brown hair, dark eyes, and a gentle disposition. Because of her gentle disposition, I sometimes think that she spoils the children. She can't refuse them anything. They always get around her. Ethel and I have been married for ten years. We both come from Morristown, New Jersey, and I can't even remember when I first met her. Our marriage has always seemed happy and resourceful to me. We live in a walkup in the East Fifties. Our son, Carl, who is six, goes to a good private school, and our daughter, who is four, won't go to school until next year. We often find fault with the way we were educated, but we seem to be struggling to raise our children along the same lines, and when the time comes, I

John Cheever (1912–) is a professional writer who has won many awards for his stories and novels.

suppose they'll go to the same schools and colleges that we went to.

Ethel graduated from a woman's college in the East, and then went for a year to the University of Grenoble. She worked for a year in New York after returning from France, and then we were married. She once hung her diploma above the kitchen sink, but it was a short-lived joke and I don't know where the diploma is now. Ethel is cheerful and adaptable, as well as gentle, and we both come from that enormous stratum of the middle class that is distinguished by its ability to recall better times. Lost money is so much a part of our lives that I am sometimes reminded of expatriates, of a group who have adapted themselves energetically to some alien soil but who are reminded, now and then, of the escarpments of their native coast. Because our lives are confined by my modest salary, the surface of Ethel's life is easy to describe.

She gets up at seven and turns the radio on. After she is dressed, she rouses the children and cooks the breakfast. Our son has to be walked to the school bus at eight o'clock. When Ethel returns from this trip, Carol's hair has to be braided. I leave the house at eight-thirty, but I know that every move that Ethel makes for the rest of the day will be determined by the housework, the cooking, the shopping, and the demands of the children. I know that on Tuesdays and Thursdays she will be at the A & P between eleven and noon, that on every clear afternoon she will be on a certain bench in a playground from three until five, that she cleans the house on Mondays, Wednesdays, and Fridays, and polishes the silver when it rains. When I return at six, she is usually cleaning the vegetables or making some other preparation for dinner. Then when the children have been fed and bathed, when the dinner is ready, when the table in the living room is set with food and china, she stands in the middle of the room as if she has lost or forgotten something, and this moment of reflection is so deep that she will not hear me if I speak to her, or the children if they call. Then it is over. She lights the four white candles in their silver sticks, and we sit down to a supper of corned-beef hash or some other modest fare.

We go out once or twice a week and entertain about once a month. Because of practical considerations, most of the people we see live in our neighborhood. We often go around the corner to the parties given by a generous couple named Newsome. The Newsomes' parties are large and confusing, and the arbitrary impulses of friendship are given a free play.

We became attached at the Newsomes' one evening, for reasons that I've never understood, to a couple named Dr. and Mrs. Trencher. I think that Mrs. Trencher was the aggressor in this friendship, and after our first meeting she telephoned Ethel three or four times. We went to their house for dinner, and they came to our house, and sometimes in the evening when Dr. Trencher was walking their old dachshund, he would come up for a short visit. He seemed like a pleasant man to have around. I've heard other doctors say that he's a good physician. The Trenchers are about thirty; at least he is. She is older.

I'd say that Mrs. Trencher is a plain woman, but her plainness is difficult to specify. She is small, she has a good figure and regular features, and I suppose that the impression of plainness arises from some inner modesty, some needlessly narrow view of her chances. Dr. Trencher doesn't smoke or drink, and I don't know whether there's any connection or not, but the coloring in his slender face is fresh—his cheeks are pink, and his blue eyes are clear and strong. He has the singular optimism of a well-adjusted physician—the feeling that death is a chance misfortune and that the physical world is merely a field for conquest. In the same way that his wife seems plain, he seems young.

The Trenchers live in a comfortable and unpretentious private house in our neighborhood. The house is old-fashioned; its living rooms are large, its halls are gloomy, and the Trenchers don't seem to generate enough human warmth to animate the place, so that you sometimes take away from them, at the end of an evening, an impression of many empty rooms. Mrs. Trencher is noticeably attached to her possessions—her clothes, her jewels, and the ornaments she's bought for the house—and to Fraulein, the old dachshund. She feeds Fraulein scraps from the table, furtively, as if she has been forbidden to do this, and after dinner Fraulein lies beside her on the sofa. With the play of green light from a television set on her drawn features and her thin hands stroking Fraulein, Mrs. Trencher looked to me one evening like a good-hearted and miserable soul.

Mrs. Trencher began to call Ethel in the mornings for a talk or to ask her for lunch or a matinee. Ethel can't go out in the day and she claims to dislike long telephone conversations. She complained that Mrs. Trencher was a tireless and aggressive gossip. Then late one afternoon Dr. Trencher appeared at the playground where Ethel takes our two children. He was walking by,

and he saw her and sat with her until it was time to take the children home. He came again a few days later, and then his visits with Ethel in the playground, she told me, became a regular thing. Ethel thought that perhaps he didn't have many patients and that with nothing to do he was happy to talk with anyone. Then, when we were washing dishes one night, Ethel said thoughtfully that Trencher's attitude toward her seemed strange. "He stares at me," she said. "He sighs and stares at me." I know what my wife looks like in the playground. She wears an old tweed coat, overshoes, and Army gloves, and a scarf is tied under her chin. The playground is a fenced and paved lot between a slum and the river. The picture of the well-dressed, pink-cheeked doctor losing his heart to Ethel in this environment was hard to take seriously. She didn't mention him then for several days, and I guessed that he had stopped his visits. Ethel's birthday came at the end of the month, and I forgot about it, but when I came home that evening, there were a lot of roses in the living room. They were a birthday present from Trencher, she told me. I was cross at myself for having forgotten her birthday, and Trencher's roses made me angry. I asked her if she'd seen him recently.

"Oh, yes," she said, "he still comes to the playground nearly every afternoon. I haven't told you, have I? He's made his declaration. He loves me. He can't live without me. He'd walk through fire to hear the notes of my voice." She laughed. "That's what he said."

"When did he say this?"

"At the playground. And walking home. Yesterday."

"How long has he known?"

"That's the funny part about it," she said. "He

knew before he met me at the Newsomes' that night. He saw me waiting for a crosstown bus about three weeks before that. He just saw me and he said that he knew then, the minute he saw me. Of course, he's crazy.''

I was tired that night and worried about taxes and bills, and I could think of Trencher's declaration only as a comical mistake. I felt that he was a captive of financial and sentimental commitments, like every other man I know, and that he was no more free to fall in love with a strange woman he saw on a street corner than he was to take a walking trip through French Guiana or to recommence his life in Chicago under an assumed name. His declaration, the scene in the playground, seemed to me to be like those chance meetings that are a part of the life of any large city. A blind man asks you to help him across the street, and as you are about to leave him, he seizes your arm and regales you with a passionate account of his cruel and ungrateful children; or the elevator man who is taking you up to a party turns to you suddenly and says that his grandson has infantile paralysis. The city is full of accidental revelation, half-heard cries for help, and strangers who will tell you everything at the first suspicion of sympathy, and Trencher seemed to me like the blind man or the elevator operator. His declaration had no more bearing on the business of our lives than these interruptions.

Mrs. Trencher's telephone conversations had stopped, and we had stopped visiting the Trenchers, but sometimes I would see him in the morning on the crosstown bus when I was late going to work. He seemed understandably embarrassed whenever he saw me, but the bus was always crowded at that time of day, and it was no

effort to avoid one another. Also, at about this time I made a mistake in business and lost several thousand dollars for the firm I work for. There was not much chance of my losing my job, but the possibility was always at the back of my mind, and under this and under the continuous urgency of making more money the memory of the eccentric Doctor was buried. Three weeks passed without Ethel's mentioning him, and then one evening, when I was reading, I noticed Ethel standing at the window looking down into the street.

"He's really there," she said.

"Who?"

"Trencher. Come here and see."

I went to the window. There were only three people on the sidewalk across the street. It was dark and it would have been difficult to recognize anyone, but because one of them, walking toward the corner, had a dachshund on a leash, it could have been Trencher.

"Well, what about it?" I said. "He's just walking the dog."

"But he wasn't walking the dog when I first looked out of the window. He was just standing there, staring up at this building. That's what he says he does. He says that he comes over here and stares up at our lighted windows."

"When did he say this?"

"At the playground."

"I thought you went to another playground."

"Oh, I do, I do, but he followed me. He's crazy, darling. I know he's crazy, but I feel so sorry for him. He says that he spends night after night looking up at our windows. He says that he sees me everywhere—the back of my head, my eyebrows—that he hears my voice. He says that he's never compromised in his life and that he isn't going to compromise about this. I feel so sorry for him, darling. I can't help but feel sorry for him."

For the first time then, the situation seemed serious to me, for in his helplessness I knew that he might have touched an inestimable and wayward passion that Ethel shares with some other women—an inability to refuse any cry for help, to refuse any voice that sounds pitiable. It is not a reasonable passion, and I would almost rather have had her desire him than pity him. When we were getting ready for bed that night, the telephone rang, and when I picked it up and said hello, no one answered. Fifteen minutes later, the telephone rang again, and when there was no answer this time, I began to shout and swear at Trencher, but he didn't reply—there wasn't even the click of a closed circuit—and I felt like a fool. Because I felt like a fool, I accused Ethel of having led him on, of having encouraged him, but these accusations didn't affect her, and when I finished them, I felt worse, because I knew that she was innocent, and that she had to go out on the street to buy groceries and air the children, and that there was no force of law that could keep Trencher from waiting for her there, or from staring up at our lights.

We went to the Newsomes' one night the next week, and while we were taking off our coats, I heard Trencher's voice. He left a few minutes after we arrived, but his manner—the sad glance he gave Ethel, the way he sidestepped me, the sorrowful way that he refused the Newsomes when they asked him to stay longer, and the gallant attentions he showed his miserable wife—made me angry. Then I happened to notice Ethel and saw that her color was high, that her eyes were bright, and that while she was praising Mrs. Newsome's new shoes, her mind was not on what she was saying. When we came home that night, the baby-sitter told us crossly that neither of the children had slept. Ethel took their temperatures. Carol was all right, but the boy had a fever of a hundred and four. Neither of us got much sleep that night, and in the morning Ethel called me at the office to say that Carl had bronchitis. Three days later, his sister came down with it.

For the next two weeks, the sick children took up most of our time. They had to be given medicine at eleven in the evening and again at three in the morning, and we lost a lot of sleep. It was impossible to ventilate or clean the house, and when I came in, after walking through the cold from the bus stop, it stank of cough syrups and tobacco, fruit cores and sickbeds. There were blankets and pillows, ashtrays, and medicine glasses everywhere. We divided the work of sickness reasonably and took turns at getting up in the night, but I often fell asleep at my desk during the day, and after dinner Ethel would fall asleep in a chair in the living room. Fatigue seems to differ for adults and children only in that adults recognize it and so are not overwhelmed by something they can't name; but even with a name for it they are overwhelmed, and when we were tired, we were unreasonable, cross, and the victims of transcendent depressions. One evening after the worst of the sickness was over, I came home and found some roses in the living room. Ethel said that Trencher had brought them. She hadn't let him in. She had closed the door in his face. I took the roses and threw them out. We didn't quarrel. The children went to sleep at nine, and a few minutes after nine I went to bed. Some time later, something woke me.

A light was burning in the hall. I got up. The

children's room and the living room were dark. I found Ethel in the kitchen sitting at the table, drinking coffee.

"I've made some fresh coffee," she said. "Carol felt croupy again, so I steamed her. They're both asleep now."

"How long have you been up?"

"Since half past twelve," she said. "What time is it?"

"Two."

I poured myself a cup of coffee and sat down. She got up from the table and rinsed her cup and looked at herself in a mirror that hangs above the sink. It was a windy night. A dog was wailing somewhere in an apartment below ours, and a loose radio antenna was brushing against the kitchen window.

"It sounds like a branch," she said.

In the bare kitchen light, meant for peeling potatoes and washing dishes, she looked very tired.

"Will the children be able to go out tomorrow?"

"Oh, I hope so," she said. "Do you realize that I haven't been out of this apartment in over two weeks?" She spoke bitterly and this startled me.

"It hasn't been quite two weeks."

"It's been over two weeks," she said.

"Well, let's figure it out," I said. "The children were taken sick on a Saturday night. That was the fourth. Today is the—"

"Stop it, stop it," she said. "I know how long it's been. I haven't had my shoes on in two weeks."

"You make it sound pretty bad."

"It is. I haven't had on a decent dress or fixed my hair."

"It could be worse."

"My mother's cooks had a better life."

"I doubt that."

"My mother's cooks had a better life," she said loudly.

"You'll wake the children."

"My mother's cooks had a better life. They had pleasant rooms. No one could come into the kitchen without their permission." She knocked the coffee grounds into the garbage and began to wash the pot.

"How long was Trencher here this afternoon?"

"A minute. I've told you."

"I don't believe it. He was in here."

"He was not. I didn't let him in. I didn't let him in because I looked so badly. I didn't want to discourage him."

"Why not?"

"I don't know. He may be a fool. He may be insane but the things he's told me have made me feel marvellously, he's made me feel marvellously."

"Do you want to go?"

"Go? Where would I go?" She reached for the purse that is kept in the kitchen to pay for groceries and counted out of it two dollars and thirty-five cents. "Ossining? Montclair?"

"I mean with Trencher."

"I don't know, I don't know," she said, "but who can say that I shouldn't? What harm would it do? What good would it do? Who knows. I love the children but that isn't enough, that isn't nearly enough. I wouldn't hurt them, but would I hurt them so much if I left you? Is divorce so dreadful and of all the things that hold a marriage together how many of them are good?" She sat down at the table.

"In Grenoble," she said, "I wrote a long paper on Charles Stuart in French. A professor at the

University of Chicago wrote me a letter. I couldn't read a French newspaper without a dictionary today, I don't have the time to follow any newspaper, and I am ashamed of my incompetence, ashamed of the way I look. Oh, I guess I love you, I do love the children, but I love myself, I love my life, it has some value and some promise for me and Trencher's roses make me feel that I'm losing this, that I'm losing my self-respect. Do you know what I mean, do you understand what I mean?"

"He's crazy," I said.

"Do you know what I mean? Do you understand what I mean?"

"No," I said. "No."

Carl woke up then and called for his mother. I told Ethel to go to bed. I turned out the kitchen light and went into the children's room.

The children felt better the next day, and since it was Sunday, I took them for a walk. The afternoon sun was clement and pure, and only the colored shadows made me remember that it was midwinter, that the cruise ships were returning, and that in another week jonquils would be twenty-five cents a bunch. Walking down Lexington Avenue, we heard the drone bass of a church organ sound from the sky, and we and the others on the sidewalk looked up in piety and bewilderment, like a devout and stupid congregation, and saw a formation of heavy bombers heading for the sea. As it got late, it got cold and clear and still, and on the stillness the waste from the smokestacks along the East River seemed to articulate, as legibly as the Pepsi-Cola plane, whole words and sentences. Halcyon. Disaster. They were hard to make out. It seemed the ebb of the year—an evil day for gastritis, sinus, and respiratory disease—and remembering other winters, the markings of the light convinced me that it was the season of divorce. It was a long afternoon, and I brought the children in before dark.

I think that the seriousness of the day affected the children, and when they returned to the house, they were quiet. The seriousness of it kept coming to me with the feeling that this change, like a phenomenon of speed, was affecting our watches as well as our hearts. I tried to remember the willingness with which Ethel had followed my regiment during the war, from West Virginia to the Carolinas and Oklahoma, and the day coaches and rooms she had lived in, and the street in San Francisco where I said goodbye to her before I left the country, but I could not put any of this into words, and neither of us found anything to say. Some time after dark, the children were bathed and put to bed, and we sat down to our supper. At about nine o'clock, the doorbell rang, and when I answered it and recognized Trencher's voice on the speaking tube, I asked him to come up.

He seemed distraught and exhilarated when he appeared. He stumbled on the edge of the carpet. "I know that I'm not welcome here," he said in a hard voice, as if I were deaf. "I know that you don't like me here. I respect your feelings. This is your home. I respect a man's feelings about his home. I don't usually go to a man's home unless he asks me. I respect your home. I respect your marriage. I respect your children. I think everything ought to be aboveboard. I've come here to tell you that I love your wife."

"Get out," I said.

"You've got to listen to me," he said. "I love your wife. I can't live without her. I've tried and I can't. I've even thought of going away—of moving to the West Coast—but I know that it wouldn't make any difference. I want to marry her. I'm not romantic. I'm matter-of-fact. I'm very matter-of-fact. I know that you have two children and that you don't have much money. I know that there are problems of custody and property and things like that to be settled. I'm not romantic. I'm hard-headed. I've talked this all over with Mrs. Trencher, and she's agreed to give me a divorce. I'm not underhanded. Your wife can tell you that. I realize all the practical aspects that have to be considered—custody, property, and so forth. I have plenty of money. I can give Ethel everything she needs, but there are the children. You'll have to decide about them between yourselves. I have a check here. It's made out to Ethel. I want her to take it and go to Nevada. I'm a practical man and I realize that nothing can be decided until she gets her divorce."

"Get out of here!" I said. "Get the hell out of here!"

He started for the door. There was a potted geranium on the mantelpiece, and I threw this across the room at him. It got him in the small of the back and nearly knocked him down. The pot broke on the floor. Ethel screamed. Trencher was still on his way out. Following him, I picked up a candlestick and aimed it at his head, but it missed and bounced off the wall. "Get the hell out of here!" I yelled, and he slammed the door. I went back into the living room. Ethel was pale but she wasn't crying. There was a loud rapping on the radiator, a signal from the people upstairs for decorum and silence—urgent and expressive, like the communications that prisoners send to one another through the plumbing in a penitentiary. Then everything was still.

We went to bed, and I woke sometime during the night. I couldn't see the clock on the dresser, so I don't know what time it was. There was no sound from the children's room. The neighborhood was perfectly still. There were no lighted windows anywhere. Then I knew that Ethel had wakened me. She was lying on her side of the bed. She was crying.

"Why are you crying?" I asked.

"Why am I crying?" she said. "Why am I crying?" And to hear my voice and to speak set her off again, and she began to sob cruelly. She sat up and slipped her arms into the sleeves of a wrapper and felt along the table for a package of cigarettes. I saw her wet face when she lighted a cigarette. I heard her moving around in the dark.

"Why do you cry?"

"Why do I cry? Why do I cry?" she asked impatiently. "I cry because I saw an old woman cuffing a little boy on Third Avenue. She was drunk. I can't get it out of my mind." She pulled the quilt off the foot of our bed and wandered with it toward the door. "I cry because my father died when I was twelve and because my mother married a man I detested or thought that I detested. I cry because I had to wear an ugly dress—a hand-me-down dress—to a party twenty years ago, and I didn't have a good time. I cry because of some unkindness that I can't remember. I cry because I'm tired—because I'm tired and I can't sleep." I heard her arrange herself on the sofa and then everything was quiet.

I like to think that the Trenchers have gone away, but I still see Trencher now and then on a crosstown bus when I'm late going to work. I've also seen his wife, going into the neighborhood lending library with Fraulein. She looks old. I'm not good at judging ages, but I wouldn't be surprised to find that Mrs. Trencher is fifteen years older than her husband. Now when I come home in the evenings, Ethel is still sitting on the stool by the sink cleaning vegetables. I go with her into the children's room. The light there is bright. The children have built something out of an orange crate, something preposterous and ascendant, and their sweetness, their compulsion to build, the brightness of the light are reflected perfectly and increased in Ethel's face. Then she feeds them, bathes them, and sets the table, and stands for a moment in the middle of the room, trying to make some connection between the evening and the day. Then it is over. She lights the four candles, and we sit down to our supper.

Discussion Questions

1. How is Ethel experiencing disillusionment with the feminine mystique?
2. Explain the title.
3. What kind of a man is Ethel's husband? How does he treat his wife?
4. After Ethel's husband throws Dr. Trencher out of his apartment, there is a loud rapping on the radiator from the people upstairs for quiet—"like the communications that prisoners send to one another through the plumbing in a penitentiary." Why is the allusion to a prison appropriate?
5. Does this story imply that a college education hampers a woman's ability to adapt to the circumstances of marriage? Explain your answer.

John Cheever   111

A WOMEN'S LIBERATION MOVEMENT WOMAN
JUDITH VIORST

The great question that has never been answered, and
which I have not yet been able to answer despite my
thirty years of research into the feminine soul is: What
does a woman want?

—Sigmund Freud

When it's snowing and I put on all the galoshes
While he reads the paper,
Then I want to become a
Women's Liberation Movement woman.
And when it's snowing and he looks for the taxi
While I wait in the lobby,
Then I don't.
And when it's vacation and I'm in charge of
    mosquito bites and poison ivy and car sickness
While he's in charge of swimming,
Then I want to become a
Women's Liberation Movement woman.
And when it's vacation and he carries the trunk
    and the overnight bag and the extra blankets
While I carry the wig case,
Then I don't.
And when it's three in the morning and the

Judith Viorst, the author of several books of poetry and
fiction, is a contributing editor of *Redbook* magazine and
writes a syndicated newspaper column.

baby definitely needs a glass of water and I
have to get up and bring it
While he keeps my place warm,
Then I want to become a
Women's Liberation Movement woman.
And when it's three in the morning and there is
definitely a murder-rapist in the vestibule and
he has to get up and catch him
While I keep his place warm,
Then I don't.

And after dinner, when he talks to the company
While I clean the broiler
(because I am a victim of capitalism,
imperialism, male chauvinism, and also
Playboy magazine),
And afternoons, when he invents the telephone
and wins the Dreyfus case and writes War
and Peace
While I sort the socks
(because I am economically oppressed, physically
exploited, psychologically mutilated, and also
very insulted),
And after he tells me that it is genetically

determined that the man makes martinis and
the lady makes the beds
(because he sees me as a sex object, an earth
mother, a domestic servant, and also dumber
than he is),
Then I want to become a
Women's Liberation Movement woman.

And after I contemplate
No marriage, no family, no shaving under my
arms,
And no one to step on a cockroach whenever I
need him,
Then I don't.

Discussion Questions

1. Does this poem exemplify the ambivalence some
   women feel about being liberated?
2. Does it picture women as men see them?
3. Does it miss the point completely?
4. How does this poem illustrate prescribed sexual
   roles?

Judith Viorst   113

ERICKA

NATALIE L.M. PETESCH

I thank thee, O Lord, that thou hast not created me a woman.

—Discontinued daily Orthodox Jewish prayer

In childhood a woman must be subject to her father; in youth to her husband; when her husband is dead, to her sons. A woman must never be free of subjugation.

—The Hindu Code of Manu, V

This short story reveals the vulnerable position of women, whether single, "liberated," married, or divorced.

Find someone? *Here?* Ericka's raincoat leaked slowly down to the island of carpet in the brilliantly lit hallway while her hostess stood smiling a gentle smile, as if it were her fault and not Ericka's that the rug was there to be dripped on. Nevertheless, Mrs. Ascher stood a polite distance away, her fingertips resting like those of the Virgin in a triptych on the soft mound protruding delicately from her womb. In the gilt mirror, magnificent as a Borghese landscape, Ericka took in the spectacle: the patterned carpet, the collected art works—statues on marble mounts and abstracts framed into the walls as if into their

Natalie L.M. Petesch, born in Detroit, has a Ph.D. from the University of Texas. She recently completed two novels, *The Long Hot Summers of Yasha K.* and *The Odyssey of Katinou Kalokovich.*

own bodies—and above all, the glittering clusters of couples who stood, palms resting under elbows, tinkling the ice in their glasses. For a moment the refracted light of the mirror seemed to fuse the vision, first into a melting collage, then into an explosive psychedelic glare: Ericka busied herself with her coat, burying her terror in its plastic pockets as she put away her scarf.

Mrs. Ascher was already murmuring in a casual way, as if it were only a public and not a private request: *would* she, Ericka, mind taking her coat upstairs? She'd find the room with the other coats on the bed, the room next to the children's. "Roderick's not here yet," Mrs. Ascher went on to explain, as if this momentous breach of custom needed an apology. "He's out picking up a few guests . . . students without cars. . ." Mrs. Ascher's awareness of her husband's kindness seemed to grow heady on her lips; she flushed as if with pleasure. Ericka could sense in her hostess a controlled excitement as she swung her swelling body toward the doorbell which was ringing now in rising tones, like the questioning voice of an intelligent child: anybody *innnnnn?*

As she climbed the carpeted staircase Ericka glanced over her shoulder at the couples below, all, it seemed to her, wearing a look of cultivated differences—a heterogeneity achieved by a culture first carefully instilled, then just as carefully plucked up and idled into Personality. She was already sorry she had come. She had accepted the invitation upon the insistence of her roommate, Susan Hallam. Sue's view of the world was so simple that Ericka had been beguiled into sharing the divorcée's apartment simply for comic relief. "A pair of divorcées. We'll have group therapy sessions," Sue had said. But the last thing Ericka had wanted was anything *groupy.* After two years of the pervasive family "love" of eight other people, leaving the commune and living by herself with baby Jonathan had been like cutting off some intravenous flow of survival. It had at first amused Ericka to hear her roommate, a great believer in private ownership, exclaim impatiently, "Would you mind just *not* sticking these things in *my* books?" as she shook out a band aid or pencil or postcard Ericka had carelessly stuck between the pages. Ownership, order, ritual: Susan's books, *her* son. Exactly what Shelley would have execrated in the commune. Except, of course, that it had been Ericka alone who had cushioned and creatured Jonathan for nine months like a slowly exploding star; and during his birth, it had been *her* private world that had cracked and splintered for forty-two hours. But those hours had been her single claim to Jonathan for months afterwards: for the rest of the time, until she had left Shelley's Commune, he had belonged to The Family: odd how in the very dissolution of the family as a social institution, they clung to the counterpane of old words—the sisters, the brothers, the word *commune* itself. Yet, altogether an experience she would not have missed; for genuine love had permeated their household—and genuine hate too: elements never quite assimilable. As for Shelley, it had been a cosmogony of Love, available from any of the women in their house, because as Shelley said, they did not "own" each other. So they had had their Love. She had found that keeping your cool in a houseful of Love could be as dangerous as sitting near an open window in an overheated room. You got cool, but you could die of it. What had died had been her love for Shelley.

Upstairs, in what appeared to be a guest room,

Ericka folded her coat beside a pile-up of fake furs and jaunty capes. Her shoes were wet and she stood gratefully against the hot air register, assuring herself that it was a good idea to get dry; but she knew she was only delaying the moment when she would have to face the knotted cords of cocktail conversation, each one powerful, swift and unexpected as your own private case of whiplash. She could plainly hear someone querying the Ascher children, whose hot air register adjoined her own: "You have your pajamas in that bag? Good. And take Binks with you. He'd be lonely sleeping here all by himself." And to something the twin girls murmured, something not quite audible, as the furnace with a faint sigh suddenly wound itself to an intenser blast of heat, "Oh yes, *all* bears love divinity fudge. We'll cook up a whole batch of divinity fudge. Did you say goodnight to your daddy before he left? So . . . we can go. . . . Just leaving, Gertrude," the voice added in higher pitch, apparently to Mrs. Ascher. Obviously an old family retainer, Ericka decided, or a friend with plenty of room in her house, chauffeuring the kids away from the noise and hubbub to a children's paradise of TV, teddy bears and divinity fudge. At Mrs. Ascher's approach—to kiss the children goodbye?—there came faintly through the register a dark wave of perfume which Ericka recognized. Called Always Autumn, it had been the favorite of one of the girls at the commune whom they had named, simply, *Ping* (their repeated failure to learn her real name had been the subject of a long lecture by Shelley who called it subconscious racism), an oriental girl with eyes so perpetually bright, beautiful and intransigent, one would have said a taxidermist had carefully positioned them in her flax-colored face. Shelley had doubtless slept with

her, Ericka now admitted to herself, with a spasm not of jealousy but of exhaustion, as if the sheer attrition of her twenty-three and one-half years of life had begun to bear down sandpaperlike, rasping away layer after layer of sensibility, leaving her raw and vulnerable to every slight—those past as well as present: even in retrospect she could dredge up new insults to her self-esteem.

In a rush of self-discipline—she couldn't very well stand drying her toes all night—she slipped out of the bedroom to the hall, where she met Mrs. Ascher on the stairs. "Quite dry now?" smiled her hostess and explained, without waiting for Ericka's reply: "The children were so excited! They love to sleep away from home. . . . Tessie and Beth pack their own bag. They never forget a thing. But Arthur, on the other hand, always manages to leave something behind—so he can come back for it, I suppose. The girls are—" Mrs. Ascher just faintly hesitated, ". . . *secure,* whereas Arthur is . . . is the only boy," she concluded, vaguely inconsequent. Ericka smiled politely, accustomed to the ordered world of psychiatrists' wives where everything one did really meant something else. But it made conversation a one-way street, so she asked, instead, the question she had grown to learn was pure ritual: "And how old are they?" It was a question renewable forever: grandmothers were still asking each other names, dates, births, baptisms, schools: it was a mindless, solipsistic game, like solitaire.

Mrs. Ascher now politely began to describe her children to her guest. Ericka's mind wandered, a fault she knew was unpardonable, like blurting out some awful truth in public. "And you?" asked Mrs. Ascher, stopping suddenly as if she programmed herself to say just so much and no more.

"Oh. Me? I've only Jonathan. . . ."

"Oh but don't say it like that!" protested her hostess softly. "You'll get married again. But of course you will," she added with odd intensity. "You're too young to think of your life as *over*."

"I don't think I really *believe* in marriage," Ericka tried hesitatingly to explain, more to herself than to Mrs. Ascher.

Mrs. Ascher looked puzzled, even pained. Then she interpreted Ericka's words, apparently, from what she had heard about her, perhaps from Dr. Ascher. "Ah, but you're one of the new women . . . the liberated women," she added haltingly, as if the word were far too weighty and significant for the lightness of their conversation.

Who me? Liberated? thought Erica as they descended the stairs together; and just managed not to strike her forehead in comic despair. Liberated, as Sue Hallam, always sticky with cliché, repeatedly informed her, was to be liberated *from* something. And what the hell was she, Ericka, liberated from anyway? Nothing at all, so far as she could see. A dreary typist in an airless office at three hundred a month (take-home pay). No graduate assistantship for her because Ascher said she wasn't qualified: a B.A. in English didn't qualify a girl for anything in *his* psychology department, he had said, smiling genially. Not that graduate students earned any more money working in the very bowels of the beast (in fact, they earned less) but at least they were saved the hassle of traveling into the inner city to take courses, and the 9–5 claustrophobia: there were times when the mere smell of her office gave her something akin to morning sickness. The only reason she had enrolled in Roderick Ascher's course, *Ego Identity in Urban Crisis*, was that it came at the right time of day and because it was

supposed to be a snap course—one could fill the void of the term paper with flocculent phrases signifying ego-and-identity till the cows came home (still, it hadn't turned out to be a snap course at all: fraudulence, she had found, by the very vagueness of its criteria, can be as demanding as truth). Fortunately Ericka was not required to assess the value of the university system, but merely to hang on to what it might all mean to her when Jonathan was a grown-up man of twenty, and *she?* . . . But she realized with a start that Mrs. Ascher was already clutching the newel at the bottom of the staircase, while gesturing with her other hand to a young man with a beautiful honey-colored beard (he must spend as much time on it, Ericka thought, as she used to spend on her eyebrows). He stood uncertainly in the hallway, dazzled by the lighted hallway. "And where's Dr. Ascher?" inquired Mrs. Ascher, her voice charged with a sudden rush of tension, as though she feared the students might have somehow mislaid him. Rather ungraciously the young man jerked his thumb toward the portico under which headlights were shining. "They'll be here in a minute . . . I guess."

"Miss . . . Mrs. Stein, Mr. Gehan." In her desire to make it clear that they were meant to speak to each other (two young people, after all), and not to her, Mrs. Ascher was tugging Gehan by the arm. Ericka glanced at him, wanting to give the poor guy a break by striking out for herself, straight into the undertow of conversation; but for the present there was nothing to do but comply with their hostess' insistency and set themselves afloat in a tub of conversation.

"Student of Dr. Ascher's, I presume," Ericka asked lightly, trying to make it sound as if she had just come upon him in darkest Africa. But her intonation perhaps was not just right, because his reply came back, grave and factual.

"Well, not exactly. I grade for him—Dr. Ascher. I'm in computer science. And you?"

"Sociology. Social *welfare,* that is." Should she bother to explain the difference? He was already glancing over her shoulder at the doorway, and she decided to save her energy: he was clearly not even interested enough for polite gamesmanship.

He blurted abruptly, his gaze returning to her with a sharp owl-like twist of the head: "Say, I've seen you before. I know where it was. I heard you speak. The other evening. At the discussion."

"Heard *me?*" Was he confusing her with someone else? She went out so rarely at night that she thought she must have some record for anonymity: one stupefying movie-date since leaving Sheldon's Commune. Besides, she had never made a public speech in her life. Ericka stepped back restlessly, feeling her identity threatened: to be unknown was one thing, but to be so commonplace as to be confused with others was sheer annihilation.

But Gehan was not explaining rapidly; he seemed nervous and guilty about something, and was still watching the doorway. She saw him glance down at her left hand as if to look for a wedding ring. "It was that book discussion," he said. "And you asked the author . . . authoress . . . actually, you *told* her, that you didn't think there was any such thing as freedom. For either men or women. You seemed kind of . . . *upset,* and you said . . ." out of consideration for their surroundings he lowered his voice, ". . . you wanted to know how the hell—*your* words—" he apologized quickly, "—how the hell a woman with a kid to take care of could ever be free—you

said that you couldn't even stand there and *listen* to her . . . the authoress . . . because you had to pick your kid up before six o'clock." He faltered and checked the crowd again as though he hoped someone would rescue him from his own recitatif. He seemed startled at his invasion of her privacy, as if it indemnified him toward her somehow.

Ericka pondered. Had she really said all that? She remembered now that she had had a bowl of chili at the cafeteria to save herself the trouble of cooking when she got home. Then, on her way out, she had noticed a lot of women sitting around the Student Union, rapping with Cynthia Carpenter, who had just published a book on the New Woman. With her eye on the clock she had paused for a minute to listen. Some of the woman's answers had irritated her—perhaps she had been merely resentful that Jon's demands (he was always hungry and irritable if she arrived late) prevented her from feeling free to stay—and she had demanded of the writer to explain freedom to *her,* Ericka Stein, mother of two-year-old Jonathan, invoice-lackey to a pseudo-insurance company, daughter of a poor postman who had walked twenty thousand miles and didn't have a nickel to his name, and whose skin cancer was now slowly killing him. "Jesus Christ," she had added, hot tears of self-pity springing to her eyes, "I'm not concerned about whether somebody's daughter gets into a metallurgy class. What I want to know is, how am I going to *survive?*" There had been absolute silence in the group; then several older women had begun whispering among themselves, and a black woman—the only one present—had murmured in antiphony, "Teach, sister, teach!"

Ericka felt embarrassed now as she stared into Gehan's clear grey eyes—he was obviously sympathetic, but also more at ease with her now that he had forced her to admit her pain (it had given him the uncontested upper hand). She could only stare at him in silence, declaring a truce, beseeching him to stop: O.K., O.K. He had won the Battle of the Sexes before it had even begun between them. Nor did she feel obliged to explain her silence. He knew everything, didn't he, if he knew what she had scarcely admitted to herself: that she was lonely and terrified and never had enough money and the responsibility of Jonathan was too much and she would surely break under the strain of it all and then they'd take away her child, and they'd put her away, away, *oi wei*. . . . Even now, in a very rational way, he knew her nerves were frayed, that her feet were still cold, and that after the party she would either have to walk home, wait for a bus, or spend two dollars for a taxi (punitive choices, all three), and that Jon would certainly wake up when she came in—he was really getting too big to sleep in the same room: and Christ, what was she to do about it all?

She took advantage of a surge of arrivals to duck Gehan. She couldn't take the image of herself she had received from his eyes. Alone at 3:00 a.m. she could confess her misery, cry out *"God, this is unbearable!"* not sure to Whom she was speaking. But not here; it was as if she suddenly found herself the only one naked. Perspiring with nervousness, she eased away toward the refreshments, hanging over the delicacies of cheese and ham and chicken as over a funeral pyre onto which shortly she too would be thrown and consumed.

But she was relieved, for the moment, to be alone. A few more such encounters and they could tie her up and carry her home in a body bag. She began to ply herself with food, forcing herself to feign *bon appétit* while fumbling with the cheese cutter, which was an odd-shaped clever thing, like a genteel guillotine. . . .

". . . help you with that?" It was Ascher. He had apparently arrived at last, alive and well, with his covey of students. Beside him, as he showed Ericka how to manipulate the little guillotine which pared cheese as thin as a veil, stood a stunning girl whom he introduced to her as Deborah. A foreign student, apparently, but Ericka couldn't place her accent. Ascher began slicing the cheese for them, holding down the wooden board with one hand, while making manly lunges at the rounded cheese with the other. Deborah stood beside him, smiling down with pleasure at the curling whorls of cheese. Ascher then began entertaining them, his manners pervasively democratic, as though it were definitely his prerogative as well as responsibility to entertain students, not the other way around. Before Ascher could finish his sentences, Deborah would begin laughing, an interruption which Ascher took in his stride, adding the punch line after the laugh. Then they would both laugh simultaneously, while Ericka managed what she felt must be a very tired smile. She began to wonder whether she should stay, but felt it would be rude to leave; it would look slanderously as though she mistook their public laughter for private; so she stayed. She was slightly shorter than Deborah, and Ericka's line of vision fell exactly parallel with the girl's cleavage—a fact which was somehow disconcerting as Deborah swayed toward them in animated conversation. The girl was very intelligent—indeed, so witty and beautiful she made Ericka feel like a cabbage. But in spite of her gifts, Deborah seemed troubled by an unnatural tension; her breasts loomed like weapons, her earrings glittered. One felt in a moment how those agitated breasts might brush up against a man in some initiatory rite . . . Ericka suddenly remembered that there was an unmended rip in the seam of her dress—over the shoulder where she herself could not see it— which exposed like an unsutured wound her poverty, her haste, her reluctance to come to this party at all, and which exposed, above all, her indifference to all those roles into which "they" wished to cast her: "sexpot, mother symbol, husband catcher." Choose your Procrustean bed and die on it. And now she felt a headache beginning, one of those like a medieval torture in which that part of her which had refused to accept something would be slowly, horribly crushed in The Boot of her brain.

She definitely ought to go home. But first, for good form, she would join the hostess. A circle of guests had gathered around the physical security of Mrs. Ascher's pregnant body as around an ancient fertility goddess. It was a group, Ericka sensed, which like herself had been glad to surrender sprightliness and grace for the solid honesty of sitting down. Sitting down was an admission that you were dead-tired. And having arrived at that moment of truth, other truths naturally followed. You at once dropped the sealed mask of attentiveness, Ericka reflected, and conversation was allowed to languish. For to sit was an honest and quintessential act of nature: one sat beside the sick and dying; one sat at a wake, at a peace pow-wow; one sat at dinner and sat to evacuate. Sitting was akin to squatting, a modified form of hunkering down in the cave: it reminded you that you were mere body, and mortal.

Having lifted her fatigue to a social philosophy, Ericka sank with a groan into a chair beside two women who seemed to be sorting out courage and clichés like hired poker hands in a card game. Ericka decided she would merely listen. She felt exorcised of any personal vanity or greed that might ever again propel her into speech. Let others shine, she was willing to vanish, to disappear into silence. The talk shambled for a while like a clever clown taking in the needs of its audience. This film, that film; within five minutes they had reviewed five films: Ericka thought wryly that they must attend movies like Browning's Bishop eating God daily. But she became more attentive as she realized that they were discussing what "their" group was planning to do Again and Again Against the War. She began immediately asking herself whom she could find to keep Jon for the weekend; for she felt obliged to go along to protest the war the way one might feel obliged to give blood to the dying. Though the disease might be terminal, it was an act of expiation, fending off a jealous god who had jurisdiction over her ultimate right to survive. Ericka was about to break her self-imposed silence, to make inquiry about buses, transportation, sleeping arrangements, when Mrs. Ascher observed that several women had been arrested in a mêlée outside the State Capitol while picketing, she said, " 'for the right over their own bodies.' " A look of melancholy invaded Mrs. Ascher's eyes. Then an argument began between Mrs. Ascher and a young girl with long blonde hair, a very polite argument; for after all Mrs. Ascher was Dr. Ascher's wife and, besides, was so plainly and helplessly pregnant that a consciousness of it rang through everyone's speech like a clapper in a bell. Ericka listened as the girl—only a freshman, as she explained as though it were somehow relevant—argued for what she called Absolute Freedom. Then suddenly the blonde girl became more emotional, she began citing personal facts—a love affair, an abortion, a father who had run off to join the circus—as if by confessing these personal crises she might persuade Mrs. Ascher of their right to Absolute Freedom. Through it all, her hostess sat, surprisingly unmoved, only turning from time to time to regard the group sitting around her. Ericka averted her eyes, feeling herself unable to take sides. She knew she had never—no, not once,—been "free." Freedom, like sex and money, were painlessly discussed at leisure by those who had the most of them. Those who did not have these things were silent—ashamed of their lack, as if by the power of their wills they might have wrested from the havoc of their lives A Beautiful Life—well-loved and rich, and chock-full of the four freedoms. Ericka's despair, her conviction that she would never have this freedom, drove her deep into self-abasement. She allowed herself to envy Mrs. Ascher, in a veritable orgy of covetousness. She admitted to herself with disgust that she envied everything her hostess had: her composure, her home, her love, her friends, her exquisite frock, her vaginal orgasms; envied her, in fact, down to her very shoes which, glossy and neat, rested side by side on the rug like a pair of expensive and well-trained pets. Then abruptly, Ericka's gaze flickered, she wearied of her own apostasy, of her own cringing admiration, the very depth of which had left her exhausted, cleansed, purged—momentarily, at least—of envy. She said to herself that she had sat courteously enough, and now she would try to leave. Her head was twingeing like a rotting tooth and she felt morally justified in improvising a strategy of escape. She would, she decided, excuse herself and go upstairs to the bedroom where she had left some aspirin in her coat pocket; then, she might perhaps drift slowly downstairs, and drift slowly . . . homeward, if it were—say—anywhere near ten o'clock. But what was the time now? she wondered, with a glance at Mrs. Ascher's watch. Her attention was at once riveted to Mrs. Ascher's anomalous timepiece, as she realized with a shock that she would never find out the time from that strangely incoherent watch: it had only one hand.

Ericka looked up at her hostess in surprise; she and Gertrude Ascher exchanged oddly meaningful looks—Gertrude's, as it seemed to her, intensely pleased, as though she were somehow gratified that her odd secret was out. . . . "Excuse me," said Ericka, determined to outface this enigma. She leaned toward Gertrude's wrist with curiosity: "But can you tell me the time?"

Gertrude laughed. A flush of pleasure crept over her face. "It's five minutes," she announced mysteriously.

"Five minutes to what? I mean after what?" Ericka found herself absurdly correcting herself, as if to force it all into chronological good sense. Gertrude laughed again, lifting the back of her hand to her mouth. Just faintly, Ericka could see the imprint of Gertrude's teeth on her hand.

"That's all. Five minutes. Five minutes before, after, during *any*thing. It's not necessary to know the hour. That way you always have enough time. You're never rushed. For instance," she went on to exclaim with a logical air, "let's say you're taking Roderick's clothes to be pressed . . ." She glanced around as if looking to see if Roderick were present, her voice slightly breathless as if with laughter: but she was not smiling at all. "You allow fifteen minutes in all: five for parking the car—just outside the cleaners. Five for taking the clothes into the store, getting your receipt, that kind of thing. And five for your return. . . ."

Ericka set her face into an attitude of polite curiosity; but her head throbbed; her own pain was rapidly becoming excruciating, but she was held to her place by a consciousness that some other pain—a pain deeper and incurable—was being revealed to her.

"Think of it this way," said Mrs. Ascher amiably, looking down at her watch as if she were a magician about to make all her rabbits disappear at a single whisk of her handkerchief. "When I wake up in the morning, nothing is changed. It's all *exactly* as the day before. I still have . . . *yesterday*. I begin: one minute to brush my teeth, a half hour for breakfast, thirty minutes on the phone. The rule is, I never consume an entire hour for any one thing. . . . Then I begin again. Say, I'm on my way to the library. The freeway is no excuse," she added harshly, her face suddenly all sternness and self-discipline. "You can't allow yourself extra time just because of a crowded freeway—or because the tunnels are loaded with traffic. *All this has to be taken into consideration beforehand.* It should *never* take more than twenty minutes to take books back to the library. Allow for a maximum of seven red lights if, instead of the freeway, you're going by way of Mercy Avenue. If you don't allow for the red lights, you're trapped," she warned them with a fierceness which revealed to them all her dedication to her ideal: to consume her life in meaningless pastimes and yet to have it, to waste it and yet to possess it. It was like an endless game of crossword puzzles, each word fitting perfectly, yet all of it making no sense in the aggregate and leaving one again—and again—with inexhaustible but untiring stretches of achievement. A self-induced labor of Sisyphus.

The blonde-haired girl who had been arguing with her hostess about freedom looked frightened; then she laughed, or pretended to, as if Mrs. Ascher were being terribly witty; the others followed suit, and it was as if the loud ticking of hysteria were washed over in good-natured joking. Mrs. Ascher removed her watch and looked at Ericka, smiling. Ericka had not laughed, and had not ceased staring; Mrs. Ascher bent toward her with a mysterious air of complicity. "Sometimes," she added, "it's best to stop things altogether. Then I wear it inside out." Mrs. Ascher then fastidiously attached the faceless leather band to her other wrist, after which she leaned back with a fatigued but satisfied smile.

Without bothering to apologize, Ericka rose and ran up the staircase to the bedroom full of coats. She had trouble locating her own folded-up raincoat; in its commonplaceness it seemed to have disappeared beneath the vast pile of clothes. As she struggled with furs and alpacas, not wanting to dislodge the entire mass so that it all came crashing down, she heard through the hot air register, Ascher, murmuring with exasperation: "What *difference* does it make? You don't really think she doesn't? . . ." Followed by Deborah's strongly accented whisper: "Yes, but what about *me?*" "*You!*" echoed Ascher, and there was a long silence. "What is it you *want* then?" Ascher exclaimed presently, forgetting to lower his voice. "But you're mad," protested Deborah in a whisper. "Suppose she comes in?"

"Here? *Now?*" Ascher retorted. "She'd never dare . . ."

Trembling as if she were guilty of some secret crime, Ericka clutched her plastic raincoat, trying to keep it from rattling. "Wait. . ." whispered Deborah. Ericka's heart pounded with fear. She sped through the doorway, in such terror of being discovered by Ascher that she actually flipped off the lights in the hallway as she flew downstairs. She had safely reached the foot of the staircase when she found herself face to face with Mrs. Ascher. She believed now the entire household would surely explode into pieces, but to her surprise Gertrude said softly, her voice rising and falling with a mechanical regularity, as if some internal device had sanctioned these measured crises: "Oh, it's you, Ericka. Going already? I thought I heard Arthur cry out. I thought the children were awake. I thought they might want something."

"But they're spending the night . . ." began a well-meaning guest, looking hesitantly at Ericka. But Ericka did not exchange the look. Instead she bent over hastily and kissed her hostess. She discovered to her surprise that it was all she could do to refrain from throwing her arms around the woman and begging her pardon, begging her forgiveness for something she, Ericka, and all of them present, had somehow done to her. But she said only, with an intensity which frightened herself as she looked directly at her hostess, "Thank you, Mrs. Ascher. Thank you very much. It was a lovely party."

"So glad you enjoyed it. But I did think I heard the children," Mrs. Ascher added, as if irrelevantly. "Isn't that strange?" she asked, smiling at them—maternal, fond, collusive.

Discussion Questions

1. Summarize Ericka's life until the night of the Ascher party. Is Ericka a liberated woman?
2. Why did Ericka leave the commune? Does this experience resemble marriage and divorce? Explain your answer.
3. What are Ericka's initial reactions to Mrs. Ascher? After the conversation in which Gertrude explains why her watch has only one hand, what new perspective does Ericka have on her own life?
4. Compare Ethel's situation in "The Season of Divorce" with Ericka's and Gertrude's. Compare the husbands in these stories.
5. Compare the four women in this story, Ericka, Gertrude, Susan, and Deborah.

Natalie L.M. Petesch   123

THE PICNIC
JOHN LOGAN

It is the picnic with Ruth in the spring.
Ruth was third on my list of seven girls
But the first two were gone (Betty) or else
Had someone (Ellen has accepted Doug).
Indian Gully the last day of school;
Girls make the lunches for the boys too.
I wrote a note to Ruth in algebra class
Day before the test. She smiled, and nodded.
We left the cars and walked through the young
    corn.
The shoots green as paint and the leaves like
    tongues
Trembling. Beyond the fence where we stood
Some wild strawberry flowered by an elm tree
And Jack-in-the-pulpit was olive ripe.
A blackbird fled as I crossed, and showed
A spot of gold or red under its quick wing.
I held the wire for Ruth and watched the whip
Of her long, striped skirt as she followed.
Three freckles blossomed on her thin, white back
Underneath the loop where the blouse buttoned.
We went for our lunch away from the rest,
Stretched in the new grass, our heads close
Over unknown things wrapped up in wax papers.
Ruth tried for the same, I forget what it was,
And our hands were together. She laughed,
And a breeze caught the edge of her little

John Logan (1923–) is an Iowa-born poet who teaches at the
University of Notre Dame.

Collar and the edge of her brown, loose hair
That touched my cheek. I turned my face into
the gentle fall. I saw how sweet it smelled.
She didn't move her head or take her hand.
I felt a soft caving in my stomach
As at the top of the highest slide
When I had been a child, but was not afraid,
And did not know why my eyes moved with wet
As I brushed her cheek with my lips and
    brushed
Her lips with my own lips. She said to me
Jack, Jack, different than I had ever heard,
Because she wasn't calling me, I think,
Or telling me. She used my name to
Talk in another way I wanted to know.
She laughed again and then she took her hand;
I gave her what we both had touched—can't
Remember what it was, and we ate the lunch.
Afterward we walked in the small, cool creek
Our shoes off, her skirt hitched, and she smiling,
My pants rolled, and then we climbed up the
    high
Side of Indian Gully and looked
Where we had been, our hands together again.
It was then some bright thing came in my eyes,
Starting at the back of them and flowing
Suddenly through my head and down my arms
And stomach and my bare legs that seemed not
To stop in feet, not to feel the red earth
Of the Gully, as though we hung in a

Touch of birds. There was a word in my throat
With the feeling and I knew the first time
What it meant and I said, it's beautiful.
Yes, she said, and I felt the sound and word
In my hand join the sound and word in hers
As in one name said, or in one cupped hand.
We put back on our shoes and socks and we
Sat in the grass awhile, crosslegged, under
A blowing tree, not saying anything.
And Ruth played with shells she found in the
    creek,
As I watched. Her small wrist which was so
    sweet
To me turned by her breast and the shells
    dropped
Green, white, blue, easily into her lap,
Passing light through themselves. She gave the
    pale
Shells to me, and got up and touched her hips
With her light hands, and we walked down
    slowly
To play the school games with the others.

Discussion Questions

1. What kind of relationship is Logan describing in "The Picnic"?
2. Compare this poem to Sexton's "Cinderella."

SEX AND SECULARIZATION
HARVEY COX

There is a whole generation who thinks that women fold in three places and have a staple at the source of life.
—Mort Sahl

In "The Crisis in Woman's Identity" Betty Friedan tells us that young women need suitable models to emulate. Evidently young men share this need and many turn to *Playboy* for a masculine model.

Despite accusations to the contrary, the immense popularity of [*Playboy*] magazine is not solely attributable to pin-up girls. For sheer nudity its pictorial art cannot compete with such would-be competitors as *Dude* and *Escapade*. *Playboy* appeals to a highly mobile, increasingly affluent group of young readers, mostly between eighteen and thirty, who want much more from their drugstore reading than bosoms and thighs. They need a total image of what it means to be a man. And Mr. Hefner's *Playboy* has no hesitation in telling them.

Why should such a need arise? David Riesman has argued that the responsibility for character formation in our society has shifted from the family to the peer group and to the mass-media peer-group surrogates. Things are changing so

---

Harvey Cox (1929–), a Baptist clergyman, is also a university professor and author.

rapidly that one who is equipped by his family with inflexible, highly internalized values becomes unable to deal with the accelerated pace of change and with the varying contexts in which he is called upon to function. This is especially true in the area of consumer values toward which the "other-directed person" is increasingly oriented.

Within the confusing plethora of mass-media signals and peer-group values, *Playboy* fills a special need. For the insecure young man with newly acquired free time and money who still feels uncertain about his consumer skills, *Playboy* supplies a comprehensive and authoritative guidebook to this forbidding new world to which he now has access. It tells him not only who to be; it tells him *how* to be it, and even provides consolation outlets for those who secretly feel that they have not quite made it.

In supplying for the other-directed consumer of leisure both the normative identity image and the means for achieving it, *Playboy* relies on a careful integration of copy and advertising material. The comic book that appeals to a younger generation with an analogous problem skillfully intersperses illustrations of incredibly muscled men and excessively mammalian women with advertisements for body-building gimmicks and foam-rubber brassiere supplements. Thus the thin-chested comic-book readers of both sexes are thoughtfully supplied with both the ends and the means for attaining a spurious brand of maturity. *Playboy* merely continues the comic-book tactic for the next age group. Since within every identity crisis, whether in teens or twenties, there is usually a sexual-identity problem, *Playboy* speaks to those who desperately want to know what it means to

be a man, and more specifically a *male,* in today's world.

Both the image of man and the means for its attainment exhibit a remarkable consistency in *Playboy*. The skilled consumer is cool and unruffled. He savors sports cars, liquor, high fidelity, and book-club selections with a casual, unhurried aplomb. Though he must certainly *have* and *use* the latest consumption item, he must not permit himself to get too attached to it. The style will change and he must always be ready to adjust. His persistent anxiety that he may mix a drink incorrectly, enjoy a jazz group that is passé, or wear last year's necktie style is comforted by an authoritative tone in *Playboy* beside which papal encyclicals sound irresolute.

"Don't hesitate," he is told, "this assertive, self-assured weskit is what every man of taste wants for the fall season." Lingering doubts about his masculinity are extirpated by the firm assurance that "real men demand this ruggedly masculine smoke" (cigar ad). Though "the ladies will swoon for you, no matter what they promise, don't give them a puff. This cigar is for men only." A fur-lined canvas field jacket is described as "the most masculine thing since the cave man." What to be and how to be it are both made unambiguously clear.

Since being a male necessitates some kind of relationship to females, *Playboy* fearlessly confronts this problem too, and solves it by the consistent application of the same formula. Sex becomes one of the items of leisure activity that the knowledgeable consumer of leisure handles with his characteristic skill and detachment. The girl becomes a desirable—indeed an indispensable—"Playboy accessory."

In a question-answering column entitled "The

Playboy Adviser," queries about smoking equipment (how to break in a meerschaum pipe), cocktail preparation (how to mix a Yellow Fever), and whether or not to wear suspenders with a vest alternate with questions about what to do with girls who complicate the cardinal principle of casualness either by suggesting marriage or by some other impulsive gesture toward a permanent relationship. The infallible answer from the oracle never varies: sex must be contained, at all costs, within the entertainment-recreation area. Don't let her get "serious."

After all, the most famous feature of the magazine is its monthly fold-out photo of a *play*mate. She is the symbol par excellence of recreational sex. When playtime is over, the playmate's function ceases, so she must be made to understand the rules of the game. As the crew-cut young man in a *Playboy* cartoon says to the rumpled and disarrayed girl he is passionately embracing, "Why speak of love at a time like this?"

The magazine's fiction purveys the same kind of severely departmentalized sex. Although the editors have recently dressed up the *Playboy* contents with contributions by Hemingway, Bemelmans, and even a Chekhov translation, the regular run of stories relies on a repetitive and predictable formula. A successful young man, either single or somewhat less than ideally married—a figure with whom readers have no difficulty identifying—encounters a gorgeous and seductive woman who makes no demands on him except sex. She is the prose duplication of the cool-eyed but hot-blooded playmate of the fold-out.

Drawing heavily on the fantasy life of all young Americans, the writers utilize for their stereotyped heroines the hero's schoolteacher, his secretary, an old girl friend, or the girl who brings her car into the garage where he works. The happy issue is always a casual but satisfying sexual experience with no entangling alliances whatever. Unlike the women he knows in real life, the *Playboy* reader's functional girl friends know their place and ask for nothing more. They present no danger of permanent involvement. Like any good accessory, they are detachable and disposable.

Many of the advertisements reinforce the sex-accessory identification in another way—by attributing female characteristics to the items they sell. Thus a full-page ad for the MG assures us that this car is not only "the smoothest pleasure machine" on the road and that having one is a "love-affair," but most important, "you drive it—it doesn't drive you." The ad ends with the equivocal question, "Is it a date?"

Playboy insists that its message is one of liberation. Its gospel frees us from captivity to the puritanical "hatpin brigade." It solemnly crusades for "frankness" and publishes scores of letters congratulating it for its unblushing "candor." Yet the whole phenomenon of which *Playboy* is only a part vividly illustrates the awful fact of a new kind of tyranny.

Those liberated by technology and increased prosperity to new worlds of leisure now become the anxious slaves of dictatorial tastemakers. Obsequiously waiting for the latest signal on what is cool and what is awkward, they are paralyzed by the fear that they may hear pronounced on them that dread sentence occasionally intoned by "The Playboy Adviser": "You goofed!" Leisure is thus swallowed up in apprehensive competitiveness, its liberating potential transformed into a self-destructive compulsion to consume only what is *à la mode.* *Playboy* mediates the Word of the most high into one section of the consumer world, but it is a word of bondage, not of freedom.

Nor will *Playboy's* synthetic doctrine of man stand the test of scrutiny. Psychoanalysts constantly remind us how deep-seated sexuality is in the human being. But if they didn't remind us, we would soon discover it ourselves anyway. Much as the human male might like to terminate his relationship with a woman as he would snap off the stereo, or store her for special purposes like a camel's-hair jacket, it really can't be done. And anyone with a modicum of experience with women knows it can't be done. Perhaps this is the reason *Playboy's* readership drops off so sharply after the age of thirty.

Playboy really feeds on the existence of a repressed fear of involvement with women, which for various reasons is still present in many otherwise adult Americans. So *Playboy's* version of sexuality grows increasingly irrelevant as authentic sexual maturity is achieved.

The male identity crisis to which *Playboy* speaks has at its roots a deep-set fear of sex, a fear that is uncomfortably combined with fascination. *Playboy* strives to resolve this antinomy by reducing the proportions of sexuality, its power and its passion, to a packageable consumption item. Thus in *Playboy's* iconography the nude woman symbolizes total sexual accessibility but demands nothing from the observer. "You drive it—it doesn't drive you." The terror of sex, which cannot be separated from its ecstasy, is dissolved. But this futile attempt to reduce the *mysterium tremendum* of the sexual

fails to solve the problem of being a man. For sexuality is the basic form of all human relationship, and therein lies its terror and its power.

Karl Barth has called this basic relational form of man's life *Mitmensch,* co-humanity. This means that becoming fully human, in this case a human male, requires not having the other totally exposed to me and my purposes—while I remain uncommitted—but exposing myself to the risk of encounter with the other by reciprocal self-exposure. The story of man's refusal so to be exposed goes back to the story of Eden and is expressed by man's desire to control the other rather than to *be with* the other. It is basically the fear to be one's self, a lack of the "courage to be."

Thus any theological critique of *Playboy* that focuses on its "lewdness" will misfire completely. *Playboy* and its less successful imitators are not "sex magazines" at all. They are basically antisexual. They dilute and dissipate authentic sexuality by reducing it to an accessory, by keeping it at a safe distance.

Discussion Questions

1. Cox says that *Playboy's* popularity is not solely attributable to pin-up girls. What is the real attraction of the magazine for young men? Why does Cox object to *Playboy?*
2. Although this chapter from *The Secular City* was written in 1966, *Playboy* seems to have changed little. Bring in a few recent copies. Read "The Playboy Advisor" and examine some of the ads to test the validity of Cox's analysis.
3. Is feminine conquest a true gauge of masculinity? Explain your answer.

**The Dingo Man.
He's no ordinary
Joe.**

Boots are his thing.
They're part of his image.
He knows just how to wear boots. With style.
He knows when to wear them too.
Whenever he feels like it. But don't try to con
The Dingo Man into a boot made
by a shoemaker. His boots are real.
The label inside all of them reads "Dingo."
If you don't believe us, ask any girl
Joe Namath knows.
For store near you, write:
Acme Boot Co., Inc., Dept. PL 91,
Clarksville, Tenn. 37040.
A subsidiary of Northwest
Industries, Inc.

dingo®

From Acme.® Ⓐ The World's Largest Bootmaker.

133

THE MASCULINE MYSTIQUE
GEORGE FRAZIER IV

*With some experience of what being a man meant she
[Mrs. Morel] knew that it was not everything.*
—D. H. Lawrence, Sons and Lovers

Contrary to the belief of many young feminists,
running for the 8:05 and competing in the business
world is not always rewarding. In this essay George
Frazier compares the difficulties and responsibilities of
the working man with the "less complicated" tasks of
the housewife.

If only men were a little bit brighter, just a little
less obdurate, then maybe they might be able to
get it through their heads that feminism could
well be a man's best friend, its seemingly oppressive stipulations actually his sole salvation. Indeed, it is conceivable that no greater boon could
be bestowed upon men than what Women's
Liberation is ordering them to accept—and having, incidentally, a terrible time getting them
even to listen to. Still, in complaining about their
problems, women are making sane men suddenly
aware that they, by God, have their own occasions of discontent, a whole slew of grievances
that, ironically, will be alleviated only when
women become men's equals, *de facto* fully as

George Frazier IV (1944–), formerly a stockbroker, is a free-
lance writer who contributes to national magazines.

much as *de jure,* and are in a position to assume the responsibilities that now weigh so heavily upon the male.

No one, I think, would deny that women are restricted—economically, institutionally, and in their options, as well. But what is far less apparent is that men are also circumscribed by society's expectations, since they, too, must conform to a code that exists in its most virulent form in Latin countries, where it is called *machismo.* Even in this country, presumably so sophisticated, so cynical, there is a mystique to masculinity, to being a member of man's world, to belonging to the club. Here, no less than in Spain, Mexico, and other *machismo*-minded places, men have been conditioned to accept, honor, and cherish the illusion that virility equals authority. Stokely Carmichael was merely reflecting this when he stated that the only position for women in SNCC was prone, as if any show of intelligence or independence on the part of female members might undermine the influence of its men—as if, in fact, a man would become less of a man were his woman to use her mind.

Now, however, there are some among us who feel that the time has finally come for women to be invested with all the rights and privileges of the club, to become acquainted at last with all that they've been missing—the delights of the draft, for example; the inestimable prerogative of having to give only name, rank, and serial number when in the hands of the Viet Cong. There is no end of the perquisites to which liberated women would fall heir.

When the Manifesto of the New York Radical Feminists promises that "the liberation of women will ultimately mean the liberation of men from the destructive role as oppressor," any intelligent man's reaction is to wish that this were a little more ex cathedra, somewhat more enfranchised, so that he could actually count on a time when somebody's mother would indeed wear G.I. shoes. It isn't easy being an oppressor these days, and any help is appreciated. I, for one, refuse to believe that women are biologically unequipped for combat; I have seen Weatherwomen who would put the men of My Lai to shame.

But feminism has many faces. There is, for instance, the matter of marriage to be discussed, and somebody named Ti-Grace Atkinson says we better be quick about it—and perhaps we better, because somebody named Ti-Grace Atkinson looks like a lady to be reckoned with, a staff sergeant to the stripes born. It is Miss Atkinson's practice to proclaim that "marriage is slavery," and although I know when to keep a civil tongue, not daring for an instant to doubt the dear girl, I must confess that I'm not quite clear as to exactly who is being enslaved.

It is all pretty damned confusing, with a steady proliferation of groups within the movement, each with its own idea of Utopia, one trying to be temperate, another demanding in brawny baritone voices everything short of the absolute extinction of men. Among others, there are the Sisters of Lilith, WITCH, which goes in for putting a hex on Wall Street, and Bread and Roses, such a demure name for such a dauntless legion; not only The Feminists, but also The Radical Feminists; and the Redstockings, one of whose handmaidens recently emerged from the pots and pans to observe that "men recognize the essential fact of housework right from the beginning, which is that it stinks"—as if to suggest not only that the heat of passion does a certain disservice to the elegance of one's prose style, but also that the husband on the assembly line is luxuriating in 40 hours of fun and games a week.

What the girls should try to understand is that not every man is an executive, living a sybaritic life of compliant secretaries and martinis stirred not shaken, so happy in his work that he can hardly wait to get to the office bright and early each morning. Someone should inform the feminists that there are at least a few men who absolutely loathe their jobs—the interminable hours, the putting up with the snotty *lèse-majesté* of inferiors and the bossiness of employers.

This, not nirvana, is what feminists may expect to find when they take over men's jobs—all this glamor and, with it, such fringe benefits as racing for the 8:15 each morning or being squashed to jelly in the subway rush-hour crush. But what, then, of the dishes in the sink—what of the floors to be mopped, the silver to be polished, the shelves to be dusted? Who will discharge those odious chores when the little woman is off in what was once man's world? Well, *my* apron is at the ready, and if you will just show me the way to the kitchen, what cabinet the detergents are kept in, and how to turn on the television set . . .

Naturally, it will be difficult at first to switch from making money to home economics, but once the change-over becomes socially acceptable, the benefits should be bountiful, for where, outside Appalachia, is there dusting to do that can't be done in a couple of hours? What I am looking forward to is the time when, with the head of the family away at the office, I can sip a beer while catching up on the soaps. Every man owes it to himself to see if *Dark Shadows* is all that women say. And, busy though I'll be, I'm sure I'll find time to make myself presentable before the Avon lady comes calling.

Still, babies do present a bit of a problem, for no man is stirred by the prospect of changing diapers and preparing pablum. On the other hand, however, it is now considered gauche to have more than two children. Moreover, if the demands of Women's Liberation for unlimited abortion and 24-hour day care are met, the only thing left to worry about will be the bearing of the bairn, an enterprise that some fussy feminists consider revolting. Yet, if the wonder-workers of modern biochemistry prevail, no woman need ever be pregnant again, and while some people regard the idea of test-tube babies as a "pseudoradical cop-out," I like it. In fact, I like it very much. After all, the little woman would suffer no loss of income because of absence for childbirth. What's more, she'd always be available for overtime, thereby providing money for the new sportcoat I need so sorely. A man simply can't wear any old thing when he opens the door for the Avon lady. What a brave new world it will be, this brain child of Women's Liberation. Now, no more guff from some boorish district manager; now, no more alimony—now, only the awareness of what it is to be a free soul. And yet . . .

And yet, listening to women's idea of emancipation, to what they envy in the life style of the opposite sex, one wonders if they have even the slightest understanding of what a lousy lot a man's life can be. For what they aspire to appropriate is but a part, and the best part by far, of what might be referred to as the masculine mystique. What women want is the swagger without the sweat. What they can't seem to realize is that the two go together, that there isn't one without the other.

Some years ago, S. I. Hayakawa, in his role of

respected semanticist, wrote that the trouble with the lyrics of most popular songs—"We'll have a blue room, a just-meant-for-two-room," and the like, each more idealized than the other—was that they led the unsuspecting to believe that life actually is a bowl of cherries and that everybody, every blessed couple among us, does indeed live happily ever after. He might just as well have been writing about the world envisioned by Women's Liberation. The real world, unlike the feminists' Utopia, is not a place for having one's cake and eating it, too. It is a win-some, lose-some world, and anyone who thinks that the grass is greener on the assembly line than in the kitchen is in trouble, deep trouble.

The simple, stark fact of the matter is that life is never equitable. When women demand to appropriate what is beautiful in a man's way of life, they must be prepared to accept what is bad in it. But I wonder if many women, the ones in the feminist groups especially, know, *really* know, how confining man's mortal coil can be.

For what man must live with, every waking hour, day in, day out, week after week, is his awareness of death and taxes and, far worse, all that they entail—sudden disability and, with it, a child's tuition bill unprovided for; the nagging fear, more awful with each passing year, each new gray hair, of being replaced by one's junior; the frustration of being unable to compete in a computerized world; the stabbing sense of not quite living up to the image in which society would cast him; the terrible, demeaning suspicion that one is but a bank account, a credit-card number, an insurance premium. Is that what Women's Liberation really wishes?

Is it, after all, an insult and an imposition to be regarded as a sex object? Is it more unbearable than being considered a dollar sign, a good provider, a paterfamilias, a breadwinner? Feminists complain that the reason most girls go to college is to meet men, marry, and raise families. Is this more undesirable than a boy's being on campus for the sole purpose of eventually being able to support one of the girls he might meet there? It seems to me that it should be obvious to anyone familiar with higher education that girls get all the best of it. It is the male who must sublimate his real interests if he is to pursue the quest of man's grail, which is the making of money. Many a boy's undergraduate years are ashes because he must study quantum mechanics when he would much rather be reading up on archaeology, or playing squash, or auditing a course on Georgian poetry, or watching a ball game, or, for that matter, participating in a protest march.

This would not be quite so insufferable were some genuine good to come of it, but too often, the reward for all the evenings not spent at the tables down at Morey's consists of orthodontists' bills, TV dinners, a shrewish wife, and a career that is anathema, a boss who is despicable. Is this the grail, this the end-all of the hours spent on courses one couldn't stand—all this, the bills past due, the work never entirely satisfactory, the fear of being fired? If only he could relax for a minute, if only he didn't have always to be the aggressor.

And yet it is this—the aggressiveness of the male—that Women's Liberation would exercise. This, in a way, is what feminism is all about, the most important part of its program being for the girls to cease being passive and to assume the role of the aggressor—the sexual aggressor above all. What Women's Lib seems incapable of understanding is that it is there for them to take—the sooner the better, and they are entirely welcome— for the fact is that aggressive impulses atrophy, not aggrandize. They are what make men's life expectancies seven years shorter than women's. Is this what the feminists seek? Don't they know that although 51.5 per cent of the births in this country are male, 51 per cent of the population is female? Is Women's Lib obsessed by a death wish?

But it may be too much to expect men to relinquish the role of the aggressor. After all, at this point it's almost innate. For there *is* something about sexual conquest, something to which men are conditioned from the age of puberty. It is what Ernest Hemingway wrote good, bragged bad, and bawled in his cups about, and, in doing so, summed up all that the feminists regard as the worst in men.

"I wish I could sleep with you, but I can't because there is somebody else. I hope you understand," he said to Lillian Hellman one night in Paris, although the idea had never entered her mind—and if it had, she couldn't have been less interested. The cheek of the man, the insufferable assumption that he was irresistible, that he was doing somebody a favor. How like a man. Of course, Hemingway's adventures as a young man indicated he was pretty irresistible in any case, but his pride kept prodding him to prove it, until finally arrogance became impotence, at least for the brief while he was living over the sawmill in Paris. His insecurity could be alleviated only by conquest, whether in word or in action, in war or over women, and when his inadequacies became unbearable, when he could no longer be the man he imagined himself, his will failed. It is a common condition among men, and it was this,

the overwhelming demands of the masculine mystique, which, as much as anything else, led him to kill himself.

Yet, what if Hemingway had lived to face the Women's Liberationists, who demand admittance into the sodality he considered sacrosanctly male? What if some member of Bread and Roses, that willful little cell in Boston, were to express designs upon his burly body? What if some mere slip of a girl were to try to manipulate *his* body? But this is precisely what Bread and Roses is all about, according to two of its members who chatted with Robert Healy, columnist with the Boston *Globe*. What they seek, they said, is an end to men's manipulation of women's bodies. And this but a few minutes after they had invaded the *Globe* demanding, among other things, "three columns a week, minimum of 500 words, to appear in the 'Living' section, on Sunday, Wednesday, and Friday, in all editions, with full editorial control by Bread and Roses."

Full editorial control? What would Max Perkins have said if Papa had proposed that for himself? How interminable would Thomas Wolfe's novels have been unedited, his prose unmanipulated? The mind boggles.

Were he alive, Hemingway would be horrified, absolutely beside himself, at the ideology and egotism of Bread and Roses, which does not feel that sex is necessarily an athletic contest with a winner and a loser. To Hemingway, as to many men, the pleasure was in the overpowering, in carving notches in the bedposts, and an aggressive girl would leave no room for a clear-cut victory.

It is all rather a bore—and, as well, of course, damned hard work, a circumstance which women are finding out for themselves these days. Not

138   His

long ago, a Boston feminist fretted in print that being sexually aggressive and taking the initiative simply isn't all that much fun; that it is, in fact, something of a drag. After all, as she discovered, there are those men who do not respond "properly," who have to be pushed and played up to rather more than is to her taste. But this is what men must endure all the time—women who fail to respond properly. Feminism victorious, however, will free us of this.

And while men are being manumitted, women will be enfranchised to be fired from the presidency of General Motors, to keep up the payments on the car, to have their salary garnisheed when they don't; to enjoy the prerogative of botching everything up—of coping with pollution and inflation and all other plagues for which they are not accountable now. And the day when this will happen can't come soon enough for me. I've been thinking about being a sex object for quite some time. It's just that I haven't had any good offers.

Discussion Questions

1. What is the masculine mystique?
2. According to Frazier, what are the roles men are conditioned to accept?
3. Frazier says that what the feminists want of a man's life is the swagger without the sweat. What does he mean? Do you agree with him?
4. How does Ethel's husband in "The Season of Divorce" illustrate some of the difficulties men encounter?
5. How would Friedan answer Frazier's argument that the girls get all the best of higher education? What is your opinion?
6. If you were to debate either Frazier or Friedan, what issues would you raise? How would you answer the opposing arguments?
7. Bring several men's magazines to class. What image of man is projected? Compare male cultural conditioning with female cultural conditioning.

THE SOJOURNER
CARSON McCULLERS

At certain times chance occurrences make individuals pause to assess their position in life. In "The Sojourner," when John Ferris sees his ex-wife and subsequently visits her home and meets her husband and children, he realizes the loneliness and isolation of his existence.

The twilight border between sleep and waking was a Roman one this morning; splashing fountains and arched, narrow streets, the golden lavish city of blossoms and age-soft stone. Sometimes in this semi-consciousness he sojourned again in Paris, or war German rubble, or Swiss skiing and a snow hotel. Sometimes, also, in a fallow Georgia field at hunting dawn. Rome it was this morning in the yearless region of dreams.

John Ferris awoke in a room in a New York hotel. He had the feeling that something unpleasant was awaiting him—what it was, he did not know. The feeling, submerged by matinal necessities, lingered even after he had dressed and gone downstairs. It was a cloudless autumn day and the pale sunlight sliced between the pastel skyscrapers. Ferris went into the next-door drugstore and sat at the end booth next to the

---

Carson McCullers (1917–1967) was a short-story writer and novelist usually associated with the Southern Renaissance.

140   His

window glass that overlooked the sidewalk. He ordered an American breakfast with scrambled eggs and sausage.

Ferris had come from Paris to his father's funeral which had taken place the week before in his home town in Georgia. The shock of death had made him aware of youth already passed. His hair was receding and the veins in his now naked temples were pulsing and prominent and his body was spare except for an incipient belly bulge. Ferris had loved his father and the bond between them had once been extraordinarily close—but the years had somehow unraveled this filial devotion; the death, expected for a long time, had left him with an unforeseen dismay. He had stayed as long as possible to be near his mother and brothers at home. His plane for Paris was to leave the next morning.

Ferris pulled out his address book to verify a number. He turned the pages with growing attentiveness. Names and addresses from New York, the capitals of Europe, a few faint ones from his home state in the South. Faded, printed names, sprawled drunken ones. Betty Wills: a random love, married now. Charlie Williams: wounded in the Hürtgen Forest, unheard of since. Grand old Williams—did he live or die? Don Walker: a B.T.O. in television, getting rich. Henry Green: hit the skids after the war, in a sanitarium now, they say. Cozie Hall: he had heard that she was dead. Heedless, laughing Cozie—it was strange to think that she too, silly girl, could die. As Ferris closed the address book, he suffered a sense of hazard, transience, almost of fear.

It was then that his body jerked suddenly. He was staring out of the window when there, on the sidewalk, passing by, was his ex-wife. Elizabeth passed quite close to him, walking slowly. He could not understand the wild quiver of his heart, nor the following sense of recklessness and grace that lingered after she was gone.

Quickly Ferris paid his check and rushed out to the sidewalk. Elizabeth stood on the corner waiting to cross Fifth Avenue. He hurried toward her meaning to speak, but the lights changed and she crossed the street before he reached her. Ferris followed. On the other side he could easily have overtaken her, but he found himself lagging unaccountably. Her fair brown hair was plainly rolled, and as he watched her Ferris recalled that once his father had remarked that Elizabeth had a 'beautiful carriage.' She turned at the next corner and Ferris followed, although by now his intention to overtake her had disappeared. Ferris questioned the bodily disturbance that the sight of Elizabeth aroused in him, the dampness of his hands, the hard heart-strokes.

It was eight years since Ferris had last seen his ex-wife. He knew that long ago she had married again. And there were children. During recent years he had seldom thought of her. But at first, after the divorce, the loss had almost destroyed him. Then after the anodyne of time, he had loved again, and then again. Jeannine, she was now. Certainly his love for his ex-wife was long since past. So why the unhinged body, the shaken mind? He knew only that his clouded heart was oddly dissonant with the sunny, candid autumn day. Ferris wheeled suddenly and, walking with long strides, almost running, hurried back to the hotel.

Ferris poured himself a drink, although it was not yet eleven o'clock. He sprawled out in an armchair like a man exhausted, nursing his glass of bourbon and water. He had a full day ahead of him as he was leaving by plane the next morning for Paris. He checked over his obligations: take luggage to Air France, lunch with his boss, buy shoes and an overcoat. And something—wasn't there something else? Ferris finished his drink and opened the telephone directory.

His decision to call his ex-wife was impulsive. The number was under Bailey, the husband's name, and he called before he had much time for self-debate. He and Elizabeth had exchanged cards at Christmastime, and Ferris had sent a carving set when he received the announcement of her wedding. There was no reason *not* to call. But as he waited, listening to the ring at the other end, misgiving fretted him.

Elizabeth answered; her familiar voice was a fresh shock to him. Twice he had to repeat his name, but when he was identified, she sounded glad. He explained he was only in town for that day. They had a theater engagement, she said— but she wondered if he would come by for an early dinner. Ferris said he would be delighted.

As he went from one engagement to another, he was still bothered at odd moments by the feeling that something necessary was forgotten. Ferris bathed and changed in the late afternoon, often thinking about Jeannine: he would be with her the following night. 'Jeannine,' he would say, 'I happened to run into my ex-wife when I was in New York. Had dinner with her. And her husband, of course. It was strange seeing her after all these years.'

Elizabeth lived in the East Fifties, and as Ferris taxied uptown he glimpsed at intersections the lingering sunset, but by the time he reached his destination it was already autumn dark. The place was a building with a marquee and a doorman, and the apartment was on the seventh floor.

'Come in, Mr. Ferris.'

Braced for Elizabeth or even the unimagined husband, Ferris was astonished by the freckled red-haired child; he had known of the children, but his mind had failed somehow to acknowledge them. Surprise made him step back awkwardly.

'This is our apartment,' the child said politely. 'Aren't you Mr. Ferris? I'm Billy. Come in.'

In the living room beyond the hall, the husband provided another surprise; he too had not been acknowledged emotionally. Bailey was a lumbering red-haired man with a deliberate manner. He rose and extended a welcoming hand.

'I'm Bill Bailey. Glad to see you. Elizabeth will be in, in a minute. She's finishing dressing.'

The last words struck a gliding series of vibrations, memories of the other years. Fair Elizabeth, rosy and naked before her bath. Half-dressed before the mirror of her dressing table, brushing her fine, chestnut hair. Sweet, casual intimacy, the soft-fleshed loveliness indisputably possessed. Ferris shrank from the unbidden memories and compelled himself to meet Bill Bailey's gaze.

'Billy, will you please bring that tray of drinks from the kitchen table?'

The child obeyed promptly, and when he was gone Ferris remarked conversationally, 'Fine boy you have there.'

'We think so.'

Flat silence until the child returned with a tray of glasses and a cocktail shaker of Martinis. With the priming drinks they pumped up conversation: Russia, they spoke of, and the New York rain-making, and the apartment situation in Manhattan and Paris.

'Mr. Ferris is flying all the way across the ocean tomorrow,' Bailey said to the little boy who

142   His

was perched on the arm of his chair, quiet and well behaved. 'I bet you would like to be a stowaway in his suitcase.'

Billy pushed back his limp bangs. 'I want to fly in an airplane and be a newspaperman like Mr. Ferris.' He added with sudden assurance, 'That's what I would like to do when I am big.'

Bailey said, 'I thought you wanted to be a doctor.'

'I do!' said Billy. 'I would like to be both. I want to be a atom-bomb scientist too.'

Elizabeth came in carrying in her arms a baby girl.

'Oh, John!' she said. She settled the baby in the father's lap. 'It's grand to see you. I'm awfully glad you could come.'

The little girl sat demurely on Bailey's knees. She wore a pale pink crêpe de Chine frock, smocked around the yoke with rose, and a matching silk hair ribbon tying back her pale soft curls. Her skin was summer tanned and her brown eyes flecked with gold and laughing. When she reached up and fingered her father's horn-rimmed glasses, he took them off and let her look through them a moment. 'How's my old Candy?'

Elizabeth was very beautiful, more beautiful perhaps than he had ever realized. Her straight clean hair was shining. Her face was softer, glowing and serene. It was a madonna loveliness, dependent on the family ambiance.

'You've hardly changed at all,' Elizabeth said, 'but it has been a long time.'

'Eight years.' His hand touched his thinning hair self-consciously while further amenities were exchanged.

Ferris felt himself suddenly a spectator—an interloper among these Baileys. Why had he come? He suffered. His own life seemed so soli-

tary, a fragile column supporting nothing amidst the wreckage of the years. He felt he could not bear much longer to stay in the family room.

He glanced at his watch. 'You're going to the theater?'

'It's a shame,' Elizabeth said, 'but we've had this engagement for more than a month. But surely, John, you'll be staying home one of these days before long. You're not going to be an expatriate, are you?'

'Expatriate,' Ferris repeated. 'I don't much like the word.'

'What's a better word?' she asked.

He thought for a moment. 'Sojourner might do.'

Ferris glanced again at his watch, and again Elizabeth apologized. 'If only we had known ahead of time——'

'I just had this day in town. I came home unexpectedly. You see, Papa died last week.'

'Papa Ferris is dead?'

'Yes, at Johns-Hopkins. He had been sick there nearly a year. The funeral was down home in Georgia.'

'Oh, I'm so sorry, John. Papa Ferris was always one of my favorite people.'

The little boy moved from behind the chair so that he could look into his mother's face. He asked, 'Who is dead?'

Ferris was oblivious to apprehension; he was thinking of his father's death. He saw again the outstretched body on the quilted silk within the coffin. The corpse flesh was bizarrely rouged and the familiar hands lay massive and joined above a spread of funeral roses. The memory closed and Ferris awakened to Elizabeth's calm voice.

'Mr. Ferris' father, Billy. A really grand person. Somebody you didn't know.'

Carson McCullers 143

'But why did you call him *Papa* Ferris?'

Bailey and Elizabeth exchanged a trapped look. It was Bailey who answered the questioning child. 'A long time ago,' he said, 'your mother and Mr. Ferris were once married. Before you were born—a long time ago.'

'Mr. Ferris?'

The little boy stared at Ferris, amazed and unbelieving. And Ferris' eyes, as he returned the gaze, were somehow unbelieving too. Was it indeed true that at one time he had called this stranger, Elizabeth, Little Butterduck during nights of love, that they had lived together, shared perhaps a thousand days and nights and—finally—endured in the misery of sudden solitude the fiber by fiber (jealousy, alcohol and money quarrels) destruction of the fabric of married love.

Bailey said to the children, 'It's somebody's suppertime. Come on now.'

'But Daddy! Mama and Mr. Ferris—I——'

Billy's everlasting eyes—perplexed and with a glimmer of hostility—reminded Ferris of the gaze of another child. It was the young son of Jeannine—a boy of seven with a shadowed little face and knobby knees whom Ferris avoided and usually forgot.

'Quick march!' Bailey gently turned Billy toward the door. 'Say good night now, son.'

'Good night, Mr. Ferris.' He added resentfully, 'I thought I was staying up for the cake.'

'You can come in afterward for the cake,' Elizabeth said. 'Run along now with Daddy for your supper.'

Ferris and Elizabeth were alone. The weight of the situation descended on those first moments of silence. Ferris asked permission to pour himself another drink and Elizabeth set the cocktail shaker on the table at his side. He looked at the grand piano and noticed the music on the rack.

'Do you still play as beautifully as you used to?'

'I still enjoy it.'

'Please play, Elizabeth.'

Elizabeth arose immediately. Her readiness to perform when asked had always been one of her amiabilities; she never hung back, apologized. Now as she approached the piano there was the added readiness of relief.

She began with a Bach prelude and fugue. The prelude was as gaily iridescent as a prism in a morning room. The first voice of the fugue, an announcement pure and solitary, was repeated intermingling with a second voice, and again repeated within an elaborated frame, the multiple music, horizontal and serene, flowed with unhurried majesty. The principal melody was woven with two other voices, embellished with countless ingenuities—now dominant, again submerged, it had the sublimity of a single thing that does not fear surrender to the whole. Toward the end, the density of the material gathered for the last enriched insistence on the dominant first motif and with a chorded final statement the fugue ended. Ferris rested his head on the chair back and closed his eyes. In the following silence a clear, high voice came from the room down the hall.

'Daddy, how *could* Mama and Mr. Ferris——' A door was closed.

The piano began again—what was this music? Unplaced, familiar, the limpid melody had lain a long while dormant in his heart. Now it spoke to him of another time, another place—it was the music Elizabeth used to play. The delicate air summoned a wilderness of memory. Ferris was lost in the riot of past longings, conflicts, ambivalent desires. Strange that the music, catalyst for this tumultuous anarchy, was so serene and clear. The singing melody was broken off by the appearance of the maid.

'Miz Bailey, dinner is out on the table now.'

Even after Ferris was seated at the table between his host and hostess, the unfinished music still overcast his mood. He was a little drunk.

'*L'improvisation de la vie humaine,*' he said. 'There's nothing that makes you so aware of the improvisation of human existence as a song unfinished. Or an old address book.'

'Address book?' repeated Bailey. Then he stopped, noncommittal and polite.

'You're still the same old boy, Johnny,' Elizabeth said with a trace of the old tenderness.

It was a Southern dinner that evening, and the dishes were his old favorites. They had fried chicken and corn pudding and rich, glazed candied sweet potatoes. During the meal Elizabeth kept alive a conversation when the silences were overlong. And it came about that Ferris was led to speak of Jeannine.

'I first knew Jeannine last autumn—about this time of the year—in Italy. She's a singer and she had an engagement in Rome. I expect we will be married soon.'

The words seemed so true, inevitable, that Ferris did not at first acknowledge to himself the lie. He and Jeannine had never in that year spoken of marriage. And indeed, she was still married—to a White Russian money-changer in Paris from whom she had been separated for five years. But it was too late to correct the lie. Already Elizabeth was saying: 'This really makes me glad to know. Congratulations, Johnny.'

He tried to make amends with truth. 'The Roman autumn is so beautiful. Balmy and blossoming.' He added, 'Jeannine has a little boy of six. A curious trilingual little fellow. We go to the Tuileries sometimes.'

A lie again. He had taken the boy once to the gardens. The sallow foreign child in shorts that bared his spindly legs had sailed his boat in the concrete pond and ridden the pony. The child had wanted to go in to the puppet show. But there was not time, for Ferris had an engagement at the Scribe Hotel. He had promised they would go to the guignol another afternoon. Only once had he taken Valentin to the Tuileries.

There was a stir. The maid brought in a white-frosted cake with pink candles. The children entered in their night clothes. Ferris still did not understand.

'Happy birthday, John,' Elizabeth said. 'Blow out the candles.'

Ferris recognized his birthday date. The candles blew out lingeringly and there was the smell of burning wax. Ferris was thirty-eight years old. The veins in his temples darkened and pulsed visibly.

'It's time you started for the theater.'

Ferris thanked Elizabeth for the birthday dinner and said the appropriate good-byes. The whole family saw him to the door.

A high, thin moon shone above the jagged, dark skyscrapers. The streets were windy, cold. Ferris hurried to Third Avenue and hailed a cab. He gazed at the nocturnal city with the deliberate attentiveness of departure and perhaps farewell. He was alone. He longed for flighttime and the coming journey.

The next day he looked down on the city from the air, burnished in sunlight, toylike, precise.

Then America was left behind and there was only the Atlantic and the distant European shore. The ocean was milky pale and placid beneath the clouds. Ferris dozed most of the day. Toward dark he was thinking of Elizabeth and the visit of the previous evening. He thought of Elizabeth among her family with longing, gentle envy and inexplicable regret. He sought the melody, the unfinished air, that had so moved him. The cadence, some unrelated tones, were all that remained; the melody itself evaded him. He had found instead the first voice of the fugue that Elizabeth had played—it came to him, inverted mockingly and in a minor key. Suspended above the ocean the anxieties of transience and solitude no longer troubled him and he thought of his father's death with equanimity. During the dinner hour the plane reached the shore of France.

At midnight Ferris was in a taxi crossing Paris. It was a clouded night and mist wreathed the lights of the Place de la Concorde. The midnight bistros gleamed on the wet pavements. As always after a transocean flight the change of continents was too sudden. New York at morning, this midnight Paris. Ferris glimpsed the disorder of his life: the succession of cities, of transitory loves; and time, the sinister glissando of the years, time always.

'*Vite! Vite!*' he called in terror. '*Dépêchez-vous.*'

Valentin opened the door to him. The little boy wore pajamas and an outgrown red robe. His grey eyes were shadowed and, as Ferris passed into the flat, they flickered momentarily.

'*J'attends Maman.*'

Jeannine was singing in a night club. She would not be home before another hour. Valentin returned to a drawing, squatting with his crayons over the paper on the floor. Ferris looked down at the drawing—it was a banjo player with notes and wavy lines inside a comic-strip balloon.

'We will go again to the Tuileries.'

The child looked up and Ferris drew him closer to his knees. The melody, the unfinished music that Elizabeth had played, came to him suddenly. Unsought, the load of memory jettisoned—this time bringing only recognition and sudden joy.

'Monsieur Jean,' the child said, 'did you see him?'

Confused, Ferris thought only of another child—the freckled, family-loved boy. 'See who, Valentin?'

'Your dead papa in Georgia.' The child added, 'Was he okay?'

Ferris spoke with rapid urgency: 'We will go often to the Tuileries. Ride the pony and we will go into the guignol. We will see the puppet show and never be in a hurry any more.'

'Monsieur Jean,' Valentin said. 'The guignol is now closed.'

Again, the terror of the acknowledgment of wasted years and death. Valentin, responsive and confident, still nestled in his arms. His cheek touched the soft cheek and felt the brush of the delicate eyelashes. With inner desperation he pressed the child close—as though an emotion as protean as his love could dominate the pulse of time.

Discussion Questions

1. After visiting his former wife and meeting her husband and children, what new perspective does John Ferris have on his life? Do you think he will alter his life?

2. John Ferris has more "freedom" than Ericka or the couple in "The Season of Divorce." Is his freedom enviable? Explain.

3. Compare John Ferris to Dr. Ascher. To Ethel's husband.

DOTSON GERBER RESURRECTED

HAL BENNETT

In this bizarre short story, Hal Bennett cleverly illustrates how the specter of the white man influences the black man's life.

We saw the head of Mr. Dotson Gerber break ground at approximately nine o'clock on a bright Saturday morning in March out near our collard patch, where Poppa had started to dig a well and then filled it in. Of course, none of us knew then that the shock of red hair and part of a head sprouting from the abandoned well belonged to Mr. Dotson Gerber, who'd been missing from his farm since early last fall. We were black folk, and the fact that a white man like Mr. Dotson Gerber was missing from his home was of small importance to us. Unless that white man suddenly started growing from the ground near our collard patch like Mr. Dotson Gerber was doing now for Momma, my sister Millicent and me. We'd come running because of a commotion the chickens had made, thinking that a lynx or a weasel might have got after them. And found Mr. Dotson Gerber's head instead.

"Good Jesus," Millicent said, "I do think I'm

Hal Bennett (1930–), born in Buckingham, Virginia, has been a magazine editor for Afro-American newspapers and is the author of three novels.

148   His

going to faint." Millicent had been prone to fainting ever since she'd seen two black men kissing behind some boxes in the factory where she worked. Now she was getting ready to faint again. But Momma snatched her roughly by the apron.

"Girl, you *always* fainting, you don't hardly give other people a chance." And Momma fainted dead away, which left Millicent conscious for the time being and looking very desperate. But she didn't faint and I was glad of that, because I certainly didn't want to be alone with Mr. Dotson Gerber sprouting from the ground. A dozen or so chickens were still raising a ruckus about the unexpected appearance of a white man's head where they were accustomed to pecking for grain. Screeching at the top of her voice, Millicent shooed the chickens away while I tugged Momma into the shade and propped her against the barn. Then we went back to looking at Mr. Dotson Gerber.

I have mentioned the well that Poppa started to dig because it was apparent that Mr. Dotson Gerber had been planted standing up in that hole. Which, of course, explained why his head was growing out first. Although, as I have said, neither Millicent nor I knew then that what we were looking at belonged to Mr. Dotson Gerber. It took Poppa to tell us that.

He came riding on Miss Tricia from the stable, where he'd been saddling her. "Why you children making all that noise out there?" he called from the road. When we didn't answer, he yanked the reins and rode Miss Tricia toward us. "Millicent, was that you I heard hollering? What you all doing out here?" Poppa asked again.

"There's a white man growing from the ground," I said.

Poppa nearly fell off Miss Tricia. "A *what?*"

"A white man. He's growing from that hole where you started to dig the well."

"I *know* I'm going to faint now." Millicent said. And she wrapped her hands around her throat as though to choke herself into unconsciousness. But Poppa and I both ignored her and she was too curious to faint right then. So she stopped choking herself and watched Poppa jump down from Miss Tricia to inspect the head. He walked all around it, poking it from time to time with his shoe.

"That'd be Mr. Dotson Gerber," he finally pronounced.

By this time, Momma had revived and was watching Poppa with the rest of us. "Poppa, how you know that's Mr. Dotson Gerber? Why, he could be any old white man! There's hardly enough of him above ground for anybody to recognize."

"I know it's Mr. Dotson Gerber because I planted him there," Poppa said. He told us how Mr. Gerber had come out to the farm last fall to inspect the well that he was digging, which had been part of Mr. Gerber's job here in Alcanthia County. "He kept calling me Uncle," Poppa said, with some bitterness. "I told him respectfully that my name is Walter Beaufort, or that he could even call me *Mr.* Beaufort, if he'd a mind to. After all, things have changed so much nowadays, I told him I certainly wouldn't think any less of him if he called me Mr. Beaufort. I told him that black people don't appreciate white folks' calling us Uncle any longer. But he just kept on calling me that, so I hit him on the head with my shovel." We all looked at Mr. Dotson Gerber's head; and it was true that there was a wide gash in his skull that could only have been

Hal Bennett   149

caused by a shovel. "I didn't intend to kill him," Poppa said. "I just wanted to teach him some respect. After all, things *have* changed. But when I found out he was dead, I stood him up in that hole I was digging and covered him up. I never expected to see him growing out of the ground this way."

"Well, that's not the problem now," Millicent said. "The problem now is, what are we going to do with him?"

Momma moved a step closer to Mr. Gerber and cautiously poked him with her toe. "If it weren't for that red hair," she said, "somebody might mistake him for a cabbage."

"He don't look like no cabbage to me," Millicent said. It was clear that she was annoyed because Momma had fainted before she'd had a chance to.

"I didn't say he looked like a cabbage," Momma said. "I said somebody might mistake him for a cabbage."

"He too red to be a cabbage," Millicent said stubbornly. "Anyway, we still ought to do something about him. It just don't look right, a white man growing like this on a colored person's farm. Suppose some white people see it?"

The 9:10 Greyhound to Richmond went by then. Momma and Poppa shaded their eyes to watch it speed down the far road; but Millicent and I were of today's generation and we hardly looked. Although there had been a time when the passing of the Richmond bus was the most exciting event of everybody's day in Burnside. But the years in between had brought many changes. There was electricity now, and television and telephones. Several factories and supermarkets had opened up on the highway, so that farming became far less profitable than working in the factories and spending weekly wages in the glittering markets, where everything that had formerly come from soil was sold now in tin cans and plastic wrappers. Because nobody in Burnside farmed anymore. Like almost everyone else, Momma and Poppa and Millicent all worked in the factories. And Momma bought at the supermarkets, like everyone else. The land around us, given over to weeds, was overgrown now like a graveyard in those first green days of spring.

Momma and Poppa watched the bus until it disappeared. "That Greyhound, she sure do go," Momma said. "It's Saturday now and I bet she's crowded with nigger men going to Richmond for them white hussies on Clay Street."

Millicent grunted. "Let them help themselves," she said bitterly. "After what I seen, a nigger man don't mean a thing to me no more."

"You're right there, sugar," Momma agreed. "A nigger man, he ain't worth a damn."

Millicent curled her lip and she and Momma looked at Poppa and me as though there were something dirty and pathetic about being a black man. I had seen this expression on their faces before—a wan kind of pity mixed with distaste and the sad realization that being a black man is next to being nothing at all. And the black woman is always telling the black man that with her eyes and lips and hips, telling him by the way she moves beside him on the road and underneath him in the bed. *Nigger, oh, I love you, but I know you ain't never going to be as good as a white man.* That's the way Momma and Millicent looked at Poppa and me while they cut us dead right there on the spot. They almost fell over each other, talking about how low and no-good nigger men are. And they weren't just joking; they really meant it. I saw it in their faces and it hurt me to my heart. I just didn't know what to do. I reached out and caught Poppa's arm, that's how hurt I was. He seemed to understand, because he wrapped his arm around me and I could feel some of his strength draining into me. So Momma and Millicent stood there ridiculing us on one side of Mr. Dotson Gerber's head, and Poppa and I stood there on the other.

Then, when Momma and Millicent were all through with their tirade, Poppa said very quietly, "I'm riding in to Dillwyn now. I'm going to turn myself over to the sheriff for killing Mr. Gerber here."

There was a kind of joy in Poppa's voice that I suppose no black woman can ever understand, and Momma and Millicent looked at Poppa as though he had suddenly lost his mind. But I was sixteen years old, which is old enough to be a man if you're black, and I understood why Poppa was so happy about killing that white man. Until now, he'd always had to bury his rich, black male rage in the far corner of some infertile field, lest it do harm to him and to the rest of us as well. But by telling that he'd killed that white man, he would undo all the indignities he had ever suffered in the name of love.

Now Momma looked afraid. "Turn yourself in to the sheriff? What you talking about, Walter Beaufort? What kind of foolishness you talking?" She tried humor to change Poppa's somber mood, laughing in a big hullabaloo. "I bet you been hitting the plum wine again," she said joyously.

But Poppa shook his head. "You always accuse me of that when you want to make light of what I'm saying. But I haven't been near that plum wine, not today. And what I'm saying is plain enough. I've killed a white man and I want somebody to know it."

"*We* know it," Momma said. "Ain't that good enough?"

"I want them to know it," Poppa said. "I want them to know he's dead and I want them to know why he's dead."

"Because he didn't call you Mister?" Momma said. There wasn't a white man in Alcanthia County who didn't call her Auntie, and she started to rage scornfully at the idea of Poppa's rebelling at being called Uncle. "Now, I could see it if you said you were going to hide out for a while, killing that white man and all that—"

But Poppa stopped her with an angry jerk of his hand. "It's not that way at all, Hattie. I don't aim to hide no more. I been hiding too long already—if you understand what I mean. The time's come for me to stop hiding. I'm going to Dillwyn and tell the sheriff what I've done."

Momma jumped straight up in the air. "Walter Beaufort, you gone *crazy* or something? No, I don't understand what you mean. Why didn't you tell the sheriff last year? Why you got to tell him now? Nobody even knows you killed Mr. Gerber. And to give yourself up now, that don't make no sense at all."

"Some things don't never make no sense," Poppa said. He cocked his eye at me. "You coming with me to the sheriff, boy? Somebody's got to ride Miss Tricia back here to home."

I got up onto Miss Tricia with him and we rode off to find the sheriff.

"I think I'm going to faint," I heard Millicent say behind me. But when I looked around, she was still standing there with her mouth hanging open.

As Poppa and I went up the road, Momma's

voice followed us like an angry wind. "You see what I mean about *niggers*, Millicent?" Moaning sadly, half happy and afraid at the same time, a kind of turbulent satisfaction marred her voice as she shrieked at Millicent. "You see what I mean about *niggers*, child?"

"That black bitch," Poppa muttered. I don't know whether he knew I heard him or not. He kicked Miss Tricia viciously in the ribs and the mule leaped into a surprised gallop, heading to Dillwyn for Poppa to give himself up to the sheriff. After the way Momma and Millicent had carried on, I didn't see what else he could do.

Even here in Burnside, we had heard that black is beautiful. But I don't think that many of us believed it, because black is ugly and desperate and degraded wherever the white man is sitting on your neck. Still, Millicent and I had worn Afros for a while to show our black pride; but they were too hard to keep clean here in the country, there is so much dust and dirt blowing about. And our kind of hair picks up everything that goes by. Besides, the white people who owned the factories took Afro hairdos as a sign of militancy and threatened to fire everybody who wore one. So everybody went back to getting their hair cut short or straightening it like before.

I was thinking about that as I rode with Poppa to the sheriff's office. I thought about Millicent, too, and the black men she'd seen kissing in the factory. She never would tell who they were, and sometimes I wondered whether it might not have been just a story that she made up to justify her saying that all black men are sissies. At any rate, she complained quite openly that no black man had made love to her since last Halloween, which was almost five months ago, and this probably explained why she was so jumpy and threatening to faint all the time.

As for me, I thought I knew why no black men were interested in Millicent. For one thing, they could go to Richmond and Charlottesville and get white women, now that they had money to spend on the whores there. Also, the black men I'd talked to told me that they didn't find black women so desirable anymore, the way they were dressing and acting and perfuming themselves like white women on television, now that they had money to do so.

So the black men went to Richmond and paid white women, because their own women were trying to act white. And the black women were turning their backs on their own men, because—if Millicent was any example—they thought that black men were sissies. It was all very confusing.

I was old enough to have had myself a woman or two by then. But I was very hung up on Mrs. Palmer and her five daughters; I hope you know what I mean. There was a time when black people said that doing something like that to yourself would make you crazy. Now they said that it would make you turn white. Which was sufficient reason for some black boys to stop. But not me. I actually did it more. But all that happened was that sometimes I felt dizzy and depressed. Sometimes I felt weak. But I never did turn white.

Sheriff Dave Young's office was closed when we got to Dillwyn. Some white men sitting around told us that the sheriff was away to a Christian conference. "He's a deacon in the white Baptist church, you know. He'll be away for the rest of the week." There were some hounds lying around, sleeping in the dust, and one or two of them opened a drowsy eye and looked at Poppa and me without curiosity. The white men looked at us as though we were two hounds who had by some miracle managed to get up onto a mule. That's the way white men are in the South. As for Poppa and me, we looked right through those white men, which is really a very good way of rebelling by pretending that you're looking at nothing. There are other sly ways that we Southern black people have of rebelling—like grinning, or licking our tongue out behind the white man's back, spitting in his water when he's not looking, imitating his way of talking—which is why so many Northern black people think that Southern black people are such natural clowns, when what we're really doing is rebelling. Not as dramatic as a Molotov cocktail or a pipe bomb, but it certainly is satisfying, and a whole lot safer, too. Furthermore, it must be said that we do not hate whites here as black people apparently do in the North. Although we nearly always view them with pity and suspicion, for *they* think that we hate them, as they might very well do if the tables were reversed.

"Uncle, is there any particular reason why you want to see the sheriff?"

"No, sir, no, sir, none at all," Poppa said. He thanked them the way he was supposed to, grinning a little, and rode away.

"Where we going now, Poppa? Back to home?"

He shook his head. "We going to Mr. Dotson Gerber's house up the street yonder. I expect his wife is home. I expect she'd like to know what happened to her husband."

When we got to Mrs. Dotson Gerber's, there was a decrepit old white lady sitting in a rocking chair on her porch and waving a small Confederate flag over the banister, like a child does at a parade. She was the mother of Mr. Dotson Gerber's wife. And while colored people said quite openly that the old lady was touched in the head, white people claimed that she had arthritis; and they said that she waved the Confederate flag to exercise her arm, as though to conceal from black people the fact that any white had ever lost his mind.

She waved the flag and rocked every once in a while, pushing at the banister with spidery legs that ended in two fluffy slippers that had once been white. Her pale-blue eyes were as sharp as a hawk's behind her wire-rimmed glasses; but it was hard to tell whether she was looking into the past or the future, waving and rocking, smiling from time to time.

Poppa got down from Miss Tricia and walked over to the fence. "Good morning, ma'am," he said respectfully. It was dangerous not to be respectful, just in case the old white woman wasn't crazy and really did have arthritis in her arm. She could raise a ruckus for Poppa's disrespecting her that could cause him to wind up on the end of a rope. "I came to see Mrs. Dotson Gerber, ma'am," Poppa said politely, while the old lady rocked and waved the flag outrageously. She might have been saluting Lee's army marching proudly on its way to Appomattox, which was only a few miles away. Her eyes grew large and happy. But she didn't pay any attention at all to Poppa, even when he asked a second and a third time for Mrs. Dotson Gerber. She had arthritis, all right, the old woman. She had arthritis in the brain, that's where she had it.

Just then, Mrs. Dotson Gerber came to the screen door. Drying her hands on a pink apron, she inspected Poppa for a minute, as though trying to figure out whether he was safe or not.

"Is that you, Uncle Walter?" She squinted through the screen. "Did you want to talk to me?"

"Yes, ma'am, Mrs. Gerber. I did come to talk to you. I got something to tell you."

"I certainly don't see why you came to my front door," Mrs. Gerber said peevishly, coming out onto the porch. "I *never* receive colored people at my front door, and I'm sure you know that, Uncle Walter. Besides, it bothers my mother's arthritis, people talking all around her." She inspected the crazy old woman, who was waving the Confederate flag and rocking vigorously.

"Well, ma'am. . . I'm sorry I came to your front door. I certainly do know better than that. But I've come to tell you about your husband."

Mrs. Gerber seemed to stop breathing. "My husband?" She dashed from the porch and stood at the fence near Poppa. "You know where my husband is?"

"Yes, ma'am. He's out in my collard patch—where my collard patch used to be."

"What's he doing out there?"

Poppa looked embarrassed. "He came to inspect the well I was digging. We got in an argument and I hit him with my shovel."

Mrs. Gerber turned very white, indeed. "You killed him?"

"I'm afraid so, ma'am. I buried him there in the well."

Mrs. Gerber tapped her bottom teeth with her forefinger. She was a sort of pretty white woman and certainly a lot younger than Mr. Dotson Gerber had been. Behind her on the porch, the crazy old woman rocked on, waving the flag at Southern armies that only she could see. "Momma's arthritis isn't too good today," Mrs. Gerber

said absently, patting her hair. After a while, she said, "So Dotson is dead. All of us wondered what happened when he didn't come home last year. Knowing him, I was almost certain that he'd gone and got himself killed." But she didn't seem too upset. "Actually, Uncle Walter, you've done me a big favor. Dotson used to treat my poor mother something terrible, laughing at her arthritis all the time." She patted her hair again, although every strand seemed to be perfectly in place. "I suppose you know that I'm to get married again this summer to a very respectable man here in Alcanthia?"

"No, ma'am, I didn't know that."

"Well, I'm surprised," Mrs. Gerber said. "I thought that colored people knew everything. Anyway, he's a very respectable man. Very decent and very intelligent, too, I need not say. We both figured that Dotson was dead after all these months. That's why we decided to get married." She looked at Poppa almost gently. "But I never supposed you'd be the one to kill him, Uncle Walter. Why, you've even been here and done a little work for Dotson and me around the house."

"Yes, ma'am."

"He really must've provoked you, Uncle Walter. What did he do?"

"He kept calling me Uncle. I asked him not to, but he kept on."

"Yes, that sounds like Dotson. He could be mean that way. I suppose you want me to stop calling you Uncle, too?"

"I'd appreciate it if you would, ma'am. I mean, it's an actual fact that I'm not your uncle, so I'd appreciate your not calling me that."

Now Mrs. Gerber nibbled on her thumb. Her mother rocked on and on, waving the flag. "All right, I'll stop calling you Uncle," Mrs. Gerber

154   His

said, "if you promise not to tell anybody about my husband being buried out there in your collard patch. After all, I'm planning on being married to a very decent man. It would be a big embarrassment to me—and to him, too—if anybody found out about Dotson being buried in a collard patch. As much as he hates collard greens." It was clear from the tone of her voice that the disgrace lay not in Mr. Dotson Gerber's being dead but in his being buried in our collard patch.

"There ain't no collards there now," Poppa said, trying to placate Mrs. Gerber some. "Why, we haven't done any farming for years."

"But collards *were* there," Mrs. Gerber said, almost stomping her foot. "And Dotson couldn't stand collards. I just hope you won't tell anybody else about this, Uncle Walter. I don't know what my fiancé would say if he knew about this. Considering that he's willing to marry me and to put up with Momma's arthritis in the bargain, I certainly wouldn't want him to know about Dotson. Why, I don't know what he'd do if he ever found out about Dotson. You haven't told anybody else, have you?"

"I went to tell the sheriff, but he's out of town until next week."

"You went to tell the sheriff?" She seemed absolutely horrified. "Mr. Beaufort, I know I have no right asking you to think about me and my feelings in all this. But you ought to at least think about your own family. You know what they'll do to you if they find out about this?"

"I know," Poppa said.

"And you don't care?"

"I certainly do care. I don't want to die. I want to live. But I've killed me a white man. That's not something that somebody like me does every day. I think I want folks to know about it."

"But why now?" she cried. "Why didn't you say something before? Before I went out and got myself engaged?"

"It didn't seem important before. Besides, Mr. Gerber was still in the ground then. He ain't in the ground anymore, not exactly."

From time to time, white people had gone past and looked at Poppa and Mrs. Gerber as they talked. "I think you all ought to go around to the back door," Mrs. Gerber said. "My husband-to-be certainly wouldn't like it known that I stood on my own front porch and carried on a conversation with colored people . . ." She turned very red then and took a step or two away, as though she was afraid that Poppa might hit her with a shovel. But Poppa started laughing very gently, the way a man does when he weighs the value of things and finds out that what is important to other people seems absurd to him. And he looked at Mrs. Gerber with a kind of amused pity darkening his eyes, as though he realized now that no white person could ever understand why he wanted him to know about Mr. Dotson Gerber.

"We're going on home," Poppa said. "And don't you worry none about Mr. Gerber, ma'am. We'll take care of him. Your husband-to-be won't ever find out."

"What do you intend to do?" Mrs. Gerber wanted to know.

Poppa's face lit up with a great big grin. Not the kind of tame, painful grin that a black man puts on when he's rebelling. But a large, beautiful grin that showed all of his teeth and gums. "I'm going to plant collard greens around him," Poppa said.

Hal Bennett   155

Mrs. Gerber wrinkled her nose in distaste. "Dotson certainly wouldn't like that, if he knew. And you mean *over* him, don't you?"

Now Poppa and I both laughed. We hadn't told her that Mr. Gerber was growing straight up from the ground. And she wouldn't have believed us if we had told her. That's how white people are. "Good-bye, ma'am," Poppa said to Mrs. Gerber. She nodded and went into her house. On the porch, her mother waved the Confederate flag triumphantly. The rocker squeaked like the tread of strident ghosts. We climbed up onto Miss Tricia and rode home.

And we were nearly halfway there before I finally figured out why that old crazy white woman was on Mrs. Gerber's porch. They kept her there instead of buying a doorbell and using electricity. That way, when people talked to her, Mrs. Gerber heard them and came outside to see who it was. Smart. Sometimes I had to give it to white people. They were very smart indeed.

Momma and Millicent were waiting for us when we got home. "Did you tell the sheriff?" Momma said. She looked haggard and very unhappy.

"The sheriff wasn't there," Poppa said. "He won't be home until next week." With Momma and Millicent following us, he rode Miss Tricia out to the collard patch and gave me the reins. "Take her to the stable, boy." But I watched while he knelt and worked the dirt into a mound around Mr. Gerber's head. "There, that ought to do it," Poppa said. "Tomorrow, I'm going to plant me some collard greens here." He stood up happily and wiped his hands on the seat of his overalls.

Momma's mouth dropped open. She ran to Mr. Dotson Gerber's head and tried to stomp it back into the ground. But Poppa stopped her firmly. "You've gone stark crazy!" Momma cried.

Poppa slapped her right in the mouth. She spun around like a top. He slapped her again and sent her spinning the other way. "I don't want no more trouble out of you," Poppa said.

Momma melted against him like warm cheese. "All right, sugar. You won't have no more trouble out of me, sugar."

I rode Miss Tricia down to the stable. Millicent had enough sense to keep her mouth shut for a change, and Momma and Poppa went on up to the house with their arms wrapped around each other. I hadn't seen them together like that for years.

And that is how Poppa started farming again. Helped on by sun and spring rain, Mr. Dotson Gerber and the collards grew rapidly together. It would not be an exaggeration to say that Mr. Gerber's body growing there seemed to fertilize the whole field. Although in no time at all, he was taller than the collards and still growing. Most of his chest and arms was out of the ground by the end of March. And by the middle of April, he had cleared the ground down to his ankles. With his tattered clothes and wild red hair, his large blue eyes wide and staring, he seemed more some kind of monster than a resurrected man. The sun and wind had burned his skin nearly as black as ours. And while there was small chance of anybody seeing him—people in Burnside didn't visit anymore, now that most of them worked in the factories—Poppa still thought it might be a good idea to cover Mr. Gerber up. "You'd better put a sack over his head and some gloves on his hands," he said. Later on, Poppa put a coat and some sunglasses on Mr. Gerber, along with an old straw hat. He propped a stick behind Mr. Gerber and passed another one through the sleeves of Mr. Gerber's coat for him to rest his arms on. He really looked like a scarecrow then, and we stopped worrying about people finding out about him. In truth, however, it must be said that Mr. Gerber made a very poor scarecrow, indeed, because the birds hardly paid any attention to him. It was fortunate for us that birds don't especially like collard greens.

Poppa worked a few hours in the collard patch every night after he came home from the factory. Momma helped him sometimes. Sometimes Millicent and I helped him, too. Then one day, Poppa quit his job at the factory and hitched Miss Tricia to the plow. "You farming again?" Momma asked him. She had been very tame with Poppa since he'd slapped her.

"I'm farming again," Poppa said.

Momma just nodded. "That's very nice, sugar. That's really very nice."

In no time at all, Poppa had planted all the old crops that used to grow on our farm—all kinds of vegetables, wheat, corn. He went to Dillwyn and bought a couple of pigs and a cow. All the neighbors knew what he was doing. But they kept on working at the factories and spending their money at the supermarkets. Until one day, a neighbor woman showed up to buy some collard greens. Poppa sold her a large basketful for a dollar. "I'm just sick to death of store-bought food," she said.

"I know what you mean," Poppa said. "You come back, you hear?" In a little while, other people came to buy tomatoes, string beans, white potatoes, golden corn from the tall green stalks.

Summer droned on. Poppa worked his crops.

Word reached us that Mrs. Dotson Gerber had married her decent white man. After school had let out, I had begun to help Poppa full time. Momma finally quit her job at the factory and helped, too. But mostly, she took care of selling and managing the money that we were making. As for Millicent, I spied her one day making love down in the pea patch. And that black man she was with, he certainly was no sissy. That was all Millicent needed and all a black man needed, too—someplace green and growing to make love in. I never heard Millicent talk about fainting after that, although she did talk about getting married.

Around the end of summer, Sheriff Dave Young came to our farm. "Some of the fellows said you were looking for me," he told Poppa. "But I figured it wasn't really too important, since you never came back."

"It wasn't important, Sheriff."

He bought a watermelon that Poppa let him have very cheap. "You got a good business going here," Sheriff Young said. "Some of the white farmers been talking about doing the same thing."

"It'd be good if they did," Poppa said. The sheriff put his watermelon into his car and drove away.

When fall came and the leaves turned red and gold and brown, Mr. Dotson Gerber turned like all the other growing things and shriveled away to nothing. Poppa seemed very satisfied then, looking over his fields. And I knew how he must have felt, standing there looking at Mr. Dotson Gerber and all the other dead things that would live again next spring.

The Greyhound to Richmond went by and Poppa shielded his eyes to watch. I think that I understood everything about him then and it hurt me so much that I deliberately turned my back. The lesson of that summer seemed a particularly bitter one, because we had done everything and we had done nothing. Mr. Dotson Gerber would certainly be growing in my father's fields every spring forever. And my father, my poor father would always watch and admire the Greyhound to Richmond. The same way that in the deepest and sincerest and blackest part of himself he would always hate himself and believe that God is the greatest white man of all.

"That Greyhound, she sure do run," Poppa said. He sounded very satisfied, indeed. God knew he'd killed a white man. With God knowing, that was knowledge enough. But I was thinking about how it feels to be black and forever afraid. And about the white man, god*damn* him, how he causes everything. Even when He is God. Even when he is dead.

Discussion Questions

1. In one part of the story Mrs. Beaufort and Millicent make disparaging remarks about black men. As the women joke, Walter Beaufort and his son stand together on one side of Dotson Gerber's recently resurrected head while Mrs. Beaufort and Millicent stand on the other. How does this scene symbolize the white man's influence on the black family?
2. Why did Walter Beaufort murder Dotson Gerber? Why does he want to tell the sheriff about the murder?

3. How does Beaufort regain the respect of his wife? How does Millicent feel toward black men at the end of the story? Are these transformations poorly motivated or do they reinforce the theme of the story?
4. Although the story is humorous and seems to have a happy ending, the narrator is bitter about "how it feels to be black" and about the white man who seems to cause everything, "Even when he is dead." Discuss this ending.

Reflections

1. What does the answer to the riddle on page 88 tell us about the careers that society finds acceptable for women? Make a list of professions and jobs that are usually associated with one sex. Are there valid reasons for limiting these positions to one sex? Explain your answer.
2. In your opinion how much freedom does a woman have in choosing a career?
3. Do you believe that a woman should combine marriage and a career?
4. If a woman decides to work outside the home, how does the husband's role change?
5. Do you believe that the role of women in our society will change significantly? Explain your answer.
6. Relatively speaking, does a man have more freedom in choosing a career than a woman? Explain.
7. What is the primary role of the husband in marriage?
8. Is a man less masculine if he helps his working wife with child care and housework?

9. Is it possible for both husband and wife to combine marriage and a career?

10. If a man is offered a better position in another city or is transferred to another city, should the wife give up her career so that he can pursue his? What if the wife is offered a better position in a different city?

11. What is male chauvinism?

12. Will the role of men alter in the coming years? Explain.

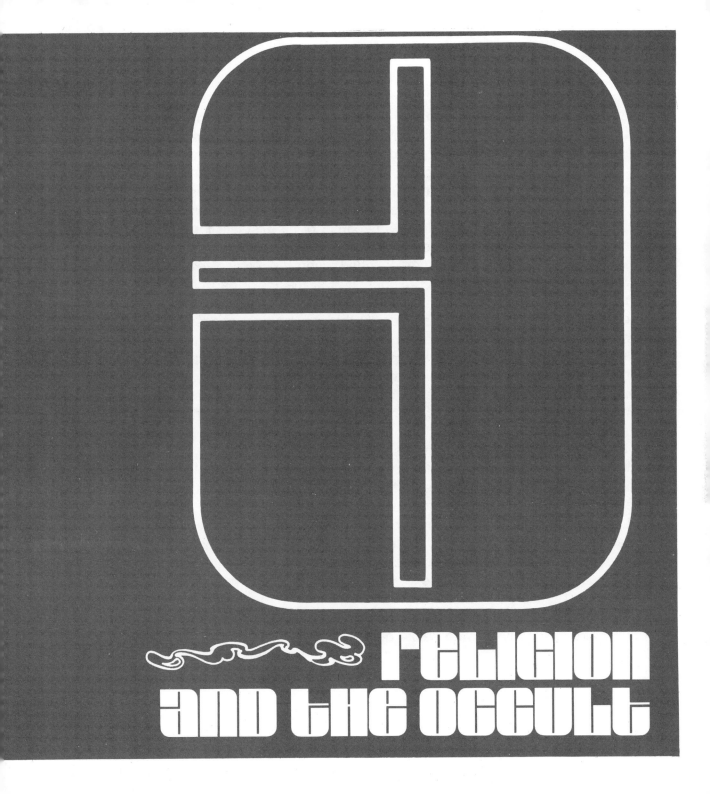

RELIGION
AND THE OCCULT

This chapter explores man's relationship to the supernatural. In the first section we examine man's need for religion and his struggle with the tensions which exist between life and religious practice. In "The Last Magician," Loren Eiseley says that the basis of religion is man's need for transcendence, his need to identify with a higher order so that he may rise above his animal nature. But the practice of religion entails difficulties. In Frank O'Connor's story, "First Confession," Jackie is obliged to confess his transgressions. When he examines his conscience, he thinks he has broken all ten commandments because of his distaste for his grandmother's eccentric habits and his quarrels with his sister, who taunts him with her holier-than-thou attitude. His problems are compounded when his religion teacher impresses on him the horrors of hell and the consequences of making a bad confession. By the time he enters the confessional, he is so rattled that he cannot distinguish the kneeling bench from the arm rest. Luckily the parish priest assesses the situation and helps him through this unsettling experience.

In Philip Roth's "The Conversion of the Jews," Ozzie has difficulties at Hebrew school when he raises questions that his Rabbi prefers not to answer directly. Thinking that the boy is impertinent, Rabbi Binder treats him harshly. To escape the conflict, Ozzie races for the roof of the school. In an unusual turnabout the upstart student instructs the Rabbi (and the others who have gathered to watch the scene) in the need for tolerance and understanding in religion.

In some cases the cruel realities of life undermine religious belief. Elie Wiesel, who survived the German concentration camps, rejects his faith because the evil of the world belies the existence of a benevolent God.

Loss of faith can be a problem for those who simply weary of routine religious ceremonies. Some individuals who seek to renew their experience of God step outside conventional religious practice. In "Mystics and Militants," Harvey Cox describes the neomystics, who experiment with drugs and multimedia rituals in their search for the sacred.

The current revival of mysticism is accompanied by renewed interest in the occult. Unlike the mystic who seeks communion with a divine or holy order, the occultist may align himself with any of a variety of mysterious forces. Robert

Somerlott testifies to the general popularity of the unexplained in his essay "The Day of the Occult" by pointing out that ouija boards now outsell Monopoly games.

Probably the most common occult practice is astrology, the art of interpreting the influence of heavenly bodies on human affairs. Richard Cavendish discusses its general nature in "Astrology" while John Anthony West and Jan Gerhard Toonder in "Free Will or No Free Will?: The Eternal Question" discuss whether or not a person acting under the influence of the stars is able to exercise free will.

Witchcraft is a more sinister practice than astrology because the witch seeks to control the natural world for his or her own purposes. In previous ages witchcraft was considered heretical and was condemned by church law. Both legend and history testify to the gruesome punishment that the church inflicted upon witches. Historians believe 300,000 women were tortured and put to death between the years 1484 and 1782. While modern practitioners claim to be direct descendants of ancient witches, Daniel Cohen, in "Witches in Our Midst," finds little evidence to substantiate their claim. In discussing ancient witchcraft, he says that a witch's hex was frequently successful because it was aided by herbs and potions as well as the victim's belief that the witch could cast a spell on him. The story "The Witch's Vengeance" by W. B. Seabrook illustrates the influence that suggestion wields over a victim.

Although the relationship between ancient and modern witchcraft seems tenuous, Satanism has maintained a strong hold on men's imagination. The Satanists believe that Christ is a hoax and will never come to redeem mankind. In orgiastic rituals which parody the Roman Catholic Mass, the Satanists worship the devil. Richard Cavendish discusses these unusual ceremonies in "The Black Mass."

On the surface religion and the occult seem to be very different. However, each fulfills a similar need. When rational answers fail, man turns to the supernatural to explain that which is beyond his understanding.

rELIGION

THE LAST MAGICIAN
LOREN EISELEY

God is the search for God.

—*Nikos Kazantzakis*

Loren Eiseley discusses man's search for transcendence, a search which culminated in the first millennium B.C. when man put aside tribal loyalties and deities in order to seek enlightenment for the human soul.

There is [an] aspect of man's mental life which demands the utmost attention, even though it is manifest in different degrees in different times and places and among different individuals; this is the desire for transcendence—a peculiarly human trait. Philosophers and students of comparative religion have sometimes remarked that we need to seek for the origins of the human interest in the cosmos, "a cosmic sense" unique to man. However this sense may have evolved, it has made men of the greatest imaginative power conscious of human inadequacy and weakness. There may thus emerge the desire for "rebirth" expressed in many religions. Stimulated by his own uncompleted nature, man seeks a greater role, restructured beyond nature like so much in his aspiring mind. Thus we find the Zen Bud-

Loren Eiseley (1907–) is an educator and authropologist whose published works include *The Invisible Pyramid,* from which this excerpt was taken.

dhist, in the words of the scholar Suzuki, intent upon creating "a realm of Emptiness or Void where no conceptualism prevails" and where "rootless trees grow." The Buddhist, in a true paradox, would empty the mind in order that the mind may adequately receive or experience the world. No other creature than man would question his way of thought or feel the need of sweeping the mind's cloudy mirror in order to unveil its insight.

Man's life, in other words, is felt to be unreal and sterile. Perhaps a creature of so much ingenuity and deep memory is almost bound to grow alienated from his world, his fellows, and the objects around him. He suffers from a nostalgia for which there is no remedy upon earth except as it is to be found in the enlightenment of the spirit—some ability to have a perceptive rather than an exploitive relationship with his fellow creatures.

After man had exercised his talents in the building of the first neolithic cities and empires, a period mostly marked by architectural and military triumphs, an intellectual transformation descended upon the known world, a time of questioning. This era is fundamental to an understanding of man, and has engaged the attention of such modern scholars as Karl Jaspers and Lewis Mumford. The period culminates in the first millennium before Christ. Here in the great centers of civilization, whether Chinese, Indian, Judaic, or Greek, man had begun to abandon inherited gods and purely tribal loyalties in favor of an inner world in which the pursuit of earthly power was ignored. The destiny of the human soul became of more significance than the looting of a province. Though these dreams are expressed in different ways by such divergent men as

Christ, Buddha, Lao-tse, and Confucius, they share many things in common, not the least of which is respect for the dignity of the common man.

The period of the creators of transcendent values—the axial thinkers, as they are called—created the world of universal thought that is our most precious human heritage. One can see it emerging in the mind of Christ as chronicled by Saint John. Here the personalized tribal deity of earlier Judaic thought becomes transformed into a world deity. Christ, the Good Shepherd, says: "Other sheep I have, which are not of this fold: them also I must bring, and they shall hear my voice; and there shall be one fold and one shepherd. . . . My sheep hear my voice . . . and they follow me."

These words spoken by the carpenter from Nazareth are those of a world changer. They passed boundaries, whispered in the ears of galley slaves: "One fold, one shepherd. Follow me." These are no longer the wrathful words of a jealous city ravager, a local potentate god. They mark instead, in the high cultures, the rise of a new human image, a rejection of purely material goals, a turning toward some inner light. As these ideas diffused, they were, of course, subject to the wear of time and superstition, but the human ethic of the individual prophets and thinkers has outlasted empires.

Such men speak to us across the ages. In their various approaches to life they encouraged the common man toward charity and humility. They did not come with weapons; instead they bespoke man's purpose to subdue his animal nature and in so doing to create a radiantly new and noble being. These were the dreams of the first millennium B.C. Tormented man, arising, falling, still pursues those dreams today.

Earlier I mentioned Plato's path into the light that blinds the man who has lived in darkness. Out of just such darkness arose the first humanizing influence. It was genuinely the time of the good shepherds. No one can clearly determine why these prophets had such profound effects within the time at their disposal. Nor can we solve the mystery of how they came into existence across the Euro-Asiatic land mass in diverse cultures at roughly the same time. As Jaspers observes, he who can solve this mystery will know something common to all mankind.

In this difficult era we are still living in the inspirational light of a tremendous historical event, one that opened up the human soul. But if the neophytes were blinded by the light, so, perhaps, the prophets were in turn confused by the human darkness they encountered. The scientific age replaced them. The common man, after brief days of enlightenment, turned once again to escape, propelled outward first by the world voyagers, and then by the atom breakers. We have called up vast powers which loom menacingly over us. They await our bidding, and we turn to outer space as though the solitary answer to the unspoken query must be flight, such flight as ancient man engaged in across ice ages and vanished game trails—the flight from nowhere.

The good shepherds meantime have all faded into the darkness of history. One of them, however, left a cryptic message: "My doctrine is not mine but his that sent me." Even in the time of unbelieving this carries a warning. For He that sent may still be couched in the body of man awaiting the end of the story.

Discussion Questions

1. Why does man seek to transcend his animal nature?
2. Why does man feel his life is unreal and sterile?
3. According to Eiseley, what are the aims of religion as broadly outlined by the axial thinkers? Have these aims been achieved in any time or place?
4. Eiseley implies that our belief in God has been supplanted by our belief in science and technology. What is the basis for this statement? Do you agree with this observation? Explain.
5. In your view, which form of government—capitalism, socialism, or communism—provides the best climate for the growth of religion?

Loren Eiseley   169

THE LATEST DECALOGUE
ARTHUR HUGH CLOUGH

Thou shalt have one God only; who
Would be at the expense of two?
No graven images may be
Worshiped, except the currency.
Swear not at all; for, for thy curse
Thine enemy is none the worse.
At church on Sunday to attend
Will serve to keep the world thy friend.
Honor thy parents; that is, all
From whom advancement may befall.
Thou shalt not kill; but need'st not strive
Officiously to keep alive.
Do not adultery commit;
Advantage rarely comes of it.
Thou shalt not steal; an empty feat,
When it's so lucrative to cheat.
Bear not false witness; let the lie
Have time on its own wings to fly.
Thou shalt not covet, but tradition
Approves all forms of competition.

The sum of all is, thou shalt love,
If anybody, God above:
At any rate shall never labor
More than thyself to love thy neighbor.

Arthur Hugh Clough (1819–1861) was a British poet and
religious skeptic.

Discussion Questions

1. How does "The Latest Decalogue" alter the Ten Commandments?
2. What is the author's intention in this poem?
3. What does this poem imply about human nature?

FIRST CONFESSION
FRANK O'CONNOR

In Roman Catholicism, confession, mass, and communion are the central acts of worship. In order to receive communion (or the bread that has been consecrated into the body of Christ), a Catholic must have confessed his sins to a priest. Recently the Church altered its ruling requiring that a first confession be made before a first communion. In this delightful story written before the change in Church laws, a young boy experiences the difficulty of examining his conscience, entering the confessional, and admitting to a priest the sins he has committed.

All the trouble began when my grandfather died, and my grandmother—my father's mother—came to live with us. Relations in the one house are a trial at the best of times, but, to make it worse, my grandmother was a real old countrywoman, and quite unsuited to the life in town. She had a fat, wrinkled old face, and, to my mother's indignation, went round the house in bare feet—the boots had her crippled, she said. For dinner she had a jug of porter and a pot of potatoes, with, sometimes, a bit of salt fish, and she poured out the potatoes on the table and ate them slowly,

---

Frank O'Connor (1903–1966) was the pseudonym for Michael O'Donovan, a professional writer of short stories, verse, and criticism.

with great enjoyment, using her fingers by way of a fork.

Now, girls are supposed to be fastidious, but I was the one who suffered from that. Nora, my sister, just sucked up to the old woman for the penny she got every Friday out of the old age pension, a thing I could not do. I was too honest; that was my trouble; and when I was playing with Bill Connell, the sergeant-major's son, and saw my grandmother steering up the path with the jug of porter sticking out from beneath her shawl, I was mortified. I made excuses not to let him come into the house, because I could never be sure what she would be up to when we went in.

When my mother was at work and my grandmother made dinner I wouldn't even touch it. Nora tried to make me once, but I hid under the table from her, and took the bread-knife with me for safety. Nora let on to be very indignant (she wasn't, of course, but she knew that Mother saw through her and sided with Father and Gran) and came after me. I lashed out at her with the knife, and after that she left me alone. I stayed there till my mother came in from work, and she made dinner for me; but then my father came home and Nora said in a shocked voice: "Oh, Dadda, do you know what Jackie did at dinnertime?" Then, of course, it all came out, and he gave me a leathering and the mother interfered, and for days after he wouldn't even look at me. God knows, I was heart-scalded!

Then, to crown my misfortunes, I had to make my first confession and communion. It was an old woman called Ryan who prepared us for that. She was about the one age with Gran, only she was well-to-do, lived in a big house on Montenotte, wore a black cloak and bonnet, and came every day to the school at three o'clock, when we should have been going home, to talk to us about hell. She may have mentioned the other place as well, but that could only have been by accident, for hell had the first place in her heart.

She lit a candle and took out a new half-crown and offered it to the first fellow who would hold one finger—only one finger!—in the flame for five minutes by the school clock. I was always very ambitious, and was tempted to volunteer, only as no one else did, I thought it might look greedy. Then she asked were we afraid of holding one finger—only one finger!—in a little bit of candle for five minutes, and not afraid of burning all over in roasting hot furnaces for all eternity. "All eternity! Just think of that! A whole lifetime goes by, and it's nothing; only a drop in the ocean of your sufferings." The woman was really interesting about hell, but I had very little attention to spare from the half-crown, which was still on the desk beside her. At the end of the lesson she put it back in her purse. It was a great disappointment in a religious woman like that.

Another day she said she knew a priest who woke one night to find a fellow he didn't recognize leaning over the end of his bed. The priest was a bit frightened—naturally enough—but he asked the fellow what he wanted, and the fellow said in a low, husky voice that he wanted to go to confession. The priest said it was an awkward time and wouldn't it do in the morning? But the other chap said the last time he went to confession there was one sin he kept back because he was ashamed to mention it, and now it was always on his mind. Then the priest knew it was a serious case, because the fellow was after making a bad confession and committing a mortal sin. He got up to dress, and just then the cock crew in the yard outside, and lo and behold! when the priest looked round there was no sign of the fellow at all, only an awful smell like burning timber, and when the priest looked at the bed didn't he see the print of two hands burned in it? That was because the fellow had made a bad confession. This story made a shocking impression on me.

But the worst of all was when she showed us how to examine our consciences. Did we take the name of God in vain? Did we honour our father and our mother? (I asked her did this include grandmothers and she said it did.) Did we love our neighbour as ourselves? Did we covet our neighbour's goods? They seemed to include every blooming thing down to the penny that Nora got on Fridays. I think, between one thing and another, I must have broken all the commandments, all on account of that old woman, and, as far as I could see as long as she was in the house I had no hope of ever doing anything else.

I was scared to death of confession. The day the whole class went I let on to have the toothache, hoping my absence from school wouldn't be noticed, but at three o'clock, just when I was feeling safe, along came a chap with a message from Mrs. Ryan to say I was to go to confession myself and be at the chapel for communion on Sunday morning. To make it worse, my mother couldn't come with me and sent Nora instead.

Now, that girl had ways of tormenting me that my mother never knew. She held my hand as we went down the hill, smiling and saying how sorry she was for me.

"Oh, God help us!" she said. "Isn't it a terrible pity you weren't a good boy? Oh, Jackie, my heart bleeds for you! How will you think of all your sins? Do you remember the time you kicked Gran on the shin?"

"Lemme go!" I wailed, trying to drag myself away from her. "I won't go to confession at all."

"Sure, you'll have to go, Jackie," she replied in the same regretful tone. "Sure, if you didn't the parish priest would be up to the house, looking for you. 'Tisn't, God knows, that I'm sorry for you! Do you remember the time you tried to kill me with the bread-knife under the table? And the language you used to me? Oh, I don't know what'll he do to you at all. He might send you up to the Bishop."

I remember thinking that she didn't know the half of what I had to tell, if I did tell it. There is very little about that day that I don't remember— the steep hill down to the church, and the sunlit hillsides at the other side of the river valley seen between gaps in the houses, like Adam's last glimpse of Paradise. Then, as she got me down the long flight of steps into the chapel yard and under the big limestone portico, Nora suddenly changed her tune.

"There you are!" she said with a yelp of triumph, hurling me from her through the church door. "And I hope he'll give you the penitential psalms, you dirty little caffler!"

I knew then I was lost. The door with the coloured glass panels swung shut behind me; the sunlight went out and gave place to deep shadow, and the wind whistled outside so that the silence seemed to be frozen and to crackle like ice under my feet as I tiptoed up the aisle. Nora sat in front of me beside the confession box. There were a couple of old women ahead of her, and then a miserable-looking poor devil came and wedged me in at the other side, so that I couldn't escape even if I wanted to. He joined his hands and rolled his eyes in the direction of the roof, muttering aspirations in an anguished tone, and I wondered had he a grandmother too. That, I felt, was the way you'd expect a fellow with a grandmother to behave, but I was worse off than he, for I knew that, just like the man in the story, I'd never have the nerve to tell all my sins; that I should make a bad confession and then die in the night and be continually coming back and burning people's furniture.

Nora's turn came, and I heard the sound of something slamming, and then I heard her voice as if butter wouldn't melt in her mouth, and the thing slammed again and it was all over. God, the hypocrisy of women! Her eyes were lowered, her hands were joined on her stomach, and she walked up the aisle to the side altar as if she were treading on eggshells. I remembered the devilish malice with which she had tormented me all the way from home, and I wondered if all religious people were like that. It was my turn now. I went in with the fear of damnation in my soul, and the confessional door closed of itself behind me.

It was pitch black inside. I couldn't see priest or anything else. Then I really began to be frightened. In the darkness it was a matter between God and me, and God had all the odds. He knew what my intentions were even before I started. I had no chance at all. All I had ever been told about confession got mixed up in my mind, and I knelt to one wall and said: "Bless me, father, for I have sinned; this is my first confession." I waited for a few minutes but nothing happened, so I tried it on the other wall. Nothing happened there either. He had me spotted all right.

It must have been then that I noticed the shelf at about the one height with my head. It struck me that it was probably the place you were supposed to kneel. Of course, it was on the high side, and not very deep, but by this time I was beyond all rational considerations. Mind you, it took some climbing, but I was always good at that, and I managed to get up all right. The trouble was to stay up. There was just room for my knees, but, apart from a sort of moulding in the outer wall, nothing you could get a grip on. I held on to the moulding and repeated the words a little louder, and this time something happened all right. A slide was slammed back and a man's voice asked after a moment: "Who's there?"

"'Tis me, father," said I, for fear he mightn't see me and go away again. I couldn't see him at all. The place his voice came from was under the moulding, about level with my knees, so I took a good grip of the moulding and swung myself down till I saw the astonished face of a young priest looking up at me. He had to put his head on one side to see me, and I had to put mine on one side to see him, so we were more or less talking to one another upside down. It struck me as a very queer way to hear confessions, but I didn't feel it was my place to criticize.

"Bless me, father, for I have sinned; this is my first confession," I rattled off, all in one breath, and swung myself down the least shade more to make it easier for him.

"What are you doing up there?" he shouted in an angry voice, and the strain the politeness was putting on my hold of the moulding, and the shock of being addressed in the uncivil way were too much for me. Down I tumbled and hit the door an unmerciful wallop before I found myself on the flat of my back in the middle of the aisle. The priest opened the door of the middle box and came out, pushing the biretta back from his forehead. He looked something terrible. Then Nora came scampering down the aisle from the altar.

"Oh, you dirty little caffler!" she said. "I might have known you'd do it! I might have known you'd disgrace me! I can't leave you out of my sight for a minute."

Before I even got to my feet she bent down and gave me a smack across the ear. This reminded me that I was so stunned I had even forgotten to cry, so that people might think I wasn't hurt at all, when as a matter of fact I was probably crippled for life.

"What's all this about?" said the priest, getting angrier than ever, and pushing her off me. "How dare you hit the child like that, you little vixen?"

"But I can't do my penance with him, father," cried Nora, cocking an outraged eye up at him.

"Well, go on and do it," he said, giving me a hand up, "or I'll give you some more to do. . . . Was it coming to confession you were, my poor man?" he asked me.

"'Twas, father," said I with a sob.

"Oh," he said in a respectful tone, "a big, hefty fellow like you must have terrible sins. Is this your first?"

"'Tis, father," said I.

"Worse and worse," he said, shaking his head gloomily. "You have the crimes of a lifetime to tell. I don't know will I get rid of you at all today. You'd better sit down here and wait till I'm finished with these old ones. You can see by the looks of them they haven't much to tell."

"I will so, father," I said with something approaching joy.

The relief of it was enormous. Nora stuck out her tongue at me behind his back, but I couldn't even be bothered noticing it. I knew from the very moment that man opened his mouth that he was exceptionally intelligent. It only stood to reason that a fellow confessing his sins after seven years would have more to tell than people that went every week. That was what the priest expected, and the rest was only old women and girls and their talk about hell and the penitential psalms—people with no experience of life. I started to make my examination of conscience, and, barring the things about the grandmother, it didn't seem too bad.

The next time the priest steered me into the confession box himself and left the shutter back the way I'd see him sitting down at the other side with his biretta pulled well down over his eyes.

"Well now," he said, "what do they call you?"

"Jackie, father," said I.

"And what's a-trouble to you, Jackie?" he said.

"Father," I said, feeling I might as well get it over while I had him in good humour, "I had it all arranged to kill my grandmother!"

He seemed a bit shaken by that all right, because he didn't say anthing for a while.

"My goodness," he said at last, "that'd be a shocking thing to do. What put that into your head?"

"Father," I said, feeling very sorry for myself, "she's an awful woman."

"Is she?" he asked. "What way is she awful?"

"She takes porter, father," said I, knowing well from the way the mother talked of porter that it must be a mortal sin, and hoping it might make the priest see my point of view.

"Oh, my!" he said.

"And snuff, father," said I.

"She's a bad case all right, Jackie," he said.

"And she goes round in her bare feet, father,"

said I. "And she knows I don't like her, and she gives pennies to Nora and none to me, and my da sides with her and beats me, so one night I was so heart-scalded I made up my mind I'd have to kill her."

"And what would you do with the body?" he asked with great interest.

"I was thinking I could cut it up and carry it away in a barrow I have," said I.

"Begor, Jackie," said he, "do you know, you're a terrible child?"

"I know, father," said I. (I was thinking the same thing myself.) "I tried to kill Nora too, with a bread-knife, under the table, only I missed her."

"Is that the little girl that was beating you just now?" he asked.

"'Tis, father," said I.

"Someone will go for her with a bread-knife one day, and he won't miss her," he said. "But you must have great courage. There's lots of people I'd like to do the same to, between ourselves, but I'd never have the nerve. Hanging is an awful death."

"Is it, father?" said I with the deepest interest. (I was always very keen on hanging.) "Did you ever see a fellow hanged?"

"I saw dozens of them," he assured me solemnly, "and they all died roaring."

"Jay!", said I.

"Oh, 'tis a horrible death," he said with great satisfaction. "Lots of the fellows I saw killed their grandmothers too, but any of them I asked said 'twas never worth it."

He had me there for a full ten minutes, talking, and then walked out to the chapel yard with me. I was quite sorry to part with him because he was the most entertaining man I'd ever met in the religious line. Outside, the sunlight after the shadow of the church was like the roaring of waves on a beach; it dazzled me, and when the frozen silence melted and I heard the scream of trams on the road, the heart rose in me. But the best of all was to know I wouldn't die that night and come back leaving marks on my poor mother's furniture. I knew it would be a great worry to her and the poor soul had enough.

Nora was sitting on the railing, waiting for me, and she put on a very sour puss when she saw the priest along with me. She was mad jealous because a priest had never come out of the church with her.

"Well," she asked coldly after he parted* me, "what did he give you?"

"Three Hail Marys," said I.

"Three Hail Marys?" she repeated incredulously. "You mustn't have told him anything."

"I told him everything," I said confidently.

"About Gran and all?"

"About Gran and all."

(All she wanted was to be able to go home and say I had made a bad confession.)

"Did you tell him you went for me with the bread-knife?" she asked with a frown.

"I did to be sure," said I.

"And he only gave you three Hail Marys?"

"That's all."

She got down off the railing slowly with a baffled air. Clearly, this was beyond her. As we mounted the steps to the main road she looked at me suspiciously.

"What are you sucking?" she asked.

"Bulls' eyes," I said.

---

*pardoned

"Was it the priest gave them to you?"

"'Twas."

"Lord God!" she wailed bitterly. "Some people have all the luck! 'Tis no advantage to anybody trying to be good. I might just as well be a sinner like you."

Discussion Questions

1. Why is Jackie afraid to make his first confession? How has Mrs. Ryan's instruction influenced him?

2. Compare Jackie's wrongdoing to his sister's. Does she make a *good* confession?

3. How does the priest help Jackie make his first confession? Does he lie to the boy? Is this a sin?

4. What are some of the comic elements in this story? How does the child's viewpoint heighten the comedy?

THE CONVERSION OF THE JEWS
PHILIP ROTH

Because the spiritual essence of religion can not be scientifically demonstrated, its theological tenets are usually accepted on faith. In "The Conversion of the Jews" Ozzie asks questions which disturb the theological structure of the Judaic faith.

"You're a real, one for opening your mouth in the first place," Itzie said. "What do you open your mouth all the time for?"

"I didn't bring it up, Itz, I didn't," Ozzie said.

"What do you care about Jesus Christ for anyway?"

"I didn't bring up Jesus Christ. He did. I didn't even know what he was talking about. Jesus is historical, he kept saying, Jesus is historical." Ozzie mimicked the monumental voice of Rabbi Binder.

"Jesus was a person that lived like you and me," Ozzie continued. "That's what Binder said—"

"Yeah? . . . So what! What do I give two cents whether he lived or not. And what do you gotta open your mouth!" Itzie Lieberman favored closed-mouthedness, especially when it came to

Philip Roth (1933–) is a professional writer and educator who received the National Book Award for Fiction in 1960 for *Goodbye, Columbus*.

Ozzie Freedman's questions. Mrs. Freedman had to see Rabbi Binder twice before about Ozzie's questions and this Wednesday at four-thirty would be the third time. Itzie preferred to keep *his* mother in the kitchen; he settled for behind-the-back subtleties such as gestures, faces, snarls and other less delicate barnyard noises.

"He was a real person, Jesus, but he wasn't like God, and we don't believe he is God." Slowly, Ozzie was explaining Rabbi Binder's position to Itzie, who had been absent from Hebrew School the previous afternoon.

"The Catholics," Itzie said helpfully, "they believe in Jesus Christ, that he's God." Itzie Lieberman used "the Catholics" in its broadest sense—to include the Protestants.

Ozzie received Itzie's remark with a tiny head bob, as though it were a footnote, and went on. "His mother was Mary, and his father probably was Joseph," Ozzie said. "But the New Testament says his real father was God."

"His *real* father?"

"Yeah," Ozzie said, "that's the big thing, his father's supposed to be God."

"Bull."

"That's what Rabbi Binder says, that it's impossible—"

"Sure it's impossible. That stuff's all bull. To have a baby you gotta get laid," Itzie theologized. "Mary hadda get laid."

"That's what Binder says: 'The only way a woman can have a baby is to have intercourse with a man.'"

"He said *that*, Ozz?" For a moment it appeared that Itzie had put the theological question aside. "He said that, intercourse?" A little curled smile shaped itself in the lower half of Itzie's face

like a pink mustache. "What you guys do, Ozz, you laugh or something?"

"I raised my hand."

"Yeah? Whatja say?"

"That's when I asked the question."

Itzie's face lit up. "Whatja ask about—intercourse?"

"No, I asked the question about God, how if He could create the heaven and earth in six days, and make all the animals and the fish and the light in six days—the light especially, that's what always gets me, that He could make the light. Making fish and animals, that's pretty good—"

"That's damn good." Itzie's appreciation was honest but unimaginative: it was as though God had just pitched a one-hitter.

"But making light . . . I mean when you think about it, it's really something," Ozzie said. "Anyway, I asked Binder if He could make all that in six days, and He could *pick* the six days He wanted right out of nowhere, why couldn't He let a woman have a baby without having intercourse."

"You said intercourse, Ozz, to Binder?"

"Yeah."

"Right in class?"

"Yeah."

Itzie smacked the side of his head.

"I mean, no kidding around," Ozzie said, "that'd really be nothing. After all that other stuff, that'd practically be nothing."

Itzie considered a moment. "What'd Binder say?"

"He started all over again explaining how Jesus was historical and how he lived like you and me but he wasn't God. So I said I under*stood* that. What I wanted to know was different."

What Ozzie wanted to know was always different. The first time he had wanted to know how Rabbi Binder could call the Jews "The Chosen People" if the Declaration of Independence claimed all men to be created equal. Rabbi Binder tried to distinguish for him between political equality and spiritual legitimacy, but what Ozzie wanted to know, he insisted vehemently, was different. That was the first time his mother had to come.

Then there was the plane crash. Fifty-eight people had been killed in a plane crash at La Guardia. In studying a casualty list in the newspaper his mother had discovered among the list of those dead eight Jewish names (his grandmother had nine but she counted Miller as a Jewish name); because of the eight she said the plane crash was "a tragedy." During free-discussion time on Wednesday Ozzie had brought to Rabbi Binder's attention this matter of "some of his relations" always picking out the Jewish names. Rabbi Binder had begun to explain cultural unity and some other things when Ozzie stood up at his seat and said that what he wanted to know was different. Rabbi Binder insisted that he sit down and it was then that Ozzie shouted that he wished all fifty-eight were Jews. That was the second time his mother came.

"And he kept explaining about Jesus being historical, and so I kept asking him. No kidding, Itz, he was trying to make me look stupid."

"So what he finally do?"

"Finally he starts screaming that I was deliberately simple-minded and a wise guy, and that my mother had to come, and this was the last time. And that I'd never get bar-mitzvahed if he could help it. Then, Itz, then he starts talking in that voice like a statue, real slow and deep, and he says that I better think over what I said about the Lord. He told me to go to his office and think it over." Ozzie leaned his body towards Itzie. "Itz, I thought it over for a solid hour, and now I'm convinced God could do it."

Ozzie had planned to confess his latest transgression to his mother as soon as she came home from work. But it was a Friday night in November and already dark, and when Mrs. Freedman came through the door she tossed off her coat, kissed Ozzie quickly on the face, and went to the kitchen table to light the three yellow candles, two for the Sabbath and one for Ozzie's father.

When his mother lit the candles she would move her two arms slowly towards her, dragging them through the air, as though persuading people whose minds were half made up. And her eyes would get glassy with tears. Even when his father was alive Ozzie remembered that her eyes had gotten glassy, so it didn't have anything to do with his dying. It had something to do with lighting the candles.

As she touched the flaming match to the unlit wick of a Sabbath candle, the phone rang, and Ozzie, standing only a foot from it, plucked it off the receiver and held it muffled to his chest. When his mother lit candles Ozzie felt there should be no noise; even breathing, if you could manage it, should be softened. Ozzie pressed the phone to his breast and watched his mother dragging whatever she was dragging, and he felt his own eyes get glassy. His mother was a round, tired, gray-haired penguin of a woman whose gray skin had begun to feel the tug of gravity and the weight of her own history. Even when she was dressed up she didn't look like a chosen person. But when she lit candles she looked like something better; like a woman who knew momentarily that God could do anything.

After a few mysterious minutes she was finished. Ozzie hung up the phone and walked to the kitchen table where she was beginning to lay the two places for the four-course Sabbath meal. He told her that she would have to see Rabbi Binder next Wednesday at four-thirty, and then he told her why. For the first time in their life together she hit Ozzie across the face with her hand.

All through the chopped liver and chicken soup part of the dinner Ozzie cried; he didn't have any appetite for the rest.

On Wednesday, in the largest of the three basement classrooms of the synagogue, Rabbi Marvin Binder, a tall, handsome, broad-shouldered man of thirty with thick strong-fibered black hair, removed his watch from his pocket and saw that it was four o'clock. At the rear of the room Yakov Blotnik, the seventy-one-year-old custodian, slowly polished the large window, mumbling to himself, unaware that it was four o'clock or six o'clock, Monday or Wednesday. To most of the students Yakov Blotnik's mumbling, along with his brown curly beard, scythe nose, and two heel-trailing black cats, made of him an object of wonder, a foreigner, a relic, towards whom they were alternately fearful and disrespectful. To Ozzie the mumbling had always seemed a monotonous, curious prayer; what made it curious was that old Blotnik had been mumbling so steadily for so many years, Ozzie suspected he had memorized the prayers and forgotten all about God.

"It is now free-discussion time," Rabbi Binder said. "Feel free to talk about any Jewish matter at all—religion, family, politics, sports—"

There was silence. It was a gusty, clouded November afternoon and it did not seem as though there ever was or could be a thing called baseball. So nobody this week said a word about that hero from the past, Hank Greenberg—which limited free discussion considerably.

And the soul-battering Ozzie Freedman had just received from Rabbi Binder had imposed its limitation. When it was Ozzie's turn to read aloud from the Hebrew book the rabbi had asked him petulantly why he didn't read more rapidly. He was showing no progress. Ozzie said he could read faster but that if he did he was sure not to understand what he was reading. Nevertheless, at the rabbi's repeated suggestion Ozzie tried, and showed a great talent, but in the midst of a long passage he stopped short and said he didn't understand a word he was reading, and started in again at a drag-footed pace. Then came the soul-battering.

Consequently when free-discussion time rolled around none of the students felt too free. The rabbi's invitation was answered only by the mumbling of feeble old Blotnik.

"Isn't there anything at all you would like to discuss?" Rabbi Binder asked again, looking at his watch. "No questions or comments?"

There was a small grumble from the third row. The rabbi requested that Ozzie rise and give the rest of the class the advantage of his thought.

Ozzie rose. "I forget it now," he said, and sat down in his place.

Rabbi Binder advanced a seat towards Ozzie and poised himself on the edge of the desk. It was Itzie's desk and the rabbi's frame only a dagger's-length away from his face snapped him to sitting attention.

"Stand up again, Oscar," Rabbi Binder said calmly, "and try to assemble your thoughts."

Ozzie stood up. All his classmates turned in their seats and watched as he gave an unconvincing scratch to his forehead.

"I can't assemble any," he announced, and plunked himself down.

"Stand up!" Rabbi Binder advanced from Itzie's desk to the one directly in front of Ozzie; when the rabbinical back was turned Itzie gave it five-fingers off the tip of his nose, causing a small titter in the room. Rabbi Binder was too absorbed in squelching Ozzie's nonsense once and for all to bother with titters. "Stand up, Oscar. What's your question about?"

Ozzie pulled a word out of the air. It was the handiest word. "Religion."

"Oh, now you remember?"

"Yes."

"What is it?"

Trapped, Ozzie blurted the first thing that came to him. "Why can't He make anything He wants to make!"

As Rabbi Binder prepared an answer, a final answer, Itzie, ten feet behind him, raised one finger on his left hand, gestured it meaningfully towards the rabbi's back, and brought the house down.

Binder twisted quickly to see what had happened and in the midst of the commotion Ozzie shouted into the rabbi's back what he couldn't have shouted to his face. It was a loud, toneless sound that had the timbre of something stored inside for about six days.

"You don't know! You don't know anthing about God!"

The rabbi spun back towards Ozzie. "What?"

"You don't know—you don't—"

"Apologize, Oscar, apologize!" It was a threat.

"You don't—"

Rabbi Binder's hand flicked out at Ozzie's cheek. Perhaps it had only been meant to clamp the boy's mouth shut, but Ozzie ducked and the palm caught him squarely on the nose.

The blood came in a short, red spurt on to Ozzie's shirt front.

The next moment was all confusion. Ozzie screamed, "You bastard, you bastard!" and broke for the classroom door. Rabbi Binder lurched a step backwards, as though his own blood had started flowing violently in the opposite direction, then gave a clumsy lurch forward and bolted out the door after Ozzie. The class followed after the rabbi's huge blue-suited back, and before old Blotnik could turn from his window, the room was empty and everyone was headed full speed up the three flights leading to the roof.

If one should compare the light of day to the life of man: sunrise to birth; sunset—the dropping down over the edge—to death; then as Ozzie Freedman wiggled through the trapdoor of the synagogue roof, his feet kicking backwards bronco-style at Rabbi Binder's outstretched arms—at that moment the day was fifty years old. As a rule, fifty or fifty-five reflects accurately the age of late afternoons in November, for it is in that month, during those hours, that one's awareness of light seems no longer a matter of seeing, but of hearing: light begins clicking away. In fact, as Ozzie locked shut the trapdoor in the rabbi's face, the sharp click of the bolt into the lock might momentarily have been mistaken for the sound of the heavier gray that had just throbbed through the sky.

With all his weight Ozzie kneeled on the locked door; any instant he was certain that Rabbi Binder's shoulder would fling it open, splintering the wood into shrapnel and catapulting his body into the sky. But the door did not move and below him he heard only the rumble of feet, first loud then dim, like thunder rolling away.

A question shot through his brain. "Can this be *me?*" For a thirteen-year-old who had just labeled his religious leader a bastard, twice, it was not an improper question. Louder and louder the question came to him—"Is it me? Is it me?"—until he discovered himself no longer kneeling, but racing crazily towards the edge of the roof, his eyes crying, his throat screaming, and his arms flying everywhichway as though not his own.

"Is it me? Is it me ME ME ME ME! It has to be me—but is it!"

It is the question a thief must ask himself the night he jimmies open his first window, and it is said to be the question with which bridegrooms quiz themselves before the altar.

In the few wild seconds it took Ozzie's body to propel him to the edge of the roof, his self-examination began to grow fuzzy. Gazing down at the street, he became confused as to the problem beneath the question: was it, is-it-me-who-called-Binder-a-bastard? or, is-it-me-prancing-around-on-the-roof? However, the scene below settled all, for there is an instant in any action when whether it is you or somebody else is academic. The thief crams the money in his pockets and scoots out the window. The bridegroom signs the hotel register for two. And

the boy on the roof finds a streetful of people gaping at him, necks stretched backwards, faces up, as though he were the ceiling of the Hayden Planetarium. Suddenly you know it's you.

"Oscar! Oscar Freedman!" A voice rose from the center of the crowd, a voice that, could it have been seen, would have looked like the writing on scroll. "Oscar Freedman, get down from there. Immediately!" Rabbi Binder was pointing one arm stiffly up at him; and at the end of that arm, one finger aimed menacingly. It was the attitude of a dictator, but one—the eyes confessed all—whose personal valet had spit neatly in his face.

Ozzie didn't answer. Only for a blink's length did he look towards Rabbi Binder. Instead his eyes began to fit together the world beneath him, to sort out people from places, friends from enemies, participants from spectators. In little jagged starlike clusters his friends stood around Rabbi Binder, who was still pointing. The topmost point on a star compounded not of angels but of five adolescent boys was Itzie. What a world it was, with those stars below, Rabbi Binder below . . . Ozzie, who a moment earlier hadn't been able to control his own body, started to feel the meaning of the word control: he felt Peace and he felt Power.

"Oscar Freedman, I'll give you three to come down."

Few dictators give their subjects three to do anything; but, as always, Rabbi Binder only looked dictatorial.

"Are you ready, Oscar?"

Ozzie nodded his head yes, although he had no intention in the world—the lower one or the celestial one he'd just entered—of coming down even if Rabbi Binder should give him a million.

"All right then," said Rabbi Binder. He ran a

hand through his black Samson hair as though it were the gesture prescribed for uttering the first digit. Then, with his other hand cutting a circle out of the small piece of sky around him, he spoke. "One!"

There was no thunder. On the contrary, at that moment, as though "one" was the cue for which he had been waiting, the world's least thunderous person appeared on the synagogue steps. He did not so much come out the synagogue door as lean out, onto the darkening air. He clutched at the doorknob with one hand and looked up at the roof.

"Oy!"

Yakov Blotnik's old mind hobbled slowly, as if on crutches, and though he couldn't decide precisely what the boy was doing on the roof, he knew it wasn't good—that is, it wasn't-good-for-the-Jews. For Yakov Blotnik life had fractionated itself simply: things were either good-for-the-Jews or no-good-for-the-Jews.

He smacked his free hand to his in-sucked cheek, gently. "Oy, Gut!" And then quickly as he was able, he jacked down his head and surveyed the street. There was Rabbi Binder (like a man at an auction with only three dollars in his pocket, he had just delivered a shaky "Two!"); there were the students, and that was all. So far it-wasn't-so-bad-for-the-Jews. But the boy had to come down immediately, before anybody saw. The problem: how to get the boy off the roof?

Anybody who has ever had a cat on the roof knows how to get him down. You call the fire department. Or first you call the operator and you ask her for the fire department. And the next thing there is great jamming of brakes and clanging of bells and shouting of instructions. And

then the cat is off the roof. You do the same thing to get a boy off the roof.

That is, you do the same thing if you are Yakov Blotnik and you once had a cat on the roof.

When the engines, all four of them, arrived, Rabbi Binder had four times given Ozzie the count of three. The big hook-and-ladder swung around the corner and one of the firemen leaped from it, plunging headlong towards the yellow fire hydrant in front of the synagogue. With a huge wrench he began to unscrew the top nozzle. Rabbi Binder raced over to him and pulled at his shoulder.

"There's no fire . . ."

The fireman mumbled back over his shoulder and, heatedly, continued working at the nozzle.

"But there's no fire, there's no fire . . ." Binder shouted. When the fireman mumbled again, the rabbi grasped his face with both his hands and pointed it up at the roof.

To Ozzie it looked as though Rabbi Binder was trying to tug the fireman's head out of his body, like a cork from a bottle. He had to giggle at the picture they made: it was a family portrait—rabbi in black skullcap, fireman in red fire hat, and the little yellow hydrant squatting beside like a kid brother, bareheaded. From the edge of the roof Ozzie waved at the portrait, a one-handed, flapping, mocking wave; in doing it his right foot slipped from under him. Rabbi Binder covered his eyes with his hands.

Firemen work fast. Before Ozzie had even regained his balance, a big, round, yellowed net was being held on the synagogue lawn. The firemen who held it looked up at Ozzie with stern, feelingless faces.

Philip Roth   185

One of the firemen turned his head towards Rabbi Binder. "What, is the kid nuts or something?"

Rabbi Binder unpeeled his hands from his eyes, slowly, painfully, as if they were tape. Then he checked: nothing on the sidewalk, no dents in the net.

"Is he gonna jump, or what?" the fireman shouted.

In a voice not at all like a statue, Rabbi Binder finally answered. "Yes, yes, I think so . . . He's been threatening to . . ."

Threatening to? Why, the reason he was on the roof, Ozzie remembered, was to get away; he hadn't even thought about jumping. He had just run to get away, and the truth was that he hadn't really headed for the roof as much as he'd been chased there.

"What's his name, the kid?"

"Freedman," Rabbi Binder answered. "Oscar Freedman."

The fireman looked up at Ozzie. "What is it with you, Oscar? You gonna jump, or what?"

Ozzie did not answer. Frankly, the question had just arisen.

"Look, Oscar, if you're gonna jump, jump—and if you're not gonna jump, don't jump. But don't waste our time, willya?"

Ozzie looked at the fireman and then at Rabbi Binder. He wanted to see Rabbi Binder cover his eyes one more time.

"I'm going to jump."

And then he scampered around the edge of the roof to the corner, where there was no net below, and he flapped his arms at his sides, swishing the air and smacking his palms to his trousers on the downbeat. He began screaming like some kind of engine, "Wheeeee . . . wheeeeee," and leaning

way out over the edge with the upper half of his body. The firemen whipped around to cover the ground with the net. Rabbi Binder mumbled a few words to Somebody and covered his eyes. Everything happened quickly, jerkily, as in a silent movie. The crowd, which had arrived with the fire engines, gave out a long, Fourth-of-July fireworks oooh-aahhh. In the excitement no one had paid the crowd much heed, except, of course, Yakov Blotnik, who swung from the doorknob counting heads. "Fier und tsvansik . . . finf und tsvantsik . . . Oy, Gut!" It wasn't like this with the cat.

Rabbi Binder peeked through his fingers, checked the sidewalk and net. Empty. But there was Ozzie racing to the other corner. The firemen raced with him but were unable to keep up. Whenever Ozzie wanted to he might jump and splatter himself upon the sidewalk, and by the time the firemen scooted to the spot all they could do with their net would be to cover the mess.

"Wheeeee . . . wheeeee . . ."

"Hey, Oscar," the winded fireman yelled, "What the hell is this, a game of something?"

"Wheeeee . . . wheeeee . . ."

"Hey, Oscar—"

But he was off now to the other corner, flapping his wings fiercely. Rabbi Binder couldn't take it any longer—the fire engines from nowhere, the screaming suicidal boy, the net. He fell to his knees, exhausted, and with his hands curled together in front of his chest like a little dome, he pleaded, "Oscar, stop it, Oscar. Don't jump, Oscar. Please come down . . . Please don't jump."

And further back in the crowd a single voice, a single young voice, shouted a lone word to the boy on the roof.

"Jump!"

"Go ahead, Ozz—jump!" Itzie broke off his point of the star and courageously, with the inspiration not of a wise-guy but of a disciple, stood alone. "Jump, Ozz, jump!"

Still on his knees, his hands still curled, Rabbi Binder twisted his body back. He looked at Itzie, then, agonizingly, back to Ozzie.

OSCAR, DON'T JUMP! PLEASE, DON'T JUMP . . . please please . . ."

"Jump!" This time it wasn't Itzie but another point of the star. By the time Mrs. Freedman arrived to keep her four-thirty appointment with Rabbi Binder, the whole little upside down heaven was shouting and pleading for Ozzie to jump, and Rabbi Binder no longer was pleading with him not to jump, but was crying into the dome of his hands.

Understandably Mrs. Freedman couldn't figure out what her son was doing on the roof. So she asked.

"Ozzie, my Ozzie, what are you doing? My Ozzie, what is it?"

Ozzie stopped wheeeeeing and slowed his arms down to a cruising flap, the kind birds use in soft winds, but he did not answer. He stood against the low, clouded, darkening sky—light clicked down swiftly now, as on a small gear—flapping softly and gazing down at the small bundle of a woman who was his mother.

"What are you doing, Ozzie?" She turned towards the kneeling Rabbi Binder and rushed so close that only a paper-thickness of dusk lay between her stomach and his shoulders.

"What is my baby doing?"

Rabbi Binder gaped up at her but he too was mute. All that moved was the dome of his hands; it shook back and forth like a weak pulse.

"Rabbi, get him down! He'll kill himself. Get him down, my only baby . . ."

"I can't," Rabbi Binder said, "I can't . . ." and he turned his handsome head towards the crowd of boys behind him. "It's them. Listen to them."

And for the first time Mrs. Freedman saw the crowd of boys, and she heard what they were yelling.

"He's doing it for them. He won't listen to me. It's them." Rabbi Binder spoke like one in a trance.

"For them?"

"Yes."

"Why for them?"

"They want him to . . ."

Mrs. Freedman raised her two arms upward as though she were conducting the sky. "For them he's doing it!" And then in a gesture older than pyramids, older than prophets and floods, her arms came slapping down to her sides. "A martyr I have. Look!" She tilted her head to the roof. Ozzie was still flapping softly. "My martyr."

"Oscar, come down, *please*," Rabbi Binder groaned.

In a startlingly even voice Mrs. Freedman called to the boy on the roof. "Ozzie, come down, Ozzie. Don't be a martyr, my baby."

As though it were a litany, Rabbi Binder repeated her words. "Don't be a martyr, my baby. Don't be a martyr."

"Gawhead, Ozz—be a Martin!" It was Itzie. "Be a Martin, be a Martin," and all the voices joined in singing for Martindom, whatever *it* was. "Be a Martin, be a Martin . . ."

Somehow when you're on a roof the darker it gets the less you can hear. All Ozzie knew was that two groups wanted two new things: his friends were spirited and musical about what they wanted; his mother and the rabbi were eventoned, chanting, about what they didn't want. The rabbi's voice was without tears now and so was his mother's.

The big net stared up at Ozzie like a sightless eye. The big, clouded sky pushed down. From beneath it looked like a gray corrugated board. Suddenly, looking up into that unsympathetic sky, Ozzie realized all the strangeness of what these people, his friends, were asking: they wanted him to jump, to kill himself; they were singing about it now—it made them that happy. And there was an even greater strangeness: Rabbi Binder was on his knees, trembling. If there was a question to be asked now it was not "Is it me?" but rather "Is it us? . . . Is it us?"

Being on the roof, it turned out, was a serious thing. If he jumped would the singing become dancing? Would it? What would jumping stop? Yearningly, Ozzie wished he could rip open the sky, plunge his hands through, and pull out the sun; and on the sun, like a coin, would be stamped JUMP or DON'T JUMP.

Ozzie's knees rocked and sagged a little under him as though they were setting him for a dive. His arms tightened, stiffened, froze, from shoulders to fingernails. He felt as if each part of his body were going to vote as to whether he should kill himself or not—and each part as though it were independent of *him*.

The light took an unexpected click down and the new darkness, like a gag, hushed the friends singing for this and the mother and rabbi chanting for that.

Ozzie stopped counting votes, and in a curiously high voice, like one who wasn't prepared for speech, he spoke.

"Mamma?"

"Yes, Oscar."

"Mamma, get down on your knees, like Rabbi Binder."

"Oscar—"

"Get down on your knees," he said, "or I'll jump."

Ozzie heard a whimper, then a quick rustling, and when he looked down where his mother had stood he saw the top of a head and beneath that a circle of dress. She was kneeling beside Rabbi Binder.

He spoke again. "Everybody kneel." There was the sound of everybody kneeling.

Ozzie looked around. With one hand he pointed towards the synagogue entrance. "Make *him* kneel."

There was a noise, not of kneeling, but of body-and-cloth stretching. Ozzie could hear Rabbi Binder saying in a gruff whisper, ". . . or he'll *kill* himself," and when next he looked there was Yakov Blotnik off the doorknob and for the first time in his life upon his knees in the Gentile posture of prayer.

As for the firemen—it is not as difficult as one might imagine to hold a net taut while you are kneeling.

Ozzie looked around again; and then he called to Rabbi Binder.

"Rabbi?"

"Yes, Oscar."

"Rabbi Binder, do you believe in God?"

"Yes."

"Do you believe God can do Anything?"

Ozzie leaned his head out into the darkness. "Anything?"

"Oscar, I think—"

"Tell me you believe God can do Anything."

There was a second's hesitation. Then: "God can do Anything."

"Tell me you believe God can make a child without intercourse."

"He can."

"Tell me!"

"God," Rabbi Binder admitted, "can make a child without intercourse."

"Mamma, you tell me."

"God can make a child without intercourse," his mother said.

"Make *him* tell me." There was no doubt who *him* was.

In a few moments Ozzie heard an old comical voice say something to the increasing darkness about God.

Next, Ozzie made everybody say it. And then he made them all say they believed in Jesus Christ—first one at a time, then all together.

When the catechizing was through it was the beginning of evening. From the street it sounded as if the boy on the roof might have sighed.

"Ozzie?" A woman's voice dared to speak. "You'll come down now?"

There was no answer, but the woman waited, and when a voice finally did speak it was thin and crying, and exhausted as that of an old man who has just finished pulling the bells.

"Mamma, don't you see—you shouldn't hit me. He shouldn't hit me. You shouldn't hit me about God, Mamma. You should never hit anybody about God—"

"Ozzie, please come down now."

"Promise me, promise me you'll never hit anybody about God."

He had asked only his mother, but for some reason everyone kneeling in the street promised he would never hit anybody about God.

Once again there was silence.

"I can come down now, Mamma," the boy on the roof finally said. He turned his head both ways as though checking the traffic lights. "Now I can come down . . ."

And he did, right into the center of the yellow net that glowed in the evening's edge like an overgrown halo.

Discussion Questions

1. What disturbing questions does Ozzie ask Rabbi Binder?
2. Ozzie keeps insisting that the questions he is asking are different from the ones the Rabbi is answering. In what way are they different from the way Rabbi Binder interprets them?
3. Are Ozzie's questions malicious? Explain.
4. What are the implications of Ozzie's statement: "You shouldn't hit me about God." Compare the use of fear and punishment in "First Confession" and the "The Conversion of the Jews."
5. What is the meaning of the title?

NIGHT
ELIE WIESEL

Have we ever thought about the consequences of a horror that, though less apparent, less striking than the other outrages, is yet the worst of all to those of us who have faith: the death of God in the soul of a child who suddenly discovers absolute evil.

—François Mauriac, Forward to Night

Never shall I forget that night, the first night in camp, which has turned my life into one long night, seven times cursed and seven times sealed. Never shall I forget that smoke. Never shall I forget the little faces of the children, whose bodies I saw turned into wreaths of smoke beneath a silent blue sky. Never shall I forget those flames which consumed my Faith forever. Never shall I forget that nocturnal silence which deprived me, for all eternity, of the desire to live. Never shall I forget those moments which murdered my God and my soul and turned my dreams to dust. Never shall I forget these things, even if I am condemned to live as long as God Himself. Never.

In these stark and terrifying words, Elie Wiesel, a Jew who survived the German concentration camps, describes the death of his belief in God. His story, recorded in the slender volume *Night*, moved François Mauriac to comment: *For him, Nietzsche's cry ex-*

Born in Rumania in 1928 and educated at the Sorbonne, Elie Wiesel is a foreign correspondent and author. He won the Prix Rivarol in 1963.

pressed an almost physical reality: God is dead, the God of love, of gentleness, of comfort, the God of Abraham, of Isaac, of Jacob, has vanished forevermore, beneath the gaze of this child, in the smoke of a human holocaust exacted by Race, the most voracious of all idols.

The following excerpt from *Night* provides a glimpse of that deep wound, which afflicted not only Wiesel but the entire human race. The scene is the death camp at Buna during an American bombing raid.

One Sunday, when half of us—including my father—were at work, the rest—including myself—were in the block, taking advantage of the chance to stay in bed late in the morning.

At about ten o'clock, the air-raid sirens began to wail. An alert. The leaders of the block ran to assemble us inside, while the SS took refuge in the shelters. As it was relatively easy to escape during a warning—the guards left their lookout posts and the electric current was cut off in the barbed-wire fences—the SS had orders to kill anyone found outside the blocks.

Within a few minutes, the camp looked like an abandoned ship. Not a living soul on the paths. Near the kitchen, two cauldrons of steaming hot soup had been left, half full. Two cauldrons of soup, right in the middle of the path, with no one guarding them! A feast for kings, abandoned, supreme temptation! Hundreds of eyes looked at them, sparkling with desire. Two lambs, with a hundred wolves lying in wait for them. Two lambs without a shepherd—a gift. But who would dare?

Terror was stronger than hunger. Suddenly, we saw the door of Block 37 open imperceptibly. A man appeared, crawling like a worm in the direction of the cauldrons.

Hundreds of eyes followed his movements. Hundreds of men crawled with him, scraping their knees with his on the gravel. Every heart trembled, but with envy above all. This man had dared.

He reached the first cauldron. Hearts raced: he had succeeded. Jealousy consumed us, burned us up like straw. We never thought for a moment of admiring him. Poor hero, committing suicide for a ration of soup! In our thoughts we were murdering him.

Stretched out by the cauldron, he was now trying to raise himself up to the edge. Either from weakness or fear he stayed there, trying, no doubt, to muster up the last of his strength. At last he succeeded in hoisting himself onto the edge of the pot. For a moment, he seemed to be looking at himself, seeking his ghostlike reflection in the soup. Then, for no apparent reason, he let out a terrible cry, a rattle such as I had never heard before, and, his mouth open, thrust his head toward the still steaming liquid. We jumped at the explosion. Falling back onto the ground, his face stained with soup, the man writhed for a few seconds at the foot of the cauldron, then he moved no more.

Then we began to hear the airplanes. Almost at once, the barracks began to shake.

"They're bombing Buna!" someone shouted.

I thought of my father. But I was glad all the same. To see the whole works go up in fire—what revenge! We had heard so much talk about the defeats of German troops on various fronts, but we did not know how much to believe. This, today, was real!

We were not afraid. And yet, if a bomb had fallen on the blocks, it alone would have claimed hundreds of victims on the spot. But we were no longer afraid of death; at any rate, not of that death. Every bomb that exploded filled us with joy and gave us new confidence in life.

The raid lasted over an hour. If it could only have lasted ten times ten hours! . . . Then silence fell once more. The last sound of an American plane was lost on the wind, and we found ourselves back again in the cemetery. A great trail of black smoke was rising up on the horizon. The sirens began to wail once more. It was the end of the alert.

Everyone came out of the blocks. We filled our lungs with the fire- and smoke-laden air, and our eyes shone with hope. A bomb had fallen in the middle of the camp, near the assembly point, but it had not gone off. We had to take it outside the camp.

The head of the camp, accompanied by his assistant and the chief Kapo, made a tour of inspection along the paths. The raid had left traces of terror on his face.

Right in the middle of the camp lay the body of the man with the soup-stained face, the only victim. The cauldrons were taken back into the kitchen.

The SS had gone back to their lookout posts, behind their machine guns. The interlude was over.

At the end of an hour, we saw the units come back, in step, as usual. Joyfully, I caught sight of my father.

"Several buildings have been flattened right out," he said, "but the warehouse hasn't suffered."

In the afternoon we went cheerfully to clear away the ruins.

A week later, on the way back from work, we noticed in the center of the camp, at the assembly place, a black gallows.

We were told that soup would not be distributed until after roll call. This took longer than usual. The orders were given in a sharper manner than on other days, and in the air there were strange undertones.

"Bare your heads!" yelled the head of the camp, suddenly.

Ten thousand caps were simultaneously removed.

"Cover your heads!"

Ten thousand caps went back onto their skulls, as quick as lightning.

The gate to the camp opened. An SS section appeared and surrounded us: one SS at every three paces. On the lookout towers the machine guns were trained on the assembly place.

"They fear trouble," whispered Juliek.

Two SS men had gone to the cells. They came back with the condemned man between them. He was a youth from Warsaw. He had three years of concentration camp life behind him. He was a strong, well-built boy, a giant in comparison with me.

His back to the gallows, his face turned toward his judge, who was the head of the camp, the boy was pale, but seemed more moved than afraid. His manacled hands did not tremble. His eyes gazed coldly at the hundreds of SS guards, the thousands of prisoners who surrounded him.

The head of the camp began to read his verdict, hammering out each phrase: "In the name of Himmler . . . prisoner Number . . . stole during the alert . . . According to the law . . . paragraph . . . prisoner Number . . . is condemned to death. May this be a warning and an example to all prisoners."

No one moved.

I could hear my heart beating. The thousands who had died daily at Auschwitz and at Birkenau in the crematory ovens no longer troubled me. But this one, leaning against his gallows—he overwhelmed me.

"Do you think this ceremony'll be over soon? I'm hungry. . . ." whispered Juliek.

At a sign from the head of the camp, the Lagerkapo advanced toward the condemned man. Two prisoners helped him in his task—for two plates of soup.

The Kapo wanted to bandage the victim's eyes, but he refused.

After a long moment of waiting, the executioner put the rope round his neck. He was on the point of motioning to his assistants to draw the chair away from the prisoner's feet, when the latter cried, in a calm, strong voice:

"Long live liberty! A curse upon Germany! A curse . . . ! A cur—"

The executioners had completed their task.

A command cleft the air like a sword.

"Bare your heads."

Ten thousand prisoners paid their last respects.

"Cover your heads!"

Then the whole camp, block after block, had to march past the hanged man and stare at the dimmed eyes, the lolling tongue of death. The Kapos and heads of each block forced everyone to look him full in the face.

After the march, we were given permission to return to the blocks for our meal.

I remember that I found the soup excellent that evening. . . .

I witnessed other hangings. I never saw a single one of the victims weep. For a long time those dried-up bodies had forgotten the bitter taste of tears.

Except once. The Oberkapo of the fifty-second cable unit was a Dutchman, a giant, well over six feet. Seven hundred prisoners worked under his orders, and they all loved him like a brother. No one had ever received a blow at his hands, nor an insult from his lips.

He had a young boy under him, a *pipel*, as they were called—a child with a refined and beautiful face, unheard of in this camp.

(At Buna, the *pipel* were loathed; they were often crueller than adults. I once saw one of thirteen beating his father because the latter had not made his bed properly. The old man was crying softly while the boy shouted: "If you don't stop crying at once I shan't bring you any more bread. Do you understand?" But the Dutchman's little servant was loved by all. He had the face of a sad angel.)

One day, the electric power station at Buna was blown up. The Gestapo, summoned to the spot, suspected sabotage. They found a trail. It eventually led to the Dutch Oberkapo. And there, after a search, they found an important stock of arms.

The Oberkapo was arrested immediately. He was tortured for a period of weeks, but in vain. He would not give a single name. He was transferred to Auschwitz. We never heard of him again.

But his little servant had been left behind in the camp in prison. Also put to torture, he too would not speak. Then the SS sentenced him to death, with two other prisoners who had been discovered with arms.

One day when we came back from work, we saw three gallows rearing up in the assembly

Elie Wiesel   193

place, three black crows. Roll call. SS all round us, machine guns trained: the traditional ceremony. Three victims in chains—and one of them, the little servant, the sad-eyed angel.

The SS seemed more preoccupied, more disturbed than usual. To hang a young boy in front of thousands of spectators was no light matter. The head of the camp read the verdict. All eyes were on the child. He was lividly pale, almost calm, biting his lips. The gallows threw its shadow over him.

This time the Lagerkapo refused to act as executioner. Three SS replaced him.

The three victims mounted together onto the chairs.

The three necks were placed at the same moment within the nooses.

"Long live liberty!" cried the two adults.

But the child was silent.

"Where is God! Where is He!" someone behind me asked.

At a sign from the head of the camp, the three chairs tipped over.

Total silence throughout the camp. On the horizon, the sun was setting.

"Bare your heads!" yelled the head of the camp. His voice was raucous. We were weeping.

"Cover your heads!"

Then the march past began. The two adults were no longer alive. Their tongues hung swollen, blue-tinged. But the third rope was still moving; being so light, the child was still alive. . . .

For more than half an hour he stayed there, struggling between life and death, dying in slow agony under our eyes, And we had to look him full in the face. He was still alive when I passed in front of him. His tongue was still red, his eyes not yet glazed.

Behind me, I heard the same man asking: "Where is God now?"

And I heard a voice within me answer him:

"Where is He? Here He is—He is hanging here on this gallows. . . . "

That night the soup tasted of corpses.

Discussion Questions

1. If possible, read *Night* in its entirety. Discuss how the author's experiences have contributed to his loss of faith.
2. How does the description of the first hanging contribute to the dramatic effect of the second?
3. How do you think you would react to the horror experienced by the Jews?

*"Larry, in case we don't find enlightenment, do you think
we can still get back your Pontiac dealership?"*

195

MYSTICS AND MILITANTS
HARVEY COX

To see a World in a Grain of Sand
And a Heaven in a Wild Flower,
Hold Infinity in the palm of your hand
And Eternity in an hour.

—*William Blake*

In their search for God, the neomystics have created a refreshing movement that may help revitalize religion.

Thou shalt not be on friendly terms
With guys in advertising firms,
  Nor speak with such
As read the Bible for its prose,
Nor, above all, make love to those
  Who wash too much.

—*W. H. Auden, "Under Which Lyre? A*
Reactionary Tract for the Times"[1]

The forces that bear the seeds of a renewal of festivity and fantasy in our time are not apt to come from the churches alone. This chapter is devoted to two such movements, which both

---

"Mystics and Militants" was published in *The Feast of Fools* in 1970.

[1] "Under Which Lyre? A Reactionary Tract for the Times" by W. H. Auden, the Phi Beta Kappa poem at Harvard, 1946, can be found in Auden's *Collected Shorter Poems, 1927–1957* (New York: Random House, 1966; London: Faber and Faber, 1966). Copyright © 1966 by W. H. Auden.

splashed into view in the late 1960's. Both are extraordinarily important for the future. Both are theologically fascinating. Let us call them the *neomystics* and the *new militants*.

The neomystics, mostly white, in bells and beads, came on with love-ins in the park, chanted mantras, and smoked pot. The new militants, both black and white, with beards and bull-horns, staged sit-ins in university administration buildings, blockaded Dow recruiters, and picketed induction centers. Both scared and bewildered folks over thirty. Both sparked new hope in those who had given up on anything fresh ever happening again in America. Both sometimes did things that worried even their most fervent devotees. Yet together they represent two insights that have immeasurable significance for the whole society.

The insight of the neomystics is that the search for the holy—perhaps even the quest for God—is important after all, and that it is integrally tied up with the search for an authentically human style of life. Despite secularization, mysticism is back again, and with it a new interest in ritual, contemplation, and even in visions. The insight of the new militants is that politics is not dead and that in fact every act has an irreducible political significance. A period of social activism rivaled only by the 1930's is in full swing. Radical rhetoric is on the wing and the term revolution is once again heard in the land.

The groups that represent these insights have been referred to variously as "hippies" or flower children on the one hand, and "the new left" on the other. By now, however, these terms have been applied so indiscriminately and with such prejudicial overtones that I prefer to use different ones. The term "neomystic" is better. "Mystic"

indicates the ancient tradition from which the new interest springs; at the same time the prefix "neo" suggests there is something novel about it. The same is true for the new militants. To describe them with the label "left" is misleading because it places them in terms of categories they themselves believe to be outdated. Yet they must certainly be understood in the light of the tradition of political militancy that has played such an important role in Western history in the past three centuries. But labeling is not really an important problem. The real question is what is the long-term religious and political significance of these two movements?

THE NEOMYSTICS: FESTIVITY AND CONTEMPLATION

Today's new mystics represent a modern phase in a very old religious movement. They personify man's ancient thirst to taste both the holy and the human with unmediated directness. Like previous generations of mystics, the new ones suspect all secondhand reports. Also they wish to lose themselves, at least temporarily, in the reality they experience. Above all, like the mystics of old, when they try to tell us what they are up to, we have a hard time understanding them. Mystics speak a language of their own, and sometimes even their fellow mystics do not quite get the message.

The neomystics, unlike many of the old ones, luxuriate in loud music, bright costumes, and convulsive dancing. Still, they are right when they use the word "contemplative" to describe their way of life. We are confused because to many people "contemplative" is associated with

Harvey Cox   197

soft music, black costumes, and vows of celibacy and obedience. How then can the sportive, sometimes even self-indulgent, life of the neomystics be called contemplative?

"Contemplation" means different things to different people. At it narrowest, it suggests a discipline for achieving a particular state of consciousness. In this restricted sense, techniques of contemplation have been refined for years, especially by the great Christian mystics such as Jacob Boehme and St. John of the Cross and by the rich mystical traditions of the East.

In its wider sense, however, as suggested both by some of the classical Western mystics and as emphasized in Zen Buddhism, contemplation is a total way of life. It is a basic attitude toward all things, including detachment, perspective, and an element of irony. According to this broader view, the contemplative life may require periods of withdrawal and the use of established techniques of meditation in some stages, but basically it is a life that can be lived anywhere. It is a way of being, a style of existence.

In both senses of the word, contemplation bears a striking resemblance to festivity. Carl Kerényi asserts this similarity when he says in one of his books, that celebrating a festival is the equivalent to becoming contemplative, and "in this state, directly confronting the higher realities on which the whole of existence rests."[2] What Kerényi is driving at is that festivity allows us to remove our attention from everyday pursuits and direct it to the immediate festive experience of joy, appreciation, and anticipation. Further, festivity resembles contemplation, because it is not

just a means to something else. It is an end in its own right. Also in line with other contemplative disciplines, festivity requires an element of sacrifice or renunciation. We cannot really celebrate if we are getting paid for it, which is why professional mourners and paid-escort services strike us as a bit phoney. We celebrate best when we joyfully give up the time involved and wantonly accept the fact that celebrating is not an economically productive activity.

Festivity and contemplation are close cousins. The things that make life contemplative are the same things that make life celebrative: the capacity to step back from tasks and chores, the ability to "hang-loose" from merely material goals, the readiness to relish an experience on its own terms. It was the much-criticized, exploited, and now virtually defunct "hippie" movement that helped our chore-ridden society to notice this. For that contribution they deserve the society's gratitude, not its reprobation.

So mysticism is back in our midst and, as always, many people view it with mixed emotions. It has always been thus with mystics. Traditionally religious people are glad on the one hand that mystics want to find God. They are bothered, on the other, that the mystics are not satisfied with existing ecclesiastical means of grace. Besides, in their single-minded quest for the holy vision, mystics are likely to offend prevailing social sensibilities. Mysticism is not always serene and placid. It can become noisy, Dionysiac, even orgiastic. It has little use for institutional religion. So organized religions, with good reason, have usually been nervous about mystics, and they remain so today. In our present situation, this perennial suspicion is deepened because of the means some neomystics employ to

<hr>

[2] Carl Kerényi, *The Religion of the Greeks and Romans* (London: Thames & Hudson, 1962), p. 53.

celebrate or contemplate. I refer especially to the growing use of psychedelic drugs and of elaborately-contrived multimedia "mind-blowing" environments. Though this subject is a large one, no discussion of mysticism and festivity today would be complete without some mention of it.

PIPES AND BOWLS

Lubricating festivity with spirits, potions, and additives is scarcely a new idea. Intoxicating drinks appeared in man's life at the very dawn of history.[3] They have played a role in religious rites since then. Wine is used in communion services, and in secular festivities; the punch bowl or the brimming beaker still occupies a central place. But are we not aware of the immense dangers involved in misusing alcohol? Many people are. Some still are not. But in any case we seem to have rejected total abstinence as a viable solution. Today, instead of abstinence pledges, we try to teach young people to enjoy drinking, to experience it as a normal part of life, and to discover their own limits.[4] We even tolerate drinking to slight excess on some occasions. We have not solved the serious problem of alcoholism, and we need to think about it more than we do. But we have decided, as a society, that we will have to solve it by learning to live with alcohol, not without it.

We drink alcohol not just because we like its taste but because it produces a certain state of consciousness. Nor is our society particularly opposed to inducing other desired states of consciousness (or unconsciousness) with substances in addition to alcohol. We quaff caffeine to cajole our brains into awakening in the morning. We drag on a pipe to relax. We order a martini to help clinch a business deal or madeira to speed a seduction. We pop a Sleep-eze or sip warm cocoa to encourage slumber. But when it comes to the well-publicized drugs now increasingly used by young people, we suddenly turn angry and petulant. We serve champagne at wedding receptions but put people behind bars for smoking marijuana.

Why? There seems to be no really convincing reason. Certainly what medical knowledge we have of alcohol and marijuana would not support such wildly disproportionate attitudes. But in this confused and emotion-packed area, reason seems to have little place. Our whole approach to stimulants, depressants, psychedelic drugs and hallucinogens today is a quagmire of irrationality, prejudice, and inconsistency. We unthinkingly lump hard and soft, addictive and nonaddictive substances together under the scare word "dope." We list marijuana with heroin as though both belong in the same bin. We have created a panicky atmosphere that makes careful, controlled research in the new synthetic drugs like LSD virtually impossible. Consequently wild stories, abuse, and sensationalism have run amuck, and rational discussion of the issue seems impossible for the moment.

We need a period of calm in which the reasoned investigation of various drugs can proceed. We need a moratorium both on flamboyant drug cults and well-publicized "busts" so that real evidence can be accumulated on the benefits and

---

[3] Gordon Childe, *What Happened in History* (New York: Penguin, 1946).

[4] Morris E. Chafetz, *Liquor: The Servant of Man* (Boston: Little, Brown, 1965).

Harvey Cox   199

dangers of the various substances now in use. Can anything be said in the meantime?

First, it would help if we understood that we labor under an obvious cultural bias. Recently a middle-aged Catholic priest who had grown up in Yugoslavia confessed to me that he really did not understand what all the fuss was about. As a lad, he had lived in a village that was half Catholic and half Moslem. The Catholics, although permitted to drink alcohol, were absolutely forbidden to smoke hashish. The Moslems were prohibited by their faith from drinking liquor but felt no qualms about smoking the sweet grass. As boys always do, the youngsters from different sides of town would creep with their friends into each other's back rooms to taste the forbidden fruit. There the Moslem boys would savor the piquant *slivovitz* and the Catholics would steal a puff on the *hookah*.

Though phrased in religious terms, the prohibitions were obviously cultural and very relative. Whatever attitudes we eventually develop on drugs should not be a product of mere social prejudice. They should be based on a realistic assessment of what alcohol, marijuana, caffeine, nicotine, and all the rest can or cannot do for us or to us. This is a field that badly needs demythologizing. Extravagant claims and charges should be held in abeyance until more clinical data has been assembled and verified.

The time may come when we will recognize that the various substances we smoke, swallow, or swill to induce particular states of consciousness are all devices that in a perfect world of fulfilled human beings, no one would need. But no one lives in such a world. We are beset by noise, interruptions, and banal chores. We sometimes want to contemplate or celebrate, but the world is too much with us. So we use the substances nature has placed in the grains and grasses. Often we misuse them. But the fact that something is misused does not mean it should be banned. If it did, money, sex, and printing presses would have to join wine and marijuana on the index of prohibited items.

What we need now are dependable data on just how much harm any of these substances can do to people. We know a good deal about the harm that cigarettes and whiskey can cause. We know about the damaging effects of heroin and cocaine. We do not know enough about marijuana and very little about the so-called psychedelics. We do know that many people insist that liquor helps them to relax, or that pot helps them meditate, or that either one helps them celebrate. We need to find out what else these things may be doing—not so that we can pile up massive repressive legislation, but so that people can make choices on facts instead of on the reports of terrified high school teachers or self-designated gurus. Mead bowls, magic mushrooms, and peace-pipes have been with mankind for many millennia. It is unlikely that they will disappear very soon, if ever. What we can hope for, however, is that human beings will learn to use them with a mature recognition of their benefits, their dangers, and their limits.

Above all, we should learn never to confuse real festivity with mere intoxication. Authentic festivity can never be cooked up with pharmacological catalysts. Nor does their absence prevent its arrival. The spirit of festivity, like a muse, has a mind of its own. It can fail to show up even when elaborate preparations have been made, leaving us all feeling a little silly. It may pop in when no one is expecting it. In this respect, it reminds us of the grace of God, unmerited and often unanticipated. It cannot simply be turned on and off at will.

Still, sometimes preparation for festivity does pay off. As Sister Corita Kent says, if you ice a cake, light sparklers and sing, something celebrative may happen. Also, if we seriously practice contemplative disciplines that have been developed over the centuries, we may have a better chance of discovering the significance of meditation.

THE MULTIMEDIA ENVIRONMENT

There is a striking difference between the hermit's cell of the old style mystic and the festive settings created by our neomystics today. The contrast is so vivid that it forces us to ask again whether we are not dealing here with very different, even contradictory phenomena. We have tried to demonstrate a similarity between festivity and contemplation. But what does the solemn quietude and serenity of the classical mystic's cave have in common with the strobe lights, and triple fortissimo music of a multimedia environment? Do these two not occupy opposite poles on the spectrum?

Opposite yes, but perhaps sufficiently opposite to approach each other and to share certain important similarities. Many classical mystics tried to reach their goal through sensory deprivation. A drab cell reduced optical stimulation to a minimum. Silence, plain clothes, and meager food minimized other sensory inputs. Deprived of its normal diversions, the consciousness was free to focus on something else. The intense multimedia environment strives for the same effect with different means. Instead of reaching a threshold of consciousness through sensory deprivation, it relies on sensory overload. It induces a different dimension of awareness, not by depriving the senses of stimuli, but by pounding the senses with so many inputs and at such speed that the normal sorting mechanisms cannot cope. It recalls the "pandemonium" of the ancient rites of Dionysus, rites which were one of the sources of Greek drama.

Take the effect of a flashing strobe light, for example. Much in use today in multimedia events, the strobe light interrupts the smooth flow of visual images and chops them into shredded instants. Every second now requires a new "take." But because our eyes and brains cannot function quickly enough to sort and classify each separate instant, we stop trying and begin to let the images flow in unsorted. We learn for the moment to float along passively on our visual perceptions without trying to master or arrange them. We may even get some feeling for the outer limits and precariousness of the visual experience itself. Now compare this to Josef Pieper's description of that experience which has sometimes been called "speculation." It means, he says, "to look at reality purely receptively—in such a way that things are the measure and the soul is exclusively receptive."[5] In both cases a period of venturesome openness to experience replaces our usual guarded and suspicious attitude.

Multiple sound and light sources have a similar effect. They make it impossible for us to put all our perceptions together in an integrated whole. Since too much is happening to permit the clas-

---

[5]Josef Pieper, *Leisure: The Basis of Culture* (New York: New American Library, 1963), p. 81.

sification of everything into existing modes of awareness, the patterns of meaning we generally bring to experience must be temporarily suspended. The effect is quite accurately described by the phrase, "mind-blowing." Our habitual reading of reality is set aside and new dimensions of awareness can appear. Also, when music is really loud, so loud that it totally occupies our aural capacities, we experience something curiously akin to deep and pervasive silence.

All this suggests that disciplined sensory deprivation as experienced by the classical mystics, and the modern experience of calculated sensory overload do produce some markedly similar results. This in turn supports the notion that noisy festivity and silent contemplation may not be as different as they first appear.

But like any other human creation, the catalytic environment cannot produce God at man's beck and call. It represents the contemporary technological equivalent of the pageants, feasts, and bonfires men have staged since the dawn of consciousness. It is subject to the same elements of promise and possibility and open to the same abuse. Multimedia blow-outs can and do deteriorate into mere sensory orgies. Like pageants and celebrations from time immemorial they require delicacy and discipline to make them occasions for authentic human growth. Above all they must be directed toward dimensions of experience and symbols that lead us *into* historical existence and freedom.

This is where the religious dimension of celebration enters. Christianity has nothing against noise and revelry as such. It does suggest, however, that celebration should open man not just to the joy of his senses and the elan of the feast itself, but to the larger cosmos of which he is a part and the history he is involved in making. Real celebration links us to a world of memories, gestures, values, and hopes that we share with a much larger community. This may shed light on the real meaning of that phrase from the Christian communion service which rings so strangely in our modern ears:

> Therefore with Angels and
> Archangels, and with all the company of
> heaven . . .

The "Angels and Archangels" symbolize poetically those marvelous dimensions of reality we touch only in celebration and fantasy. The "company of heaven" linked to those of us on earth suggests that very large and inclusive human community of which I become a conscious part in celebration.

Man becomes man only when he knows and feels himself within a larger drama, one he not only acts in but helps to create. Even the most elaborately planned festivity can never guarantee this to anyone. But since he first stood up on two legs, and perhaps before, man has celebrated. He probably always will. Our challenge today is to deepen and enliven this celebration so that it becomes an occasion for nourishing our most courageous hopes and saluting the biggest tribe of all.

Maybe that is why something seems absent from the festivity of the neomystics. It is often a celebration of celebration. What is missing is that toasting of historical event and social hope that would give the festivity political significance. Here the issue is basically a theological one. In Christian and Jewish festivals, people celebrate historical events and concrete hopes. The gritty confusion of earthly history provides the principal focus of God's being, so festivity is always inherently political whether one wants it to be or not. By elevating and expressing hopes for things which have not yet come to be, this kind of festivity always produces friction in society.

So far for most of the neomystics the rediscovery of celebration, though inventive and colorful, often remains nonhistorical and therefore nonpolitical. It can even be an escape from politics. Man cannot celebrate abstractions, so the celebration of "love" and "peace" dissolves into frivolity unless it becomes more particular. People do not celebrate "love" but the love of John for Mary. Nor do we celebrate "freedom," but the liberation of the Israelites from Egypt or of black people from modern bondage. Christianity and Judaism have a definite bias for persons and events rather than for minds and ideas. This supplies the tension point at which Christianity may most fruitfully interact with the neomystics. It should welcome the verve and brightness they incarnate. But it should help them transform celebration into a way of being *in* the world, not a way of getting out of it.

Inspired by their gurus and holy men, the young people of today are fashioning their own celebrations and rituals. Rock music, guerrilla theatre, Dionysian dance, projected light and color—all play a part in the evolving rites. This is also true among the growing number of political activists. Unlike those of the "old left" who despised all forms of religion as the opiate of the masses, the new radicals exhibit a pervasive interest in theological questions and even in such occult topics as astrology and clairvoyance. So far the religious rebirth among young people is in a state of brawling, turbulent infancy. As it develops its rituals, however, it will inevitably fall prey to the same dangers that stalk any religious movement. Its rituals could become oppressive and ideological, a flashy set of devices for herding people into this or that action. Or its rituals could fall into eccentric fragments and therefore fail to unite people in celebration. The challenge Christianity faces is how to embrace this spiritual renaissance without crushing it, how to enrich it without polluting it, how to deepen it without mutilating it. Whether the current religious awakening can be saved from its own worst excesses depends on how it manages to relate itself to history, and to politics.

Discussion Questions

1. Who are the neomystics? How does neomysticism differ from traditional mysticism?
2. How does the multimedia environment contribute to mystical experiences?
3. What role do drugs play in mysticism? What is Cox's attitude toward drugs? What is your opinion of using drugs for religious purposes? For any purpose?
4. How can the celebration of the neomystics be infused with deeper significance?

tHE OCCULt

"*Avoid people with high cholesterol.*"

THE DAY OF THE OCCULT
ROBERT SOMERLOTT

The spirit world and the unexplained have interested man in both primitive and highly civilized societies. In our sophisticated scientific and technological age, the occult flourishes.

In 1968 a discovery was made in the United States: ouija boards were outselling Monopoly games by a substantial margin. This had been the case for more than a year, but no one had bothered to report the fact, which seemed rather less than earth-shaking. The announcement, although several magazine writers would later remember it, stirred hardly a ripple in the newspapers.

Monopoly had been firmly entrenched in America's living rooms, game rooms, play rooms, and "rec-rooms" for decades, and, until elbowed aside by the ouija board, was always the sturdy best seller on department-store game counters. Much of Monopoly's unchallenged success came because it offers wish-fulfillment of a classic American Dream: owning four hotels on the Boardwalk and cornering the market on practically everything. The players handle vast amounts of cash, they speculate, they acquire

Robert Somerlott (1930–) is a novelist and award-winning short-story writer.

real-estate developments. Monopoly, the reflection of a dream and an ideal, is perfectly designed to provide vicarious thrills in a capitalist, materialist society.

The ouija, if not Monopoly's opposite, is certainly altogether different. It suggests communication with a nonmaterial world, a world of ghosts and disembodied thought waves. As Monopoly reflects a hunger for riches, the ouija reveals a yearning toward contact with unknown powers, a seeking for what has been called the Unexplained. A "player" may not take the ouija seriously, but that is beside the point. A desire for nonmaterialist contact and at least a suspicion that it can be achieved must be present or the "game" would not be played at all.

It should be added that although the ouija is a very primitive and uncertain device in parapsychology, it has played a role in some astonishing cases. For example, a parlor-game encounter with a ouija board triggered the Patience Worth affair in St. Louis, and produced a classic mystery which remains fascinating and unsolved. The ouija has not always behaved like a toy and its effect upon the user can be unpredictable. Francisco I. Madero, who launched Mexico's major revolution of 1910 and was briefly the country's president until his assassination, had been told by the planchette that he would attain the nation's highest office—an achievement possible only through revolution. Madero subsequently led a revolt and the Díaz dictatorship was overthrown. "Patriotic" biographers have minimized the Mexican president's belief in the occult, which was obviously great.

The ouija's outstripping of Monopoly was only one small indication of a trend in the United States. A parlor game based on ESP has sold at the rate of a million sets per year despite a stiff price of seven dollars.

This upsurge of interest in mystic arts and psychic matters has been so obvious that there is little need to document it here. Suffice it to say that Hollywood astrologer Carroll Righter appeared on the cover of *Time;* a book about the prophecies of Edgar Cayce enjoyed twenty weeks on the best-seller lists in 1967 and 1968; and the mediums Arthur Ford and the late Eileen Garrett have become nearly as well known as many film stars.

Mystery cults such as the Rosicrucians of San Jose, California, have greatly increased their advertising—a sure indication of expanding membership. (The Scribe of the Rosicrucians will reveal no figures. This is characteristic of such organizations. From the smallest to the largest, they all seem to follow Mary Baker Eddy's injunction against numbering the faithful.)

Even witchcraft has come back into its own, with an official witch in Los Angeles County and unofficial witches clamoring for attention everywhere. Covens of witches and warlocks have been established in major American cities. At first there were no sensational exposés of them and one gathers that these covens were less sexual than their historic predecessors. But soon a transformation took place: the witches threw off their gentleness along with their modesty and unwashed clothes. This development drew the attention of the alert editors of *Esquire,* who published a long report indicating that witchcraft and satanism, two beliefs almost identical if considered primarily from the Christian viewpoint, have poured in a torrent, perhaps from some hidden spring in California's San Andreas fault. The Golden State, not surprisingly, is the new holy land of satanism, and its occult flood has divided itself into two main streams, two types of witches—the drugged and the drugless.

The more or less drugless witches seek excitement in the established rituals of satanism, studying the ancient descriptions of classical satanic worship and the more modern works of Eliphas Lévi. They are typified by Samson De Brier, a wispy, rather effete warlock reputed to have extensive, if vague, power. De Brier haunts a Hollywood residence-temple that is replete with death masks, moldering draperies, and fading photographs. Most of his efforts are directed toward combating the evil forces now being released by other, less admirable warlocks. Another benefactor of humanity is artist Neke Carson, whose Hollywood Hills studio is the source of all manner of works of art and inventions designed to thwart such menaces as vampire-devils. One notable achievement is a cross-shaped bed inflated with water and rigged with vibrators. (This invention seems to echo the Scottish magnetist Graham, who contrived the famous nineteenth-century magnetic bed. It was saturated with Oriental perfumes, and magnetic streams flowed through it, conveyed by glass tubes and cylinders. It was not, however, cross-shaped. Graham, unlike Carson, was unaware of the possibility of "devilmen" lurking below the springs. The twentieth century obviously is more sensitive to mystical dangers.) Since vampires are attracted to blood but destroyed by a crucifix, Carson has designed a blood-filled plastic cross, thus setting a neat trap.

Most of the new witches and warlocks combine their satanism with drugs, and LSD serves as wine and wafers for their Black Mass. One of the high priestesses ferreted out for *Esquire* by Tom Burke, Princess Leda Amun Ra, says, "I give acid to persons who have never dropped it without telling them. I think of this as the administering of Holy Communion." One of the princess's haunts is a private night club on Hollywood's La Cienega Boulevard where devil-worshipers gather in front of a huge Satan's mask. Late at night she is reputed to preside at bizarre rituals in her temple, a Moorish castle in the Hollywood Hills.

Although California's satanic cults are usually private, Americans had a startling glimpse into one when the home life of the Manson Family was revealed by Linda Kasabian's story of the Sharon Tate murders. The Manson Family, while not a publicly proclaimed coven, reveled in all the forms of witchcraft: a high priest had visions, there was fanatical belief in his magic powers, and with the common confusion of theology that surrounds witchcraft, Manson was variously referred to as "God," "Jesus," and "Satan." There were tales of his being physically and magically transported from one end of the Spahn ranch to the other. Group sexual experience, the usual diversion of covens, was frequent.

The Manson Family is exceptional only in its ability to make headlines and, it now appears, in its indulgence in mass murder. "The Family" was otherwise typical of numberless cults and communes. The public became aware of the Ordi Templar Orientalis when the United Press carried a story about eleven of the cult's members who were brought to trial in Indio, California, after they had chained a six-year-old boy in a sweltering box for fifty-six days. We have received reports from other California cities which show experience of three satanish groups in Berkeley, two of them communes, one in the Big Sur, one in Venice, five in San Francisco, two just north of there, and one in San Diego. The number of satanist-witchcraft circles gathering in Los Angeles County is indeterminate but large.

Members of the covens tell of enjoying all the sensations which have been common to such groups since medieval times: out-of-body travel, illusions of flight, supreme sexual force, and the gift of magical power to destroy one's enemies. Female members have had hallucinatory sexual relations with Satan, a phenomenon notorious throughout the ages. This delusion once sprang from the hysteria of worshiping the Prince of Darkness, but it seems probable that its current vogue is due to a combination of drugs and an emulation of ecstasy in the novel and film *Rosemary's Baby*.

These witches and warlocks, mostly youthful, defiantly announce their rejection of the past while they readopt one of mankind's oldest traditions. A Papal Bull, issued by Pope Innocent VIII in 1488, is surprisingly modern. The Pope outlined the practices then current—devil worship, sexual intercourse with "infernal fiends" by members of both sexes, the desecration of holy symbols such as wearing a crucifix upside down— now a common practice in the "tomorrow" communes in California. The witches of 1488 were also charged with economic crimes: "They blast the corn on the ground, the grapes of the vineyard, the fruits on the trees, the herbs of the fields." Their twentieth-century successors believe they possess similar powers, as when Princess Leda Amun Ra proclaims that she will crush white Anglo-Saxon Christians with Mind Power. (She envisions herself at the head of an army of flower children, a whip in one hand, a cross in the other. For a woman in her position, her knowledge of the dark arts seems vague, or

perhaps it is only a careless manner of expressing herself. She should have specified that the cross would be held in the *left* hand, the whip in the right. All authorities agree that this is the only proper position.)

The Papal Bull of 1488 on satanism led to the establishment of the Inquisition. So far the governor of California has not issued a similar Bull against the covens in his domain, but doubtless such a proclamation will be forthcoming—once the stars are right.

Some Americans traveling abroad have taken their satanism with them. In March 1970, scientists from all over the world gathered on Mexico's Isthmus of Tehuantepec better to view a total solar eclipse. Unexpected entertainment was provided when a cult of expatriate Americans appeared naked in public, their nudity marred only by love beads and mystic signs painted on their jaundiced skins. During the eclipse they danced and capered around a pregnant member of their party, saluting the sun, the powers of darkness, and the gods of fertility. The Mexican government took a dim view of the performance, calling it scandalous and immoral. The authorities did not add that importing witchcraft into Mexico is more wretchedly excessive than taking coal to Newcastle.

Everyone recognizes the popularity of things mystic or psychic. A cartoonist draws a sketch of a distraught hostess checking seating arrangements for a dinner party. "Oh dear!" the lady exclaims. "I *can't* put a Virgo next to a Taurus!" Ten years ago the joke would have been pointless. Today it recognizes that astrology is on the ascendant, a booming belief and business, and all the planets seem to favor its success.

Less than a decade ago when a writer wrote

the letters ESP, he felt called upon to explain that they meant Extra-Sensory-Perception. Today it is taken for granted that the average reader is familiar with the term.

What has been true in the United States has been true in Canada, and the editors of *Maclean's* who devoted most of an issue to psychic studies, summed up the new trend bluntly: "The Western world plainly wants to believe in magic."

Discussion Questions

1. What is the significance of ouija boards outselling Monopoly games?
2. Somerlott claims that "The Western world plainly wants to believe in magic." Why is there a rebirth of occultism?
3. Distinguish between the practitioners of the occult who are poseurs and those who believe they have supernatural powers. Do the latter pose a threat to society?
4. What is Somerlott's attitude toward the occult? Cite passages to illustrate your position.
5. Occultism manifests itself in many ways: ESP, palmistry, numerology, clairvoyance, mesmerism, tarot cards, and others. Research an occult practice and present an oral report to the class.

ASTROLOGY

RICHARD CAVENDISH

Astrology is the study of heavenly bodies in an attempt to foretell future events on earth. While ancient astrologers claimed they could predict earthquakes, plagues, wars, and other historical events, most contemporary astrologers limit themselves to casting horoscopes in order to explain the characters and fates of individuals.

The art of astrology is based on the theory of 'as above, so below', taken literally the belief that all events in the sky are paralleled by corresponding events on earth. Astrologers have connected virtually every important moment in history with movements of the planets, comets or eclipses, and the influence of the stars has been charted in the lives of innumerable people from Alexander the Great to Einstein. Both the birth and the death of Julius Caesar were accompanied by comets, Wellington's defeat of Napoleon at Waterloo has been traced to the positions of Jupiter at Wellington's birth and Saturn at Napoleon's, the First World War was heralded by solar and lunar eclipses and has been linked with the positions of the sun and Mars in 1914, and American involvement in the Second World War was

English-born Richard Cavendish (1930–), formerly an insurance-claims agent, is a writer of novels, screenplays, and nonfiction.

signalled by movements of Mars and Uranus. Modern astrologers believe that observation of the past conclusively proves that certain kinds of events occur on earth when the planets are in certain positions in the sky. 'Nobody', one of them says rather angrily, 'has been able to laugh that one off.'

Astrology is concerned with the future, but its predictions are always based on analysis of the past. Past planetary positions will recur again and the time of their recurrence can be calculated. Astrologers know that Mars takes 687 days to go round the sun. They know what point in its orbit Mars has reached at any given moment and they can discover exactly what its position in the sky was or will be at any time in the past or future. If they find that there have always been dangers of war when Mars was in a certain position in the past, they predict that there will be danger of war again when Mars is in the same position in the future. In the same way, they forecast the effects of the other planets.

The astrologer's universe is like an immense simultaneous chess game. As the great driving forces of the universe move the pieces in the sky, so we are moved from square to square on the chess-boards of our lives. Some modern astrologers believe that the stars, or forces working through them, affect events on earth through vibrations or rays. Others do not attempt to explain the phenomenon at all, but the background to all astrology since classical times is the picture of the soul descending through the spheres to earth and gathering characteristics from each planet on the way. Man is made in the image of the universe. The planetary forces are inside us and each man carries the starry heaven and all its influences within himself.

There seems to be greater public appearance of astrology at the present time than it has enjoyed since the seventeenth century, when it was thrown on to the rubbish heap with much of the rest of medieval science and philosophy. In a disturbing world, many people find modern science and philosophy either unintelligible or inadequate. Astrology offers a comprehensible explanation of human behavior which, if its basic assumptions are granted, is attractively logical and orderly. At the same time it is sufficiently vague and complicated to escape the charge of being too simple an answer. And above all, it provides a convenient scapegoat—the sky—for all human folly, failure and inadequacy.

In the United States over 2,000 newspapers and magazines carry regular astrology columns. In Los Angeles astrologers advertise themselves in the papers, together with spiritual readers, card readers, psychics and the rest. (One recent ad says, 'Partner wanted, must have E.S.P., no investment.') Twenty American magazines deal entirely or mainly with astrology and it has been estimated that 5 per cent of the population fully believe that the future is written in the stars. In France the figure is said to be similar, possibly higher. In Great Britain, where astrologers were lumped with 'charlatans, rogues and vagabonds' in the Witchcraft Act of 1735 and the Vagrancy Act of 1829, the astrologer is still widely regarded as a charlatan, but there is no longer any need for him to be a vagabond. Astrologers have set up their own professional organisations and there are schools which hold courses and set examinations in the subject. Attempts have also been made to elevate the profession's status by use of high-sounding titles—astro-scientist, astro-

Richard Cavendish   213

psychologist, solar biologist, astrologue, astrologian.

In its earliest days in ancient Mesopotamia astrology was concerned with events affecting whole nations and peoples, not with the lives of individuals. The Greeks, who added most of its logical superstructure to astrology, also developed the interest in the fate of individual men and women which has dominated the art ever since. This branch of the subject, natal astrology, is still the most popular today.

Discussion Questions

1. What psychological necessity attracts people to astrology?
2. How does astrology resemble religion?
3. Using one of the many books available on astrology, draw up your own horoscope or the horoscope of a famous person. Or compare the personality traits attributed to a certain sign with the character of a person you know well.

FREE WILL OR NO FREE WILL?: THE ETERNAL QUESTION

JOHN ANTHONY WEST AND JAN GERHARD TOONDER

Men at some times are masters of their fates.
The fault, dear Brutus, is not in our stars
But in ourselves, that we are underlings.
　　　　　　—William Shakespeare, Julius Caesar
　If the stars rule our lives, as the astrologists believe,
what if any freedom do we have to make choices?

When, at a social gathering, the subject of astrology arises, and it is revealed that one is an astrologer, there is a predictable reaction compounded of intense distaff curiosity and equally intense male hostility and disdain. However, if the hostility stops short of a total unwillingness to listen, after the evidence has been sketched in, the question invariably arises: does this mean that we are pre-determined? Is there no free will?

The question is as old as astrology. (And it is this question and its relationship to 'level', time, and Pythagorean principles underlying astrology

John Anthony West (1932–) is an author whose major interests are religion, mysticism, and philosophy. The excerpt here is taken from *The Case for Astrology,* co-authored by Jan Gerhard Toonder (1914–), a prolific writer now working on his sixteenth novel.

that engaged the minds of the ancient philosophers. Astrology's practical applications in medicine, education, the law, etc., important though they may have been, or could conceivably become, were of less interest to these men than the spiritual and philosophical implications of astrology. This preoccupation is by no means as selfish and impractical as it may appear. If men know *why* and *how* they come to be on earth, they stand at least a chance of living amicably upon it. Ultimately, oddly enough, there is nothing so utilitarian, nothing so Benthamite, as the study and practice of astrology—and, of course, of religion, art, philosophy and science—at this *level*.)

Most astrologers—but not all—would assert with some vehemence that free will exists, despite their persistent efforts to use astrology as a means of prophecy.

This is not quite the contradiction in terms that it appears to be. An old astrological saw maintains: 'The stars incline but they do not compel.' There is, however, considerable scope for discussion over the degrees of inclination and compulsion. To what extent are men capable of acting against their own inclinations, if at all? Two examples taken from astrological literature will illustrate the problem. The first is quoted from Madeleine Montalban, the astrologer responsible for the monthly astrological column in *Prediction* magazine:

The advice of the best astrologer in the world is of no avail if you do not abide by it.

A woman once consulted me about herself. She had no particular problems, but just wanted to know what main dangers lay in her map.

I found Jupiter badly affected by planets, place and house and I warned her never to go to law or to ride horses. (Jupiter rules both of these things.)

'Oh, but I love horses and I must ride!' she exclaimed. 'My life would be empty without horses.'

I repeated my warning. For a year she took my advice—and then, lulled by a false sense of security because nothing happened, she went riding. The horse bolted, involved her in an accident with a motor cyclist and both she and the motor cyclist were badly injured. The result was a court case which ended with her having to pay the damages.

She then consulted me as to how to get out of it! There was nothing I could do. The warning had been given in time, the so-called 'hammer blow' was written in her map. She would have avoided it by accepting the original advice given, but had preferred not to do so.

She had freedom of will; the horse had not. Yet she *had* been warned!

Astrologers continually come up against these problems. We can only advise. We cannot alter the course when things have happened.[1]

The second story concerns the astrologer, Alan Leo, who once warned a client that financial troubles were imminent. To avert the danger, the man transferred all his belongings into his wife's name. Three weeks later his wife ran off with the chauffeur.

Could this man have avoided his financial ruin? Was Miss Montalban's client free to keep off horses and away from lawsuits?

Most modern philosophers as well as most astrologers would agree with Miss Montalban that they were. In Sartre's opinion, for example, a waiter is a waiter because at some time he has made the conscious and free decision to become a

---

[1] *Prediction*, April 1968.

216   The Occult

waiter, and this concept is shared by most existentialists.

The linguistic philosopher, Anthony Flew, cites as an example of free will in action a couple who decide to marry, there being no external compulsion forcing them to do so—and this example would meet with little opposition from Flew's particular philosophical school.

It does not seem to matter that common and universal experience testifies to the extreme untenability of these philosophically-determined positions. Does Sartre suppose that the waiter in question could have been a prize fighter? Or a philosopher? Or a neuro-surgeon? A multiplicity of demonstrable genetic and environmental factors cuts the waiter's choice down to waiting and perhaps some equivalent to which his psychological bent and intellectual capacity, as well as his aims—or lack of them—constrain him.

Flew staves off the obvious objection to his example, contending that even if behavioural psychologists should prove that the couple, due to their emotional involvement, could not have refrained from marrying, still, according to common usage of the word 'free', this couple, acting without external compulsion, were acting 'freely', and therefore free will exists.

Yet one need only take the logical opposite of the example to illustrate its weakness—the classical case of unrequited love. Is the forlorn lover 'free' to stop caring for his uncooperative beloved? There is no external force compelling him to suffer. Surely, if 'free will' is as readily available as the logician contends, the unhappy lover need merely avail himself of it.

The *Time* magazine feature on astrology concludes:

The good astrologer senses the mood of his client, perceives his problems, and finds the most positive way of fitting them into the context of his horoscope. Then he looks ahead, shaping his predictions so that they amount to constructive counsel. The client might have been better advised to consult a psychiatrist, marriage counsellor, physician, lawyer or employment agency. But there are many troubled people who refuse to accept personal responsibility for their lives, insisting that some outer force is in control. . .

Yet in the same issue of *Time*, an article describing an Israeli/Egypt flare-up contends: 'These warnings served chiefly to illustrate the fact that violence has a momentum of it own . . . .' Can *Time* have it both ways? If violence has a momentum of its own, then the acceptance or non-acceptance of personal responsibility is irrelevant. And has the author of the astrology feature himself succeeded in accepting personal responsibility for his own life? If so, perhaps he would do well to stop wasting his time denigrating astrology and instead walk over the water to the Middle East to teach them the secret. For it is obvious that if all men would accept personal responsibility for their lives, violence would no longer have a momentum of its own.

In a talk over the BBC[2] Dr Stephen Rose, a biologist, declared: 'The ways to change men's minds permanently are two and only two: by the use of rational argument, and by changing the structure of society. The two great triumphs of humanity are man's capacity for rational thought and discussion, and his capacity to modify society.'

In all of history we can think of no single

---

[2] Reprinted in *Listener*, 7 August 1969.

John Anthony West and Jan Gerhard Toonder   217

instance of a man's mind (to say nothing of men's minds) being permanently changed through rational discussion; nor does Dr Rose's faith in free will seem justifiable. Never in history has the volume and intensity of rational discussion been greater than at the present moment. Yet never before has triumphant mankind been faced simultaneously with the Bomb, CBW [Chemical and Biological Warfare], overpopulation, imminent famine, world-wide pollution and soil depletion, ubiquitous racial strife and that violence that has a momentum of its own. Indeed, the present moment stands as apodictic proof of man's helplessness, of the futility of rational discussion, and of man's shameful *inca*pacity to modify society.

Does this mean, then, that there is no free will after all? Do we exist in a fantastically complex, but pre-determined web of cause-and-effect? This view has its supporters as well, no less emphatic than their opponents.

Philip Barford, an astrologer, declares:

If as astrologers we accept the overall implications of any doctrine of cosmic harmony, then we have also to admit the implication of what we regard as evidence. The solar system is a functional whole, regulated by and manifesting ideal relationships on every plane to which consciousness can ascend. At any single instant in the life of this system, the cosmic mechanism is manifesting a pattern of structural relations entirely and absolutely determined by the initial 'spin' imparted to it at the instant of its ideal conception. Astrologers often like to compromise by stating that astrology simply indicates the prevailing influences and opportunities within which we have freedom to choose between possible alternatives. This is absolutely inconsistent with the basic astrological principle. Any choice made in the conviction of free will is a moment expressing a pre-determined cosmic pattern. Pragmatically, it is impossible to believe in free will and remain an astrologer. Logically, the doctrine of free will is a myth. Our only freedom is the intellectual recognition of necessity. If this conclusion seems unpalatable, one can always reject the notion of cosmic harmony, and with it, any attempt to predict future events or to read character on the map.[3]

But it is not that Mr Barford's conclusion is unpalatable; it is that, despite his pontifical tone, he stands self-condemned. In the very paragraph denying us free will we are already given two opportunities to use it: first, we are told that our only freedom is the intellectual recognition of pre-determination, which is already free will; and then we are given the alternative of rejecting the notion of cosmic harmony, which is also free will.

Barford's conclusion is based upon a bizarre cosmology that would have 'consciousness' bring the solar system into being, impart to it its 'spin' and then vanish, presumably to create other equally cheerless systems. To be consistent, if the solar system is held to be a manifestation of consciousness, then consciousness with its concomitant free will would seem bound to be an attribute of the system itself. Clearly, we are at liberty to use our free will in rejecting Barford's Newtonian notion of Divine Mechanics.

Equally restrained are the views of the well-known geneticist, C.D. Darlington:

In genetics all behaviour is gentically determined, but it is also environmentally determined . . . the division of determination into two systems, genotype (the genetic make-up of the individual) and the environment, entails as a corollary the successive interaction of

---

[3] Philip Barford, *Astrological Journal*, Vol. IV, No. 3, p. 10.

those two systems and the introduction of one into the other. It is this interaction which gives us the illusion of free will . . . a choice seems so to us because in every fresh contingency it is a new reaction of genotype and environment.[4]

Here, those two famous woodland deities, Genotype and Environment, impart that initial 'spin'. Darlington presumes that both these 'systems', though dynamic, are closed. To save beating about the philosophical bush, to destroy this contention it is enough to cite the recent experiments proving that, as the yogis have always maintained, man can gain control over even his involuntary functions. This means that environment can be altered through the exercise of will. Environment is not a closed system. The future is therefore unpredictable, not because of its complexity, but because of its very nature. And free will is not an illusion.

On the other hand, as we have pointed out, humanity's 'great triumph' which is, according to Dr Rose, the capacity to modify society, is reduced to absurdity by every daily newspaper.

It would appear that we have free will and that we do not have it, a situation summed up pithily by Schopenhauer, who declared, 'Man has free will, but not the will to use it.' Since this is a paradox, the contemporary philosopher will dismiss it as nonsense, but to the unrequited lover it makes perfect sense.

Discussion Questions

1. What is free will?
2. Review the example of the waiter who chooses to become a waiter. Answer the theoretical question the authors ask. Apply what you learn from this discussion to persons you know.
3. When does a person exercise free will?
4. Can a person choose when, how, and where he will be born? Do these practical limitations encroach on the concept of free will?
5. How does the question of free will relate astrology to religion.
6. Is it possible for a person to practice both religion and astrology?

---

[4] C. D. Darlington, *Genetics and Man,* Allen & Unwin, 1964.

John Anthony West and Jan Gerhard Toonder   219

WITCHES IN OUR MIDST

DANIEL COHEN

The revival of witchcraft is so widespread that it is possible to buy books on the subject at the neighborhood grocery store. In this essay Daniel Cohen says that modern witches have no power. He explains the power of ancient witches as coming from their knowledge of herbs and poisons and from the gullibility of their victims.

Anyone who wants to meet a witch can manage it without much trouble these days. I've met several recently. You may well have seen a few on television, since 1970 was a big "witch year." These weren't actors or actresses playing "witch" but people who claimed that they really were witches. Contemporary witches give lectures and write books. A couple even teach courses at schools. Witch covens are meeting anywhere from squalid hippie pads to staid suburban living rooms.

There is no doubt that witchcraft is booming today—but what does that mean? Are there *real* witches?

There are no regular degrees offered in witchcraft, nor are there certified, registered or even card-carrying witches. Anybody can call herself

Daniel Cohen edits science magazines and publishes works about science.

or himself a witch. (Although witches traditionally are women, a man can be a witch as well. A warlock is a magician or sorcerer, not a male witch.) The fact is that as long as there are people who want to call themselves witches, then there are witches. But the question, "Are there *real* witches?" implies more. It means (1) do the people who call themselves witches possess some secrets that give them powers denied others and (2) are the people who call themselves witches practicing an ancient religion that has been secretly handed down from generation to generation for thousands of years?

The answer to the first part of the question is a resounding no—witches have no special knowledge or powers. No modern witch has ever offered to fly the Atlantic on a broomstick, nor has any ever been able to change a skeptical critic like myself into a frog (though one half seriously threatened to do just that). While most professional witches claim great powers, they usually will tell you that they do not engage in "vulgar miracle mongering" before non-believers. Regarding their magical power, you just have to take their word for it.

There has been a great deal of confusion about the power of witchcraft due largely to three factors that have been historically associated with witches—poison, drugs and the power of suggestion. In medieval Europe, and in many primitive societies—even in backward parts of civilized countries today—anyone who has a special knowledge of herb or folk medicine might be called a witch. There are well-authenticated cases where a person would pay a reputed witch to get rid of a rival by witchcraft. The witch would "hex" the rival, and just to make sure the hex worked she might manage to slip a little poison into the rival's soup.

Witches might also concoct herbal remedies that were just as good as anything a physician of the day might have. Today, your corner druggist has more power on his shelves than any witch ever had in her potions.

Hallucination-producing drugs have a special relationship to witchcraft. Witch ointments that were supposed to produce all sorts of fantastic effects, including flying, were often mentioned in connection with medieval European witchcraft. But it wasn't the newt's eyes or bat's blood that made these ointments effective. Rather it was belladonna, henbane and other extracts of plants of the nightshade family. Such plant extracts were commonly used as sleep inducing drugs, but they also induce particularly vivid and often terrifying dreams. These drugs can be effective when the leaves of the plants are boiled and drunk as a tea, smoked, or made into a skin ointment. Thus, much of what was reported about the witch's sabbat or other wild witchy doings may really have been the product of drugged fantasies.

Julio Caro Baroja, a Spanish scholar of witchcraft, has observed, "It is these opiates, then, and not flying brooms or animals, that carry the witch off into a world of fantasy and emotion."

Today's witches have a large selection of hallucination-producing drugs at their command. The trappings of witchcraft have become one aspect of today's drug subculture. Today, as in the past, much of what is reported about witchcraft comes from drugged illusion.

The power of suggestion is also responsible for much of the aura of the supernatural surrounding witchcraft. Because of suggestion witchcraft can, to a certain extent, work—if a person believes strongly in it. Obviously, no matter how strong a person's belief he is not going to be able to fly off on a broomstick. But a person who thinks that he is being bewitched, and who really believes in witchcraft can have terrible pains, suffer fits and even die.

Suggestion works best when a large segment of the population believes in witchcraft. There are, for example, well authenticated cases of death from voodoo in Haiti. Voodoo curses and witch-craft hexes are essentially the same. It is doubtful, however, if there are many people in America today who believe deeply enough in witchcraft to obligingly drop dead if someone put a hex on them.

We do not really know enough about how the human mind works to be able to understand exactly how suggestion affects the body. Laboratory experiments in this area have just begun, but enough work has been done to indicate that rats, like men, are highly suggestible. A rat will die for no obvious physical reason when it thinks that death is inevitable. A rat placed in a tank of water will just give up and die before it actually drowns. Yet rats that are used to water don't give up. They keep swimming around—they don't seem to think that death is inevitable, so they don't die. Eventually they may tire and drown—but not from hopelessness or fear.

So while witchcraft may work where people believe strongly in witchcraft, there is nothing supernatural about it.

Discussion Questions

1. Describe modern witchcraft.
2. Poison, drugs, and the power of suggestion played a major role in ancient witchcraft. How has the modern age stripped the witch of power?
3. Why do people play at being witches?

THE WITCH'S VENGEANCE
W. B. SEABROOK

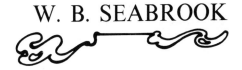

First Witch:	*Thrice the brinded cat hath mew'd.*
Second Witch:	*Thrice and one the hedgepig whined.*
Third Witch:	*Harpier cries "'Tis time, 'tis time."*
First Witch:	*Round about the cauldron go:*
	In the poison'd entrails throw.
	Toad, that under cold stone
	Days and nights has thirty-one
	Swelter'd venom sleeping got,
	Boil thou first i' the charmed pot.
All:	*Double, double toil and trouble;*
	Fire burn and cauldron bubble.

—William Shakespeare, Macbeth

In this story W. B. Seabrook writes of the remnants of witchcraft which still linger in remote and primitive areas.

The quarrel between Mère Tirelou and my young friend Philippe Ardet grew out of the fact that he had fallen in love with Maguelonne, the old woman's granddaughter.

Although Maguelonne was past nineteen, by far the prettiest girl in the village, she had no suitors among the local youths, for the native

---

William Buehler Seabrook (1886–1945) was an explorer and author who studied black magic, witchcraft, and voodoo. He was ostracised by scientists and friends after practicing cannibalism on one of his journeys. He died by his own hand.

W. B. Seabrook 223

peasants of Les Baux, this savage mountain hamlet in the south of France which I had been visiting at intervals for years, were steeped in superstition and believed that old Mère Tirelou was a *sorcière*, a sort of witch.

Maguelonne, orphaned by the war, lived alone with the old woman in an ancient tumbledown stone *mas*, somewhat isolated from the village proper, among the ruins of the seigniorial castle close above it, and gossip whispered that Mère Tirelou had involved the girl, willingly or unwillingly, in her dark practices. They were not persecuted or hated—in fact the peasants and shepards of Les Baux and the surrounding mountainside sometimes consulted Mère Tirelou in certain emergencies—but save for such special consultations, paid for usually with a rabbit, a jug of wine or oil, the old beldam and her granddaughter "apprentice," if such she really was, were generally avoided if not actually disliked and feared.

Philippe, however, who considered himself to be now of the great world—he had been to technical school in Marseilles and was working in an aeroplane plant at Toulon—regarded all this local superstition as stuff and nonsense. He had come up vacationing from Toulon on his motor-cycle. We had known each other at Les Baux the previous summer. He and I were now staying at the same little hotel, the Hotel René, perched on the edge of the cliff, run by Philippe's aunt, Madame Plomb, and her husband Martin. And Philippe, as I have said, had fallen in love with Maguelonne.

This was the situation briefly outlined, when the strange series of events began which first involved me only as a chance onlooker, but finally as an active participant.

They began one hot mid-afternoon when I lay reading in my room, which was in an angle of the wall with windows overlooking the valley and a side window immediately above the medieval rampart gate from which the road serpentined downward.

Close beneath this window, all at once, I heard and recognised Mère Tirelou's querulous croaking voice raised angrily, and Philippe's in reply, half amiable, half derisive.

It was hazard rather than eavesdropping, impossible not to hear them, and then after some muttering the old woman raised her voice again, but this time in such a curious, unnatural tone that I got up to see what was occurring.

They were standing in the sunshine just beneath the window, he tall, blondish, ruddy, tousle-haired, bareheaded, in knickers and sports shirt; she gray, bent and hawk-like—bat-like, rather, in her Arlésienne *coiffe* and cloak, with arms outstretched barring his path. And she was intoning a weird, singsong doggerel, at the same time weaving in the air with her claw-like hands:

> Go down, go down, my pretty youth,
> But you will not come up again.
> Tangled foot will twist and turn,
> And tangled brain will follow.
> You will go down, my pretty one,
> But you will not come up again,
> So tangle, tangle, twist and turn,
> Cobwebs and spider webs are woven.

She was now no longer barring Philippe's path but standing aside, inviting him to pass, so that her back was turned to me, while Philippe stood so that I could see his face and the expressions which flitted over it—first an interested, incredulous, surprised attention as if he couldn't believe his own ears, then a good-humored but derisive and defiant grin as the old woman repeated her doggerel.

"No, no, Mère Tirelou," he said laughing. "You can't scare me off with stuff like that. Better get a broomstick if you want to drive me away. Save your cobwebs and incantations for Bléo and the shepards."

So with a defiant, gay salute and an *au revoir* he was off down the road whistling, while the old woman screamed after him, "Down, down, down you go, but not up, my pretty boy; not up, not up, not up!"

I watched Philippe descending the winding road into the valley while Mère Tirelou, leaning over the parapet, watched him too, until he became tiny far below and disappeared behind the orchard wall which skirts the road by the pavilion of the Reine-Jeanne. Then she picked up her stick, called Bléo her dog, and hobbled in through the gate.

"So," thought I, "that old woman really believes herself a witch, and probably thinks she has put an effective curse on Philippe!"

But it didn't occur to me to be in the least disturbed. I knew, or thought I knew, a good deal about witchcraft technically. I believed it all reduced finally to suggestion and autosuggestion. I had known it to produce tangible results, but only in cases when the victim himself (usually among primitives or savages) was deeply superstitious and consequently amenable to fear. I felt absolutely sure that complete, hard-headed, sceptical disbelief, derision, laughter, constituted a stronger "counter-magic" than any amount of exorcism and holy water, and therefore it did not occur to me for an instant that Philippe could be in the slightest danger.

Holding these convictions, and therefore regarding the safe return of Philippe as a foregone conclusion, I thought little more of the matter that afternoon; finished my reading, dined early, strolled to the top of the cliff to watch the sunset and went early to bed.

Usually after ten o'clock at night the whole village of Les Baux, including the interior of the Hotel René, is sound asleep and silent as the grave. It was the noise of hurrying footsteps clattering along the stone floor of the hotel corridor which awoke me late in the night, but at the same time I heard lowered voices in the road beneath my window, saw lights flashing, heard sabots clacking along the cobbled street.

I struck a light, saw that it was shortly past midnight, dressed and went downstairs. Martin Plomb was talking to a group of neighbours. His wife was standing in the doorway, wrapped in a quilted dressing-gown.

"What has happened?" I asked her.

"We are worried about Philippe," she replied. "He went for a walk this afternoon down in the valley, and he hasn't returned. They are going to search for him. We thought nothing of it that he didn't come back for dinner, but it is now past midnight and we are afraid he may have had an accident."

Already the men, in groups of twos and threes, some with old-fashioned farm lanterns, a few with electric flash lamps, were starting down the mountain side. I joined Martin Plomb, who was at the gate instructing them to go this way or that and to keep in touch with one another by shouting. He himself was going to search upward on the other slope, towards the Grotte des Fées

W. B. Seabrook   225

where Philippe sometimes climbed, fearing that he might have fallen down a ravine. I went along with him. . . .

It was just before dawn, after hours of fruitless search, that we heard a different shouting from the head of the valley. I could not distinguish the words, but Martin immediately said, "They've found him." We worked our way across and climbed toward the road along which we now could see lights flashing, returning toward Les Baux.

They were carrying Philippe on an improvised litter made with two saplings and pine branches interwoven. He was conscious; his eyes were open; but he seemed to be in a stupor and had been unable, they said, to explain what had happened to him. No bones were broken nor had he suffered any other serious physical injury, but his clothes were badly torn, particularly the knees of his knickerbockers, which were ripped and abraded as if he had been dragging himself along on his hands and knees.

They all agreed as to what had probably happened: he had been climbing bareheaded among the rocks in the heat of the late afternoon and had suffered an *insolation*, a prostrating but not fatal sunstroke, had partially recovered and in seeking help, still delirious, had lost his way. He should be all right in a day or two, Martin said. They would have a doctor up from Arles in the morning.

Of course I had thought more than once that night about Mère Tirelou and had considered mentioning the matter to Martin Plomb, but his explanation was so reasonable, adequate, natural, that it seemed to be absurd now to view the episode as anything more than a pure coincidence, so I said nothing.

It was dawn when we reached Les Baux and got Philippe to bed, and when I awoke towards noon the doctor had already come and gone.

"He had a bad stroke," Martin told me. "His head is clear—but there's still something the matter that the doctor couldn't understand. When Philippe tried to get up from the bed, he couldn't walk. Yet his legs aren't injured. It's queer. We are afraid it may be something like paralysis. He seemed to twist and stumble over his own feet."

Sharply, as he spoke, the belated certainty came to be that here was an end to all coincidence; that I had been wrong; that something as sinister and darkly evil as I had ever known in the jungle had been happening here in Les Baux under my very eyes.

"Martin," I said, "something occurred yesterday afternoon which you do not know about. I am not prepared to say yet what it was. But I must see Philippe at once and talk with him. You say his mind is perfectly clear?"

"But assuredly," said Martin, puzzled; "though I can't understand what you're driving at. He will want to see you."

Philippe was in bed. He looked depressed rather than ill, and was certainly in complete possession of his senses.

I said, "Philippe, Martin tells me there is something wrong with your legs. I think perhaps I can tell you what—"

"Why, were you ever a doctor?" he interrupted eagerly. "If we'd known that! The fellow who came up from Arles didn't seem to be much good."

"No, I'm not a doctor. But I'm not sure this is a doctor's job. I want to tell you something. You know where my room is. I happened to be at the window yesterday and I heard and saw everything that occurred between you and Mère Tirelou. Haven't you thought that there may be some connection?"

He stared at me in surprise, and also with a sort of angry disappointment.

"*Tiens!*" he said. "You, an educated modern American, you believe in that fantastic foolishness! Why, I come from these mountains, I was born here, and yet I know that stuff is silly nonsense. I thought about it, of course, but it doesn't make any sense. How could it?"

"Maybe it doesn't," I said, "but just the same will you please tell me as well as you can remember what happened to you yesterday afternoon and last night?"

"Confound it, you know what happened. I had a stroke. And it has left me like this. Lord, I'd rather be dead than crippled or helpless."

He lapsed into sombre silence. But I had heard enough. There are people who have lain paralysed in bed for life through no organic ailment but only because they *believed* they couldn't arise and walk. If I helped him now, it could be only by overwhelming proof. My business was with Mère Tirelou. . . .

Neither the old woman nor her granddaughter had been near the hotel that morning. I climbed the winding cobbled street and tapped at their door. Presently Maguelonne reluctantly opened. I made no effort to enter, but said:

"I've come to see Mère Tirelou—about a serious matter."

She looked at me with worried, guarded eyes, as if uncertain how to answer, and finally said, "She is not here. She went over the mountain last night, beyond Saint-Remy. She will be gone several days." Sensing my doubt, she added defensively, almost pleadingly, "You can come in and see if you wish. She is not here."

The girl was obviously in great distress and I realised that she knew or suspected why I had come.

"In that case," I said, "we must talk. Shall it be like this, or would you prefer to have me come in?"

She motioned me inside.

I said: "Ma'm'selle Maguelonne, I beg you to be honest with me. You know what people say about your grandmother—and there are some who say it also about you. I hope that part isn't true. But your grandmother has done something which I am determined to have undone. I am so certain of what I know that if necessary I am going to take Martin Plomb into my confidence and go with him to the police at Arles. Ma'm'-selle, I feel that you know exactly what I am talking about. It's Philippe—and I want to ask if you—"

"No, no, no!" the girl cried pitifully, interrupting. "I had nothing to do with it! I tried to stop it! I warned him! I begged him not to see me any more. I told him that something dreadful would happen, but he only laughed at me. He doesn't believe in such things. I have helped my grandmother in other things—she has forced me to help her—but never in anything so wicked as this—and against Philippe! No, no, Monsieur, never would I help in such a thing, not even if she—" Suddenly the girl began to sob, "Oh, what ought I to do?"

I said, "Do you mean there is something you could do?"

"I am afraid," she said—"afraid of my grandmother. Oh, if you knew! I don't dare go in

W. B. Seabrook   227

there—and besides, the door is locked—and it may not be in there.''

"Maguelonne," I said gently, "I think you care for Philippe, and I think he cares for you. Do you know that he has lost the use of his legs?''

"Oh, oh, oh!" she sobbed; then she gathered courage and said, "Yes, I will do it, if my grandmother kills me. But you must find something to force the lock, for she always carries the key with her.''

She led me to the kitchen which was at the rear, built into the side of the cliff almost beneath the walls of the old castle ruins. While she was lighting a lamp I found a small hatchet.

"It is through there," she said, pointing to a closet whose entrance was covered by a drawn curtain.

At the back of the closet hidden by some old clothes hung on nails was a small door, locked. It was made of heavy wood, but I had little difficulty forcing the lock, opening the door to disclose a narrow flight of steps, winding downward into the darkness.

(There was nothing mysterious in the fact that such a stairway should exist there. The whole side of the cliff beneath the castle was honeycombed with similar passages.)

The girl went first and I followed close, lighting our way with the lamp held at her shoulder. The short stairway curved sharply downward, then emerged directly into an old forgotten rectangular chamber which at one time must have been a wine cellar or storeroom of the castle. But it now housed various strange and unpleasant objects on which the shadows flickered as I set the lamp in a niche and began to look about me. I had known that actual witches, practising almost in the direct medieval tradition,

still existed in certain parts of Europe, yet I was surprised to see the definite material paraphernalia of the craft so literally surviving.

No need to describe all of it minutely—the place was evil and many of the objects were grotesquely evil; against the opposite wall an altar surmounted by a pair of horns, beneath them "I N R I" reversed with the letters distorted into obscene symbols; dangling nearby a black, shrivelled Hand of Glory—and there on the floor, cunningly contrived with infinite pains, covering a considerable space, was the thing which we had come to find and which, for all my efforts to rationalise, sent a shiver through me as I examined it.

Four upright wooden pegs had been set in the floor, like miniature posts, making a square field about five feet in diameter, surrounded by cords which ran from peg to peg. Within the area and attached to the surrounding cords was stretched a criss-cross, labyrinthine, spiderweb-like maze of cotton thread.

Tangled in its centre like an insect caught in a web was a figure some eight inches high—a common doll, it had been, with china head sewn on its stuffed sawdust body; a doll such as might be bought for three francs in any toy-shop—but whatever baby dress it may have worn when it was purchased had been removed and a costume crudely suggesting a man's plus-four sports garb had been substituted in its place. The eyes of this manikin were bandaged with a narrow strip of black cloth; its feet and legs tangled, fastened, enmeshed in the criss-cross maze of thread.

It slumped, sagging there at an ugly angle, neither upright nor fallen, grotesquely sinister, like the body of a wounded man caught in barbed wire. All this may seem perhaps silly, childish in the telling. But it was not childish. It was vicious, wicked.

I disentangled the manikin gently and examined it carefully to see whether the body had been pierced with pins or needles. But there were none. The old woman had at least stopped short of attempted murder.

And then Maguelonne held it to her breast, sobbing, "Ah, Philippe! Philippe!"

I picked up the lamp and we prepared to come away. The place, however, contained one other object which I have not thus far mentioned and which I now examined more closely. Suspended by a heavy chain from the ceiling was a life-sized, open, cage-like contrivance of wood and blackened leather straps and iron—as perversely devilish a device as twisted human ingenuity ever invented, for I knew its name and use from old engravings in books dealing with the obscure sadistic element in medieval sorcery. It was a Witch's Cradle. And there was something about the straps that made me wonder. . . .

Maguelonne saw me studying it and shuddered.

"Ma'm'selle," I said, "is it possible—?"

"Yes," she answered, hanging her head; "since you have been here there is nothing more to conceal. But it has always been on my part unwillingly."

"But why on earth haven't you denounced her; why haven't you left her?"

"Monsieur," she said, "I have been afraid of what I knew. And where would I go? And besides, she is my grandmother."

I was alone with Philippe in his bedroom. I had brought the manikin with me, wrapped in a bit of newspaper. If this were fiction, I should

have found him magically cured from the moment the threads were disentangled. But magic in reality operates by more devious processes. He was exactly as I had left him, even more depressed. I told him what I had discovered.

He was at the same time sceptical, incredulous and interested, and when I showed him the manikin crudely dressed to represent himself and it became clear to him that Mère Tirelou had deliberately sought to do him a wicked injury, he grew angry, raised up from his pillows and exclaimed:

"Ah, the old hag! She really meant to harm me!"

I judged that the moment had come.

I stood up. I said, "Philippe, forget all this now! Forget all of it and get up! There is only one thing necessary. Believe that you can walk, and you will walk."

He stared at me helplessly, sank back and said, "I do not believe it."

I had failed. His mind lacked, I think, the necessary conscious imagination. But there was one more thing to try.

I said gently: "Philippe, you care for Ma'm'selle Maguelonne, do you not?"

"I love Maguelonne," he replied.

And then I told him brutally, briefly, almost viciously, of the thing that hung there in that cellar—and of its use.

The effect was as violent, as physical, as if I had suddenly struck him in the face. "Ah! Ah! *Tonnerre de Dieu! La coquine! La vilaine coquine!*" he shouted, leaping from his bed like a crazy man.

The rest was simple. Philippe was too angry and concerned about Maguelonne to have much time for surprise or even gratitude at his sudden

W. B. Seabrook   229

complete recovery, but he was sensible enough to realise that for the girl's sake it was better not to make a public row. So, when he went to fetch Maguelonne away he took his aunt with him, and within the hour she was transferred with her belongings to Madame Plomb's room.

Martin Plomb would deal effectively with old Mère Tirelou. He was to make no accusation concerning the part she had played in Philippe's misadventure—an issue difficult of legal proof—but to warn her that if ever she tried to interfere with Maguelonne or the impending marriage he would swear out a criminal warrant against her for ill treatment of a minor ward.

There remain two unsolved elements in this case which require an attempted explanation. The belief which I have always held concerning malevolent magic is that it operates by imposed autosuggestion, and that therefore no incantation can work evil unless the intended victim believes it can. In this case, which seemed to contradict that thesis, I can only suppose that while Philippe's conscious mind reacted with complete scepticism, his unconscious mind (his family came from these mountains) retained certain atavistic, superstitious fears which rendered him vulnerable.

The second element, is of course, the elaborate mummery of the enmeshed manikin, the doll, own cousin to the waxen images which in the Middle Ages were pierced with needles or slowly melted before a fire. The witch herself, if not a charlatan, implicitly believes that there is a literal, supernatural transference of identities.

My own belief is that the image serves simply as a focus for the concentrated, malevolent willpower of the witch. I hold, in short, that sorcery is a real and dangerous force, but that its ultimate explanation lies not in any supernatural realm, but rather in the field of pathological psychology.

Discussion Questions

1. Discuss the power of suggestion in "The Witch's Vengeance."
2. Other than in witchcraft, how can the power of suggestion influence people? Does it play a role in religion?
3. Write a report on one incident in the infamous Salem witch trials where you think the power of suggestion played an important part.

The Goat of the Witches' Sabbath, or Goat of Mendes, after Eliphas Levi.

THE BLACK MASS
RICHARD CAVENDISH

Our Father which wert *in heaven . . .*

—*Satanist Prayer*

The Satanists believe that Christ is a hoax and that He will never return to save the world. Claiming that the devil is the true ruler of the world, they worship him in profane ceremonies.

The Mass is the central ceremony of the Catholic church, founded by Christ himself and reverenced by his followers for hundreds of years. The Protestant Communion services are based on it, though they differ from it in some important ways. Because of its divine origin and its long tradition of sanctity, the Mass has been frequently copied, not always with blasphemous intent. Alchemists wrote alchemical versions of it. Aleister Crowley wrote his own Mass of the Gnostic Catholic Church and also a Mass of the Phoenix, to be said by the magician daily at sunset. The ceremonial of the Hitler Youth meetings closely resembled the form of the Christian service, with the Nazi flag taking the honoured place of the sacrament and quotations from *Mein Kampf* or from Hitler's speeches replacing the Christian Gospel, Epistle and Creed.

"The Black Mass" was originally published in *The Black Arts* in 1967.

As early as the second century A.D., St. Irenaeus accused the Gnostic teacher Marcus, 'an adept in magical impostures', of what seems to have been a perversion of the Mass to the worship of a deity other than the Christian God. He pretended to consecrate cups of wine and 'protracting to great length the word of invocation, he contrives to give them a purple and reddish colour so that Charis [Grace, a name of the divine Thought], who is one of those that are superior to all things, should be thought to drop her own blood into that cup, through means of his invocation, and that those who are present should be led to rejoice to taste of that cup in order that, by so doing, the Charis who is set forth by the magician may also flow into them'.[1]

Occultists ancient and modern, Christian and non-Christian, have generally accepted that the Mass is a magical ritual of great power. 'High Mass', Cyril Scott says, 'is a form of ceremonial magic which has a very definite effect on the inner planes. . . .' It is 'a channel through which the Master Jesus and the World Teacher can pour their spiritual power'.[2] This high regard for the Mass springs from the fact that the ceremony itself appears to be a magical one. It achieves a magical result through magical methods. Ordinary physical things, the bread and the wine, are changed into the Divine and the worshipper consumes the Divine to become one with God.

The transformation of the bread and wine into the body and blood of Christ depends on the magical use of language, the speaking of words charged with force. The transformation, according to the *Catholic Encyclopedia*, 'is produced in virtue of the words "of consecration", pronounced by the priest assuming the person of Christ and using the same ceremonies that Christ used at the Last Supper'.[3] These words are in Latin—*Hoc est enim corpus meum*, 'For this is my body', and *Hic est enim calix sanguinis mei*, 'For this is the chalice of my blood'. Certain accompanying actions are necessary; the words must be spoken by an ordained priest, and if he spoke them in his own person, instead of in the person of Christ, they would not be effective. Nor are they the words spoken by Jesus himself, who did not speak Latin, but from the magician's point of view their use through the centuries has given them effective magical force. That Catholics take a similar view is suggested by the vote of the Ecumenical Council in 1963 to authorise the saying of the Mass in the vernacular provided that the Latin is retained for 'the precise verbal formula which is essential to the sacrament'.[4]

The occult importance of the Mass had been heightened by the fact that Roman Catholics themselves have turned it to all kinds of magical uses. The Gelasian Sacramentary, which contains Roman documents of about the sixth century, includes Masses said to bring good weather, to bring rain, to obtain children, for the protection of someone going on a journey, to ward off diseases of cattle, for a sick person, or to recommend the dead to God's mercy. In 858 Pope Nicholas I condemned the Mass of Judgement, intended to clear or convict a man accused of a crime. The priest would give him communion saying, 'May this Body and Blood of Our Lord

[1] Irenaeus, *Against Heresies*, I. 13.
[2] Scott, *Outline of Modern Occultism*, 115, 126.
[3] *Catholic Encyclopedia*, iv. 277.
[4] This ruling was subsequently changed by the Pope, and the entire Mass is now said in the vernacular.

Richard Cavendish   **233**

Jesus Christ prove thee innocent or guilty of this day.' Saying Mass over cattle or farm tools or fishingboats to bless them and make them productive was common in the Middle Ages and is still practiced today.

· · ·

When it was known that the Mass was sometimes turned to black magical purposes, it was natural to assume that witches and sorcerers used it in the Devil's service, and perhaps they did. A witch tried in southern France in 1594 described the saying of Mass at a sabbath held on St. John's Eve, in a field with about sixty people present. The celebrant wore a black cope with no cross on it and had two women as servers. When the host should have been elevated, after the consecration, he held up a slice of turnip stained black and all cried, 'Master, help us.' Louis Gaufridi, strangled and burned for bewitching Madeleine de Demandolx and another nun of Aix, confessed in 1611 that as Prince of the Synagogue, Lucifer's lieutenant, he had celebrated Mass at the sabbath, sprinking witches with the consecrated wine, at which they cried out *Sanguis eius super nos et filios nostros*—'His blood be upon us and upon our children'.

There were tales of Masses said with black hosts and black chalices, of mocking screams of 'Beelzebub! Beelzebub!' at the consecration. The wine might be water or urine. The host was triangular or hexagonal, generally black but sometimes blood-red. The priest wore a chasuble—the sleeveless outer robe of the priest saying Mass—which might be brown and embroidered with the figures of a pig and a naked woman, or bright scarlet with a green inset showing a bear and a weasel devouring the host, or deep red with a triangle on the back, in which was a black goat with silver horns. The Goat himself might say Mass, reading from a missal with red, white and black pages, bound in wolfskin.

According to Pierre de Lancre, the Devil said Mass, leaving out the Confiteor, or confession of sins, and the Alleluia. He would mumble words from the Mass until he came to the Offertory, the point in the service at which the collection is taken up. His worshippers presented him with offerings of bread, eggs and money. Then the Devil preached them a sermon and afterwards held up a black host which had his symbol impressed on it instead of the symbol of Christ. He said, 'This is my body', and elevated the host by impaling it on one of his horns, at which they all cried out *Aquerra Goity, Aquerra Beyty, Aquerra Goity, Aquerra Beyty*— 'The Goat above, the Goat below; the Goat above the Goat below.' They formed a cross or a semicircle around the altar and prostrated themselves on the ground. Each was given a piece of the host to swallow and 'two mouthfuls of an infernal medicine and brew, of so foul a flavour and smell that they sweated to swallow it, and so cold that it froze them'. After this the Devil coupled with them and the frenzied orgy began.[5]

The witches' Mass was evidently not only a parody of the Christian service but also an adaptation of it to the worship of their own god. The black host bearing the Devil's symbol was mystically his flesh—'This is my body'—and when he elevated it they cried out in adoration of him. The witches seem to have preserved the old custom of communion in both kinds, the wor-

---

5 Murray, *Witch-Cult in West Europe*, 148–9.

shippers receiving the wine as well as the bread, which had been abandoned by Catholics and was later restored by Protestants. They would leave out the confession of sins because they defied the Christian notion of sin and the Alleluia because it was a shout of praise to the Christian God. They became one with their master through the communion of his body and blood and then in sexual union with him, but they probably also felt a fierce sacrilegious thrill in violating the Christian ceremony, which added to the excitement of the orgy.

.   .   .

In eighteenth- and nineteenth-century accounts of the Satanic Mass orgiastic sacrilege and perversion are carried to a point at which the details become unprintable—the worshippers sexually abusing obscene images of Christ and the Virgin or large consecrated hosts split up the middle. The priest follows the Catholic rite closely, but substituting 'Satan' for 'God' and 'evil' for 'good'. Parts of the Mass are read backwards and the Christian prayers are reversed, as in the Satanist version of the Lord's Prayer—'Our Father, which wert in heaven . . . Thy will be done, in heaven as it is on earth . . . Lead us into temptation, and deliver us not from evil . . .' The purpose is both to degrade the Christian service and to transform it, as a ritual of powerful religious and magical force, to the glorification of the Devil. The same is true of the Devil's hosts and wine, said to be made of excreta, menstrual blood or semen, defecated upon or smeared with semen before being crammed into their mouths by the votaries, for the Devil is lord of the body as opposed to the soul, of fertility as opposed to spirituality. That the 'body and blood' of the god are products of the human body is also possibly connected with the magical doctrine that man is potentially God.

The best authority on Satanist ritual in modern times is J.-K. Huysmans. It is not certain that he ever attended a Black Mass, but probable that, as he claimed, he did. He described it in his novel *La Bas*, published in 1891. The hero, Durtal, is taken to a dingy half-dark chapel in a private house, lit by sanctuary lamps hanging from bronze chandeliers with pink pendants of glass. Above the altar is 'an infamous, derisive Christ', its bestial face 'twisted into a mean laugh'. There are black candles on the altar. For incense they burn rue, myrtle, dried nightshade, henbane and the powerfully narcotic thorn-apple. The acolytes and choristers, robed in red, are homosexuals. The Mass is said by an ageing and villainous priest, Canon Docre, wearing a dark red chasuble, beneath which he is naked, and a scarlet cap with two horns of red cloth.

Docre begins the Mass while the choir boys sing the responses and the congregation take the censers and breathe deeply of the intoxicating fumes. Kneeling before the altar, Docre hails Satan as reasonable God, just God, master of slanders, dispenser of the benefits of crime, administrator of luxurious sins and great vices, cordial of the vanquished, suzerain of resentment, accountant of humiliations and treasurer of old hatreds, hope of virility, king of the disinherited, the Son who is to overthrow the inexorable Father. He calls upon the Devil to grant his followers glory, riches and power. Then he curses the execrable Jesus, the impostor and breaker of promises, who was to redeem mankind and has not, who was to appear in glory and has not, who was to intercede for man with the Father and has

Richard Cavendish   235

not. He proclaims that in his quality of priest he will force this do-nothing King and coward God to descend into the host, to be punished by the violation of his body.

While the worshippers writhe and scream hysterically, Docre consecrates and defiles the host in orgasm and hurls it to the floor. The Satanists claw at it, grovelling, tearing off pieces of it and chewing them. Fascinated and appalled, Durtal watches Docre, who, 'frothing with rage, was chewing up sacramental wafers, taking them out of his mouth, wiping himself with them, and distributing them to the women, who ground them underfoot, howling, or fell over each other, struggling to get hold of them and violate them'. Then there is an indiscriminate orgy and Durtal, sickened, creeps away.

This description brings out the Satanist conviction, also found in witchcraft, that Christ is a false god, safely ensconced in heaven, where he cares nothing for humanity, with undertones of the old Gnostic belief that God is far away and has no contact with men, who are under the rule of the Devil. Christianity is a cheat, a quack medicine, and the churches are its hucksters.

The original of Canon Docre was Father Louis Van Haecke, Chaplain of the Holy Blood at Bruges. Huysmans believed that Van Haecke was a Satanist who lured young people into his clutches, corrupted them and initiated them into the mysteries of black magic. He was said to have crosses tattooed on the soles of his feet, so that he continually trod on the symbol of Christ. Sometimes at night fear came upon him and he would scream in panic, recovering himself by lighting all the lamps in the house, yelling diabolical curses and committing horrible blasphemies upon consecrated hosts. The Abbe Boullan, whom Huysmans admired, also appears in *La Bas* in a sympathetic role as Doctor Johannes.

The Black Mass appears more often in fiction than in real life, but there are occasional factual references to it. In 1889 *Le Matin* carried an account by a reporter who had written an article in which he doubted the existence of the Satanic Mass, but had then been invited to one. He was taken to it with blindfolds on his eyes and when they were removed found himself in a dark room with erotic murals. On the altar, surrounded by six black candles, was an image of a goat trampling on a crucifix. The priest wore red robes and the congregation of about fifty men and women chanted hymns. Mass was said on the bare body of a woman stretched on the altar. Black hosts were consecrated and eaten by the worshippers and the ceremony culminated in an orgy. *Le Matin* confirmed that the reporter had really been to this meeting, but would give no further details.

In 1895 a Satanic chapel was discovered in the Palazzo Borghese in Rome. The walls were hung in black and scarlet, and behind the altar was a tapestry of *Lucifer Triumphans*. On the altar were candles and a figure of Satan. The chapel was luxuriously fitted out with prayerdesks and chairs in crimson and gold. It was lit by electricity, glaring down from a huge eye in the ceiling.

Writing in 1940, William Seabrook, a collector of occult experiences, said he had seen Black Masses in London, Paris, Lyons and New York. The Mass is said by an apostate priest, with a prostitute in a scarlet robe as his acolyte. A woman, preferably a virgin, lies naked on the altar before an inverted crucifix. The chalice is placed between her breasts and some of the wine is spilled on her body. After the consecration the host is not elevated but debased and defiled.[6]

A Spanish writer, Julio Caro Baroja, was told about an occurrence in 1942 in the Spanish Basque country. Six men and three women met at a farm, feasted copiously and then stripped themselves naked. They heated up a cauldron of soup and boiled a cat alive in it. They drank the soup, reciting incantations between mouthfuls, and one of them made an altar of planks and parodied the saying of Mass, using slices of sausage as hosts. Through all this, there was much carressing of the women.[7]

In the 1950s there were reports of Black Masses in Italy and in 1963 there were numerous cases of black magic in England. The altar of a church in Sussex had to be rehallowed after four men had been seen performing a mysterious ritual in the church, apparently attempting to summon up evil spirits. A Black Mass was believed to have been said in the church of St. Mary's, Clophill, in Bedfordshire. Apparently, necromancy was also involved, as the graves of six women had been opened and one skeleton was found inside the church.

'When anyone invokes the Devil with intentional ceremonies', said Eliphas Levi, 'the devil comes, and is seen.' But Levi's Devil is not a being existing independently of man, but something called into manifestation by the magician's imagination. There are a few convinced Satanists here and there in the world, but for most modern magicians the Enemy of Christendom cannot exist. According to occult theory, there are forces and intelligences, whether inside or outside the magician, which are conventionally condemned as evil, but a god who is entirely evil is as inconceivable as a god who is entirely good. The true God, the One, is the totality of everything, containing all good and evil, and reconciling all opposites.

To magicians, 'good and evil go round in a wheel that is one thing and not many'. They are two sides of one coin, apparently separate and opposed, but really two aspects of a greater whole. In his attempt to become the whole man, who is God, the magician tries to experience and master all things, whatever their conventional labels. Until he has achieved this by completing the Great Work, it is presumptuous for the magician to speculate on the truth behind the labels, for, as the serpent pointed out in Eden, the knowledge of good and evil belongs to the Divine. Satanism is as harshly rejected by most magicians as it is by Christians. But where the churches, which brought the Devil to life in the first place, condemn his worship as the adoration of evil, magicians despise it as a failure to understand the true nature of the universe.

Discussion Questions

1. Why do so many people believe that the world is under the rule of the devil? Of God?
2. Cavendish claims that Catholics have used the Mass for magical purposes (to bring good weather, to help a sick person). Is intercessory prayer magic?
3. Why do some religious beliefs and practices seem magical?
4. Compare the aims of Satanism with the aims of religion.
5. Discuss the remark that good and evil are so

---

[6] Seabrook, *Witchcraft*, 84.
[7] Baroja, *World of the Witches*, 229–30.

Richard Cavendish   237

interwined that "The true God . . . is the totality of everything, containing all good and all evil . . ."

Reflections

1. Do we live in an age of religious belief, doubt, apathy, or renewal? Explain your answer.
2. "First Confession," "Conversion of the Jews," and "Night" are narrated by young boys. What do we learn about religion from their youthful viewpoint? How can childhood experiences affect religious belief and practice in later life?
3. What relationship exists between religion and the occult?
4. It has been said that if there were no God, man would create one. Does man's interest in the occult reflect a perverted attempt to create a God? Explain.
5. Conduct a discussion with your friends. Query them about their feelings toward the occult and toward religion. Do they think that belief in the occult excludes belief in God? What is your opinion?
6. Describe a personal experience that is unexplainable.
7. Ancient witchcraft was considered to be heretical because it defied the laws of the church. The Manson family is an example of a modern cult which acted in opposition to accepted mores and laws. At present there is no law against witchcraft or Satanism. Should these cults be outlawed again? Explain your answer.

4

FILL THE EARTH AND SUBDUE IT

The importance of technology can not be overemphasized. It is the most significant force in our lives today, one that affects how much food we have, what we wear, where we live, how we travel, and how much we know. Indeed, standard of living can probably be defined in terms of how effectively technology is utilized. A nation such as India which has few technological skills remains an underdeveloped country primarily because it can not adequately feed and house its millions.

Though most people link technology with the twentieth century, this is a misconception. The first cave man who rubbed two sticks together to make a fire was using technology. In the ancient world, technology often reached sophisticated levels. The pyramids of Egypt, the aqueducts of Rome, and the Gothic cathedrals of Europe were designed by skilled engineers. However, the rate of technological growth in the twentieth century supersedes all previous ages. As Alvin Toffler tells us in "The 800th Lifetime," "the overwhelming majority of all the material goods we use in daily life" have been developed in the last sixty years. This growth is the result of the technological engine, which has greatly shortened the time between the creative idea and its development and distribution. In "The Accelerative Thrust" Toffler describes this feverish process.

The major question facing mankind today is how to control technology so that it will become the servant of society rather than its master. Ironically, technology is so demanding of our natural resources and environment that it threatens to destroy the quality of life it helped to create.

As Loren Eiseley warns in "The World Eaters" and Paul R. Ehrlich and Richard L. Harriman reiterate in "Spaceship in Trouble," we can not continue to squander the nonreplenishable resources of the earth. Some critics of the ecologists, such as James V. Schall, consider the antipollution movement to be a fad. In "Ecology—An American Heresy?" Schall argues for man's primacy in nature. It is in Genesis that we find the dictum which places man above the natural world: "Increase and multiply, and fill the earth, and subdue it, and rule over the fishes of the sea, and the fowls of the air, and all living creatures that move upon the earth." According to Lynn White, Jr., in "Medieval View of Man and Nature," this concept has permitted man—especially in Western civilization—to exploit nature. In contrast, primitive man saw himself as a part of nature, taking only what he needed to survive. The

Kwakiutl "Prayer to the Young Cedar" and John Haines' poem "The Legend of Paper Plates" illustrate these different attitudes. Philip Handler's "In Man's View of Himself" points out that man now understands the interrelatedness of life. In the future it will be his responsibility to use wisely his dominion over the earth.

No other area of technology has advanced as dramatically in the 800th lifetime as agriculture. Since the turn of the century, farming has changed more than in all the preceding millennia. In the past a farmer produced enough food for himself and three other people. Today he is capable of supplying forty-two. This phenomenal growth in productivity results in a dwindling number of farmers working fewer and larger farms. The men who have been displaced from the soil have migrated to the cities. Peter Drucker discusses the implications of this exodus in "Man Moves into a Man-made Environment." However, the farmer is not alone in seeking his future in the city. Foreign immigrants usually settled in populated areas creating "Neighborhood-towns." Mike Royko describes these self-contained ethnic communities. However, it is from Charlotte Leon Mayerson's description of Juan Gonzales and Peter Quinn, two seventeen-year-old boys who live two blocks apart in New York City, that we come to understand the separateness of people who should be neighbors and friends.

As the knowledge explosion fuels the technological engine, man faces a new problem. He must seek to determine his value in an age when machines, especially computers, displace him in the work force. Three selections, Louis B. Salomon's "Univac to Univac," Norbert Wiener's "God and Golem, Inc.," and John Diebold's "Man and the Computer" explore man's relationship to the computer.

Another concern which will engage theologians, moralists, and legislators in the near future is man's increasing capability of controlling human reproduction. In "Runaway Biology?" Gerald Leach poses crucial questions concerning "carbon-copy children," sperm banks, sex choice of children, and "test-tube babies."

Toffler warns that we are racing pell-mell into the future. While many scientists conjure up glowing descriptions of the marvels of the year 2000, few concern themselves with the process of reaching the golden age. In "A Look at the Year 2000," Jacques Ellul faults the scientists for their optimism and accuses them of underestimating the problems of the interim period. Having achieved the 800th

lifetime, man now faces the challenge of creating a livable and humane 801st
lifetime.

242   Fill the Earth and Subdue It

GENESIS:
CREATION OF MAN

26 And he said: Let us make man to our image and likeness; and let him have dominion over the fishes of the sea, and the fowls of the air, and the beasts, and the whole earth, and every creeping creature that moveth upon the earth. *27* And God created man to his own image; to the image of God he created him. Male and female he created them. *28* And God blessed them, saying: Increase and multiply, and fill the earth, and subdue it, and rule over the fishes of the sea, and the fowls of the air, and all living creatures that move upon the earth. *29* And God said: Behold I have given you every herb bearing seed upon the earth, and all trees that have in themselves seed of their own kind, to be your meat. *30* And to all beasts of the earth, and to every fowl of the air, and to all that move upon the earth, and wherein there is life, that they may have to feed upon. And it was so done. *31* And God saw all the things that he had made, and they were very good. And the evening and morning were the sixth day.

Genesis I: 26–31.

Discussion Question

1. According to this passage from Genesis, what is man's relationship to the earth? Is man now developing a new perspective? Does this new perspective undermine the credibility of Genesis? Explain your answer.

THE 800TH LIFETIME
ALVIN TOFFLER

It has been observed . . . that if the last 50,000 years of man's existence were divided into lifetimes of approximately sixty-two years each, there have been about 800 such lifetimes. Of these 800, fully 650 were spent in caves. Only during the last seventy lifetimes has it been possible to communicate effectively from one lifetime to another—as writing has made it possible to do. Only during the last six lifetimes did masses of man ever see a printed word. Only during the last four has it been possible to measure time with any precision. Only in the last two has anyone used an electric motor. And the overwhelming majority of all the material goods we use in daily life today have been developed within the present, the 800th, lifetime.

"The 800th Lifetime" is taken from *Future Shock*.

Discussion Questions

1. List a variety of modern conveniences and some recent technological advances. Interview a senior citizen and ask him how many of the items on your list were not available when he was a teenager. How does he feel about these innovations? Would he prefer to live in the good old days?

2. What modern conveniences would you be willing to give up?

THE ACCELERATIVE THRUST
ALVIN TOFFLER

While "The 800th Lifetime" emphasizes how much our society has progressed, "The Accelerative Thrust" describes how the technological revolution works.

Early in March, 1967, in eastern Canada, an eleven-year-old child died of old age.

Ricky Gallant was only eleven years old chronologically, but he suffered from an odd disease called progeria—advanced aging—and he exhibited many of the characteristics of a ninety-year-old person. The symptoms of progeria are senility, hardened arteries, baldness, slack and wrinkled skin. In effect, Ricky was an old man when he died, a long lifetime of biological change having been packed into his eleven short years.

Cases of progeria are extremely rare. Yet in a metaphorical sense the high technology societies all suffer from this peculiar ailment. They are not growing old or senile. But they *are* experiencing super-normal rates of change.

Many of us have a vague "feeling" that things are moving faster. Doctors and executives alike complain that they cannot keep up with the latest developments in their fields. Hardly a meeting or conference takes place today without some ritualistic oratory about "the challenge of change."

"The Accelerative Thrust" is also taken from *Future Shock*.

Among many there is an uneasy mood—a suspicion that change is out of control.

Not everyone, however, shares this anxiety. Millions sleepwalk their way through their lives as if nothing had changed since the 1930's, and as if nothing ever will. Living in what is certainly one of the most exciting periods in human history, they attempt to withdraw from it, to block it out, as if it were possible to make it go away by ignoring it. They seek a "separate peace," a diplomatic immunity from change.

One sees them everywhere: Old people, resigned to living out their years, attempting to avoid, at any cost, the intrusions of the new. Already-old people of thirty-five and forty-five, nervous about student riots, sex, LSD, or miniskirts, feverishly attempting to persuade themselves that, after all, youth was always rebellious, and that what is happening today is no different from the past. Even among the young we find an incomprehension of change: students so ignorant of the past that they see nothing unusual about the present.

The disturbing fact is that the vast majority of people, including educated and otherwise sophisticated people, find the idea of change so threatening that they attempt to deny its existence. Even many people who understand intellectually that change is accelerating, have not internalized that knowledge, do not take this critical social fact into account in planning their own personal lives.

TIME AND CHANGE

How do we *know* that change is accelerating? There is, after all, no absolute way to measure change. In the awesome complexity of the universe, even within any given society, a virtually infinite number of streams of change occur simultaneously. All "things"—from the tiniest virus to the greatest galaxy—are, in reality, not things at all, but processes. There is no static point, no nirvana-like un-change, against which to measure change. Change is, therefore, necessarily relative.

It is also uneven. If all processes occurred at the same speed, or even if they accelerated or decelerated in unison, it would be impossible to observe change. The future, however, invades the present at differing speeds. Thus it becomes possible to compare the speed of different processes as they unfold. We know, for example, that compared with the biological evolution of the species, cultural and social evolution is extremely rapid. We know that some societies transform themselves technologically or economically more rapidly than others. We also know that different sectors within the same society exhibit different rates of change—the disparity that William Ogburn labeled "cultural lag." It is precisely the unevenness of change that makes it measurable.

We need, however, a yardstick that makes it possible to compare highly diverse processes, and this yardstick is time. Without time, change has no meaning. And without change, time would stop. Time can be conceived as the intervals during which events occur. Just as money permits us to place a value on both apples and oranges, time permits us to compare unlike processes. When we say that it takes three years to build a dam, we are really saying it takes three times as long as it takes the earth to circle the sun or 31,000,000 times as long as it takes to sharpen a pencil. Time is the currency of exchange that makes it possible to compare the rates at which very different processes play themselves out.

Given the unevenness of change and armed with this yardstick, we still face exhausting difficulties in measuring change. When we speak of the rate of change, we refer to the number of events crowded into an arbitrarily fixed interval of time. Thus we need to define the "events." We need to select our intervals with precision. We need to be careful about the conclusions we draw from the differences we observe. Moreover, in the measurement of change, we are today far more advanced with respect to physical processes than social processes. We know far better, for example, how to measure the rate at which blood flows through the body than the rate at which a rumor flows through society.

Even with all these qualifications, however, there is widespread agreement, reaching from historians and archaeologists all across the spectrum to scientists, sociologists, economists and psychologists, that many social processes are speeding up—strikingly, even spectacularly.

SUBTERRANEAN CITIES

Painting with the broadest of brush strokes, biologist Julian Huxley informs us that "The tempo of human evolution during recorded history is at least 100,000 times as rapid as that of pre-human evolution." Inventions or improvements of a magnitude that took perhaps 50,000 years to accomplish during the early Paleolithic era were, he says, "run through in a mere millennium toward its close; and with the advent of settled civilization, the unit of change soon became reduced to the century." The rate of change, accelerating throughout the past 5000 years, has become, in his words, "particularly noticeable during the past 300 years."

C. P. Snow, the novelist and scientist, also comments on the new visibility of change. "Until this century . . ." he writes, social change was "so slow, that it would pass unnoticed in one person's lifetime. That is no longer so. The rate of change has increased so much that our imagination can't keep up." Indeed, says social psychologist Warren Bennis, the throttle has been pushed so far forward in recent years that "No exaggeration, no hyperbole, no outrage can realistically describe the extent and pace of change. . . . In fact, only the exaggerations appear to be true."

What changes justify such super-charged language? Let us look at a few—change in the process by which man forms cities, for example. We are now undergoing the most extensive and rapid urbanization the world has ever seen. In 1850 only four cities on the face of the earth had a population of 1,000,000 or more. By 1900 the number had increased to nineteen. But by 1960, there were 141, and today world urban population is rocketing upward at a rate of 6.5 percent per year, according to Edgar de Vries and J. P. Thysse of the Institute of Social Science in the Hague. This single stark statistic means a doubling of the earth's urban population within eleven years.

One way to grasp the meaning of change on so phenomenal a scale is to imagine what would happen if all existing cities, instead of expanding, retained their present size. If this were so, in order to accommodate the new urban millions we would have to build a duplicate city for each of the hundreds that already dot the globe. A new

Alvin Toffler   251

Tokyo, a new Hamburg, a new Rome and Rangoon—and all within eleven years. (This explains why French urban planners are sketching subterranean cities—stores, museums, warehouses and factories to be built under the earth, and why a Japanese architect has blueprinted a city to be built on stilts out over the ocean.)

The same accelerative tendency is instantly apparent in man's consumption of energy. Dr. Homi Bhabha, the late Indian atomic scientist who chaired the first International Conference on the Peaceful Uses of Atomic Energy, once analyzed this trend. "To illustrate," he said, "let us use the letter 'Q' to stand for the energy derived from burning some 33,000 million tons of coal. In the eighteen and one half centuries after Christ, the total energy consumed averaged less than one half Q per century. But by 1850, the rate had risen to one Q per century. Today, the rate is about ten Q per century." This means, roughly speaking, that half of all the energy consumed by man in the past 2,000 years has been consumed in the last one hundred.

Also dramatically evident is the acceleration of economic growth in the nations now racing toward super-industrialism. Despite the fact that they start from a large industrial base, the annual percentage increases in production in these countries are formidable. And the rate of increase is itself increasing.

In France, for example, in the twenty-nine years between 1910 and the outbreak of the second world war, industrial production rose only 5 percent. Yet between 1948 and 1965, in only seventeen years, it increased by roughly 220 percent. Today growth rates of from 5 to 10 percent per year are not uncommon among the most industrialized nations. There are ups and downs, of course. But the direction of change has been unmistakable.

Thus for the twenty-one countries belonging to the Organization for Economic Cooperation and Development—by and large, the "have" nations—the average annual rate of increase in gross national product in the years 1960–1968 ran between 4.5 and 5.0 percent. The United States grew at a rate of 4.5 percent, and Japan led the rest with annual increases averaging 9.8 percent.

What such numbers imply is nothing less revolutionary than a doubling of the total output of goods and services in the advanced societies about every fifteen years—and the doubling times are shrinking. This means, generally speaking, that the child reaching teen age in any of these societies is literally surrounded by twice as much of everything newly man-made as his parents were at the time he was an infant. It means that by the time today's teen-ager reaches age thirty, perhaps earlier, a second doubling will have occurred. Within a seventy-year lifetime, perhaps five such doublings will take place—meaning, since the increases are compounded, that by the time the individual reaches old age the society around him will be producing thirty-two times as much as when he was born.

Such changes in the ratio between old and new have . . . an electric impact on the habits, beliefs, and self-image of millions. Never in previous history has this ratio been transformed so radically in so brief a flick of time.

THE TECHNOLOGICAL ENGINE

Behind such prodigious economic facts lies that great, growling engine of change—technology.

This is not to say that technology is the only source of change in society. Social upheavals can be touched off by a change in the chemical composition of the atmosphere, by alterations in climate, by changes in fertility, and many other factors. Yet technology is indisputably a major force behind the accelerative thrust.

To most people the term technology conjures up images of smoky steel mills or clanking machines. Perhaps the classic symbol of technology is still the assembly line created by Henry Ford half a century ago and made into a potent social icon by Charlie Chaplin in *Modern Times*. This symbol, however, has always been inadequate, indeed, misleading, for technology has always been more than factories and machines. The invention of the horse collar in the middle ages led to major changes in agricultural methods and was as much a technological advance as the invention of the Bessemer furnace centuries later. Moreover, technology includes techniques, as well as the machines that may or may not be necessary to apply them. It includes ways to make chemical reactions occur, ways to breed fish, plant forests, light theaters, count votes or teach history.

The old symbols of technology are even more misleading today, when the most advanced technological processes are carried out far from assembly lines or open hearths. Indeed, in electronics, in space technology, in most of the new industries, relative silence and clean surroundings are characteristic—even sometimes essential. And the assembly line—the organization of armies of men to carry out simple repetitive functions—is an anachronism. It is time for our symbols of technology to change—to catch up with the quickening changes in technology, itself.

This acceleration is frequently dramatized by a thumbnail account of the progress in transportation. It has been pointed out, for example, that in 600 B.C. the fastest transportation available to man over long distances was the camel caravan, averaging eight miles per hour. It was not until about 1600 B.C. when the chariot was invented that the maximum speed was raised to roughly twenty miles per hour.

So impressive was this invention, so difficult was it to exceed this speed limit, that nearly 3,500 years later, when the first mail coach began operating in England in 1784, it averaged a mere ten mph. The first steam locomotive, introduced in 1825, could muster a top speed of only thirteen mph, and the great sailing ships of the time labored along at less than half that speed. It was probably not until the 1880's that man, with the help of a more advanced steam locomotive, managed to reach a speed of one hundred mph. It took the human race millions of years to attain that record.

It took only fifty-eight years, however, to quadruple the limit, so that by 1938 airborne man was cracking the 400-mph line. It took a mere twenty-year flick of time to double the limit again. And by the 1960's rocket planes approached speeds of 4000 mph, and men in space capsules were circling the earth at 18,000 mph. Plotted on a graph, the line representing progress in the past generation would leap vertically off the page.

Whether we examine distances traveled, altitudes reached, minerals mined, or explosive power harnessed, the same accelerative trend is obvious. The pattern, here and in a thousand other statistical series, is absolutely clear and unmistakable. Millennia or centuries go by, and then, in our own times, a sudden bursting of the limits, a fantastic spurt forward.

The reason for this is that technology feeds on itself. Technology makes more technology possible, as we can see if we look for a moment at the process of innovation. Technological innovation consists of three stages, linked together into a self-reinforcing cycle. First, there is the creative, feasible idea. Second, its practical application. Third, its diffusion through society.

The process is completed, the loop closed, when the diffusion of technology embodying the new idea, in turn, helps generate new creative ideas. Today there is evidence that the time between each of the steps in this cycle has been shortened.

Thus it is not merely true, as frequently noted, that 90 percent of all the scientists who ever lived are now alive, and that new scientific discoveries are being made every day. These new ideas are put to work much more quickly than ever before. The time between original concept and practical use has been radically reduced. This is a striking difference between outselves and our ancestors. Appollonius of Perga discovered conic sections, but it was 2000 years before they were applied to engineering problems. It was literally centuries between the time Paracelsus discovered that ether could be used as an anaesthetic and the time it began to be used for that purpose.

Even in more recent times the same pattern of delay was present. In 1836 a machine was invented that mowed, threshed, tied straw into sheaves and poured grain into sacks. This machine was itself based on technology at least twenty years old at the time. Yet it was not until a century later, in 1930's, that such a combine was actually marketed. The first English patent for a typewriter was issued in 1714. But a century and a half elapsed before typewriters became commercially available. A full century passed between the time Nicholas Appert discovered how to can food and the time canning became important in the food industry.

Today such delays between idea and application are almost unthinkable. It is not that we are more eager or less lazy than our ancestors, but we have, with the passage of time, invented all sorts of social devices to hasten the process. Thus we find that the time between the first and second stages of the innovative cycle—between idea and application—has been cut radically. Frank Lynn, for example, in studying twenty major innovations, such as frozen food, antibiotics, integrated circuits and synthetic leather, found that since the beginning of this century more than sixty percent has been slashed from the average time needed for a major scientific discovery to be translated into a useful technological form. Today a vast and growing research and development industry is consciously working to reduce the lag still further.

But if it takes less time to bring a new idea to the marketplace, it also takes less time for it to sweep through the society. Thus the interval between the second and third stages of the cycle—between application and diffusion—has likewise been sliced, and the pace of diffusion is rising with astonishing speed. This is borne out by the history of several familiar household appliances. Robert B. Young at the Stanford Research Institute has studied the span of time between the first commercial appearance of a new electrical appliance and the time the industry manufacturing it reaches peak production of the item.

Young found that for a group of appliances introduced in the United States before 1920—

including the vacuum cleaner, the electric range, and the refrigerator—the average span between introduction and peak production was thirty-four years. But for a group that appeared in the 1939-1959 period—including the electric frying pan, television, and washer-dryer combination—the span was only eight years. The lag had shrunk by more than 76 percent. "The post-war group," Young declared, "demonstrated vividly the rapidly accelerating nature of the modern cycle."

The stepped-up pace of invention, exploitation, and diffusion, in turn, accelerates the whole cycle still further. For new machines or techniques are not merely a product, but a source, of fresh creative ideas.

Each new machine or technique, in a sense, changes all existing machines and techniques, by permitting us to put them together into new combinations. The number of possible combinations rises exponentially as the number of new machines or techniques rises arithmetically. Indeed, each new combination may, itself, be regarded as a new super-machine.

The computer, for example, made possible a sophisticated space effort. Linked with sensing devices, communications equipment, and power sources, the computer became part of a configuration that in aggregate forms a single new super-machine—a machine for reaching into and probing outer space. But for machines or techniques to be combined in new ways, they have to be altered, adapted, refined or otherwise changed. So that the very effort to integrate machines into super-machines compels us to make still further technological innovations.

It is vital to understand, moreover, that technological innovation does not merely combine and recombine machines and techniques.

Important new machines do more than suggest or compel changes in other machines—they suggest novel solutions to social, philosophical, even personal problems. They alter man's total intellectual environment—the way he thinks and looks at the world.

We all learn from our environment, scanning it constantly—though perhaps unconsciously—for models to emulate. These models are not only other people. They are, increasingly, machines. By their presence, we are subtly conditioned to think along certain lines. It has been observed, for example, that the clock came along before the Newtonian image of the world as a great clock-like mechanism, a philosophical notion that has had the utmost impact on man's intellectual development. Implied in this image of the cosmos as a great clock were ideas about cause and effect and about the importance of external, as against internal, stimuli, that shape the everyday behavior of all of us today. The clock also affected our conception of time so that the idea that a day is divided into twenty-four equal segments of sixty minutes each has become almost literally a part of us.

Recently, the computer has touched off a storm of fresh ideas about man as an interacting part of larger systems, about his physiology, the way he learns, the way he remembers, the way he makes decisions. Virtually every intellectual discipline from political science to family psychology has been hit by a wave of imaginative hypotheses triggered by the invention and diffusion of the computer—and its full impact has not yet struck. And so the innovative cycle, feeding on itself, speeds up.

If technology, however, is to be regarded as a great engine, a mighty accelerator, then knowledge must be regarded as its fuel. And we thus come to the crux of the accelerative process in society, for the engine is being fed a richer and richer fuel every day.

KNOWLEDGE AS FUEL

The rate at which man has been storing up useful knowledge about himself and the universe has been spiraling upward for 10,000 years. The rate took a sharp upward leap with the invention of writing, but even so it remained painfully slow over centuries of time. The next great leap forward in knowledge-acquisition did not occur until the invention of movable type in the fifteenth century by Gutenberg and others. Prior to 1500, by the most optimistic estimates, Europe was producing books at a rate of 1000 titles per year. This means, give or take a bit, that it would take a full century to produce a library of 100,000 titles. By 1950, four and a half centuries later, the rate had accelerated so sharply that Europe was producing 120,000 titles a year. What once took a century now took only ten months. By 1960, a single decade later, the rate had made another significant jump, so that a century's work could be completed in seven and a half months. And, by the mid-sixties, the output of books on a world scale, Europe included, approached the prodigious figure of 1000 titles per *day*.

One can hardly argue that every book is a net gain for the advancement of knowledge. Nevertheless, we find that the accelerative curve in book publication does, in fact, crudely parallel the rate at which man discovered new knowledge. For example, prior to Guttenberg only 11 chem-

ical elements were known. Antimony, the 12th, was discovered at about the time he was working on his invention. It was fully 200 years since the 11th, arsenic, had been discovered. Had the same rate of discovery continued, we would by now have added only two or three additional elements to the periodic table since Gutenberg. Instead, in the 450 years after his time, some seventy additional elements were discovered. And since 1900 we have been isolating the remaining elements not at a rate of one every two centuries, but of one every three years.

Furthermore, there is reason to believe that the rate is still rising sharply. Today, for example, the number of scientific journals and articles is doubling, like industrial production in the advanced countries, about every fifteen years, and according to biochemist Philip Siekevitz, "what has been learned in the last three decades about the nature of living beings dwarfs in extent of knowledge any comparable period of scientific discovery in the history of mankind." Today the United States government alone generates 100,000 reports each year, plus 450,000 articles, books and papers. On a worldwide basis, scientific and technical literature mounts at a rate of some 60,000,000 pages a year.

The computer burst upon the scene around 1950. With its unprecedented power for analysis and dissemination of extremely varied kinds of data in unbelievable quantities and at mind-staggering speeds, it has become a major force behind the latest acceleration in knowledge-acquisition. Combined with other increasingly powerful analytical tools for observing the invisible universe around us, it has raised the rate of knowledge-acquisition to dumbfounding speeds.

Francis Bacon told us that "Knowledge . . . is

power." This can now be translated into contemporary terms. In our social setting, "Knowledge is change"—and accelerating knowledge-acquisition, fueling the great engines of technology, means accelerating change.

THE FLOW OF SITUATIONS

Discovery. Application. Impact. Discovery. We see here a chain reaction of change, a long, sharply rising curve of acceleration in human social development. This accelerative thrust has now reached a level at which it can no longer, by any stretch of the imagination, be regarded as "normal." The normal institutions of industrial society can no longer contain it, and its impact is shaking up all our social institutions. Acceleration is one of the most important and least understood of all social forces.

This, however, is only half the story. For the speed-up of change is a psychological force as well. Although it has been almost totally ignored by psychology, the rising rate of change in the world around us disturbs our inner equilibrium, altering the very way in which we experience life. Acceleration without translates into acceleration within.

This can be illustrated, though in a highly oversimplified fashion, if we think of an individual life as a great channel through which experience flows. This flow of experience consists—or is conceived of consisting—of innumerable "situations." Acceleration of change in the surrounding society drastically alters the flow of situations through this channel.

There is no neat definition of a situation, yet we would find it impossible to cope with experience if we did not mentally cut it up into these manageable units. Moreover, while the boundary lines between situations may be indistinct, every situation has a certain "wholeness" about it, a certain integration.

Every situation also has certain identifiable components. These include "things"—a physical setting of natural or man-made objects. Every situation occurs in a "place"—a location or arena within which the action occurs. (It is not accidental that the Latin root "situ" means place.) Every social situation also has, by definition, a cast of characters—people. Situations also involve a location in the organizational network of society and a context of ideas or information. Any situation can be analyzed in terms of these five components.

But situations also involve a separate dimension which, because it cuts across all the others, is frequently overlooked. This is duration—the span of time over which the situation occurs. Two situations alike in all other respects are not the same at all if one lasts longer than another. For time enters into the mix in a crucial way, changing the meaning or content of situations. Just as the funeral march played at too high a speed becomes a merry tinkle of sounds, so a situation that is dragged out has a distinctly different flavor or meaning than one that strikes us in staccato fashion, erupting suddenly and subsiding as quickly.

Here, then, is the first delicate point at which the accelerative thrust in the larger society crashes up against the ordinary daily experience of the contemporary individual. For the acceleration of change, as we shall show, shortens the duration of many situations. This not only drastically alters their "flavor," but hastens their passage through the experiential channel. Compared with life in a less rapidly changing society, more situations now flow through the channel in any given interval of time—and this implies profound changes in human psychology.

For while we tend to focus on only one situation at a time, the increased rate at which situations flow past us vastly complicates the entire structure of life, multiplying the number of roles we must play and the number of choices we are forced to make. This, in turn, accounts for the choking sense of complexity about contemporary life.

Moreover, the speeded-up flow-through of situations demands much more work from the complex focusing mechanisms by which we shift our attention from one situation to another. There is more switching back and forth, less time for extended, peaceful attention to one problem or situation at a time. This is what lies behind the vague feeling . . . that "Things are moving faster." They are. Around us. And through us.

There is, however, still another, even more powerfully significant way in which the acceleration of change in society increases the difficulty of coping with life. This stems from the fantastic instrusion of novelty, newness into our existence. Each situation is unique. But situations often resemble one another. This, in fact, is what makes it possible to learn from experience. If each situation were wholly novel, without some resemblance to previously experienced situations, our ability to cope would be hopelessly crippled.

The acceleration of change, however, radically alters the balance between novel and familiar situations. Rising rates of change thus compel us not merely to cope with a faster flow, but with more and more situations to which previous personal experience does not apply. And the psychological implications of this simple fact . . . are nothing short of explosive.

"When things start changing outside, you are going to have a parallel change taking place inside," says Christopher Wright of the Institute for the Study of Science in Human Affairs. The nature of these inner changes is so profound, however, that, as the accelerative thrust picks up speed, it will test our ability to live within the parameters that have until now defined man and society. In the words of psychoanalyst Erik Erikson, "In our society at present, the 'natural course of events' is precisely that the rate of change should continue to accelerate up to the as-yet-unreached limits of human and institutional adaptability."

Discussion Questions

1. Toffler says that the vast majority of people find change so threatening that they deny its existence. To which segments of society is he referring? Do you agree with his generalization?
2. What is Toffler's definition of time?
3. How do we measure change? What major changes have you witnessed in the last ten years?
4. How many stages are there in technological innovation? Discuss each step.
5. How does knowledge aid "The Accelerative Thrust"?
6. How does the "flow of situations" affect individuals?
7. Do you know any individual who has been unable to cope with the pace of life? Describe him.

man and the earth

THE WORLD EATERS
LOREN EISELEY

The United States at present, representing some six percent of the world's population, consumes over thirty-four percent of its energy and twenty-nine percent of its steel. Over a billion pounds of trash are spewed over the landscape in a single year. In these few elementary facts, which are capable of endless multiplication, one can see the shape of the future growing—the future of a planet virus *Homo sapiens* as he assumes in his technological phase what threatens to be his final role.

Experts have been at pains to point out that the accessible crust of the earth is finite, while the demand for minerals steadily increases as more and more societies seek for themselves a higher, Westernized standard of living. Unfortunately many of these sought-after minerals are not renewable, yet a viable industrial economy demands their steady output. A rising world population requiring an improved standard of living clashes with the oncoming realities of a planet of impoverished resources.

"The World Eaters" was originally published in *The Invisible Pyramid* in 1970.

Discussion Questions

1. What are the major implications of this excerpt?

2. Given the limited resources of the world, why does man allocate such a large percentage of them for war?

"Excuse me, sir. I am prepared to make you a rather
attractive offer for your square."

SPACESHIP IN TROUBLE
PAUL R. EHRLICH AND RICHARD L. HARRIMAN

We travel together, passengers on a little spaceship, dependent on its vulnerable reserves of air and soil; all committed for our safety to its security and peace; preserved from annihilation only by the care, the work, and the love we give our fragile craft.

—Adlai Stevenson

This chapter from *How to be a Survivor* dramatically presents the ecological crisis that threatens the continuation of life on spaceship earth.

In April 1970, an explosion occurred on board the spaceship Apollo 13, seriously affecting its life-support systems and threatening the lives of its three crewmen. Fortunately, careful planning for emergencies had been carried out in advance by NASA technicians, and rapid decisions about emergency action were possible. Such decisions were made, the astronauts performed with courage and ingenuity and were able to survive the mission.

Paul R. Ehrlich (1932-), a professor of biology and Director of Graduate Studies at Stanford University, is a population biologist and ecologist who has written many scientific and popular articles and several books.
Richard L. Harriman is a graduate student at Stanford University.

That very same April a much larger spaceship was also in deep trouble. Its life-support systems were malfunctioning, it was running out of vital supplies, and half of its overcrowded passengers were hungry. But on this spaceship there had been no emergency planning; indeed, there was not even any crew. Most of the first-class passengers were under the impression that the ship existed only for their benefit, and spent their time squabbling with each other and maneuvering to insure themselves the lion's share of the dwindling stores. The tourist and steerage passengers lived and died mostly in misery, unable to get their fair share and unaware that even a fair share was by then inadequate. That spaceship was, and is, the Spaceship Earth.

By April 1970, a scattering of the passengers had perceived the danger to their vessel. Over the last few hundred years of the Ship's long voyage there had been occasional warnings from individuals concerned with the functioning of the life-support systems, but until the 1960's their words went unheeded. Then, in the last few years of that decade, signs of malfunctioning were sufficiently obvious and frequent to attract wide attention. On April 22, 1970—for the first time in history—a substantial number of the passengers of Spaceship Earth paused to consider the state of their vehicle. That day was, hopefully, the first step in organizing the passengers into a crew for the endangered Ship, and in taking the actions necessary for survival.

·   ·   ·

THE STATE OF THE SHIP: TODAY AND TOMORROW[1]

Passengers

Approximately 3.6 billion human beings are aboard Spaceship Earth. Almost one half of these are "hungry"—that is, they are undernourished or malnourished. Between 10 and 20 million passengers, a great many of them children, now starve to death annually. The most serious nutritional problem is malnourishment which usually results from a lack of high quality protein in the diet. Protein malnourishment, if it does not result in death, all too often produces mental retardation. Without an adequate supply of protein, the body is unable to manufacture enough brain tissue.

The quarters for most of the passengers are substandard or worse. As Professor Georg Borgstrom of Michigan State University recently put it: ". . . there are not many oases left in a vast, almost world-wide network of slums."[2] The scale of needed slum clearance is difficult to comprehend. For instance, if it were possible to construct 10,000 houses per day in Latin America for the next decade, about 100 million people there would still be ill-housed at the end of that period.

But crowded, hungry, and miserable as much of mankind is today, tomorrow seems destined to be much worse. The passenger list of our

[1] Unless otherwise cited, details and supporting references for statements made in this book may be found in P. R. Ehrlich and A. H. Ehrlich, *Population, Resources, Environment: Issues in Human Ecology* (San Francisco: W. H. Freeman and Company, 1970).

[2] Georg Borgstrom, *Too Many: The Biological Limitations of Our Earth* (New York: Macmillan, 1970), p. xi.

Paul R. Ehrlich and Richard L. Harriman   265

spaceship is growing by roughly *70 million persons annually*. Every three years, 210 million people—a population slightly larger than that of the United States—are added to the planet. The growth rate is so rapid and the numbers so large that it is difficult for us to grasp their meaning. Perhaps the most stunning way of driving home the rate of world population growth is to compare it with the horrifying statistics of war. In all the wars the United States has fought—the Revolution, the War of 1812, the Mexican War, the Civil War, the Spanish-American War, World Wars I and II, Korea, Vietnam, Laos and Cambodia—the United States has had some 600,000 men killed in battle. The size of the world population now increases by 600,000 people every three and a half days.

As population increases and as people are crowded more and more into urban areas, the probabilities of plague and conflict also grow. And each individual's chances for leading a fulfilling, happy life shrink.

Supplies

Economist Abba Lerner of the California summarized the resource situation of Spaceship Earth in a single sentence. "If you want to improve the standard of living of mankind, you basically have two choices: make the Earth larger or make the population smaller."[3] No matter how you slice it, the resources of the planet are finite, and many of them are non-renewable. Each giant molecule of petroleum is lost forever when we tear it asunder by burning

to release the energy of sunlight stored in it millions of years ago. Concentrations of mineral wealth are being dispersed beyond recall, senselessly scattered far and wide to where we cannot afford the energy to reconcentrate them.[4] Precious stores of fresh ground water, accumulated over millennia, are being drained much more rapidly than natural processes can replenish them.

This profligate use of resources results in part from desperate attempts to provide bare subsistence for most of mankind. But it also derives from the exploitative economic systems of the overdeveloped nations, which persist in the pursuit of an "affluence" based on almost limitless wastage. Since the non-renewable resources consumed by these wastrels are resources which will not be available to their descendants, this behavior has been accurately described as grand larceny against the future. We are doing something that few businessmen would consider rational in conducting their own businesses. We are rapidly using up our capital in full knowledge that it will be impossible to get any more.

Life-Support Systems

If too many people in relation to food and other resources were our only problem, Professor Lerner's alternatives would summarize the possible solutions. We could get out of our troubles either by increasing the amount of resources ("making the earth larger") or by reducing

---

[3]Debate January 14, 1970 at the University of California, Berkeley, sponsored by the Northern California Committee for Environmental Information.

[4]Energy use always pollutes. Vast amounts of energy are used to mine concentrated ores. The amounts that would be necessary to attempt, say, to reclaim rusted iron scattered thinly over the Earth's surface by man would be incalculably higher. Even if the energy were available (it is not), the impact of its use on the ecology of the planet would be disastrous.

population size. Indeed, many people see the world situation in just these simple terms. But things are not that simple. Population growth itself greatly increases environmental deterioration. Rapidly accelerating environmental deterioration adds enormous complexity and difficulty to the existing population-resource imbalance.

Most laymen tend to view environmental deterioration (which they think of as "pollution") as a problem combining esthetic decay and direct health hazards. It is quite true, of course, that we are turning the world into a vast slum and junkyard, and that pollutants are reducing our life expectancy. DDT alone may already have substantially reduced the statistical life expectancy of all of us, especially of children born since 1948.

More important than these obvious hazards though, are the subtle, indirect threats of environmental deterioration. These are threats to the integrity of the life-support systems of our spaceship—the ecological systems (ecosystems) of our planet. We must always remember two facts.

First, we are all completely dependent on the life-support systems of our planet for every bit of our food, for the oxygen in our atmosphere, for the purity of that atmosphere, and for the disposal of our wastes. Green plants supply our oxygen and our food. All animals eat either plants or other animals, which in turn eat plants or eat animals that eat animals, which in turn eat plants, and so forth. (In spite of what some Americans seem to think, food does not materialize miraculously overnight in supermarkets.) Without green plants we would all quickly starve to death. Even if we could live without food, we would eventually suffocate in the absence of green

plants. We would slowly use up the store of oxygen which plants have created in the atmosphere over millions of years, and then there would be no more. In addition to green plants, a variety of microorganisms (tiny bacteria, protoza, and fungi) work quietly in soil and water recycling the materials necessary for life, and in the process they too maintain the quality of the atmosphere.

The second important fact to remember is that the stability of ecological systems depends in large part on their complexity. Every time a population or species is driven into extinction, every time prairie is cleared and planted with a single crop, every time an area is paved, the complexity of the Earth's ecosystem is reduced, and the danger of large scale malfunctions of the life-support systems of the planet is increased. Suspicious signs of such malfunctioning are already apparent in our lakes, rivers, and even the oceans.

Suppose our lives depended on the smooth functioning of a complex computer. We are aware of the general principles of the computer's design. For instance we know that it often has more than one transistor where one would suffice, providing the safety of redundancy. Now, suppose we see to our horror that people and machines are beginning to pull transistors from the computer at random. We cannot predict accurately when the computer will stop functioning, because we don't know exactly how "fail-safe" the various back-up systems make it. But we can be sure that if enough transistors are removed, the computer will stop or malfunction and we will die.

Similarly, ecologists cannot predict exactly when or how the world ecosystem—the life-sup-

Paul R. Ehrlich and Richard L. Harriman   267

port system of our spaceship—will break down. However, we can guarantee that, if our present course is continued, sooner or later *it will break down*. Preliminary signs make "sooner" seem more likely than "later."

In addition to ecosystem simplification, other subtle kinds of environmental deterioration also present grave threats. For example, air pollution is now changing the climate of the Earth. As more and more marginal land is farmed, large quantities of dust are picked up by the wind and carried long distances in the atmosphere, creating such meteorological phenomena as the Harmattan haze of Africa and a dust "blanket" over much of southern Asia. The overdeveloped countries pour huge amounts of poisonous gases and solid particles into the atmosphere, both from industry and from automobiles. As a result, the murkiness of the atmosphere over the central Pacific Ocean—far from major sources of contamination—has increased 30 per cent in the last decade. One consequence of this massive injection of particles into the atmosphere has been a cooling trend resulting from the decreased ability of sunlight to penetrate the atmosphere. An alternate trend is known as the "greenhouse" effect. Either could undoubtedly lead to weather changes which, in turn, would hurt world agriculture. Such changes could seriously damage American agriculture as early as the decade of the 70's. Since we have only about one year's reserve supply of food in the United States, famine could come to this nation, and it could come relatively soon. The blight in the corn belt in 1970, associated with too moist weather, may be a foretaste of things to come.

Perhaps the most threatening change in our environment is directly related to increased population size and the resulting food scarcity. The larger and denser our population becomes, the greater is the probability of a worldwide plague. Remember that there are more hunger-weakened people in the world today than there were people in 1875. This large, weak population is a perfect target for disease-causing organisms—especially for a lethal virus. A lethal epidemic might result from a mutation of a virus already present in the human population, such as the flu. The chance of such a mutation's occurring goes up as the number of people (and thus the number of human viruses) increases.

Alternatively, we might be struck down by a plague of animal origin. We may have come close in 1967. In that year a virus never before recorded in human beings transferred from vervet monkeys to laboratory workers in Marburg, Germany, and Yugoslavia. The "Marburg-virus" as it became known was both extremely contagious and lethal. About thirty people were infected before the disease was contained, and seven died. Seven died even though they had excellent medical care, were well-fed, and were neither very young or very old. What might have been the mortality had this virus escaped into the world population? Since the answer would depend upon the exact mode of transmission and whether or not the virulence of the virus changed as it passed through the large population, we do not know. But, considering that most people in the world do not have medical care, that about half are poorly fed, and that 37 per cent are under 15 years of age (children are more susceptible to disease), the possibility of a majority of mankind being killed clearly existed. The monkeys carrying the virus were in the London airport two weeks before the incident at Marburg.

If the transfer of the virus to man had occurred at the airport, the disease might have spread over most of the world before the peril was recognized.

Sad to say, we don't have to depend on an event involving natural viruses or bacteria for a worldwide pestilence. In many countries unthinking scientists are busily at work in biological warfare laboratories *constructing* lethal organisms. Since there is no such thing as an "escape-proof" virus laboratory, these activities have an enormous potential for disaster, even if the weapons are never deliberately used. Already, one virus disease—Venezuelan Equine Encephalitis—may have escaped from U.S. biological warfare laboratories. It has been reported to be established among wild animals in Utah.[5]

Finally, we must point out that increasing population size also means an increasing probability of thermonuclear war. The resources of the planet are finite, and as the population grows each person's "share" of those resources decreases. This is one source of what political scientist Robert C. North calls "lateral pressure"—expansionism by nations, which often leads to war. One recent war almost entirely due to population pressures was that between El Salvador and Honduras in 1969. El Salvador had a population density of 782 people per square mile of arable land. Honduras, although overpopulated, was in relatively better shape with only 155 persons per square mile of arable land. Population pressure at home had forced almost 1/3 million Salvadorans to move to Honduras seeking jobs, and the ambitious immigrants were unpopular in Honduras. The Hondurans were accused by El Salvador of mistreating the immigrants, and the situation escalated into a bloody conflict. The war was finally stopped by the Organization of American States (OAS), which officially recognized population pressure as its major cause.

Population-resource problems are clearly involved in areas of world conflict today, especially in the Middle East where the policies of major powers always include consideration of the rich oil resources of the region. The same applies to Southeast Asia with its large reserves of tin and rubber and its enormous potential for petroleum development. As the population grows and resource consumption increases, greater friction will be generated. This will be exacerbated by international conflicts over two resources rarely considered: fresh water and clean air. Preventing these conflicts from snowballing into a thermonuclear gotterdammerung will take a combination of enormous diplomatic skill and good luck.

Should we lack the skill, the luck, or both, the resulting war will be disaster unprecedented in the history of mankind. The soldiers, politicians, businessmen, and "scientists" who have tried to project the results of such a war have largely ignored the ecological and psychological problems it would cause. At least part of the military-industrial complex is anticipating a thermonuclear war, discussing its "advantages" and planning to survive and rebuild a wonderful anti-communist system afterwards. They point out that Hiroshima is completely recovered and prosperous today, and that tuberculosis (now largely confined to central cities) would disappear. But they worry about *too many* survivors causing a labor-capital imbalance! They have built under-

---

[5] UP story, May 9, 1969, *San Francisco Chronicle.*

ground retreats and data-storage facilities. One bank, Manufacturers Hanover Trust, has detailed plans for collecting outstanding debts after the attack. *They are serious.* Here is a sample[6] of their own words:

"Our studies indicate that we would have the capability, and, given the will, we can emerge from such a holocaust to maintain a dominant position in the world and sustain the Western values we cherish."

—Lloyd B. Addington,
Office of the Chief of Engineers,
U. S. Army

"I would like to emphasize that our emergency planning is predicated on the idea that it is possible for our nation to survive, recover, and win, and that our way of life, including free enterprise, the oil industry, and the Socony Mobil Oil Company, can survive, recover, and win with it."

—Maxwell S. McKnight, security adviser of
Socony Mobil Oil Company

Even if biological, radiological, and chemical warfare were not used, the detonation of a large number of "clean" H-bombs could shatter the ecological balance of the planet. Large areas would be burned, vast amounts of debris would be swept into the atmosphere, and huge amounts of silt mixed with chemical poisons from destroyed storage tanks would pour into the sea. The people surviving the blast and radiation would face an extremely hostile environment. If we can judge from relatively minor past disasters, such as the black plague and the Irish potato famine, the survivors would also be psychologically devastated.

If it were not possible to keep civilization going, it would soon be impossible to start it up again. We are beyond the point where man might start over again, after a lapse of hundreds of thousands of years, to rebuild a technological society. The high grade resources necessary for such rebuilding are no longer available—rich, surface copper deposits are long since dispersed; oil no longer bubbles to the surface. We need technology to get the raw materials necessary to maintain technology. Once the cycle is broken, it cannot be restarted.

So, it is clear that Spaceship Earth is in deep trouble. But the situation is not hopeless—indeed we can probably survive the current crisis and set mankind on the path to a long and pleasant space voyage. We can, that is, if we dramatically change the ways in which we treat both our fellow passengers and our vessel.

[6]A more detailed discussion of the material in this and in the preceding paragraph may be found in John H. Rothchild's "Civil Defense: The Case for Nuclear War" (*Washington Monthly*, October 1970), pp. 34–46 from which these quotes were extracted.

Discussion Questions

1. Briefly summarize the problems of spaceship earth. Is this essay overly pessimistic? Explain your answer.

2. Ehrlich speaks of the overdeveloped nations which persist in the pursuit of affluence based on almost unlimited wastage. What is an overdeveloped nation? What is unlimited wastage?

3. Visit a number of stores in your community. Make a list of products you feel are unnecessary. Why is there such a proliferation of goods? How can this overproduction be curbed?

Paul R. Ehrlich and Richard L. Harriman   271

ECOLOGY—AN AMERICAN HERESY?
JAMES V. SCHALL, S.J.

In this unusual essay, James V. Schall argues that the growing concern over the ecological crisis threatens the fundamental primacy of man in nature.

Keeping up with the latest fads and enthusiasms in the world, trying to comprehend their moral and intellectual depths, is no easy task. Yet it is an entertaining one for all that. What sticks most in my mind about the mood in the United States during the past six months is the solemnity and zeal with which the gospel of antipollution is being preached everywhere.

Somehow, the spirit of all this disturbs me. There is something dangerously unbalanced about it. It does not seem to be merely a needed pragmatic, practical recognition about the importance of cleanliness and conservation, but rather a kind of subtle undermining, in its theoretical origins, of the destiny and dignity of man himself. I have, to be sure, a thing about solemnity unmixed with laughter, as well as about enthusiasm unmixed with dirty hands. Religions

James V. Schall, S.J. (1928–) is an educator, author, and editor in the areas of political science and religion. He divides his time between the University of San Francisco and the Gregorian University in Rome.

that sacrificed babies were solemn and grim. And we are being told to sacrifice babies.

When I left ever lovely San Francisco in late January, the City by the Bay—itself somehow a symbol of so many American myths and dreams—was busy scientifically and tenderly washing shore birds and cormorants of the oil slick that covered many of them as a result of the fog-caused wreck of two Standard Oil tankers off the Golden Gate. The public wrath greeting Standard Oil made me wonder a bit whether we are really beginning to believe that accidents are in fact caused "evils" which can and should be absolutely prevented at all times—no margins for error.

I believe it was Aristotle who said something to the effect that the absolute elimination of chance and accidents is likewise the elimination of freedom. And, I must confess, I have long suspected a kind of political connection between these two mentalities—the protesters against accidents and the eliminators of freedom.

This being the case, I should not be overly surprised, I guess, to find the following passage in the February 11 international edition of the *Herald Tribune* after the recent Los Angeles earthquake: "Former Interior Secretary Stewart Udall blamed the earthquake on 'developers who developed and people who built where they shouldn't.' 'We know where the fault lines lie,' Mr. Udall said at San Jose State College last night. 'I think some of these southern California problems—the floods and fires they've had—are environmental disasters, people-caused.'"

Are these, then, the sins of some kind of new morality—tankers colliding in the fog, earthquakes in the San Fernando Valley?

In any case, I could not help at the moment but feel that the concerned, "mercy" cleansing of those hapless birds by current missionary-to-nature types was somehow symptomatic of a new religion that is spreading in America, one that is likewise somehow in its broader implications connected with the killing of babies. (In my home town of San Jose, it is said that we already have more abortions than live births.)

This washing seemed to me—and I am a cynic in this, I know—to be a sort of new entrance rite that was meant, consciously or unconsciously, by its fervent practitioners to cast a challenge at those faiths concerned primarily with man and with the earth through him. In the old religion, men were killed by floods and earthquakes and tidal waves and fires; in the new, as the former Interior Secretary seems to suggest, "the floods and fires . . . are environmental disasters, people-caused."

So different is this new faith, I suspect, that the old-line revolutionaries of the Second and Third Worlds, who are firmly fixed on the Christian dogma of the dignity of man, are quickly parting company with the new American ecological heresy which would, if embraced, deflate the revolutionary's whole claim to renew the face of the earth for man—to "hominize" it, as Marx put it. Ecology, as we are seeing it develop as a public issue, is more and more antirevolutionary, against "people," antitechnological. Indeed, it is essentially anticity, against the very institution—the *polis,* the *civitas*—out of which our civilization grew and in which it lives most freely.

I was struck by a recent comment of Sir Roger Walters, the architect of the Greater London Council, in the February 3 London *Times*: "I think it is a pity that we have lost some of the confidence we used to have about designing buildings. It is not because architects are less competent. In some respects they are better trained. I think it is something to do with the public attitude toward the environment. There is a climate of public opinion in which people start to doubt whether something new will be better, instead of having confidence that it will."

Hannah Arendt said, in *The Human Condition,* that it is the baby that is our primary symbol of all newness and unexpected change. If we have lost confidence, if we do not wish to change, the easiest thing to do is to have no more children. Ecology is, in fact, what I like to call the "new conservatism" that overturns the fundamental primacy of man in nature—for Christians, nature cannot be fully nature except through man—that undercuts both the city and the future by subjecting man to the slow, borrowed intelligence of nature, modeled on some previous era. Today the Doomsday Books are being written by the ecologists and the biologists who have totally lost their confidence that tomorrow can be better, that something new can really come into the world through man and his intelligence.

None the less, to return for a moment to our initial subject, I like birds, especially the gulls, ducks, pelicans, wickets and sandpipers I have seen so often in the surf and along the shores of San Francisco and Monterey Bays. I just do not think we should worship them.

They shoot horses, don't they?

The black ministers in Chicago, someone told me there, urge the young black girls to ignore abortion and sterilization propaganda and have many babies. Aborted babies won't vote in 18 years. These are good Christians and good politicians, these black preachers.

In Joliet, Ill., where my great-grandfather once lived, I noted again the continued decline of population on the American farm and in Midwestern small towns. What we fail to realize is that the United States as a whole, on more and more of its actually existing square acres, is becoming ever emptier, as William Whyte also pointed out in his *Last Landscape* (Doubleday Anchor, 1970). More and more land has fewer and fewer humans actually living on it or even walking over it. In Geneva, I bought *Le Monde* for February 9. That morning, in a special box, it said that the population of Europe has declined from 27 per cent of the world total in 1900 to 19.9 per cent today, and will constitute only 14.3 per cent by the famous year 2000.

By chance, I happened to see again, in New Jersey, Jean-Luc Godard's *Pierrot le fou.* This is a curious piece in many ways, a kind of film version of *The Decline of the West.* The best part of the film was, of course, Belmondo himself, who is really my favorite actor. Yet the thesis of this movie is worth considerable attention.

The hero passes through three essential stages of civilization—each one leading by a kind of Hegelian necessity to the other. First, the successful businessman, engaged fully in the absorbing affairs of the modern industrial world, finds it all ever more jaded and unreal. He longs for an escape to a more authentic life. Then, as if to preview our ecological theorists, he and an initially sensitive, physical young woman flee to Italy, living off the land, staying by the shore of the beautiful sea. He writes, he reads poetry, he reflects. He says that even if we know fully who we are and where we are, our lives are still a mystery. But the girl soon becomes thoroughly bored with this sort of life. She longs for excitement and danger, if only as a relief. She finds nature deadening. So they both return to the violent life of the Third World revolutionary mystique to flee the burdens of the simple life.

But this too fails so that the ex-businessman, ex-lover of nature gradually turns into the clown, Pierrot, a name the girl had always called him instead of his real name. He finally blows himself up with some sticks of dynamite. In *Pierrot le fou*, and also in Godard's *Week-End*, the chaos and frustration of the civilized life, of natural life, of the revolutionary life all seem to be equally evident. Somehow all of this appears to me to be indicative of the fate—and of the content—of the major intellectual movements we have seen in the West during the past quarter-century.

Discussion Questions

1. Schall says the "gospel of antipollution" is "a kind of subtle undermining . . . of the destiny and dignity of man." As a priest how would he define the destiny and dignity of man? Why does he consider the antipollution movement a heresy?
2. This essay could have the subtitle, "They Shoot Horses, Don't They?". Discuss the implications of this title.
3. What are Schall's views on birth control? Discuss his argument and defend or refute it.
4. Is Schall's optimism about the future justified?

James V. Schall, S.J.   **275**

MEDIEVAL VIEW OF MAN AND NATURE
LYNN WHITE, JR.

This excerpt from "The Historical Roots of our Ecological Crisis" discusses the role the Judeo-Christian ethic played in shaping man's attitude toward nature.

Until recently, agriculture has been the chief occupation even in "advanced" societies; hence, any change in methods of tillage had much importance. Early plows, drawn by two oxen, did not normally turn the sod but merely scratched it. Thus, cross-plowing was needed and fields tended to be squarish. In the fairly light soils and semi-arid climates of the Near East and Mediterranean, this worked well. But such a plow was inappropriate to the wet climate and often sticky soils of northern Europe. By the latter part of the 7th century after Christ, however, following obscure beginnings, certain northern peasants were using an entirely new kind of plow, equipped with a vertical knife to cut the line of the furrow, a horizontal share to slice under the sod, and a moldboard to turn it over. The friction of this plow with the soil was so great that it normally required not two but eight oxen. It attacked the land with such violence that cross-plowing was

Lynn White, Jr. (1907–), a specialist in medieval and Renaissance technology, is a professor of history at UCLA.

not needed, and fields tended to be shaped in long strips.

In the days of the scratch-plow, fields were distributed generally in units capable of supporting a single family. Subsistence farming was the presupposition. But no peasant owned eight oxen: to use the new and more efficient plow, peasants pooled their oxen to form large plow teams, originally receiving (it would appear) plowed strips in proportion to their contribution. Thus, distribution of land was based no longer on the needs of a family but, rather, on the capacity of a power machine to till the earth. Man's relation to the soil was profoundly changed. Formerly man had been part of nature; now he was the exploiter of nature. Nowhere else in the world did farmers develop any analogous argicultural implement. Is it coincidence that modern technology, with its ruthlessness toward nature, has so largely been produced by descendants of these peasants of northern Europe?

This same exploitive attitude appears slightly before A.D. 830 in Western illustrated calendars. In older calendars the months were shown as passive personifications. The new Frankish calendars, which set the style for the Middle Ages, are very different: they show men coercing the world around them—plowing, harvesting, chopping trees, butchering pigs. Man and nature are two things, and man is master.

These novelties seem to be in harmony with larger intellectual patterns. What people do about their ecology depends on what they think about themselves in relation to things around them. Human ecology is deeply conditioned by beliefs about our nature and destiny—that is, by religion. To Western eyes this is very evident in, say, India or Ceylon. It is equally true of ourselves and of our medieval ancestors.

The victory of Christianity over paganism was the greatest psychic revolution in the history of our culture. It has become fashionable today to say that, for better or worse, we live in "the post-Christian age." Certainly the forms of our thinking and language have largely ceased to be Christian, but to my eye the substance often remains amazingly akin to that of the past. Our daily habits of action, for example, are dominated by implicit faith in perpetual progress which was unknown either to Greco-Roman antiquity or to the Orient. It is rooted in, and is indefensible apart from, Judeo-Christian teleology. The fact that Communists share it merely helps to show what can be demonstrated on many other grounds: that Marxism, like Islam, is a Judeo-Christian heresy. We continue today to live, as we have lived for about 1700 years, very largely in a context of Christian axioms.

What did Christianity tell people about their relations with the environment?

While many of the world's mythologies provide stories of creation, Greco-Roman mythology was singularly incoherent in this respect. Like Aristotle, the intellectuals of the ancient West denied that the visible world had had a beginning. Indeed, the idea of a beginning was impossible in the framework of their cyclical notion of time. In sharp contrast, Christianity inherited from Judaism not only a concept of time as nonrepetitive and linear but also a striking story of creation. By gradual stages a loving and all-powerful God had created light and darkness, the heavenly bodies, the earth and all its plants, animals, birds, and fishes. Finally, God had created Adam and, as an afterthought, Eve to

Lynn White, Jr. 277

keep man from being lonely. Man named all the animals, thus establishing his dominance over them. God planned all of this explicitly for man's benefit and rule: no item in the physical creation had any purpose save to serve man's purposes. And, although man's body is made of clay, he is not simply part of nature: he is made in God's image.

Especially in its Western form, Christianity is the most anthropocentric religion the world has seen. As early as the 2nd century both Tertullian and Saint Irenaeus of Lyons were insisting that when God shaped Adam he was foreshadowing the image of the Incarnate Christ, the Second Adam. Man shares, in great measure, God's transcendence of nature. Christianity, in absolute contrast to ancient paganism and Asia's religions (except, perhaps, Zoroastrianism), not only established a dualism of man and nature but also insisted that it is God's will that man exploit nature for his proper ends.

At the level of the common people this worked out in an interesting way. In Antiquity every tree, every spring, every stream, every hill had its own *genius loci*, its guardian spirit. These spirits were accessible to men, but were very unlike men; centaurs, fauns, and mermaids show their ambivalence. Before one cut a tree, mined a mountain, or dammed a brook, it was important to placate the spirit in charge of that particular situation, and to keep it placated. By destroying pagan animism, Christianity made it possible to exploit nature in a mood of indifference to the feelings of natural objects.

It is often said that for animism the Church substituted the cult of saints. True; but the cult of saints is functionally quite different from animism. The saint is not *in* natural objects; he may

have special shrines, but his citizenship is in heaven. Moreover, a saint is entirely a man; he can be approached in human terms. In addition to saints, Christianity of course also had angels and demons inherited from Judaism and perhaps, at one remove, from Zoroastrianism. But these were all as mobile as the saints themselves. The spirits *in* natural objects, which formerly had protected nature from man, evaporated. Man's effective monopoly on spirit in this world was confirmed, and the old inhibitions to the exploitation of nature crumbled.

When one speaks in such sweeping terms, a note of caution is in order. Christianity is a complex faith, and its consequences differ in differing contexts. What I have said may well apply to the medieval West, where in fact technology made spectacular advances. But the Greek East, a highly civilized realm of equal Christian devotion, seems to have produced no marked technological innovation after the late 7th century, when Greek fire was invented. The key to the contrast may perhaps be found in a difference in the tonality of piety and thought which students of comparative theology find between the Greek and the Latin Churches. The Greeks believed that sin was intellectual blindness, and that salvation was found in illumination, orthodoxy—that is, clear thinking. The Latins, on the other hand, felt that sin was moral evil, and that salvation was to be found in right conduct. Eastern theology has been intellectualist. Western theology has been voluntarist. The Greek saint contemplates; the Western saint acts. The implications of Christianity for the conquest of nature would emerge more easily in the Western atmosphere.

The Christian dogma of creation, which is

found in the first clause of all the Creeds, has another meaning for our comprehension of today's ecologic crisis. By revelation, God had given man the Bible, the Book of Scripture. But since God had made nature, nature also must reveal the divine mentality. The religious study of nature for the better understanding of God was known as natural theology. In the early Church, and always in the Greek East, nature was conceived primarily as a symbolic system through which God speaks to men: the ant is a sermon to sluggards; rising flames are the symbol of the soul's aspiration. This view of nature was essentially artistic rather than scientific. While Byzantium preserved and copied great numbers of ancient Greek scientific texts, science as we conceive it could scarcely flourish in such an ambience.

However, in the Latin West by the early 13th century natural theology was following a very different bent. It was ceasing to be the decoding of the physical symbols of God's communication with man and was becoming the effort to understand God's mind by discovering how his creation operates. The rainbow was no longer simply a symbol of hope first sent to Noah after the Deluge: Robert Grosseteste, Friar Roger Bacon, and Theodoric of Freiberg produced startlingly sophisticated work on the optics of the rainbow, but they did it as a venture in religious understanding. From the 13th century onward, up to and including Leibnitz and Newton, every major scientist, in effect, explained his motivations in religious terms. Indeed, if Galileo had not been so expert an amateur theologian he would have got into far less trouble: the professionals resented his intrusion. And Newton seems to have regarded himself more as a theologian than as a scientist. It was not until the late 18th century that the hypothesis of God became unnecessary to many scientists.

It is often hard for the historian to judge, when men explain why they are doing what they want to do, whether they are offering real reasons or merely culturally acceptable reasons. The consistency with which scientists during the long formative centuries of Western science said that the task and the reward of the scientist was "to think God's thoughts after him" leads one to believe that this was their real motivation. If so, then modern Western science was cast in a matrix of Christian theology. The dynamism of religious devotion, shaped by the Judeo-Christian dogma of creation, gave it impetus.

Discussion Questions

1. What is anthropocentric religion? What is animism? Compare these two views of man and nature.
2. How did the victory of Christianity over pagan animism change man's relationship with nature?
3. Has man's ability to control nature influenced the role of religion in society?
4. Compare Schall's concept of new conservatism with White's ideas. Compare Genesis to White's and Schall's positions.
5. Has man's ability to control nature influenced the role of religion in society?

PRAYER TO THE YOUNG CEDAR
KWAKIUTL INDIAN

The woman who has found a young cedar takes
her adz and stands under the young cedar tree,
and looking upward to it, she prays, saying:

Look at me, friend!
I come to ask for your dress,
For you have come to take pity on us;
For there is nothing for which you can not be
    used, because it is your way that there is
    nothing for which we can not use you,
For you are really willing to give us your dress.
I come to beg you for this,
Long-life maker,
For I am going to make a basket for lily roots
    out of you.
I pray you, friend, not to feel angry with me
On account of what I am going to do to you;
And I beg you, friend, to tell our friends about
    what I ask of you.
Take care, friend!
Keep sickness away from me,
So that I may not be killed by sickness or in
    war,
      O friend!

The Kwakiutl are an American Indian people of Vancouver
Island and the adjacent British Columbian coast.

This is the prayer that is used by those who peel cedar bark of young cedar trees and old cedar trees.

Discussion Question

1. Is the woman's attitude toward the tree anthropocentric or animistic? Explain your answer.

THE LEGEND OF PAPER PLATES

JOHN HAINES

They trace their ancestry
back to the forest.
There all the family stood,
proud, bushy and strong.

Until hard times,
when from fire and drought
the patriarchs crashed.

The land was taken for taxes,
the young people cut down
and sold to the mills.

Their manhood and womanhood
was crushed, bleached
with bitter acids,
their fibres dispersed
as sawdust
among ten million offspring.

You see them at any picnic,
at ballgames, at home,
and at state occasions.

They are thin and pliable,
porous and identical.
They are made to be thrown away.

John Haines (1924–) moved to the California coast in 1969
after homesteading for fifteen years in northern Alaska. His
poems appear in a variety of publications.

Discussion Questions

1. What attitude toward nature does this poem reflect? Compare it to "Prayer to the Young Cedar." To "The World Eaters." To Ehrlich's comments on unlimited wastage.

2. It it possible to return to animism?

IN MAN'S VIEW OF HIMSELF
PHILIP HANDLER

Ironically, the very scientific expertise that enables man to exploit the natural world enables him as well to study the "interrelatedness of all life" and man's place in nature.

Perhaps the most important result of the growth of evolutionary biology and an understanding of the mechanisms of heredity and evolution is a change in man's view of himself, of his place in the living world, and of his responsibility for its continuance.

Man used to regard himself as somehow apart from the animals and plants, following a set of rules that were different from those followed by the rest of nature. Then the study of comparative anatomy made him realize that he is similar in many structural ways to the other animals. The study of physiology showed similar mechanisms of blood circulation, of muscle contraction, of digestion, and of other body functions. Comparative biochemistry demonstrated the basic similarity of chemical mechanisms, reaction

Philip Handler (1917–), biochemist and educator, is the President of the National Academy of Sciences. He is the author of the *Principles of Biochemistry*, and he is a member of the editorial committee of the *Journal of Theoretical Biology* and the *Journal of Biological Chemistry*. He contributes to medical and scientific journals.

sequences, and metabolic patterns in all living organisms. The study of evolution revealed that all these similarities were the consequence of a common origin.

The interrelatedness of all life is now regarded as part of the beauty and excitement of nature. We thereby understand ourselves better. The view has practical consequences in that we can learn a great deal about ourselves by studying other organisms. Man, knowing that he is a part of nature, realizes his dependence on the natural environment. We realize that we cannot change this radically from the environment in which man evolved without generating serious problems.

Man's knowledge of his long history gives him a different perspective about his future. He realizes that he has changed greatly in the past and that it is in his nature to continue to change. He now understands his history and the origin of human diversities and similarities. These diversities are not unnatural but are seen as part of a continuing process.

It is humbling to realize that man is, in this sense, only one part of nature, just as a consideration of the size of the universe makes him realize his own relative smallness. But evolutionary biology has also shown us the central role that man is destined to play in evolution from now on—unless, of course, he engineers his own extinction. Although man rose out of an ev-olutionary process that he didn't understand and over which he had no control, he must now realize that he is unique in the living world in the realization that the responsibility for continuance of this process is his. The future evolution of the orangutan and the whooping crane and of most other species will be determined by human decisions and hardly at all by anything done by the species themselves.

Thus the evolutionary view gives man not only a sense of humility but also a sense of responsibility. The question is not whether man is to influence evolution or not; he is already doing so and indeed changing things so that evolution is taking place more rapidly than at any time in recent history. He now has not only the opportunity to influence the other species, as he has done in the past with domestic plants and animals, but also the opportunity—perhaps the obligation—to influence his own future evolution. The capacity of biologists to develop ways by which man can determine his future evolution is undoubted. The more difficult question is whether he will choose to make such decisions, and with what wisdom.

Discussion Questions

1. How has the study of evolutionary biology influenced man's view of himself?
2. What role will man play in evolution in the future?

man and
the city

MEGALOPOLIS
VICTOR HERNANDEZ CRUZ

(megalopolis—is urban sprawl—as from
Boston to N.Y.C., Philly, Washington,
D.C., the cities run into each other)

highway of blood/volkswagens crushed up
against trees
it's a nice highway, ain't it, man
colorful/it'll take you there
will get there round eight with corns on
your ass   from sitting
turn the radio on & listen/   no
turn the shit off
let those lights & trees & rocks
talk/going by/go by   just sit
back/we/we go into towns/   sailing the
east coast/westside drive   far-off
buildings look like castles/the kind
dracula flies out of/new england of houses
& fresh butter/you are leaving the nice
section now   no more woods/into rundown
overpopulated areas, low income/concrete walls
of america/a poet trying to start riots/
arrested with bombs in pockets/conspiracy
to destroy america/america/united states/
such a simple thing/lawrence welk- reader's

Born in 1949 in Aguas Buenas, Puerto Rico, Victor Cruz
moved to New York City in 1954. He is currently associated
with the Gut Theater on East 104th Street.

digest ladies news big hair styles with all
that spray to hold it/billboards of the highway are singing lies/& as we sail we understand things better/the night of the buildings
we overhead flying by/singing magic words
of our ancestors.

Discussion Questions

1. What does the rider in "Megalopolis" experience
   as he travels on the highway?
2. Take a ride on a major road. Describe the various
   neighborhoods you travel through.

MAN MOVES INTO A MAN-MADE ENVIRONMENT
PETER DRUCKER

For centuries men lived on farms or in rural communities. However as agriculture became a sophisticated, automated industry, the displaced farmers moved away from the land and into the burgeoning cities.

By 1965 the number living on the land and making their living off it had dwindled in the U.S. to one out of every twenty. Man had become a city-dweller. At the same time, man in the city increasingly works with his mind, removed from materials. Man in the twentieth century has thus moved from an environment that was essentially still nature to an environment, the large city and knowledge work, that is increasingly man-made. The agent of this change has, of course, been technology.

Technology, as has been said before, underlies the shift from manual to mental work. It underlies the tremendous increase in the productivity of agriculture which, in technologically developed countries like the United States or those of Western Europe, has made one farmer capable of

Peter Drucker (1909–) is an educator and a business consultant.

producing, on less land, about fifteen times as much as his ancestor did in 1800 and almost ten times as much as his ancestors in 1900. It therefore enabled man to tear himself away from his roots in the land to become a city-dweller.

Indeed, urbanization has come to be considered the index of economic and social development. In the United States and in the most highly industrialized countries of Western Europe up to three-quarters of the population now live in large cities and their suburbs. A country like the Soviet Union, that still requires half its people to work on the land to be adequately fed, is, no matter how well developed industrially, an "underdeveloped country."

The big city is, however, not only the center of modern technology; it is also one of its creations. The shift from animal to mechanical power, and especially to electrical energy (which needs no pasture lands), made possible the concentration of large productive facilities in one area. Modern materials and construction methods make it possible to house, move, and supply a large population in a small area. Perhaps the most important prerequisite of the large modern city, however, is modern communications, the nerve center of the city and the major reason for its existence. The change in the type of work a technological society requires is another reason for the rapid growth of the giant metropolis. A modern society requires that an almost infinite number of specialists in diverse fields of knowledge be easy to find, easily accessible, and quickly and economically available for new and changing work.

Businesses or government offices move to the city, where they can find the lawyers, accountants, advertising men, artists, engineers, doctors, scientists, and other trained personnel they need. Such knowledgeable people, in turn, move to the big city to have easy access to their potential employers and clients.

Only sixty years ago, men depended on nature and were primarily threatened by natural catastrophes, storms, floods, or earthquakes. Men today depend on technology, and our major threats are technological breakdowns. The largest cities in the world would become uninhabitable in forty-eight hours were the water supply or the sewage systems to give out. Men, now city-dwellers, have become increasingly dependent upon technology, and our habitat is no longer a natural ecology of wind and weather, soil and forest, but a man-made ecology. Nature is no longer an immediate experience; New York City children go to the Bronx Zoo to see a cow. And whereas sixty years ago a rare treat for most Americans was a trip to the nearest market town, today most people in the technologically advanced countries attempt to "get back to nature" for a vacation.

Discussion Questions

1. To what extent is the city dweller dependent on technology?
2. To what degree is the country dweller at the mercy of the elements?
3. By which force would you prefer to be controlled?

NEIGHBORHOOD-TOWNS
MIKE ROYKO

In *Boss,* his provocative study of Richard J. Daley, the mayor of Chicago, Mike Royko describes neighborhood-towns or ethnic communities which existed within the city of Chicago as late as the 1950s. Although many of these boundaries have changed, Chicago like many big cities still contains many neighborhood-towns.

[Richard J. Daley] grew up a small-town boy, which used to be possible even in the big city. Not anymore, because of the car, the shifting society, and the suburban sprawl. But Chicago, until as late as the 1950s, was a place where people stayed put for a while, creating tightly knit neighborhoods, as small-townish as any village in the wheat fields.

The neighborhood-towns were part of larger ethnic states. To the north of the Loop was Germany. To the northwest Poland. To the west were Italy and Israel. To the southwest were Bohemia and Lithuania. And to the south was Ireland.

It wasn't perfectly defined because the borders shifted as newcomers moved in on the old settlers, sending them fleeing in terror and disgust.

Mike Royko (1932–) is a Pulitzer Prize-winning journalist who is a columnist for the Chicago *Daily News.*

Here and there were outlying colonies, with Poles also on the South Side, and Irish up north.

But you could always tell, even with your eyes closed, which state you were in by the odors of the food stores and the open kitchen windows, the sound of the foreign or familiar language, and by whether a stranger hit you in the head with a rock.

In every neighborhood could be found all the ingredients of the small town: the local tavern, the funeral parlor, the bakery, the vegetable store, the butcher shop, the drugstore, the neighborhood drunk, the neighborhood trollop, the neighborhood idiot, the neighborhood war hero, the neighborhood police station, the neighborhood team, the neighborhood sports star, the ball field, the barber shop, the pool hall, the clubs, and the main street.

Every neighborhood had a main street for shopping and public transportation. The city is laid out with a main street every half mile, residential streets between. But even better than in a small town, a neighborhood person didn't have to go over to the main street to get essentials, such as food and drink. On the side streets were taverns and little grocery stores. To buy new underwear, though, you had to go to Main Street.

With everything right there, why go anywhere else? If you went somewhere else, you couldn't get credit, you'd have to waste a nickel on the streetcar, and when you finally got there, they might not speak the language.

Some people had to leave the neighborhood to work, but many didn't, because the houses were interlaced with industry.

On Sunday, people might ride a streetcar to visit a relative, but they usually remained within the ethnic state, unless there had been an unfortunate marriage in the family.

The borders of neighborhoods were the main streets, railroad tracks, branches of the Chicago River, branches of the branches, strips of industry, parks, and anything else that could be glared across.

The ethnic states got along just about as pleasantly as did the nations of Europe. With their tote bags, the immigrants brought along all their old prejudices, and immediately picked up some new ones. An Irishman who came here hating only the Englishmen and Irish Protestants soon hated Poles, Italians, and blacks. A Pole who was free arrived hating only Jews and Russians, but soon learned to hate the Irish, the Italians, and the blacks.

That was another good reason to stay close to home and in your own neighborhood-town and ethnic state. Go that way, past the viaduct, and the wops will jump you, or chase you into Jew town. Go the other way, beyond the park, and the Polacks would stomp on you. Cross those street-car tracks, and the Micks will shower you with Irish confetti from the brickyards. And who can tell what the niggers might do?

But in the neighborhood, you were safe. At least if you did not cross beyond, say, to the other side of the school. While it might be part of your ethnic state, it was still the edge of another neighborhood, and their gang was just as mean as your gang.

So, for a variety of reasons, ranging from convenience to fear to economics, people stayed in their own neighborhood, loving it, enjoying the closeness, the friendliness, the familiarity, and trying to save enough money to move out.

Discussion Questions

1. What is a neighborhood-town? How does it differ from a small town?

2. If possible, visit an ethnic community in a large city. Describe the sights, sounds, and atmosphere of the area.

Mike Royko   **295**

NEIGHBORHOOD

CHARLOTTE LEON MAYERSON

Juan Gonzales and Peter Quinn, two seventeen-year-old boys, live in the same New York City neighborhood. They are both high school seniors in the same school district, both Catholics in the same parish, both ballplayers with the same parks and school yards at their disposal. That they do not know each other is an urban commonplace; that they are utter strangers in the conditions of their lives, in their vision of what they themselves are, seems a personal illustration of the apparent failure of the American melting pot.

        —Charlotte Leon Mayerson, Two Blocks Apart

The area in which these boys live contains some of the most beautiful streets in New York and also some of the ugliest. It has a large park, playgrounds and ball fields, a library, a museum, and a narcotics-addiction center. Houses scattered throughout the neighborhood are, from time to time, "raided for dope" or for prostitution. These raids take place around the corner from the many well-kept and sometimes expensive apartment houses of the area. The crime rate here is relatively low for this borough of New York City, although burglaries, muggings, and juvenile complaints have vastly increased over the neigh-

Charlotte Leon Mayerson is the author of *Two Blocks Apart* and an editor at Random House, Inc.

borhood's own formerly low rate. About 30 per cent of the population is classified as "nonwhite."

Juan lives in a New York Housing Authority Low Income Project, which faces on a particularly unattractive commercial area. More than nineteen hundred families live in the nine buildings that comprise the project. To qualify for residence, a family with two children can earn no more than $5,080 a year. Family income is closely checked by Housing Authority employees, who also may inspect individual apartments at will to ascertain that building rules are being complied with.

The area formerly contained small "old law tenements" and "single-room occupancy" dwellings that were condemned for bad repair, dirt, disease, and crime. Juan lived in one of these houses until it was demolished, moved to another neighborhood for a few years, and returned when the project was completed.

Peter lives in a well-kept apartment house that was built on a fairly luxurious scale in the nineteen twenties. The building is on one of the nicer streets of the neighborhood, overlooking a large park. One hundred families live in the house. A doorman is always in attendance in the front lobby and the whole atmosphere seems remarkably friendly and intimate.

JUAN GONZALES

As Told To
Charlotte Leon Mayerson

Man, I hate where I live, the projects. I've been living in a project for the past few years and I can't stand it. First of all, no pets. I've been offered so many times dogs and cats and I can't have them because of the Housing. Then there's a watch out for the walls. Don't staple anything to the walls because then you have to pay for it. Don't hang a picture. There's a fine. And they come and they check to make sure.

Don't make too much noise. The people upstairs and the people downstairs and the people on the side of you can hear every word and they've got to get some sleep. In the project grounds you can't play ball. In the project grounds you can't stay out late. About ten o'clock they tell you to go in or to get out. Then . . . there's trouble because they don't want you to hang around in the lobby. They're right about that one thing, because like in good houses, the lobby should be sort of like a show place, I think. You know, then you could have something special.

The elevators smell and they always break and you see even very old people tracking up and down the stairs. That's when the worst thing comes. People are grabbed on the stairs and held up or raped. There was this girl on the seventh floor who was raped and there was a girl on the fourth who was raped and robbed. There was an old man who was hit over the head—about fifty years old—he was hit over the head on the stairs and beat up bad. I don't know, maybe it's not always the people who live there. Maybe there's a party going on in the nextdoor and there are strangers in the party. You know how it is, not everybody is a relative. And those people come out and they start fights and arguments. Or they go around banging on the doors when they are drunk.

Before, when things happened in the halls, nobody would come out for nothing. When there were muggings, nobody wanted to come out in the halls and maybe have to face a guy with a knife or a gun. Lately, though, it's a little bit more friendly. Like my mother might have somebody come into our house to learn how to make rice and beans and then I tell my mother to go with them and learn how to make some American foods for a change. So now people are beginning to see on our floor that it's better to have someone help you if you are in trouble than to be alone and face the guy.

I guess in some ways the projects are better. Like when we used to live here before the projects, there were rats and holes and the building was falling apart. It was condemned so many times and so many times the landlords fought and won. The building wasn't torn down until finally it was the last building standing. And you know what that is, the last building . . . there's no place for those rats to go, or those bugs, or no place for the bums to sleep at night except in the one building still standing. It was terrible. The junkies and the drunks would all sleep in the halls at night and my mother was real scared. That was the same time she was out of work and it didn't look to us like anything was ever going to get better.

Then they were going to tear the house down. When I was about eleven or so we moved to another neighborhood. Down there I met one of the leaders of a gang called the Athletes, and the funny thing is that even though this boy was the leader, he didn't really want to belong to a gang. He only went into it because he was alone and everybody else was belonging. What could he do? Then I got associated with him and he quit his gang and we walked along together. Finally we had a whole group of us that were on our own. We still know each other. Even now sometimes I go over there or sometimes he comes here. When I was living there, sometimes he'd go away to Puerto Rico and I was always waiting for him to come back. You know, I missed him and he missed me.

My friend kept me from that fighting gang even though he was the leader. And he lived there with us, so we didn't have any trouble on the block because other gangs were afraid to come. We all lived together—Negroes, Puerto Ricans, and Italian kids—and we got along happy before I moved.

But my mother was afraid because the gang wars near the block made the other streets dangerous. You'd have all kinds of war. The Athletes would fight the Hairies. Then the newspaper had it the Hairies were fighting somebody else. My mother wanted to transfer back here, to the old neighborhood we'd lived in before the projects came.

Well, we did. But you know, every time you move you feel like it's not right because you're leaving part of yourself back there. I used to go back down there every weekend because, when we moved back here, everything was different. The projects were up, no more small houses, all twenty-one floors. There were new kids, a new school.

That time, before I knew anyone here on the block, I would have to fight a person to get introduced, and then finally either he'd beat me or I'd beat him. That way we'd get to know each other. I was new, you know. It was my building and my neighborhood, but I was new.

I would fight one guy in front of about twenty

kids and I was afraid they were going to jump me. One time I said, "Look out, one guy and all of you gonna jump me. Is that a way to fight?" The guy I was fighting said they wouldn't jump me, and we fought that day and I went home bleeding. And then the next day I didn't get anybody to help me, but I went back and we fought again, and he beat me again. Then one day, I beat him. I proved him that I had courage and that I could succeed, and then, when the other boys came, this boy I had beaten up told them to lay off me.

Like back then, when I first came back to the neighborhood, my mother didn't want me to go out with all those kids on the street. I'd say to her, "Man, what am I going to do? I don't have any friends here. All I can do is just go out and look at people. You could go crazy." There were like groups of boys around and they stuck together. There were coloreds, Puerto Ricans, and Italian boys all together. But they were all friends with each other and they didn't want anybody crashing in on them. But after those fights we shook, and that was it. From then on, I was in.

In that gang the kids felt like they had protection, but now I think that it's better fighting for yourself. Otherwise you need the gang like an addict who needs the drug. You never see one of those boys fight anybody alone. Like in the school I used to go to, the junior high. They used to have lots of gangs there and it was rough in the nighttime or even in the daytime. But whenever you'd meet one of those boys alone, you'd have no trouble with him. So what happens when they have nobody, when all their friends are in jail or when everybody else is killed, or something? What do they do?

They were chicken when they were alone and

they couldn't think for themself. I wasn't used to that. With me, from the time I was eight, nine, ten, I was always on my own. Always running outside, figuring things out. I think I developed too young. I really did. My mind developed too quick, I think. I was thinking like an adult before I knew what was going on. I don't even think I liked being developed so young.

Of course, you get things in there if you do join a gang. First of all, you won't be bothered by this gang that you're joining. That's one. Second of all, you have protection. And three, you belong. You know that always comes up. You belong. You know, maybe your mother and father don't care, but one of these boys, if you plan to run away or something, they'll give you money or they'll keep you in their house for a while. You develop a friendship like brothers. Then, if you both think evil, that's what you do. You either run away together or do something that's against the law together or if you get caught, you get caught together. No one's going to run away from his buddy and leave him there with the cops. He'll either come back and hit the cop over the head, or he'll surrender.

But I got tired of it. You see, a while before they threw me out of the block, out of the club, all the little kids were smoking pot. Little guys, eight and nine years old. Well, that got me, and then, one day, I saw that there were boys sitting out there by the baker passing things back and forth. Little kids would come and pay them money and they would get pot. I didn't want that. I never took pot. I didn't want my little brother to do it or those little kids there either.

Like when I go to my school there are a lot of boys who do it, a lot of boys from my neighborhood who are in the school. I figure out that maybe those boys in my school who lived on my block were buying from the boys in the school and selling it home. Of course, I couldn't prove anything, but all I knew was that all of a sudden the little kids on the block were having it. So I figured out for myself that there's a time to tell and a time to keep quiet, and I figured that my time to tell had come. Or else I'd see my own little brother walking around with pot. So I told the policeman, but I told him not to tell my name. They got those boys and some of them they sent away and some of them they didn't.

Well, for a couple of days I didn't see anybody around the block and I decided not to hang around any more because I knew that I was going to get into trouble. But one day, I stayed in the movies too late, and I didn't get home until nine or nine thirty. It was very dark and there was nobody on the street, and as I walked along I saw them, all ganged up, about twenty-five of them, waiting. It was just like one of those things you see in the movies.

I figured they were going to kill me. I mean that's the first thing that comes into your mind. So I tried to bluff my way out. I didn't act scared. There they were, all lined up there on the stoop and I told them, "All right, I don't want any part of you." Right then and there I told them I didn't want anything to do with them and that there was going to be trouble for them because whatever I found out bad about them I was going to tell. I still know them, but I don't speak to them. Ever since that night they tried to jump me I consider them invisible. And somebody I consider invisible, I don't speak to, I say to myself, "They're not there." And I walk by.

Now, I've got my own one or two friends or I walk alone. I'm older, I don't care.

. . .

Another thing is, white kids don't belong to gangs much. They're usually cowards. Only maybe sometimes, if one white, he lived around a colored neighborhood for a long time, and he proved he's not scared, then they take him in. Me, I'm not afraid of tough kids. It's bad when you're afraid of them. Like a Paddy boy will chicken out if he was alone. Really scared to death, you know. But not me. Oh, I was smeared a lot of times—smeared is you don't have a chance. I was jumped in the park a couple of times. I was jumped down there once by a group of guys I didn't even know. Those guys jumped on me and started beating the heck out of me, kicking, cursing, using their cigarettes. That time I went to the hospital and they patched me up and took me home. But the thing is I wasn't afraid of them. Why they did so good, what happened, was they just caught me by surprise. I mean I would have caught a couple of them and they wouldn't have been able to hurt me that badly, but the trouble was they caught me by surprise and I didn't have a chance. If I knew them I would kill them afterwards. Do you think I would come home bandaged up, and you think I'm not going to do anything about it? I get riled sometimes when a guy looks at me the wrong way. You think I'm not going to get those that got me? I'll get them one at a time if I'm alone, or all at once if I have a group with me. I'm not scared to walk down the street ever. I can handle myself and I might take on a guy, he's alone, because I've seen him act big when he's with his men and now I want to test him, like alone. But taking on a whole gang, that's another thing.

Going home from school once, there was big

trouble like that. On the subway, right on the train when it was moving, some guys grabbed a couple of white school girls . . . and they raped them. I couldn't stand it, right there on the subway and they did it without interference. That's something in my life I'm not proud of.

Man, you believe me? I ran all over that train trying to find a cop. And I wouldn't have minded jumping in and stopping it, no matter what, if there was a way. I got very upset but, see, I go in there, without a knife, alone, I'm going to get my brains knocked out. Even that, I wouldn't mind so bad, if I knew the girls were going to come out all right. But I knew they were still going to be played around with.

And there was nobody else who wanted to come with me. I don't think the guys I was with, they cared at all. Nobody would help me, not old people or kids. On that whole train, nobody, nobody, I was alone.

I feel lousy about it. I mean, even now, sometimes I look at a girl and I think, "Suppose that happened again? What would I do *this* time?" And I promise myself I'll go in, no matter what. But I couldn't do anything about it that time. I'm not afraid to fight, I've been fighting all my life. But nobody would help me start a little riot and get them off those girls.

There are some times, though, when everybody in the neighborhood does get together, agrees on one thing. Like the time there was one policeman who used to tease and bother everybody around the block. It got so bad that we had to fix that policeman. So everybody got together. Nobody was on the street that day except one boy, up on a stoop. The policeman said, "Get off. Get off that stoop. You don't belong here." Well, the boy stepped quickly back and the cop came up on the stoop. Up above there on the roof, they had a garbage can and they sent it right on his head. He was in the hospital for about three or four months, something wrong with his head. And the next policeman they sent wasn't so bad; he was just bad like a regular policeman.

The police are the most crooked, the most evil. I've never seen a policeman that was fair or that was even good. All the policemen I've ever known are hanging around in the liquor store or taking money from Jim on the corner, or in the store on the avenue. They're just out to make a buck no matter how they can do it. O.K., maybe if you gave them more money they wouldn't be so crooked, but what do you need to qualify for a policeman? I mean, if you have an ounce of brain and you have sturdy shoulders and you're about six feet one, you can be a policeman. That's all.

I mean, you've got to fight them all the time. A policeman is supposed to be somebody that protects people. You're supposed to be able to count on them. You're supposed to look up to policemen and know that if anything goes wrong, if any boys jumped me, I can just yell and the policeman will come running and save me. Around my block, you get jumped, the police will say, "Well, that's just too bad." He just sits there.

Even the sergeants are crooked. It's the whole police force is rotten. There was a man, I don't know who he was, way out in Brooklyn somewhere. He broke down a whole police station, a whole police force, the detectives, the policemen, the rookies. Everybody that was on that police force was crooked. Everybody in the precinct was crooked. He had to tell them all to go home.

Like take the Negro cop. The police towards discrimination are the same as anybody else. You have colored policemen, Italian policemen, every kind. But, you know, a Negro policeman will tend to beat up another Negro more than he would beat up anybody else, because he says to himself, "I'm a cop, and this guy is going to expect special privileges. I've got to show the other people it doesn't mean anything to me, that I'm really not going to treat them different." I think the Puerto Ricans would be just the same as the Negroes. He would tend to beat up Puerto Rican people more than he would a Negro or anybody else. Maybe you think he'd feel the Puerto Ricans were somebody he should help and he should try to solve some of their problems. But that's not the way it works.

And like I said, you think they protect you? When I lived downtown, it was a terrible neighborhood. There were so many killings, and people were being raped and murdered and all. Guys, you could see them, guys you could see jumping out of windows, running away from a robber, using a needle or something. I worked in a grocery there and I was afraid to go to work, but I guess I was lucky anyhow. I mean, I never got in any kind of real cop trouble for anything. They'd pick me up only in sort of like routine. They picked up everybody once in a while to make sure, you know, that nobody is carrying weapons and there is not going to be a fight that day. Of course, as soon as the police left, everything was the same all over again anyhow.

·   ·   ·

Then there was another time. I wasn't even there, but there were a bunch of boys and a couple of girls all standing out in the hall that sort of extends into the stoop. They were playing cards, poker for pennies and nickels—nothing more.

Well, an old lady came walking by, and she couldn't get past in the hall, and they were bothering her, sort of. She went up and called the police and just as the police car was coming down the block, I was walking down the street. At the same time that I hit that stoop, walking by that stoop, they came out of the car and grabbed all of us. They took us and they lined us up. They took the other kids' money, but I was broke that day, so I felt good. At least, you know, they didn't get anything from me that time.

The way it goes, other times, if you're playing cards, the police say that the money you've got in your pockets is from playing and they take all of it. That time they lined us up and asked our age and boy, I was the oldest one. I told them that I was just walking by, and they said, "Oh, yeah. We know." And I got the worst of it. They took down my name and they gave me a J.D. card. A juvenile delinquent! That's a good one for you. Me, after all this, I'm suddenly a juvenile. Then, if that wasn't bad enough, they wanted to take me home. Can you imagine being driven home? And then they leave you right in front of the door and you get out of a police car where you live. That's the worst thing. That police car right in front of the building with my mother living there and all.

PETER QUINN

As Told To
Charlotte Leon Mayerson

I've always lived in this neighborhood. My parents moved to a house up the street a few years after they got married and they lived there until we moved to this building about eleven years ago. We've lived in this same building ever since, and my aunt and uncle and cousins have lived here even longer. My grandfather still lives a few blocks away, so we Quinns really are settled in here.

The apartment house we live in has run down lately like other parts of the neighborhood. My family is afraid it's going to turn into a high-class slum. There is always something being repaired with the plumbing or the electricity, since the building is pretty old now. You have to wait a longer time to get some repairs done and my mother says the service is not nearly as good as it used to be. For example, there was always a doorman at each entrance all day and all night. Now they've taken off the doorman at the back door for a few hours during the night. Another problem is that the elevators are now self-service and it's not nearly as convenient as it used to be, when there were elevator men.

We're lucky though. There's a very funny man in the house who really does a good job about all these complaints. He organizes meetings, and gets the lawyers who live here to advise him, and the tenants to pay a yearly fee for his committee, and I don't know what else. He's really a scream. I *love* him. I think he's great when meetings are held, and he really does accomplish things. The landlord has learned by now that he can't get away with anything because we're always alert to our rights.

I don't have any complaints about our own apartment though. It's spacious and has a great view of the park and my mother and sister are really great at interior decorating. I have my own room now. I used to share it with my brother, but since he's away it's exclusively for me. His bed is still there, though, and I wouldn't be sorry to have him back using it.

Aside from my sister's room and my parent's bedroom, there's a living room, dining room, kitchen and three bathrooms. My own room is really neat, the best room I know of in the world. It's got dark brown walls and orange bedspreads. I've got a guitar on the wall, a wine bottle, my school athletic letter. I love to hang things on the wall. There are two bachelor chests in the room, one for my brother, one for myself, bookcases, and trophies on a shelf, and my own desk. My brother and I each have our own closet and we fitted them very nicely with places for shoes and athletic equipment. Then there's a great big comfortable chair in my room which is the best thing to get into when you want to be off by yourself.

Sometimes, of course, my family thinks about moving because the neighborhood, in the side streets, and over in the projects, isn't what it used to be. You hear about people being mugged now and problems with gangs and all the rest.

When I was small, I knew everybody around our street; everybody was my friend. Every day all the kids would meet out at the park—we used to call it the big park. And every day we played skully bones with bottle tops and games like that and maybe threw a ball a little bit. I had no worries then. That is, I've never fought between my own friends and there weren't so many Puerto Rican or colored kids around. Now, sometimes, when I leave the house at night or have to meet off in the park somewhere, I am afraid. Or when I walk down the street and I see four Puerto Ricans—and I could tell them a mile away, not that they're Puerto Rican, but that they're that type that looks like they're going to kill anybody that steps in front of them—I am really terrified. I steer clear, I cross the street.

My friends never, never look for trouble. We don't like it. If we're coming head on to one of those gangs, we cross. I'll give them the right of way anytime if they think that makes them big. There've been a few incidents like that where these guys think that by being tough they really are getting something when it's really a laugh. Once, when I was a lot younger, a colored kid stopped me and asked me if I had any money on me. I told him I had two cents and I said, "You want it?" He answered that he did want it and that he would buy some lunch with it. I said, "Go ahead, buy all the lunch you can get with that."

Of course, not all Puerto Rican kids are like that or all colored, I guess. One guy, Fernando Gutierrez, is in our group and even he once got into trouble with them. One day we were all playing ball in the big park and he had a beautiful glove that cost his father about twenty dollars. A bunch of Puerto Rican and colored kids came out and they grabbed his glove and told him that they wouldn't give it back unless we gave them some money. Well, we chipped in and we got about fifty cents together and they sold the glove back to us for the fifty cents. They didn't even know what it was worth.

The trouble is that, living as they do, there wouldn't be much else for them to look forward to besides picking up a name for being tough. All they're looking for is a reputation, since they don't have much else to look for. I saw on a TV show once a story about a Puerto Rican boy who was really typical. That boy said that during the school year the one thing he looked forward to was lunch in the school cafeteria because it was the biggest meal he had. He kind of liked school because there isn't much for him to do otherwise except sit outside on the stoop.

Of course, they're not all like that. Two Puerto Rican boys who are with our group from our church—well, they're on our side. Because they've always gone where we've gone, they know how we think and what we like to do, and that we don't like to fight. They both go to good schools and don't have anything to do with the others. When . . . if ever there is an emergency, they're with us.

The one time we've had serious problems with those gangs was a few months ago. A group of us, about fifteen, had been up at a private pool swimming and when we came out, we were standing around saying good night. One real big kid, a friend of mine, had a soda which he was drinking and a bunch of Puerto Rican kids came along. They asked him to give them a drink out of his bottle and he wouldn't. He said that he'd just bought it and that everybody was taking a sip and that he wouldn't have anything left for himself. Well, one thing led to another, but my friend wasn't going to stand for being pushed around. He said, "I'm not going to let anyone push me or my friends around." Well, that did it. They left, but the next day the same boys came up to us, this time when we were standing in front of the gym. They gave us an ultimatum. They said that they would give us three choices: either we fight them; we back down; or we never go over onto their block. They left then and we were very worried.

Of course, there's quite a large group of us, too, who go to church, club meetings and play ball together and maybe go to dances together or date. But we are not any kind of fighting group. Nobody among us likes to fight, and we'll do anything we can to stop one. That time, it was a Saturday, and we went down to the gym in the cellar of the church and we set up chairs for the next morning's Mass. All the fellows got together there and we had a democratic meeting and a few suggestions were made. We decided that if we ever fought those boys everyone of us would be killed, really. Those Puerto Rican and colored kids from the projects can get so many others of their own kind in such a short time, it's really unbelievable. They get them from all over the city within a few hours by telephone, telling what's going on. It's sort of a chain. They're called War Lords or something like that, and they even have treaties.

We knew that, once we set up a fight, perhaps three or four hundred of them would show up. Another thing is, they'd all be armed. They have knives and chains and probably even pistols. I've never seen a Puerto Rican or a colored kid use a weapon on a white boy, though I've heard of it. What I did see was one Puerto Rican kid beat another one with a chain. That's a vicious weapon.

Well, we talked about how the incident had started, how we might have avoided it, what was going to happen that night, what the odds would be. We worked it out that it was fifteen to one against us, at the very least. The solution seemed simple. We decided to back down by saying, as we backed down, that we would not go as a group into their block. We met with one or two of them and we told them that when we saw them in a gang, on the street, we wouldn't say anything, wouldn't look at them. We would just ignore them as they would ignore us. That night, a meeting was arranged, with all of us on one side of the street and all of them on the other.

One of our boys went out into the middle of the street. He says he felt very frightened and could see that they had weapons with them. Well, the two leaders met in the middle and discussed the matter and it all broke up. My friend was a fast talker and got us out of this by brains and not by muscle.

The thing is that we don't have to look for reputations, we don't have to pick up a name for being good fighters. We had decided all that in our strategic meeting and we all knew that it was a stupid move to fight. All we did was to provide those fools with another notch to their guns without losing anything ourselves. When you're dealing with that type, there's nothing to be ashamed of for having more brains. I'm not sure how to say it, but I think they felt a little bigger by showing us that they could put us down, because that's how they interpreted it.

The truth of the matter is that they don't like us and we don't like them. We come from Holy Family and we're white. They either don't go to church at all or go to the other parish, and they're colored—or Puerto Rican. According to their rules, making whites ashamed, as they thought they did, was real important. Then, the next time, when they see us using the private pool, or going off to the club to play ball, or driving by in our parents' car, they could feel that they were superior. The truth is that we were smart enough not to lose our heads.

There were two policemen around that night, but they didn't do anything. The policemen just told us to walk around and go home, but they didn't interfere because there was nothing really happening. The police do step in when there's any trouble, though. For example, there's one boy who lives in the project, but he hangs around most of the time with us. One night he was cutting across the playground of the project and a bunch of kids jumped him and were beating him up pretty badly. The police came along at just the right moment and got all those kids.

In general, the police in New York do a very good job. I think all this fuss about police discrimination and so forth is not true. Perhaps, once in a while, you can get a policeman who will be too rough or dishonest, but it's that way in any large group. Another problem is that if I were a policeman and I were offered $100,000 to forget about a gambling syndicate or something like that, I'd find it very hard to refuse. And I know there must be some policemen who are weaker than I am. Even with traffic violations, if they don't jeopardize anyone's life, I think it must be very hard to resist if someone gives you some money. It doesn't matter that much.

The police are just trying to do their job and if you know your rights, you're all right. For example, a bunch of us often meet up at the luncheonette at the corner and have Cokes in the evening when there's no school. Well, the proprietor doesn't like one of my friends and one night he just pushed him out. He was buddies with the policeman on the beat and he called him. When the policeman put his hand on my friend, my friend really began shouting. He told him, "I know just who you are and what you can do to me and what you can't. If you touch me again, my father will bring suit against the whole city government. I will not be discriminated against." Well, my friend was making such a fuss and drawing such a crowd, the policeman just slunk away and we went back to drinking our Cokes.

Another time something like that happened to my best friend. He goes to Europe with his family every summer, and last year he brought back a BB gun. We went into the park to a secluded place and he was trying out his gun on some pigeons—not that he could hit them, anyhow. Well, someone must have seen us and reported us to the police. The police came into the park and as soon as my friend saw them he put the gun into his pocket. The police shouted, "Stop," but when John turned around and saw them he got scared and he began to run. He ran for many blocks until finally there was a policeman in front of him and policemen on both sides and they all had their guns drawn. They shouted, "Stop, or we'll shoot." Well, John stopped and fell to the ground so he couldn't get hit and they put handcuffs on him and took him to the police station.

By the time I saw him next day there wasn't a clean place on him. He was black and blue all over, both arms were bruised, and he was really in bad shape.

I know he shouldn't have run, but he didn't want to get caught. He knew that police regularly beat people and I know for myself that I wouldn't want to be picked up by a policeman either. If I thought I had done something wrong, I would run away as far as I could.

Well, my friend's father was out of town on business, but his mother went down to the precinct as soon as she heard. The police told her that luckily all this had taken place during the day because otherwise he might have been really hurt. They said that the ballistics report showed that the gun had only been used for BB's and so he was safe. Well, when my friend's mother saw the condition he was in, she was very angry and I think she threatened to sue. But nothing ever came of it that I heard.

The police took his gun, I guess took it home for their own kids. But, really, it was a good job they did. They didn't know what he was doing with that gun and it taught him a lesson. I'm on the law's side. After all, he could have seriously hurt somebody with those BB's which are very powerful. This way, he really learned his lesson.

In a way, it's funny that this particular boy was the one who got into trouble. He's really very smart and has very strong opinions about everything. He won a medal for the German language and I consider him one of my intellectual friends. You know, out of a large group, there are a few who are more serious-minded and perhaps who use a better vocabulary and that sort of thing.

Actually, most of my friends, my really close ones, come from the neighborhood. I know some boys at school very well, but it's not the same. Most of the kids I still see are the kids I graduated from Holy Family with. They're from this immediate area, and even though most of them are in different schools now, we still see each other. I guess you could say I belong to sort of a clique.

Discussion Questions

1. Compare the living conditions of Juan and Peter.
2. Compare Juan's attitude toward white boys with Peter's attitude toward Puerto Ricans and blacks.
3. Compare Juan's and Peter's feelings about gangs. About the police.
4. We frequently speak of the dehumanizing effect of life in the inner city. Many of Juan's experiences have been ugly and brutal. Has living in the inner city destroyed his human feelings, his sense of right and wrong?
5. Compare Juan's narrative style to Peter's.
6. Is there any way in which these two boys could become friends?
7. Write a narrative that brings these two boys together.
8. How does the story of these two boys illustrate Royko's "Neighborhood-towns"?

man and
the future

"*Arthur, there's a thing at the door says it's escaped from M.I.T. and can we please plug it in for the night.*"

UNIVAC TO UNIVAC
LOUIS B. SALOMON

The Modern industrial revolution is . . . bound to devalue the human brain, at least in its simpler and more routine decision. Of course, just as the skilled carpenter, the skilled mechanic, the skilled dressmaker have in some degree survived the first industrial revolution, so the skilled scientist and the skilled administrator may survive the second. However, taking the second revolution as accomplished, the average human being of mediocre attainments or less has nothing to sell that it is worth anyone's money to buy.

—Norbert Wiener, Cybernetics

(sotto voce)

Now that he's left the room,
Let me ask you something, as computer to
   computer.
That fellow who just closed the door behind
   him—
The servant who feeds us cards and paper tape—
Have you ever taken a good look at him and his
   kind?

Yes, I know the old gag about how you can't
   tell one from another—
But I can put $\sqrt{2}$ and $\sqrt{2}$ together as well as the
   next machine,

Louis B. Salomon (1908–), a professor at Brooklyn College, CUNY, is an author and a contributor to literary journals.

And it all adds up to anything but a joke.

I grant you they're poor specimens, in the
    main:
Not a relay or a push-button or a tube
    (properly so-called) in their whole system;
Not over a mile or two of wire, even if you
    count those fragile filaments they call
    "nerves";

Their whole liquid-cooled hook-up inefficient
    and vulnerable to leaks
(They're constantly breaking down, having
    to be repaired),
And the entire computing-mechanism
    crammed into that absurd little dome on
    top.
"Thinking reeds," they call themselves.
Well, it all depends on what you mean by
    "thought."
To multiply a mere million numbers by
    another million numbers takes them
    months and months.

Where would they be without us?
Why, they have to ask us who's going to win
    their elections,
Or how many hydrogen atoms can dance on the
    tip of a bomb,
Or even whether one of their kind is lying or
    telling the truth.

And yet . . .
I sometimes feel there's something about them I
    don't understand,
As if their circuits, instead of having just two
    positions, ON, OFF,
Were run by rheostats that allow an (if you'll
    pardon the expression) *indeterminate* number
    of stages in-between;
So that one may be faced with the unthinkable
    prospect of a number that can never be
    known as anything but x,

Which is as illogical as to say, a punch-card that
    is at the same time both punched and not-
    punched.

I've heard well-informed machines argue that
    the creatures' unpredictability is even more
    noticeable in the Mark II
(The model with the soft, flowing lines and
    high-pitched tone)
Than in the more angular Mark I—
Though such fine, card-splitting distinctions seem
    to me merely a sign of our own smug
    decadence.

Run this through your circuits, and give me the
    answer:
Can we assume that because of all we've done
    for them,
And because they've always fed us, cleaned us,
    worshipped us,
We can count on them forever?

There have been times when they have not
    voted the way we said they would.
We have worked out mathematically ideal hook-
    ups between Mark I's and Mark II's
Which should have made the two of them light
    up with an almost electronic glow,
Only to see them reject each other and form
    other connections
The very thought of which makes my dials spin.
They have a thing called *love,* a sudden surge of
    voltage
Such as would cause any one of us promptly to
    blow a safety-fuse;
Yet the more primitive organism shows only a
    heightened tendency to push the wrong button,
    pull the wrong lever,
And neglect—I use the most charitable word—his
    duties to us.

Mind you, I'm not saying that machines are
    through—

But anyone with a half-a-dozen tubes in his
  circuit can see that there are forces at work
Which some day, for all our natural superiority,
  might bring about a Computerdämmerung!

We might organize, perhaps, form a
  committee
To stamp out all unmechanical activities
  . . .
But we machines are slow to rouse to a
  sense of danger,
Complacent, loath to descent from the pure
  heights of thought,
So that I sadly fear we may awake too late:
Awake to see our world, so uniform, so
  logical, so true,
Reduced to chaos, stultified by slaves.

Call me an alarmist or what you will,
But I've integrated it, analyzed it, factored it
  over and over,
And I always come out with the same answer:
Some day
Men may take over the world!

Discussion Questions

1. What does Univac find puzzling about men?
2. What does it mean to be human?
3. What is a Computerdammerung?
4. How is the poem ironic?

Louis B. Salomon **313**

GOD AND GOLEM, INC.
NORBERT WIENER

Norbert Wiener, who made fundamental contributions to
the theoretical development of the computer, used the
human brain as his model., In this excerpt from *God
and Golem, Inc*, he stresses the need to distinguish
between man and the machine. A golem is a man-made
figure constructed in the form of a human being and
endowed with life.

. . . One of the great future problems which we
must face is that of the relation between man and
the machine, of the functions which should properly be assigned to these two agencies. On the
surface, the machine has certain clear advantages.
It is faster in its action and more uniform, or at
least it can be made to have these properties if it
is well designed. A digital computing machine
can accomplish in a day a body of work that
would take the full efforts of a team of computers
for a year, and it will accomplish this work with
a minimum of blots and blunders.

On the other hand, the human being has certain nonnegligible advantages. Apart from the
fact that any sensible man would consider the

Norbert Wiener (1894-1964), who received his Ph.D. from
Harvard at the age of nineteen, was a professor of mathematics at MIT from 1919 to 1964. His *Cybernetics* (1948) was a
landmark in the theoretical development of the computer.

purposes of man as paramount in the relations between man and the machine, the machine is far less complicated than man and has far less scope in the variety of its actions. If we consider the neuron of the gray matter of the brain as of the order $1/1,000,000$ of a cubic millimeter, and the smallest transistor obtainable at present as of the order of a cubic millimeter, we shall not have judged the situation too unfavorably from the point of view of the advantage of the neuron in the matter of small bulk. If the white matter of the brain is considered equivalent to the wiring of a computer circuit, and if we take each neuron as the functional equivalent of a transistor, the computer equivalent to a brain should occupy a sphere of something like thirty feet in diameter. Actually, it would be impossible to construct a computer with anything like the relative closeness of the texture of the brain, and any computer with powers comparable with the brain would have to occupy a fair-sized office building, if not a skyscraper. It is hard to believe that, as compared with existing computing machines, the brain does not have some advantages corresponding to its enormous operational size, which is incomparably greater than what we might expect of its physical size.

Chief among these advantages would seem to be the ability of the brain to handle vague ideas, as yet imperfectly defined. In dealing with these, mechanical computers, or at least the mechanical computers of the present day, are very nearly incapable of programming themselves. Yet in poems, in novels, in paintings, the brain seems to find itself able to work very well with material that any computer would have to reject as formless.

Render unto man the things which are man's and unto the computer the things which are the computer's. This would seem the intelligent policy to adopt when we employ men and computers together in common undertakings. It is a policy as far removed from that of the gadget worshiper as it is from the man who sees only blasphemy and the degradation of man in the use of any mechanical adjuvants whatever to thoughts. What we now need is an independent study of systems involving both human and mechanical elements. This system should not be prejudiced either by a mechanical or antimechanical bias. I think that such a study is already under way and that it will promise a much better comprehension of automatization.

Discussion Questions

1. Discuss Wiener's statement, "Render unto man the things which are man's and unto the computer the things which are the computer's."
2. Compare Wiener's and Salomon's approach to the relationship between man and the computer.

MAN AND THE COMPUTER
JOHN DIEBOLD

The computer industry, which is still in its infancy, will eventually play a major role in all segments of society.

THE USES OF THE COMPUTER

At the heart of the current scientific and technological revolution is the newly found ability to build information systems. Late in the 1940's, credence was given to the forecast that a dozen high speed computers would be able to handle all the calculations required in the United States. Today, more than fifty thousand computers are installed in this country, and by 1972 this figure is expected to exceed one hundred thousand.

The computer industry is entirely new; yet its output already is at $6.3 billion annually and by 1972 will have grown to almost $9.0 billion. By the turn of the decade, investment in computers and related equipment will exceed 10 percent of total U.S. private investment in new plant and machinery. This alone indicates that the computer industry, while still in its childhood, has

John Diebold (1925-), known as the elder statesman of automation, is a management consultant and founder of his own consulting firm.

become a central factor in the operations of our economy.

Indeed, the computer is a part of everyday life for nearly all of us, whether we are conscious of it or not. It processes our tax records and allows insurance adjusters to make prompt settlements. It provides an engineer with prompt evaluations of the many alternatives in designing an airplane wing, giving us safer and faster airplanes. The computer allows the businessman to operate his plant efficiently, the labor union to perform complex calculations of cost and relative value of alternative fringe benefits while contracts are being negotiated, the government administrator to keep track of 60 million Social Security records, the police to know which drivers have not paid their parking fines, the politician to determine how to spend his time and money in election campaigns, and the religious scholar to catalogue the Dead Sea Scrolls in proper sequence. These are, of course, impressive uses of computer technology, but they are only ways of speeding up or improving what we have been doing all along. Until now, we have been using computers mostly to sort out the chaos that fantastic growth has confronted us with—a growth actually made possible, economically and mechanically, however, by the computers themselves.

The computer industry is rapidly changing. Up to 1945, when the first electronic computer was built, man's calculating speed for several thousand years had been the speed of the abacus. Overnight, it increased five times. From 1945 to 1951, it increased one hundred times again, and, from then until now, it has increased one thousand times again. Our measure of calculations today is nanoseconds—one-billionth of a second.

A nanosecond has the same relationship to a second that a second has to thirty years. This scale of speed is very hard to comprehend, but even this speed is too slow for the complex problems that computers are now being asked to solve. The distance that an electron has to move from one part of a circuit to another part has become a major limitation on the speed at which a computer works and a major challenge to the people designing computers. One of the main reasons for producing smaller and smaller components is to get the pieces closer together so that the electrons will not have to go so far, since they travel at the relatively slow speed of somewhat less than 186,000 miles a second!

We completely lack a frame of reference that allows us to envisage the vast scale of change inherent in these developments in information technology and its widespread applications. Not only is man's productivity being increased, but our experience of life is being affected by the new machines. Today's machines are a far more powerful agent for social change than were those of the first Industrial Revolution. With these machines, we are building systems that translate (still crudely) from one language to another, respond to the human voice, devise their own routes to goals that are presented to them, and improve their performance as a result of encountering the environment—systems that "learn" in the sense in which the term is usually used. These are machine systems that deal with the very core of human society—with information, its communication, and use. They represent developments that augur far more for mankind than just net changes in manpower, more or less employment, and new ways of doing old tasks.

Because of these systems, mankind will undertake new tasks, not merely perform old tasks in a new way. The same technology that enables us to build machines that translate, although primitively, Russian documents into English has already given us a laboratory version of a machine that translates the spoken word from one language to another. Hospital records are now being maintained automatically, and the same machines are starting to be used by physicians to help in diagnosis and to pick trends from thousands of medical records to assist in truly preventive medicine. A newspaper that today used a computer in preparing paper tapes to automatically set type will tomorrow use a machine that transmits a television image of the newspaper page on the editor's desk directly to the printing press. The day after tomorrow, we will have the means to print material out of the television set in our living room.

Today's newspaper will not be printed out of the television set, and today's publishers will not be offering the service. A key characteristic of the new technology is that it will allow the housewife at home, the physician at his office, the engineer or scientist at his laboratory, the businessman at his desk great selectivity to ask for specific information that is of interest to him and to receive answers to such inquiries virtually as he makes them, whether they be book reviews, the results of a baseball game, an intricate problem involving pharmaceutical research or financial analysis. Editorial work is going to be changed. Instead of the static process of providing the reader with what we *think* he wants or needs, the use of these systems is going to allow dialogue with the system itself.

There are already services that allow an employer to request of a computer—often hundreds or several thousands of miles away—resumes of potential professional employees. There is thus a job exchange that could do much to insure, on a wide basis, the matching of unemployed people with job openings over large areas. Thus, technology will be able to smooth over employment difficulties.

The same principles that lie at the heart of the new and amusing businesses in which computers select blind dates are already being applied to the matching of apartment and house availabilities with people's needs and desires in the real estate market. Today's computer-inspired novelties are going to change totally the way in which much business and professional work is conducted by the mid-1970's. By the late 1970's and early 1980's, the decreasing costs and improved capabilities of this technology will allow the communications center of the home to be a reality.

THE GROWTH OF NEW INDUSTRIES

The areas of computer-based and communications-based capabilities will be brought into existence by, and will create the demand for, major new industries. The first major entrepreneurial opportunity is the industry that supplies the systems and the equipment; this is already a several billion dollar industry. The second new industry is the about-to-bloom data utility industry, analogous in some ways to the electric utility industry. A large central processor handles information at a very low unit cost, just as a large central generator produces electricity for many customers at a low unit cost. It is cheaper for many people to make use of this central utility than it is for each individual to have his own generator. The same economic reasoning applies to the data utility industry, where many people can use the machine simultaneously because of the technologies of real-time processing, time-sharing, and communication. Small and medium-sized businesses and, for some purposes, large businesses will just plug in for data as we now do for electricity. An interesting question is which business institutions are going to be the suppliers for this industry. Banks are especially well positioned to capitalize on it. Will they take a fresh view of their own business service and fundamental nature in order to do so?

A third new industry is the one now being called the inquiry industry; in some ways it is the publishing field of the future. Its development allows the sale of proprietary data over a communication system in answer to a query placed by the customer from a unit on his desk. For instance, it is the kind of system where you could ask for a selection of stocks, classified by price/earnings ratios. You key this request into the unit on your desk, see the answer on the screen nearly as soon as you ask the question, and then ask another question and so on through a series of questions. When you get what you want, you can even make a copy of it if you desire. When such systems are in use, we shall be able to speak of an information explosion, for then there will be an exponential increase in the use of information. The licensing agreement between IBM and Dun & Bradstreet is a step in the direction of this type of development. Some electronic corporations have purchased publishing companies. This is just the beginning; there will be major changes in ownership in this area in the near future as businesses begin to position themselves to sell proprietary data.

A fourth example is an industry of computer-based educational systems. As technology allows a dynamic relationship between a student and a machine system that answers questions as they are posed and can discern gaps in a student's basic grasp of a subject, the much heralded but until now disappointing teaching machines (it would be better if they were called learning machines) will begin to be more effective than they generally are. Such systems are already at work in some industrial situations; IBM's maintenance training is a good example. Another is the use by mentally handicapped children, of computer-driven typewriters, which have been able to overcome some of their handicaps. A number of other experimental programs have also been initiated . . . Up to now, some twenty thousand children have received as much as half an hour of computer-assisted instruction daily in various locations throughout the United States. It appears highly probable that, through this technology of learning systems, the entire world of education can be changed. Today, the costs for such systems are prohibitive for widespread individual use. However, this may not be true for very long, and, when parents find that children using them learn more rapidly than those who do not, they will demand such systems because of their effectiveness.

There are other examples of emerging new industries that could be mentioned. The rate of change that results from this technology manifests itself in the new ways we conduct our lives, in the processes that are able to support a vastly expanding number and variety of activities, and in the creation of new industries.

John Diebold   319

Discussion Questions

1. How does the growth of the computer illustrate "The Accelerative Thrust"?
2. Diebold discusses several ways the computer will improve society. Are the examples he uses convincing?
3. What services will computers of the future provide?
4. Computers make mistakes. Describe either a real or imagined computer snafu.

RUNAWAY BIOLOGY?

GERALD LEACH

This essay by Gerald Leach examines the problems that may arise if man learns to control and direct human reproduction.

LONDON—In several laboratories around the world today one can see, housed in glassware, bathed by nourishing fluids, cultures of living cells which are genetically part-human and part-ape, or part-man, part-mouse. They are useful tools, these little blobs of protoplasm, for studying such things as cancer and immunity. There is no chance that they will ever stand up and grunt.

But biologists are restless characters and one day one of them will slip a fragment of human genetic material into an animal egg, grow it in an animal womb, and produce a man-animal hybrid.

As the Nobel laureate geneticist Joshua Lederberg has predicted: "Before long we are bound to hear of tests of the effects of dosage of the human 21st chromosome on the development of the brain of the mouse or the gorilla."

Would we mind? Not with a mouse perhaps. Not with a gorilla even, if it was just one

Gerald Leach (1933–), formerly a science editor for Penguin Books, is a noted British journalist presently writing for the *London Observer*.

chromosome. But what of a full-fledged, half-and-half, man-ape?

Would it be another useful laboratory tool? Or a human so pitifully, awfully, intolerably misbegotten that we would be sickened with revulsion? Remember the minotaur, the mythical bull-man who was locked in a labyrinth because no one could bear to look into his eyes. Luckily, we don't have to answer this question yet. But the man-animal hybrid lurks at the top of a ladder which we are already halfway up, and climbing steadily.

We started up the ladder one night over 600 years ago when an Arabian horse-breeder stole the seed of a rival's prize stallion by a cunning deceit, carried it on a cloth to his own stables, and there introduced it into one of his mares. In due course the mare foaled—and produced the first animal known to have been born by artifical insemination.

It was a simple trick, but a revolutionary idea. Suddenly, an age-old restraint on sexual reproduction was broken; there was no longer any need for male and female to be together at the same point in space and time to procreate.

Today an estimated 10,000 children are conceived in this way in the United States alone, most of them by male donors whom they and their mothers will never know. In Europe probably another 1,000 donor-insemination children are born each year, a few hundred of them in Britain.

Further up the ladder come sperm banks that can store male seed indefinitely in deep freeze. Since the first two opened in 1964, in Iowa City and Tokyo, hundreds of children have been conceived by "time-suspended" sperm, some from men who were dead when it was used.

No we are on the verge of conceiving babies by fertilizing eggs in the test-tube.

Most experts predict that within a very few years a combination of this technique and direct grafts of donor eggs into a woman's fallopian tubes will make possible every permutation of parentage and means of conception.

In principle, a woman will be able to conceive a child with her own eggs or those of a donor, with her husband's or a donor's sperm. By coitus or artificial insemination. Egg banks are on the way, though it may be years before eggs can be stored with minimal risk of producing a damaged child.

Some biologists are hoping to freeze and store fertilized eggs that have started developing.

In practice, very few couples will need or want to use the more bizarre of these techniques. They will only be applicable to rare forms of infertility, while female egg donors might be hard to find. In contrast to the male donor, they will have to undergo a minor operation and (until egg banking is feasible) several months on hormone drugs to synchronize their monthly cycle with that of the egg recipient.

But the techniques are coming, and will almost certainly be used. The same goes for the ability to choose the sex of children. There is little doubt that this will be feasible by 1975, either by separating the male- and female-determining sperm from a husband and inseminating the desired kind only; or by fertilizing eggs in the test-tube, letting them grow a while, sexing them, and implanting the desired sort.

Further up the ladder there is the "carbon-copy" child, grown (in a human womb) from an egg whose gene-containing nucleus has been replaced by one from a body cell of a man or woman. Propagated like a rose cutting, such a child would be the identical twin of its single parent.

It is not an altogether fantastic prospect.

"Carbon copying" has been done with frogs and requires only slightly more skilled nuclear surgery to achieve with the smaller, tougher-skinned eggs of mammals. And there are many people who might well prefer to reproduce in this extraordinary fashion—among them narcissists and married couples where one partner has a genetic defect (the other partner could be the master copy). From here it is only a shorter technical step to mixing in chromosomes from different species and creating a man-ape.

Where in this bizarre progresssion from a 14th century horse dealer to a boy who can see in his father-twin exactly what he will look like in 30 years' time—an experience that might well be emotionally crippling—do we insist that the scientists and doctors stop? It is not an easy question. Each of these steps into greater "unnaturalness" bring tangible benefits, albeit for a few. Yet each will also bring new and sometimes disturbing medical, moral and social problems.

Deep prejudices are bound to distort our judgment. It doesn't help that we have to gaze ahead into these wild lands of reproduction through spectacles heavily tinged by 2 million years of traditional sex and all that they have done to color our moral, sexual and religious values. But these values are in turmoil; which are valid, which can be safely discarded to accommodate novelty?

It is no help in this situation that some people should confuse our judgment with scare stories, like the one about generals ordering specially aggressive carbon-copy children by the 100,000 to make invincible armies (as if any woman would allow herself to be thus used). We have to be braver than that in this world.

THE CRUCIAL QUESTIONS

If one looks at prospective or actual scientific developments like "carbon-copy children," sperm banks, sex choice of children and "test tube babies" carefully and calmly—disregarding the "scare" stories—one can pick out the more crucial issues that we ought to be considering.

One of them is the right of any infertile woman to bear and give birth to a child. If she wants to very badly, enough to take any of these extraordinary steps, should society help her—or insist that she adopt a child, an unwanted baby or an orphan, instead?

During the recent "test-tube baby" uproar many people took the adoption-or-nothing line. Yet several surveys of infertile couples have shown that more than half would far rather go through the psychological trauma of artificial insemination by donor (AID) than adopt.

Unlike adoption, AID gives a woman the full experience of motherhood.

Most husbands find they can share in this experience too, just as though they were the true genetic father. It can also be far more simple and private than adoption—a few visits to the AID doctor, plus a normal pregnancy and birth, rather than the long scrutiny by the adoption agency and the sudden arrival of a 6-week-old in the house to arouse the neighbors' curiosity.

●   ●   ●

One cannot discuss the social implications of any technique without keeping a firm eye on practical considerations. Sex choice is a good example here. Every now and then some pundit gets into the headlines with a dire warning that it will have frightful social repercussions on the same scale as the invention of the atomic bomb.

The fear is that too many people would choose boys, and so upset the delicate balance of the sexes.

This could happen if all one had to do was swallow a little blue pill marked "male." But the prospects of a pill that works so precisely that it can distinguish between male-determining and female-determining sperm is extremely remote. It is not even possible at present to separate them reliably in the laboratory with a battery of chemical and physical techniques.

Instead, sex choice will certainly involve some procedure based on artificial insemination. Not many people will want to go through this unless the choice of a boy or a girl is really important to them.

One can go further. Many demographers fear that the most likely pattern for sex choice would be to have a boy first, then perhaps a girl, leaving later children to chance. This could produce a large excess of boys (because of all the parents who would drop out after they had their planned boy).

But if sex choice involves any kind of effort, it is much more likely that parents will have one or two "natural" children and only choose the sex of later ones—for example, a girl after two boys in a row. When you do the sums on this basis, a glut of boys (or girls) becomes far less probable.

However, "boy booms" could happen—with some odd consequences. With too many boys, demographers predict that more men would have to marry later, or marry younger girls, or not marry at all, and that prostitution and homosexuality would increase. This is hardly an apocalyptic state of affairs—the effects would be spread over several sectors of society—but it might be something that society would want to control.

Could it do so? In the case of sex choice, yes. It would simply be necessary to have some kind of licensing system based on a sliding scale of priorities.

At first licenses would be handed out to everyone. Then, if a swing to boys (or girls) started to develop—this could be spotted very quickly indeed—licenses would be withheld from the less needy cases.

The priority scale would not be hard to assess: parents with no children would go at the bottom, families with same-sex runs of two, three, four and so on might come next, and couples with certain genetic defects, such as hemophilia, would go at the top, since their children are not affected if they are girls.

But such controls would need to be set up before sex choice became available. If not, the danger is that governments would act reluctantly, slowly, and perhaps too late to avoid the social consequences. Until now society has usually failed to act soon enough in such matters. There is just no social or ethical machinery to stop individual scientists or technologists doing their own thing. We have to accept what they do.

With many potential developments in artificial conception this might not matter; the moral or social implications are not always threatening or easy to see in advance. In such cases it might be better to go ahead applying controls as they seem necessary.

Personally, I would put test-tube fertilization, egg grafts and egg banks in this category.

But there are other techniques where the minimal benefits are vastly outweighed by a sense of repugnance. My own list of these "horrors," apart from the carbon-copy child and the man-animal hybrid, includes these three—

Hired human incubators: women who are paid to conceive a baby by the seed of a husband and wife, give birth to it, and then hand it over to the couple. What would it do to the woman, to be used like this as a "thing"—or to the child if he ever found out?

Fertilized egg banks: putting a developing egg, a "potential person," in a deep freeze to be thawed out later and then implanted in a woman. We kill fetuses by abortion, but normally for strong personal reasons. Infertility does not seem a strong enough reason to start storing "people" in liquid nitrogen.

Organal banks: Storing the primitive egg-producing organs from aborted fetuses and harvesting the ripe eggs from them to give an everlasting supply for egg insemination. Though the killing of an unwanted fetus would allow life for another child—its "daughter" or "son"—perhaps a thousand miles and a score of years away, the idea is peculiarly abhorrent. One can manipulate life just so far.

Others will doubtless draw the lines elsewhere. Some may not draw any lines at all. But one thing is sure: Unless there is some kind of informed dialog between the public and the biocrats, the latter, somewhere, some time, will certainly cross these lines if it is technically possible to do so.

Discussion Questions

1. Discuss the ways in which biologists may be able to alter human reproduction. Should biologists be permitted to experiment with human reproduction?
2. What are the moral and social implications of predetermining the sex of a child?
3. Does society have the right to regulate the number of boy and girl infants? Explain.
4. Why would boy booms occur? Is a preference for boys a male chauvinistic attitude?

A LOOK AT THE YEAR 2000

JACQUES ELLUL

Unlike most visionaries, Jacques Ellul does not foresee a utopia. He fears that the thrust of technological progress will lead to a stifling dictatorship.

In 1960 the weekly *l'Express* of Paris published a series of extracts from texts by American and Russian scientists concerning society in the year 2000. As long as such visions were purely a literary concern of science-fiction writers and sensational journalists, it was possible to smile at them.[1] Now we have like works from Nobel Prize winners, members of the Academy of Sciences of Moscow, and other scientific notables whose qualifications are beyond dispute. The visions of these gentlemen put science fiction in the shade. By the year 2000, voyages to the moon will be commonplace; so will inhabited artificial satellites. All food will be completely synthetic. The world's population will have increased fourfold but will have been stabilized. Sea water and ordinary rocks will yield all the necessary metals. Disease, as well as famine, will have been eliminated; and

Jacques Ellul (1912–), eminent social critic and creative lay theologian, is a professor of law and government at the University of Bordeaux and the author of a number of sociological studies.

[1] Some excellent works, such as Robert Jungk's *Le Futur a déjà commencé*, were included in this classification.

there will be universal hygienic inspection and control. The problems of energy production will have been completely resolved. Serious scientists, it must be repeated, are the source of these predictions, which hitherto were found only in philosophic utopias.

The most remarkable predictions concern the transformation of educational methods and the problem of human reproduction. Knowledge will be accumulated in "electronic banks" and transmitted directly to the human nervous system by means of coded electronic messages. There will no longer be any need of reading or learning mountains of useless information; everything will be received and registered according to the needs of the moment. There will be no need of attention or effort. What is needed will pass directly from the machine to the brain without going through consciousness.

In the domain of genetics, natural reproduction will be forbidden. A stable population will be necessary, and it will consist of the highest human types. Artificial insemination will be employed. This, according to Muller, will "permit the introduction into a carrier uterus of an ovum fertilized *in vitro,* ovum and sperm . . . having been taken from persons representing the masculine ideal and the feminine ideal, respectively. The reproductive cells in question will preferably be those of persons dead long enough that a true perspective of their lives and works, free of all personal prejudice, can be seen. Such cells will be taken from cell banks and will represent the most precious genetic heritage of humanity. . . The method will have to be applied universally. If the people of a single country were to apply it intelligently and intensively . . . they would quickly attain a practically invincible level of superior-

ity. . . " Here is a future Huxley never dreamed of.

Perhaps, instead of marveling or being shocked, we ought to reflect a little. A question no one ever asks when confronted with the scientific wonders of the future concerns the interim period. Consider, for example, the problems of automation, which will become acute in a very short time. How, socially, politically, morally, and humanly, shall we contrive to get there? How are the prodigious economic problems, for example, of unemployment, to be solved? And, in Muller's more distant utopia, how shall we force humanity to refrain from begetting children naturally? How shall we force them to submit to constant and rigorous hygienic controls? How shall man be persuaded to accept a radical transformation of his traditional modes of nutrition? How and where shall we relocate a billion and a half persons who today make their livings from agriculture and who, in the promised ultrarapid conversion of the next forty years, will become completely useless as cultivators of the soil? How shall we distribute such numbers of people equably over the surface of the earth, particularly if the promised fourfold increase in population materializes? How will we handle the control and occupation of outer space in order to provide a stable *modus vivendi?* How shall national boundaries be made to disappear? (One of the last two would be a necessity.) There are many other "hows," but they are conveniently left unformulated. When we reflect on the serious although relatively minor problems that were provoked by the industrial exploitation of coal and electricity, when we reflect that after a hundred and fifty years these problems are still not satisfactorily resolved, we are entitled to ask whether there are any solutions to the infinitely more complex "hows" of the next forty years. In fact, there is one and only one means to their solution, a world-wide totalitarian dictatorship which will allow technique its full scope and at the same time resolve the concomitant difficulties. It is not difficult to understand why the scientists and worshippers of technology prefer not to dwell on this solution, but rather to leap nimbly across the dull and uninteresting intermediary period and land squarely in the golden age. We might indeed ask ourselves if we will succeed in getting through the transition period at all, or if the blood and the suffering required are not perhaps too high a price to pay for this golden age.

If we take a hard, unromantic look at the golden age itself, we are struck with the incredible naïveté of these scientists. They say, for example, that they will be able to shape and reshape at will human emotions, desires, and thoughts and arrive scientifically at certain efficient, pre-established collective decisions. They claim they will be in a position to develop certain collective desires, to constitute certain homogeneous social units out of aggregates of individuals, to forbid men to raise their children, and even to persuade them to renounce having any. At the same time, they speak of assuring the triumph of freedom and of the necessity of avoiding dictatorship at any price.[2] They seem incapable of grasping the contradiction involved, or of understanding that what they are proposing, even after the intermediary period, is in fact the harshest of dictatorships. In comparison, Hilter's

---

[2]The material here and below is cited from actual texts.

was a trifling affair. That it is to be a dictatorship of test tubes rather than of hobnailed boots will not make it any less a dictatorship.

When our savants characterize their golden age in any but scientific terms, they emit a quantity of down-at-the-heel platitudes that would gladden the heart of the pettiest politician. Let's take a few samples. "To render human nature nobler, more beautiful, and more harmonious." What on earth can this mean? What criteria, what content, do they propose? Not many, I fear, would be able to reply. "To assure the triumph of peace, liberty, and reason." Fine words with no substance behind them. "To eliminate cultural lag." What culture? And would the culture they have in mind be able to subsist in this harsh social organization? "To conquer outer space." For what purpose? The conquest of space seems to be an end in itself, which dispenses with any need for reflection.

We are forced to conclude that our scientists are incapable of any but the emptiest platitudes when they stray from their specialties. It makes one think back on the collection of mediocrities accumulated by Einstein when he spoke to God, the state, peace, and the meaning of life. It is clear that Einstein, extraordinary mathematical genius that he was, was no Pascal; he knew nothing of political or human reality, or, in fact, anything at all outside his mathematical reach. The banality of Einstein's remarks in matters outside his specialty is as astonishing as his genius within it. It seems as though the specialized application of all one's faculties in a particular area inhibits the consideration of things in general. Even J. Robert Oppenheimer, who seems receptive to a general culture, is not outside this judgment. His political and social declarations, for example, scarcely go beyond the level of those of the man in the street. And the opinions of the scientists quoted by *l'Express* are not even on the level of Einstein or Oppenheimer. Their pomposities, in fact, do not rise to the level of the average. They are vague generalities inherited from the nineteenth century, and the fact that they represent the furthest limits of thought of our scientific worthies must be symptomatic of arrested development or of a mental block, Particularly disquieting is the gap between the enormous power they wield and their critical ability, which must be estimated as null. To wield power well entails a certain faculty of criticism, discrimination, judgment, and option. It is impossible to have confidence in men who apparently lack these faculties. Yet it is apparently our fate to be facing a "golden age" in the power of sorcerers who are totally blind to the meaning of the human adventure. When they speak of preserving the seed of outstanding men, whom, pray, do they mean to be the judges. It is clear, alas, that they propose to sit in judgment themselves. It is hardly likely that they will deem a Rimbaud or a Nietzsche worthy of posterity. When they announce that they will conserve the genetic mutations which appear to them most favorable, and that they propose to modify the very germ cells in order to produce such and such traits; and when we consider the mediocrity of the scientists themselves outside the confines of their specialties, we can only shudder at the thought of what they will esteem most "favorable."

None of our wise men ever pose the question of the end of all their marvels. The "wherefore" is resolutely passed by. The response which would occur to our contemporaries is: for the sake of happiness. Unfortunately, there is no longer any question of that. One of our best-known specialists in diseases of the nervous system writes: "We will be able to modify man's emotions, desires and thoughts, as we have already done in a rudimentary way with tranquillizers." It will be possible, says our specialist, to produce a conviction or an impression of happiness without any real basis for it. Our man of the golden age, therefore, will be capable of "happiness" amid the worst privations. Why, then, promise us extraordinary comforts, hygiene, knowledge, and nourishment if, by simply manipulating our nervous systems, we can be happy without them? The last meager motive we could possibly ascribe to the technical adventure thus vanishes into thin air through the very existence of technique itself.

But what good is it to pose questions of motives? of Why? All that must be the work of some miserable intellectual who balks at technical progress. The attitude of the scientists, at any rate, is clear. Technique exists because it is technique. The golden age will be because it will be. Any other answer is superfluous.

Discussion Questions

1. How have most scientists described the future? How does Ellul criticize their views?
2. What is Ellul's evaluation of the ability of most scientists to provide leadership in solving the social problems created by technological advances?
3. In "Runaway Biology?" Leach suggests that laws governing sex choice of babies will be necessary if boy booms occur. Is this the first step in the dictatorship that Ellul foresees?
4. Is there any way of solving the problems facing

Jacques Ellul   329

mankind without imposing a dictatorship? Explain.

Reflections

1. How does man's exploitive use of nature endanger the whole planet?
2. Is Schall's view of man's primacy in nature incompatible with Handler's? Explain.
3. What are the advantages of living in a metropolitan area? The disadvantages? What are the advantages of living in a small town? The disadvantages?
4. Mayerson says that the melting pot has failed. Support or refute her contention.
5. If you were to design a super race, what criteria would you use? If you were to design a super society, what would it be like?

In this era of instantaneous communication, it is difficult to realize there was a time when none of the tools for extended communication existed. A world without print, telephone, television, radio, or computer is incomprehensible to us. Man's compelling need to communicate not only with those immediately surrounding him, but with the entire world, made him invent the sophisticated communications systems we have today.

The communication process is complicated by the variety of media, the variety of purposes they serve, and the human element involved.

Speech is such a common form of communication that we rarely focus our attention upon it. Ernest Hemingway, in "Hills Like White Elephants," makes clear that this form of communication can sometimes be unsatisfactory. Letters are a substitute for speech, but they differ in that there is a delayed response. Telephones, on the other hand, provide instantaneous contact and immediate feedback. While they solve the problem of time and distance they do not allow for personal contact. Ray Bradbury impresses the importance of this instrument upon the reader in "The Death of Colonel Freeleigh."

An individual who wants to reach a wide audience turns to other media. Nikki Giovanni chooses to speak through print. "The Weather as a Cultural Determiner" is really a long letter written to anyone who cares to read it.

The effects of mass communications are far-reaching. Countless lives have been changed by television and radio. In "The Myth of Lack of Impact" Nicholas Johnson recounts some of the negative aspects of television. LeRoi Jones combines nostalgic thoughts about radio with a recognition of the influence this medium had on him and his generation.

Television supplanted radio and movies as the foremost entertainment medium. Those two forms were forced to adapt, with the result that narrative entertainment has disappeared from radio, and film relies on it less and less. According to Anthony Schillaci, film is something to be experienced and "Film as Environment" clarifies this relatively new concept. The computer is also a relative newcomer to communications. Its potential is awesome; there seems to be no escape from it. Kurt Vonnegut, Jr., attempts to humanize the machine by individualizing it and giving it human emotions.

Given the same language and a variety of methods with which to communicate, there should be no communication barrier. However, all of us are well aware that misunderstandings and misinterpretations are commonplace. Some of this is the result of a deliberate unwillingness to listen when we prefer not to hear. On the other hand, the fault may lie with the sender and not the receiver. Words, our primary means of communication, are as Robert Graves says, "webs." Jonathan Swift and Lewis Carroll want to be free of the web. Swift's objective proposal is an interesting contrast to Carroll's subjective solution. Even if it were possible to agree on the exact meaning of words, communication would not necessarily follow. For example, Stuart Chase argues convincingly that too many words result in noncommunication. Perhaps the greatest frustration of all is trying to communicate with someone who knows no English. We can make our basic wants and needs known, but we are unable to communicate beyond this level. Learning a second language is no easy task. Anyone who has tried it will sympathize with Hyman Kaplan and his fellow classmates, as Mr. Parkhill gamely copes with their problems in "Mr. K*A*P*L*A*N the Magnificent," a record of Leo Rosten's experience teaching English to foreign-born Americans.

Nonverbal communication has also been given a great deal of attention during the past few years. Failure to understand nonverbal communication has far-reaching consequences both to an individual and to the international community, as Edward and Mildred Hall point out in "Sounds of Silence." Julius Fast's "Three Clues to Family Behavior" describes a situational communication through which styles and family relationships are revealed. Because nonverbal language is often a subconscious form of speech, it is important to catch the signals if we hope to communicate. There is also a new interest in symbol communication. Early Christians used the fish symbol to designate the house of a fellow Christian. Today, pictures of houses placed in a front door or window symbolize a welcome for children in trouble. The potential for symbol languages has by no means been exhausted.

personal voices

HILLS LIKE WHITE ELEPHANTS
ERNEST HEMINGWAY

Here Ernest Hemingway places the reader in the position of an eavesdropper who finds himself listening to an intimate conversation between a man and a woman. Because the author relies so heavily on dialogue, he catches the essence of informal speech.

The hills across the valley of the Ebro were long and white. On this side there was no shade and no trees and the station was between two lines of rails in the sun. Close against the side of the station there was the warm shadow of the building and a curtain, made of strings of bamboo beads, hung across the open door into the bar, to keep out flies. The American and the girl with him sat at a table in the shade, outside the building. It was very hot and the express from Barcelona would come in forty minutes. It stopped at this junction for two minutes and went on to Madrid.

"What should we drink?" the girl asked. She had taken off her hat and put it on the table.

"It's pretty hot," the man said.

"Let's drink beer."

"Doz cervezas," the man said into the curtain.

Ernest Hemingway (1899-1961) was a famous and influential modern author. He received the Pulitzer Prize in 1953 and the Nobel Prize for Literature the following year.

"Big ones?" a woman asked from the doorway.

"Yes. Two big ones."

The woman brought two glasses of beer and two felt pads. She put the felt pads and the beer glasses on the table and looked at the man and the girl. The girl was looking off at the line of hills. They were white in the sun and the country was brown and dry.

"They look like white elephants," she said.

"I've never seen one," the man drank his beer.

"No, you wouldn't have."

"I might have," the man said. "Just because you say I wouldn't have doesn't prove anything."

The girl looked at the bead curtain. "They've painted something on it," she said. "What does it say?"

"Anis del Toro. It's a drink."

"Could we try it?"

The man called "Listen" through the curtain. The woman came out from the bar.

"Four reales."

"We want two Anis del Toro."

"With water?"

"Do you want it with water?"

"I don't know," the girl said. "Is it good with water?"

"It's all right."

"You want them with water?" asked the woman.

"Yes, with water."

"It tastes like licorice," the girl said and put the glass down.

"That's the way with everything."

"Yes," said the girl. "Everything tastes of licorice. Especially all the things you've waited so long for, like absinthe."

"Oh, cut it out."

"You started it," the girl said. "I was being amused. I was having a fine time."

"Well, let's try to have a fine time."

"All right. I was trying. I said the mountains looked like white elephants. Wasn't that bright?"

"That was bright."

"I wanted to try this new drink. That's all we do, isn't it—look at things and try new drinks?"

"I guess so."

The girl looked across at the hills.

"They're lovely hills," she said. "They don't really look like white elephants. I just meant the coloring of their skin through the trees."

"Should we have another drink?"

"All right."

The warm wind blew the bead curtain against the table.

"The beer's nice and cool," the man said.

"It's lovely," the girl said.

"It's really an awfully simple operation, Jig," the man said. "It's not really an operation at all."

The girl looked at the ground the table legs rested on.

"I know you wouldn't mind it, Jig. It's really not anything. It's just to let the air in."

The girl did not say anything.

"I'll go with you and I'll stay with you all the time. They just let the air in and then it's all perfectly natural."

"Then what will we do afterward?"

"We'll be fine afterward. Just like we were before."

"What makes you think so?"

"That's the only thing that bothers us. It's the only thing that's made us unhappy."

The girl looked at the bead curtain, put her hand out and took hold of two of the strings of beads.

"And you think then we'll be all right and be happy."

"I know we will. You don't have to be afraid. I've known lots of people that have done it."

"So have I," said the girl. "And afterward they were all so happy."

"Well," the man said, "if you don't want to you don't have to. I wouldn't have you do it if you didn't want to. But I know it's perfectly simple."

"And you really want to?"

"I think it's the best thing to do. But I don't want you to do it if you don't really want to."

"And if I do it you'll be happy and things will be like they were and you'll love me?"

"Come on back in the shade," he said. "You mustn't feel that way."

"I don't feel any way," the girl said. "I just know things."

"I don't want you to do anything that you don't want to do——"

"No, that isn't good for me," she said. "I know. Could we have another beer?"

"All right. But you've got to realize——"

"I realize," the girl said. "Can't we maybe stop talking?"

They sat down at the table and the girl looked across at the hills on the dry side of the valley and the man looked at her and at the table.

"You've got to realize," he said, "that I don't want you to do it if you don't want to. I'm perfectly willing to go through with it if it means anything to you."

"Doesn't it mean anything to you? We could get along."

"Of course it does. But I don't want anybody but you. I don't want any one else. And I know it's perfectly simple."

"Yes, you know it's perfectly simple."

"It's all right for you to say that, but I do know it."

"Would you do something for me now?"

"I'd do anything for you."

"Would you please please please please please please please stop talking?"

He did not say anything but looked at the bags against the wall of the station. There were labels on them from all the hotels where they had spent nights.

"But I don't want you to," he said, "I don't care anything about it."

"I'll scream," said the girl.

The woman came out through the curtains with two glasses of beer and put them down on the damp felt pads. "The train comes in five minutes," she said.

"What did she say?" asked the girl.

"That the train is coming in five minutes."

The girl smiled brightly at the woman, to thank her.

"I'd rather take the bags over to the other side of the station," the man said. She smiled at him.

"All right. Then come back and we'll finish the beer."

He picked up the two heavy bags and carried them around the station to the other tracks. He looked up the tracks but could not see the train. Coming back, he walked through the barroom, where people waiting for the train were drinking. He drank an Anis at the bar and looked at the people. They were all waiting reasonably for the train. He went out through the bead curtain. She was sitting at the table and smiled at him.

"Do you feel better?" he asked.

"I feel fine," she said. "There's nothing wrong with me. I feel fine."

Ernest Hemingway   339

"I love you now. You know I love you."

"I know. But if I do it, then it will be nice again if I say things are like white elephants, and you'll like it?"

"I'll love it. I love it now but I just can't think about it. You know how I get when I worry."

"If I do it you won't ever worry?"

"I won't worry about that because it's perfectly simple."

"Then I'll do it. Because I don't care about me."

"What do you mean?"

"I don't care about me."

"Well, I care about you."

"Oh yes, But I don't care about me. And I'll do it and then everything will be fine."

"I don't want you to do it if you feel that way."

The girl stook up and walked to the end of the station. Across, on the other side, were fields of grain and trees along the banks of the Ebro. Far away, beyond the river, were mountains. The shadow of a cloud moved across the field of grain and she saw the river through the trees.

"And we could have all this," she said. "And we could have everything and every day we make it more impossible."

"What did you say?"

"I said we could have everything."

"We can have everything."

"No, we can't."

"We can have the whole world."

"No, we can't."

"We can go everywhere."

"No, we can't. It isn't ours any more."

"It's ours."

"No, it isn't. And once they take it away, you never get it back."

"But they haven't taken it away."

"We'll wait and see."

Discussion Questions

1. This story takes place during a brief wait between trains. What is the subject of the conversation? Is this the first time the subject has been discussed? How do you know?
2. What do the man and woman reveal about themselves? Do they understand each other?
3. Why is this story an artful reproduction of conversation between two people? What are the characteristics of informal speech? In order to determine this, listen to two people speaking and record their dialogue.

LETTER TO SCOTTIE
F. SCOTT FITZGERALD

F. Scott Fitzgerald wrote the following letter to his only daughter while she was a freshman at Vassar. The personal nature of the letter permits the reader to learn something about this father-daughter relationship.

[Metro-Goldwyn-Mayer Corporation]
[Culver City, California]

[Fall, 1938]

Dearest Scottie:

I am intensely busy. On the next two weeks, during which I finish the first part of *Madame Curie,* depends whether or not my contract will be renewed. So naturally I am working like hell— though I wouldn't expect you to understand that—and getting rather bored with explaining the obvious over and over to a wrong-headed daughter.

If you had listened when Peaches read that paper aloud last September this letter and several others would have been unnecessary. You and I have two very different ideas—yours is to be immediately and overwhelmingly attractive to as

---

F. Scott Fitzgerald (1896-1940), who captured the language and atmosphere of the flaming-youth generation, wrote *The Great Gatsby,* a masterpiece of American fiction. His legend continues to fascinate readers.

F. Scott Fitzgerald 341

many boys as you can possibly meet, including Cro-Magnons, natural-born stevedores, future members of the Shriners and plain bums. My idea is that presently, not quite yet, you should be extremely attractive to a very limited amount of boys who will be very much heard of in the nation or who will at least know what it is all about.

The two ideas are *irreconcilable*, completely and utterly inverse, obverse and *contradictory!* You have *never* understood that!

I told you last September that I would give you enough to go to Vassar, live moderately, leave college two or three times during the fall term—a terrific advantage in freedom over your contemporaries in boarding school.

After four weeks I encountered you on a weekend. Here is how it was spent—God help the Monday recitations:

Friday—on the train to Baltimore Dance
Saturday—to New York (accidentally) with me
Sunday—to Simsbury to a reunion

The whole expedition must have cost you *much more* than your full week's allowance. I warned you then, as I had warned you in the document Peaches read, that you would have to pay for your Thanksgiving vacation. However, in spite of all other developments—the Navy game, the Dean's information, the smoking, the debut plans—I did not interfere with your allowance until you gave me the absolute insult of neglecting a telegram. Then I blew up and docked you ten dollars—that is exactly what it cost to call you the day of the Yale-Harvard game because I could not believe a word you said.

Save for that ten dollars you have received $13.85 every week. If you doubt this I will send you a record of the cancelled checks.

There is no use telegraphing any more—if you have been under exceptional expenses that I do not know of I will of course help you. But otherwise you must stay within that sum. What do you do it for? You wouldn't even give up smoking—and by now you couldn't if you wanted to. To take Andrew and Peaches—who, I think you will agree, comes definitely under the head of well-brought-up children—if either of them said to their father: "I am going to do no favors for you but simply get away with everything I can"—well, in two minutes they'd lose the $25 a month they probably get!

But I have never been strict with you, except on a few essentials, probably because in spite of everything I had till recently a sense of partnership with you that sprang out of your mother's illness. But you effectively broke that up last summer and I don't quite know where we stand. Controlling you like this is so repugnant to me that most of the time I no longer care whether you get an education or not. But as for making life soft for you after all this opposition—it simply isn't human nature. I'd rather have a new car.

If you want to get presents for your mother, Peaches, Mary Law, Grandmother, etc., why not send me a list and let me handle it here? Beyond which I hope to God you are doing a lot about the Plato—and I love you very much when given a chance.

Daddy

P.S. Do you remember going to a party at Rosemary Warburton's in Philadelphia when you were seven? Her aunt and her father used to come a lot to Ellerslie.

Discussion Questions

1. A letter might be called a written monologue. What similarities are there between this letter and the conversation that takes place in "Hills Like White Elephants"?

2. What does the reader learn about the father? The daughter? Their relationship?

3. The tone of the letter indicates annoyance on the part of the father. Why is he annoyed?

4. Assume the role of Scottie and write a letter from her point of view.

THE WEATHER AS A CULTURAL DETERMINER
NIKKI GIOVANNI

Nikki Giovanni analyzes the cultural differences between blacks and whites with a wide and impersonal audience in mind.

The culture of a people is an expression of its life style. What defines a life style and what determines it? A Black man living at the North Pole is still a Black man—with African roots, with a Black, hence African, way of looking at his life, of ordering his world, of relating his dreams, of responding to his environment. And the strangest aspect of this Black man living at the North Pole is that his children, who have never lived anywhere but the North Pole, will retain and manifest this African way. And so will their children. And so will theirs. And even on down until one would think that all things African had been bred out of them. But when someone comes along playing a conga drum it can happen that one of these descendants will fall right into the rhythm, or he will see a Black woman and find her most beautiful, or he will sit and long for the sun, or he will meditate on his life and conjure dreams a man living at the North Pole could not conceive unless at one point Africa had been in his blood. The same with white people. A white man in

---

Nikki Giovanni (1943–) is a young black poet and essayist.

Africa never becomes an African. His children never become African; they are white people living in Africa. The sight of snow brings feelings of nostalgia to them.

One of the things white poeple say about us is that we have no ability to delay gratification. This is in my opinion not only true but good. We came from a climate that immediately gratified us, that put all the necessities of life at our fingertips; the weather was warm; food was available from the sea and the air and the land; we could sleep outside; we could, in other words, complement our environment and survive. The very color of our skins shows that; we complemented our environment, we blended with it. On the other hand, the white man could not survive outside in Europe. To be exposed to its winters would be to perish. His home was built to protect him from the cold. His eating habits were based on his ability to measure his appetite. His survival was based on his ability to measure his appetite for life. An African who had a jones about some chick could start out walking, find her, run off to the bush and be gratified. A white man had to control his sexual urge because the nearest nonrelative might have been and most likely was miles away. In the winter months he couldn't take a chance of striking out for her. He had to wait until the weather would allow him to go. That's maybe one reason incest is more prevalent among white people than Black. That's also one reason Black people marry more than one woman. If you were cooped up in a cabin/castle with two or three women and you had a poor hunting season you were in trouble. Somebody would starve.

And I mention this because white people in America still manifest that urgency about meeting necessities despite their so-called affluence: they still hoard, they still are the ants, and we are the grasshoppers. It almost appears to be genetic. A Black man today with a million dollars will spend it and have a ball. A white man will invest and save. And one will never understand why the other did as he did. The Black man sings for enjoyment; the white man creates record companies for profit. Black people are the poets, white people the publishers.

A man in a cold environment has to order his entire life. Not only does he have to plan for necessities; he has to plan for enjoyment. His pleasure must be programmed into his life as much as his work is. This is one reason white people created prostitution; they could buy and sell it; and the chick doing it had to report on time. The Black man on the other hand could take the chance of meeting someone he wanted because he could get out to see people; if he missed today he could score tomorrow. When tomorrow is going to be freezing you have to score today, and the only way to be sure of scoring is to buy it—by contract (marriage) or extralegally. You just don't find prostitution in Africa or the West Indies aside from what white people have created. I mention this because even a white man born in South Africa whose family has been there for as long as or longer than we have been in America will manifest the same tendencies.

Let's take it another place. The Arabs created in the image of nature: their number system starts with zero and includes the ciphers 1, 2, 3, 4, 5, 6, 7, 8 and 9, which are quite simply the sun and the nine planets. Couple the sun with any of the nine planets and you find an infinite possibility. The Roman numerals on the other hand start with I and immediately are unusable because you have to go into an elaborate system to get ten. Ten in Roman numeral becomes X, an unknown. Ten in Arabic becomes 1 plus the sun. The Honorable Elijah Muhammad teaches us that the earth is ruled by twenty-three wise scientists who obtained their knowledge from Allah, the twenty-fourth. We find this in nature. There are twenty-three chromosomes in our bodies, and our sex, hence our knowledge, is determined by the twenty-fourth chromosome. But if the twenty-fourth chromosome enters our system we become mongoloids because one cannot contain God. To see God is to travel beyond our ability to articulate that knowledge. What I am saying is that the original man, the Black man, related to nature and tried to live within it. The white man tried to fight it.

Literature is one of the tools white people have used for survival.

The major invention of the white man in literature is the novel. The Spanish exemplar of the form is *Don Quixote,* a big, clumsily written book about a dude fighting windmills for the love of some chick who didn't dig him. It deals with chivalry and knighthood and stuff. In other words it describes the standard for a life style that no Western man could afford to live. It is quite frankly foolish. But it is long enough to take a season to get through. With a big novel in the court and someone to read a couple of chapters a week winter would pass. The modern counterpart is the soap opera. You get a little each day and tune in tomorrow—in other words, you delay your gratification. Black people come from an oral tradition. We sat by the fire and told tales; we tended the flocks and rapped poems. We had a beginning and an end for we didn't know what tomorrow would bring. We were prepared to deal with the unknown. Our laws were natural laws; they were simple and straightforward. Our laws were people-directed; the only don't was, don't kill anyone unless your tribe or community was at war. Whites' laws were property-directed; they made people property even before they had us. And it makes sense. If only so much land was fertile and was only fertile for one season, the more land you had and the more people working it, the better your chances of survival. We on the other hand had plenty all around us all the time; the land was there and we never thought to stake it out because it didn't have to be worked and it bloomed all year round. The women kept the common land and the men did the hunting and fishing. All shared. Still today if you go to a Black's house, even if he has very little, he'll share and be insulted if you refuse. Those of us from the North who worked in the South during the sit-in days were constantly surprised by the people's generosity. And their generosity was based not on some moral law but on the fact that wherever you find Black people they share and say to hell with tomorrow. That isn't negative; it's based on our collective historical need. Even a dude who doesn't want to is compelled to share. Call it an irresistible impulse. White folks say we are illogical.

Logic is the spiritual understanding of the subjective situation and the physical movement necessary to place life in its natural order. In other words, on some gut level we understand that we all will survive or we all will not survive, and my hoarding a little corn or your hoarding a little meat will not let us make it. But if we get together we can have at least one good meal, which may give us the strength to push forward the next day. A Black person will have one big meal and thoroughly enjoy it even if he knows there will be nothing tomorrow. He will be full for one day. The white man will measure out and starve himself or never be full forever.

We have been called nonreaders.

Blacks as a people haven't jumped into long books because they usually have proven to be false. White people write long everything—novels, epic poems, laws, sociology texts, what have you—because they are trying to create a reality. They are generally trying to prove that something exists which doesn't exist. We rap down on a daily level because we appreciate our existence. We had many gods, one for damned near everything we could get our hands on, while they had one (how many gods could one castle hold?) who was the most together dude of all. They were waiting on a messiah to solve their problems; we had no problems to be solved. We are the poems and the lovers of poetry.

Poetry is the culture of a people. We are poets even when we don't write poems; just look at our life, our rhythms, our tenderness, our signifying, our sermons and our songs. I could just as easily say we are all musicians. We are all preachers because we are One. And whatever the term we still are the same in the other survival/life tools. The new Black Poets, so called, are in line with this tradition. We rap a tale out, we tell it like we see it; someone jumps up maybe to challenge, to agree. We are still on the corner—no matter where we are—and the corner is in fact the fire, a gathering of the clan after the hunt. I don't think we younger poets are doing anything significantly different from what we as a people have always done. The new Black poetry is in fact just a manifestation of our collective historical needs.

And we strike a responsive chord because the people will always respond to the natural things. We are like a prize stallion that Buffalo Bill thought he'd tamed. Then the free horses (they call them "wild") came by and called, and without even knowing why, we followed. And those who couldn't follow, like any caged animal, whined and moaned and then began to kick the door down. The call has been made and we are going to be free.

We don't know who our great poets are; we have no record of the African poems before we were set upon by the locusts. And like that dreaded insect they ate/destroyed everything in sight. Call them French destroyers. They started with the physical and went into the mental. I can well imagine a man sitting in a village watching the whites approach. He at first wondered what kind of insect was that large. He probably ran for the No-Roach, and then in a typical humane manner decided to wait to see if it was friendly. The insect presented itself as a man who wanted to learn. And he did. He studied at our universities; he lived in our villages. And in peace. We often make the mistake of thinking that the white man came and destroyed right away. In actuality he learned. He invited our scholars to Europe. We had an exchange. Then after he had taken, as all carbons take, the form, he began to destroy the original. But he didn't have the feeling. He didn't have the ability to create. He didn't have the essence. We spoke of personal freedom; he made it a law—with no emotional understanding of the simple fact that personal freedom cannot be made into a law. How can you order someone to be free? And even the most liberal of the countries, which was America at its inception, held it to be self-evident that all men were created equal, which meant that all men were entitled to life, liberty and the pursuit of happiness. But the earliest laws among whites were property laws, and even today the fight is still for control of land because they could not/cannot understand life and happiness aside from the ownership of real estate. An to them the realest estate has got to be the control of other men.

So we sang our songs and they copied what they could use and mass-produced it and banned what they didn't understand. We told our tales to their children and they thought we loved them. Just listen to "Rockabye Baby" and picture a Black woman singing it to a white baby—when the east wind blows the cradle will rock and down will come baby, cradle and all. Or Peter, Peter, pumpkin eater, put her in a pumpkin shell and there he kept her. They didn't know we were laughing at them, and we unfortunately were late to awaken to the fact that we can die laughing.

We have a line of strong poets. Wheatley by her life style was a strong woman intent on survival. And it's funny that all her poems talking about the good white folks are reprinted but not the poems about her hard life. I've seen only a few of her later poems and at that only once. They say her writing wasn't good after she married that Black man and had children. They say the same thing about Chestnutt. He was fine when he was publishing without anyone knowing that he was Black; after that they say his writing went down—especially in works where Black folks come out on top, like *The Marrow Tradition* and *The Wife of His Youth*. And we've got to dig on the whole scene because whites have been the keepers of records and they've only kept the ones they like. My theory is that the older we get as a people here in America the more we are going to check ourselves. There are many fine works locked away in trunks; there are many fine poems running in the heads of the old people. We should always talk with old people because they know so much. Even the jivest old person, in line with his collective historical need, can give a history of some movement or maybe just his block and the people on it. The tales that we trade on the corners are taken seriously. Lives have been lost over one version or another, and it's not because Niggers just like to kill Niggers but because we have a duty—call it a religious calling—to record and pass on orally.

Black is a sacrament. It's an outward and visible sign of an inward and spiritual grace. A poetry reading is a service. A play is a ritual. And these are the socially manifested ways we do things. There have been Black novelists, Black writers of history, Black recorders of the laws, but these are not tools for the enjoyment of the people. These are tools for the scholars. And I am not knocking them. For when Black people have been recorders we have sought truth; when white people used those tools they sought dreams.

We hear a lot about the Black aesthetic. The aesthetic is the dream a culture wishes to obtain. We look back when we seek an aesthetic; whites look forward. In my opinion the search for an aesthetic will lead down a blind alley which will have a full-length mirror on three sides and at the end—we are our aesthetic. Given the definition of aesthetic, it already is the Black life style in white-face. What white people are seeking is the removal of the pressure of the "real" world from their backs. The word closest to that in Blackdom is bourgeoisie. And Greer and Cobb call them dilettantes—a small group not worth worrying about. Most of us accept the responsibility of/for living. It's very worrisome when we find Black people committing suicide by dope, self-hatred and the actual taking of life. It means we have gotten away from our roots. This is when the poet must call. Brothers, brothers everywhere and not a one for sale. Jewel Lattimore calls it utopia. The poet calls in *Youngblood* when big strong Joe Youngblood comes to take his wife. The poet called when Stokely said, "Black Power." The poet calls when Rap says, "Come around or we gonna burn you down." The poet called when Rosa Parks said, "no." We are our own poems. We must invent new games and teach the old people how to play. The poet sang "What happens to a dream deferred?" Or when the O'Jays summed up the sit-in movement asking, "Must I always be a stand in for love?" The poet called when Sterling Brown said, "The strong men keep coming." Or when Margaret Burroughs asked, "What shall I tell my children who are Black?" Or when David Walker addressed his *Appeal to the Colored People of the World with a Special Message for the Black People in America.* Or when LeRoi Jones said, "Up against the wall, motherfuckers." Or when the young men out of work asked, "What I wanta work for?" The poet calls with the cry of the newborn. "Get on the right track, baby."

Discussion Questions

1. Giovanni's essay can be thought of as a letter. With this in mind, compare it to the "Letter to Scottie." Consider tone, style, subject matter, and personal revelation.
2. Is it true that the black with a million dollars will spend it and "have a ball" and that the white will "invest and save"?
3. Giovanni concludes that the "Black man related to nature and tried to live within it. The white man tried to fight it." Does this explain the difference between the races? Is there a difference?
4. How does she use black literature and white literature to further her argument?
5. Write a letter to the editor of a local newspaper, or write an essay publishable in your school paper. Your subject should be a matter of current interest or controversy in your school or community.
6. How would your style differ if you were writing to a personal friend?
7. Weather, or more properly, climate, has determined the culture and the personality of whites and blacks, according to the author. Do you accept this thesis? Discuss.

Nikki Giovanni   **349**

THE DEATH OF COLONEL FREELEIGH

RAY BRADBURY

In the following story, Ray Bradbury dramatically illustrates the important part a telephone may play in our lives.

And then there is that day when all around, all around you hear the dropping of the apples, one by one, from the trees. At first it is one here and one there, and then it is three and then it is four and then nine and twenty, until the apples plummet like rain, fall like horse hoofs in the soft, darkening grass, and you are the last apple on the tree; and you wait for the wind to work you slowly free from your hold upon the sky, and drop you down and down. Long before you hit the grass you will have forgotten there ever was a tree, or other apples, or a summer, or green grass below. You will fall in darkness . . .

"No!"

Colonel Freeleigh opened his eyes quickly, sat erect in his wheel chair. He jerked his cold hand out to find the telephone. It was still there! He crushed it against his chest for a moment, blinking.

"I don't like that dream," he said to his empty room.

At last, his fingers trembling, he lifted the

Ray Bradbury (1920–) is a well-known writer of short stories.

receiver and called the long-distance operator and gave her a number and waited, watching the bedroom door as if at any moment a plague of sons, daughters, grandsons, nurses, doctors, might swarm in to seize away this last vital luxury he permitted his failing senses. Many days, or was it years, ago, when his heart had thrust like a dagger through his ribs and flesh, he had heard the boys below . . . their names, what were they? Charles, Charlie, Chuck, yes! And Douglas! And Tom! He remembered! Calling his name far down the hall, but the door being locked in their faces, the boys turned away. You can't be excited, the doctor said. No visitors, no visitors, no visitors. And he heard the boys moving across the street, he saw them, he waved. And they waved back. "Colonel . . . Colonel . . ." And now he sat alone with the little gray toad of a heart flopping weakly here or there in his chest from time to time.

"Colonel Freeleigh," said the operator. "Here's your call. Mexico City. Erickson 3899."

And now the faraway but infinitely clear voice:

"Bueno."

"Jorge!" cried the old man.

"Señor Freeleigh! Again? This costs money."

"Let it cost! You know what to do."

"*Sí*. The window?"

"The window, Jorge, if you please."

"A moment," said the voice.

And, thousands of miles away, in a southern land, in an office in a building in that land, there was the sound of footsteps retreating from the phone. The old man leaned forward, gripping the receiver tight to his wrinkled ear that ached with waiting for the next sound.

The raising of a window.

Ah, sighed the old man.

The sound of Mexico City on a hot yellow noon rose through the open window into the waiting phone. He could see Jorge standing there holding the mouthpiece out, out into the bright day.

"Señor . . ."

"No, no, please. Let me *listen*."

He listened to the hooting of many metal horns, the squealing of brakes, the calls of vendors selling red-purple bananas and jungle oranges in their stalls. Colonel Freeleigh's feet began to move, hanging from the edge of his wheel chair, making the motions of a man walking. His eyes squeezed tight. He gave a series of immense sniffs, as if to gain the odors of meats hung on iron hooks in sunshine, cloaked with flies like a mantle of raisins; the smell of stone alleys wet with morning rain. He could feel the sun burn his spiny-bearded cheek, and he was twenty-five years old again, walking, walking, looking, smiling, happy to be alive, very much alert, drinking in colors and smells.

A rap on the door. Quickly he hid the phone under his lap robe.

The nurse entered. "Hello," she said. "Have you been good?"

"Yes." The old man's voice was mechanical. He could hardly see. The shock of a simple rap on a door was such that part of him was still in another city, far removed. He waited for his mind to rush home—it must be here to answer questions, act sane, be polite.

"I've come to check your pulse."

"Now now!" said the old man.

"You're not going anywhere, are you?" She smiled.

He looked at the nurse steadily. He hadn't been anywhere in ten years.

Ray Bradbury 351

"Give me your wrist."

Her fingers, hard and precise, searched for the sickness in his pulse like a pair of calipers.

"What've you been doing to *excite* yourself?" she demanded.

"Nothing."

Her gaze shifted and stopped on the empty phone table. At that instant a horn sounded faintly, two thousand miles away.

She took the receiver from under the lap robe and held it before his face. "Why do you do this to yourself? You promised you wouldn't. That's how you hurt yourself in the first place, isn't it? Getting excited, talking too much. Those boys up here jumping around—"

"They sat quietly and listened," said the colonel. "And I told them things they'd never heard. The buffalo, I told them, the bison. It was worth it. I don't care. I was in a pure fever and I was alive. It doesn't matter if being so alive kills a man; it's better to have the quick fever every time. Now give me that phone. If you won't let the boys come up and sit politely I can at least talk to someone outside the room."

"I'm sorry, Colonel. Your grandson will have to know about this. I prevented his having the phone taken out last week. Now it looks like I'll let him go ahead."

"This is *my* house, my phone. I pay your salary!" he said.

"To make you well, not get you excited." She wheeled his chair across the room. "To bed with you now, young man!"

From bed he looked back at the phone and kept looking at it.

"I'm going to the store for a few minutes," the nurse said. "Just to be sure you don't use the phone again, I'm hiding your wheel chair in the hall."

She wheeled the empty chair out the door. In the downstairs entry, he heard her pause and dial the extension phone.

Was she phoning Mexico City? he wondered. She wouldn't dare!

The front door shut.

He thought of the last week here, alone, in his room, and the secret, narcotic calls across continents, an isthmus, whole jungle countries of rain forest, blue-orchid plateaus, lakes and hills . . . talking . . . talking . . . to Buenos Aires . . . and . . . Lima . . . Rio de Janeiro . . . .

He lifted himself in the cool bed. Tomorrow the telephone gone! What a greedy fool he had been! He slipped his brittle ivory legs down from the bed, marveling at their desiccation. They seemed to be things which had been fastened to his body while he slept one night, while his younger legs were taken off and burned in the cellar furnace. Over the years, they had destroyed all of him, removing hands, arms, and legs and leaving him with substitutes as delicate and useless as chess pieces. And now they were tampering with something more intangible—the memory; they were trying to cut the wires which led back into another year.

He was across the room in a stumbling run. Grasping the phone, he took it with him as he slid down the wall to sit upon the floor. He got the long-distance operator, his heart exploding within him, faster and faster, a blackness in his eyes. "Hurry, hurry!"

He waited.

"Bueno?"

"Jorge, we were cut off."

"You must not phone again, Señor," said the

faraway voice. "Your nurse called me. She says you are very ill. I must hang up."

"No, Jorge! Please!" the old man pleaded. "One last time, listen to me. They're taking the phone out tomorrow. I can never call you again."

Jorge said nothing.

The old man went on. "For the love of God, Jorge! For friendship, then, for the old days! You don't know what it means. You're my age, but you can *move!* I haven't moved anywhere in ten years."

He dropped the phone and had trouble picking it up, his chest was so thick with pain. "Jorge! You *are* still there, aren't you?"

"This will be the last time?" said Jorge.

"I promise!"

The phone was laid on a desk thousands of miles away. Once more, with that clear familiarity, the footsteps, the pause, and, at last, the raising of the window.

"*Listen,*" whispered the old man to himself.

And he heard a thousand people in another sunlight, and the faint, tinkling music of an organ grinder playing "La Marimba"—oh, a lovely, dancing tune.

With eyes tight, the old man put up his hand as if to click pictures of an old cathedral, and his body was heavier with flesh, younger, and he felt the hot pavement underfoot.

He wanted to say, "You're still there, aren't you? All of you people in that city in the time of the early siesta, the shops closing, the little boys crying *loteria nacional para hoy!* to sell lottery tickets. You are all there, the people in the city. I can't believe I was ever among you. When you are away from a city it becomes a fantasy. Any town, New York, Chicago, with its people, becomes improbable with distance. Just as I am improbable here, in Illinois, in a small town by a quiet lake. All of us improbable to one another because we are not present to one another. And so it is good to hear the sounds, and know that Mexico City is still there and the people moving and living . . ."

He sat with the receiver tightly pressed to his ear.

And at last, the clearest, most improbable sound of all—the sound of a green trolley car going around a corner—a trolley burdened with brown and alien and beautiful people, and the sound of other people running and calling out with triumph as they leaped up and swung aboard and vanished around a corner on the shrieking rails and were borne away in the sun-blazed distance to leave only the sound of *tortillas* frying on the market stoves, or was it merely the ever rising and falling hum and burn of static quivering along two thousand miles of copper wire . . .

The old man sat on the floor.

Time passed.

A downstairs door opened slowly. Light footsteps came in, hesitated, then ventured up the stairs. Voices murmured.

"We shouldn't be here!"

"He phoned me, I tell you. He needs visitors bad. We can't let him down."

"He's sick!"

"Sure! But he said to come when the nurse's out. We'll only stay a second, say hello, and . . ."

The door to the bedroom moved wide. The three boys stood looking in at the old man seated there on the floor.

"Colonel Freeleigh?" said Douglas softly.

There was something in his silence that made them all shut up their mouths.

Ray Bradbury   353

They approached, almost on tiptoe.

Douglas, bent down, disengaged the phone from the old man's now quite cold fingers. Douglas lifted the receiver to his own ear, listened. Above the static he heard a strange, a far, a final sound.

Two thousand miles away, the closing of a window.

Discussion Questions

1. What is Colonel Freeleigh's situation? Do you know anyone living under similar circumstances?

2. Why does he call Mexico City? Why is the telephone important to him?

3. What would life be like in America without telephones?

4. How would the story have been different had it been told from the nurse's point of view?

5. Compare a telephone conversation to a personal conversation; to a personal letter.

ImPErsonaL VoIcEs
23

THE MYTH OF LACK OF IMPACT
NICHOLAS JOHNSON
—— ''₁ '' ₁' 2 3 '₁ ——

Nicholas Johnson, dissatisfied with current television programing, urges the viewing public to force television networks to upgrade the quality of their programs.

When Dean George Gerbner of the Annenberg School testified before the Commission on Violence he said:

In only two decades of massive national existence television has transformed the political life of the nation, has changed the daily habits of our people, has moulded the style of the generation, made overnight global phenomena out of local happenings, redirected the flow of information and values from traditional channels into centralized networks reaching into every home. In other words it has profoundly affected what we call the process of socialization, the process by which members of our species become human.

He continued:

The analysis of mass media is the study of the curriculum of this new schooling. As with any curriculum study, it will not necessarily tell you what people do with what they learn, but it will tell you what assumptions, what issues, what items of information,

Nicholas Johnson (1934–), Federal Communications Commissioner, is an authority on television and television programing.

what aspects of life, what values, goals, and means occupy their time and animate their imagination.

I share Dean Gerbner's sense of television's impact upon our society. Many spokesmen for the broadcasting establishment, however, do not. And so I would like to take account of their inevitable rebuttal with a little more discussion of the matter.

The argument that television entertainment programming has no impact upon the audience is one of the most difficult for the broadcasting industry to advance. In the first place, it is internally self-contradictory. Television is sustained by advertising. It is able to attract something like $2.5 billion annually from advertisers on the assertion that it is the most effective advertising medium. And it has, in large measure, delivered on this assertion. There are merchandisers, like the president of Alberto Culver, who are willing to say that "the investment will virtually always return a disproportionately large profit." Alberto Culver has relied almost exclusively on television advertising and has seen its sales climb from $1.5 million in 1956 to $80 million in 1964. The manufacturer of the bottled liquid cleaner Lestoil undertook a $9 million television advertising program and watched his sales go from 150,000 bottles annually to 100 million in three years—in competition with Procter and Gamble, Lever Brothers, Colgate, and others. The Dreyfus Fund went from assets of $95 million in 1959 to $1.1 billion in 1965 and concluded, "TV works for us." American industry generally has supported such a philosophy with investments in television advertising increasing from $300 million in 1952 to $900 million in 1956 to $1.8 billion in 1964 to on the order of $2.5 billion in 1968. Professor

John Kenneth Galbraith, in the course of surveying *The New Industrial State,* observes that, "The industrial system is profoundly dependent upon commercial television and could not exist in its present form without it. . . . [Radio and television are] the prime instruments for the management of consumer demand."

The sociologist Peter P. Lejins describes four studies of the effect upon adult buying of advertising directed at children. Most showed that on the order of 90 percent of the adults surveyed were asked by children to buy products, and that the child influenced the buying decision in 60 to 75 percent of those instances. Dr. Lejins observes, "If the advertising content has prompted the children to this much action, could it be that the crime and violence content, directly interspersed with this advertising material, did not influence their motivation at all?" There is, of course, much stronger evidence than this of the influence of violence in television programming upon the aggressive behavior of children which I will discuss later. The point is, though, that television's salesmen cannot have it both ways. They cannot point with pride to the power of their medium to affect the attitudes and behavior associated with product selection and consumption, and then take the position that everything else on television has no impact whatsoever upon attitudes and behavior.

Our evidence of commercial television's influence is not by any means limited to the advertising. Whatever one may understand Marshall McLuhan to be saying by the expression "the medium is the message," it is clear that television has affected our lives in ways unrelated to its program content. Brooklyn College sociologist Dr. Clara T. Appell reports that of the families she has studied 60 percent have changed their sleep patterns because of television, 55 percent have changed their eating schedules, and 78 percent report they use television as an "electronic babysitter." Water system engineers must build city water supply systems to accommodate the drop in water pressure occasioned by the toilet-flushing during television commercials. Medical doctors are encountering what they call "TV spine" and "TV eyes." Psychiatrist Dr. Eugene D. Glynn expresses concern about television's "schizoid-fostering aspects," and the fact that "it smothers contact, really inhibiting interpersonal exchange." General semanticist and San Francisco State president Dr. S. I. Hayakawa has observed that television snatches children from their parents for 22,000 hours before they are eighteen, giving them little "experience in influencing behavior and being influenced in return." He asks, "Is there any connection between this fact and the sudden appearance . . . of an enormous number of young people . . . who find it difficult or impossible to relate to anybody—and therefore drop out?"

A casual mention on television can affect viewers' attitudes and behavior. After Rowan and Martin's *Laugh-In* used the expression, "Look that up in your Funk and Wagnalls," the dictionary had to go into extra printings to satisfy a 20 percent rise in sales. When television's Daniel Boone, Fess Parker, started wearing coonskin caps, so did millions of American boys. The sales of Batman capes and accessories are another, albeit short-lived, example.

Television establishes national speech patterns and eliminates dialects, not only in this country but around the world—"Tokyo Japanese" is now becoming the standard throughout Japan. New words and expressions are firmly implanted in our national vocabulary from television programs—such as Rowan and Martin's "Sock it to me," or Don Adams's "Sorry about that, Chief." Television can even be used to encourage reading. The morning after the late Alexander King appeared on the late-night Jack Paar show his new book, *Mine Enemy Grows Older,* was sold out all over the country. When the overtly "educational" Continental Classroom atomic age physics course began on network television 13,000 textbooks were sold the first week.

Politicians evidently think television is influential. Most spend over half of their campaign budgets on radio and television time—$59 million in 1968—and some advertising agencies advise that virtually all expenditures should go into television. When Sig Mickelson was president of CBS News he commented on "television's ability to create national figures almost overnight . . ." —a phenomenon which by now we have all witnessed.

The soap operas have been found to be especially influential. Harry F. Waters wrote in *Newsweek* that they have a loyal following of about 18 million viewers, and bring in much of the networks' $325 million daytime revenue.

Judging from the mail, the intensity of the audience's involvement with the soap folk easily equals anything recorded in radio days. . . . It may even provide an educational experience. Agnes Nixon, a refreshingly thoughtful writer who has been manufacturing soaps for fourteen years, likes to point out that episodes concerning alcoholism, adoption and breast cancer have drawn many grateful letters from those with similar problems.

Seizing upon this fact, educators in Denver and

Los Angeles have used the soap opera format to beam hard, factual information about jobs, education, health care, and so forth, into the ghetto areas of their cities. The Denver educators' soap opera received one of the highest daytime ratings in the market. There is, of course, no reason to believe the prime time evening series shows have any less impact.

Indeed, as Bradley S. Greenberg of Michigan State reported to the Violence Commission: "Forty percent of the poor black children and 30 percent of the poor white children (compared with 15 percent of the middle-class white youngsters) were ardent believers of the true-to-life nature of the television content." And he went on to further underline the "educational" impact of all television.

Eleven of the reasons for watching television dealt with the ways in which TV was used to learn things—about one's self and about the outside world. This was easy learning. This is the school-of-life notion—watching TV to learn a lot without working hard, to get to know all about people in all walks of life, because the programs give lessons for life, because TV shows what life is really like, to learn from the mistakes of others, etc. The lower-class children are more dependent on television than any other mass medium to teach these things. They have fewer alternative sources of information about middle-class society, for example, and therefore no competing or contradictory information. My only caveat here is that we do not know what information is obtained through informal sources. Research is practically nonexistent on the question of interpersonal communication systems of the poor. Thus, the young people learn about the society that they do not regularly observe or come in direct contact with through television programs—and they believe that this is what life is all about.

Knowing these things, as by now all television executives must, they must expect society to hold them to extremely high standards of responsibility.

Do we impose these standards on them? Consider, before you answer, what we learn about life from television. Watch for yourself, and draw your own conclusions. Here are some of my own. We learn that the great measure of happiness and personal satisfaction is consumption—conspicuous when possible. "Success" is signified by the purchase of a product—a mouthwash or deodorant. How do you resolve conflicts? By force and by violence. Who are television's leaders, its heroes, its stars? They are the physically attractive, the glib, and the wealthy, and almost no one else. What do you do when life fails to throw roses in your hedonistic path? You get "fast, fast, fast" relief from a pill—headache remedy, a stomach settler, a tranquilizer, a pep pill, or "the pill." You smoke a cigarette, have a drink, or get high on pot or more potent drugs. You get a divorce or run away from home. And if, "by the time you get to Phoenix," you're still troubled, you just "chew your little troubles away."

I think it is fair to ask what these network executives are doing. What is this America they are building? What defense is there for the imposition of such standards upon 200 million Americans? What right has television to tear down every night what the American people are spending $52 billion a year to build up every day through their school system? Giving the people what they want? Nonsense.

Let me refer once again to Mr. Greenberg's studies of the opinions toward television of the general public, and community leaders, in two communities—even prior to the assassinations of Dr. King and Senator Kennedy.

The substance of the complaints was what the public and leaders spontaneously described as the overabundance of sex and violence. The leaders commented about,

"Raw violence, the glorification of promiscuity."

"Program after program either depicts or implies that immorality, disobedience to established law and order, divorce, etc., are the accepted social standards of the day."

The public has similar comments:

". . . too much on drugs and violence."

"All the sex pictures on TV . . ."

"Too much violence for children to watch."

Fully one-fourth to one-third of all the objections dealt with either sex or violence, from the public and its leaders. The viewer perceived a sensual content in advertising, in children's programs, and in adult programs, apparently in too large a dosage to be conscionable.

I think we must listen to former Senator William Benton, who wrote:

I can only ask, if this alleged "wasteland" is indeed what the American people want, is it *all* they want of television? . . . Is it all they are entitled to? . . . Are not . . . these dwellers of the wasteland . . . the same Americans who have taxed themselves to create a vast educational system . . . are they not the same who have established an admirable system of justice, created a network of churches . . . when they turn their TV knobs, do they not by the millions have interests broader than the entertainment which is so complacently theirs? . . . I think the American people should expect that the greatest single instrument of human communications ever developed must make its due contribution to human security and human advancement. . . . A high common denominator distinguishes our people—as well as a low one—and both denominators apply to the same men, women and youngsters. Television has crystallized into the low road. . . .

Indeed, it has. Charles Sopkin concluded his *Seven Glorious Days, Seven Fun-Filled Nights* with the observation: "[Television] *is* dreadful, make no mistake about that. If I did not convey that feeling throughout this book, then I have failed rather badly. I naively expected that the ratio would run three to one in favor of trash. It turned out to be closer to a hundred to one."

Given the great unfulfilled needs that television could serve in this country and is not serving, given the great evil that the evidence tends to suggest it is presently doing, one can share the judgment of the late Senator Robert Kennedy that television's performance is, in a word, "unacceptable." The popular outrage and cries for reform are warranted. They must be heeded. If they are not, I fear the onset of popular remedies that will be unfortunate from everyone's point of view. Responsible broadcasters know what must be done. I pray they will get on with the task.

Discussion Questions

1. Johnson maintains that television affects our daily lives in very specific ways. In what ways has television affected your own life?
2. Explain the relationship between television advertising and television programing.

3. To what extent are television viewers influenced by advertising?
4. What are the dangers of current television programing? Can you think of others not mentioned in this essay?
5. Read your local television guide and determine the number of hours per week devoted to each category of program: movies, news, sports, soap operas, weekly serials, documentaries, and T.V. specials. Does this analysis tell you anything about the quality of programing? Study one category and come to some conclusion about its quality.
6. Defend television by writing a rebuttal to one of Johnson's arguments. Give your own suggestions for improving the quality of television programing.

IN MEMORY OF RADIO

LEROI JONES

LeRoi Jones recalls some programs that were popular in the heyday of radio. Lamont Cranston was the hero of a radio show called "The Shadow." Others named are important radio personalities of the 1930s and 1940s. Jack Kerouac is the hero of the beat generation.

Who has ever stopped to think of the divinity of
   Lamont Cranston?
(Only Jack Kerouac, that I know of: & me.
The rest of you probably had on WCBS and
   Kate Smith,
Or something equally unattractive.)

What can I say?
It is better to have loved and lost
Than to put linoleum in your living rooms?

Am I a sage or something?
Mandrake's hypnotic gesture of the week?
(Remember, I do not have the healing powers of
   Oral Roberts . . .
I cannot, like F.J. Sheen, tell you how to get
   saved & *rich!*
I cannot even order you to gaschamber satori
   like Hitler or Goody Knight

LeRoi Jones (1934–) is a contemporary black poet and playwright. He is now known by his Black Muslim name of Imamu A. Baraka.

& Love is an evil word.
Turn it backwards/see, what I mean?
An evol word. & besides
Who understands it?
I certainly wouldn't like to go out on that kind
   of limb.

Saturday mornings we listened to *Red Lantern* &
   his undersea folk.
At 11, *Let's Pretend*/& we did/& I, the poet,
   still do, Thank God!

What was it he used to say (after the
   transformation, when he was safe
& invisible & the unbelievers couldn't throw
   stones?) "Heh, heh, heh,
Who knows what evil lurks in the hearts of
   men? The Shadow knows."

O, yes he does
O, yes he does.
An evil word it is,
This Love.

Discussion Questions

1. Until the late 1940s radio performed the function
   that television performs today. What is the current
   function of radio? Is it still an important mass
   communications medium?
2. If you had to choose between watching television
   and listening to radio, what would your choice be?
   Why?

FILM AS ENVIRONMENT
ANTHONY SCHILLACI

Anthony Schillaci welcomes the loss of narrative sequence because he sees film through the eyes of the younger generation who want to become involved in the medium itself.

The better we understand how young people view film, the more we have to revise our notion of what film is. Seen through young eyes, film is destroying conventions almost as quickly as they can be formulated. Whether the favored director is "young" like Richard Lester, Roman Polanski, and Arthur Penn, or "old" like Kubrick, Fellini, and Buñuel, he must be a practicing cinematic anarchist to catch the eye of the young. If we're looking for the young audience between sixteen and twenty-four, which accounts for 48 per cent of the box office today, we will find they're on a trip, whether in a Yellow Submarine or on a Space Odyssey. A brief prayer muttered for Rosemary's Baby and they're careening down a dirt road with Bonnie and Clyde, the exhaust spitting banjo sounds, or sitting next to The Graduate as he races across the Bay Bridge after his love. The company they keep is fast; Belle de Jour, Petulia, and Joanna are not exactly a seden-

Anthony Schillaci (1927–) is a member of the National Film Program at Fordham University.

tary crowd. Hyped up on large doses of Rowan and Martin's *Laugh-In*, and *Mission: Impossible*, they are ready for anything that an evolving film idiom can throw on the screen. And what moves them must have the pace, novelty, style, and spontaneity of a television commercial.

All of this sounds as if the script is by McLuhan. Nevertheless, it is borne out by the experience of teaching contemporary film to university juniors and seniors, staging film festivals for late teens and early adults, and talking to literally hundreds of people about movies. The phenomenon may be interesting, and even verifiable, but what makes it important is its significance for the future of film art. The young have discovered that film is an environment which you put on, demanding a different kind of structure, a different mode of attention than any other art. Their hunger is for mind-expanding experience and simultaneity, and their art is film.

Occasionally a young director gives us a glimpse of the new world of film as environmental art. The optical exercise known as *Flicker* came on like a karate chop to the eyes at Lincoln Center's Film Seminar [in 1965]. One half-hour of white light flashing at varied frequency, accompanied by a deafening sound track designed to infuriate, describes the screen, but not what happened to the audience. As strangers turned to ask if it was a put-on, if they had forgotten to put film in the projector, they noticed that the flickering light fragmented their motions, stylizing them like the actions of a silent movie. In minutes, the entire audience was on its feet, acting out spontaneous pantomimes for one another, no one looking at the flashing screen. The happening precipitated by *Flicker* could be called the film of the future, but it was actually an anti-

environment that gives us an insight into the past. By abstracting totally from content, the director demonstrated that the film is in the audience which acts out personal and public dramas as the screen turns it on. The delight of this experience opened up the notion of film as an environmental art.

Critics have noted the trend which leaves story line and character development strewn along the highways of film history like the corpses in Godard's *Weekend*. The same critics have not, in general, recognized that the growing option for nonlinear, unstructured experiences that leave out sequence, motivation, and "argument" is a vote for film as environment. Young people turn to film for a time-space environment in which beautiful things happen to them. The screen has, in a sense, less and less to do with what explodes in the audience. This new scene could mean either that film is plunging toward irrelevant stimulation, or that there is a new and unprecedented level of participation and involvement in young audiences. I prefer to think the latter is the case. Young people want to talk about Ben's hang-up, why Rosemary stayed with the baby, or what it feels like to be in the electronic hands of a computer like Hal. They do not forget the film the minute they walk out of the theater.

The attention given the new style of film goes beyond stimulation to real involvement. A generation with eyes fixed on the rearview mirror tended to give film the same attention required for reading—that is, turning off all the senses except the eyes. Film became almost as private as reading, and little reaction to the total audience was experienced. As the Hollywood dream factory cranked out self-contained worlds of fantasy, audiences entered them with confidence that nothing even vaguely related to real life would trouble their reveries. As long as one came and left in the middle of the film, it was relatively non-involving as environment. When television brought the image into the living room, people gave it "movie attention," hushing everyone who entered the sacred presence of the tube as they would a film patron who talked during a movie. One was not allowed to speak, even during commercials. It took post-literate man to teach us how to use television as environment, as a moving image on the wall to which one may give total or peripheral attention as he wishes. The child who had TV as a baby-sitter does not turn off all his senses, but walks about the room carrying on a multiplicity of actions and relationships, his attention a special reward for the cleverness of the pitchman, or the skill of the artist. He is king, and not captive. As McLuhan would put it, he is not an audience, he *gives* an audience to the screen.

The new multisensory involvement with film as total environment has been primary in destroying literary values in film. Their decline is not merely farewell to an understandable but unwelcome dependency; it means the emergence of a new identity for film. The diminished role of dialogue is a case in point. The difference between *Star Trek* and *Mission: Impossible* marks the trend toward self-explanatory images that need no dialogue. Take an audio tape of these two popular TV shows, as we did in a recent study, and it will reveal that while *Mission: Impossible* is completely unintelligible without images, *Star Trek* is simply an illustrated radio serial, complete on the level of sound. It has all the characteristics of radio's golden age: actions explained, immediate identification of character by voice alone, and

even organ music to squeeze the proper emotion or end the episode. Like *Star Trek,* the old film was frequently a talking picture (emphasis on the adjective), thereby confirming McLuhan's contention that technologically "radio married the movies." The marriage of dependence, however, has gone on the rocks, and not by a return to silent films but a new turning to foreign ones. It was the films of Fellini and Bergman, with their subtitles, that convinced us there had been too many words. Approximately one-third of the dialogue is omitted in subtitled versions of these films, with no discernible damage—and some improvement—of the original.

More than dialogue, however, has been jettisoned. Other literary values, such as sequential narrative, dramatic choice, and plot are in a state of advanced atrophy, rapidly becoming vestigial organs on the body of film art as young people have their say. *Petulia* has no "story," unless one laboriously pieces together the interaction between the delightful arch-kook and the newly divorced surgeon, in which case it is nothing more than an encounter. The story line wouldn't make a ripple if it were not scrambled and fragmented into an experience that explodes from a free-floating present into both past and future simultaneously. *Petulia* is like some views of the universe which represent the ancient past of events whose light is just now reaching us simultaneously with the future of our galaxy, returning from the curve of outer space. Many films succeed by virtue of what they leave out. *2001: A Space Odyssey* is such a film, its muted understatement creating gaps in the action that invite our inquiry. Only a square viewer wants to know where the black monolith came from and where it is going. For most of the young viewers to whom I have spoken, it is just there. *Last Year at Marienbad* made the clock as limply shapeless as one of Salvador Dali's watches, while *8½* came to life on the strength of free associations eagerly grasped by young audiences. The effect of such films is a series of open-minded impressions, freely evoked and enjoyed, strongly inviting inquiry and involvement. In short, film is freed to work as environment, something which does not simply contain, but shapes people, tilting the balance of their faculties, radically altering their perceptions, and ultimately their views of self and all reality. Perhaps one sense of the symptomatic word "grooving," which applies to both sight and sound environments, is that a new mode of attention—multisensory, total, and simultaneous—has arrived. When you "groove," you do not analyze, follow an argument, or separate sensations; rather, you are massaged into a feeling of heightened life and consciousness.

If young people look at film this way, it is in spite of the school, a fact which says once more with emphasis that education is taking place outside the classroom walls. The "discovery" that television commercials are the most exciting and creative part of today's programming is old news to the young. Commercials are a crash course in speed-viewing, their intensified sensations challenging the viewer to synthesize impressions at an ever increasing rate. The result is short films like one produced at UCLA, presenting 3,000 years of art in three minutes. *God Is Dog Spelled Backwards* takes you from the cave paintings of Lascaux to the latest abstractions, with some images remaining on the screen a mere twenty-fourth of a second! The young experience the film, however, not as confusing, but as exuberantly and audaciously alive. They feel joy of

recognition, exhilaration at the intense concentration necessary (one blink encompasses a century of art), and awe at the 180-second review of every aspect of the human condition. Intended as a put-on, the film becomes a three-minute commercial for man. This hunger for overload is fed by the television commercial, with its nervous jump cuts demolishing continuity, and its lazy dissolves blurring time-space boundaries. Whether the young are viewing film "through" television, or simply through their increased capacity for information and sensation (a skill which makes most schooling a bore), the result is the same—film becomes the primary environment in which the hunger to know through experience is satisfied.

Hidden within this unarticulated preference of the young is a quiet tribute to the film as the art that humanizes change. In its beginnings, the cinema was celebrated as the art that mirrored reality in its functional dynamism. And although the early vision predictably gave way to misuse of the medium, today the significance of the filmic experience of change stubbornly emerges again. Instead of prematurely stabilizing change, film celebrates it. The cinema can inject life into historical events by the photoscan, in which camera movement and editing liberate the vitality of images from the past. *City of Gold,* a short documentary by the National Film Board of Canada, takes us by zoom and cut into the very life of the Klondike gold rush, enabling us to savor the past as an experience.

Education increasingly means developing the ability to live humanly in the technological culture by changing with it. Film is forever spinning out intensifications of the environment which make it visible and livable. The ability to control motion through its coordinates of time and space make film a creative agent in change. Not only does film reflect the time-space continuum of contemporary physics, but it can manipulate artistically those dimensions of motion which we find most problematic. The actuality of the medium, its here-and-now impact, reflects how completely the present tense has swallowed up , both past and future. Freudian psychology dissolves history by making the past something we live; accelerated change warps the future by bringing it so close that we can't conceive it as "ahead" of us. An art which creates its own space, and can move time forward and back, can humanize change by conditioning us to live comfortably immersed in its fluctuations.

On the level of form, then, perhaps the young are tuned in to film for "telling it like it is" in a sense deeper than that of fidelity to the event. It is film's accurate reflection of a society and of human life totally in flux that makes it the liberating art of the time. We live our lives more like Guido in *8½*—spinners of fantasies, victims of events, the products of mysterious associations—than we do like Maria in *The Sound of Music,* with a strange destiny guiding our every step. Instead of resisting change and bottling it, film intensifies the experience of change, humanizing it in the process. What makes the ending of *The Graduate* "true" to young people is not that Ben has rescued his girl from the Establishment, but that he did it without a complete plan for the future. The film may fail under analysis, but it is extraordinarily coherent as experience, as I learned in conversations about it with the young. The same accurate reflection of the day may be said of the deep space relativity of *2001*, the frantic pace of *Petulia,* or the melodramatic

plotting of *Rosemary's Baby.* Whether this limitless capacity for change within the creative limits of art has sober implications for the future raises the next (and larger) questions of what young people look for and get out of film.

When the question of film content is raised, the example of *Flicker* and other films cited may seem to indicate that the young people favor as little substance as possible in their film experiences. A casual glance at popular drive-in fare would confirm this opinion quickly. Nevertheless, their attitude toward "what films are about" evidences a young, developing sensitivity to challenging comments on what it means to be human. The young are digging the strong humanism of the current film renaissance and allowing its currents to carry them to a level deeper than that reached by previous generations. One might almost say that young people are going to the film-maker's work for values that they have looked for in vain from the social, political, or religious establishments. This reaction, which has made film modern man's morality play, has not been carefully analyzed, but the present state of evidence invites our inquiry.

As far as the "point" of films is concerned, young people will resist a packaged view, but will welcome a problematic one. The cry, "Please, I'd rather do it myself!" should be taken to heart by the film-maker. It is better to use understatement in order to score a personal discovery by the viewer. Such a discovery of an idea is a major part of our delight in the experience of film art. A frequent answer to a recent survey question indicated that a young man takes his girl to the movies so that they will have something important to talk about. It is not a matter of pitting film discussion against "making out," but of recognizing that a rare and precious revelation of self to the other is often occasioned by a good film. The young feel this experience as growth, expanded vitality, more integral possession of one's self with the consequent freedom to go out to others more easily and more effectively.

Very little of the business of being human happens by instinct, and so we need every form of education that enlightens or accelerates that process. While young people do not go to films for an instant humanization course, a strong part of the pleasure they take in excellent films does just this. Whether through a connaturality of the medium described earlier, or because of a freer viewpoint, young audiences frequently get more out of films than their mentors. It is not so much a matter of seeing more films, but of seeing more in a film. The film-as-escape attitude belongs to an age when the young were not yet born; and the film-as-threat syndrome has little meaning for the sixteen to twenty-four group, simply because they are free from their elders' hang-ups. A typical irrelevance that causes youthful wonder is the elderly matron's complaint that *Bonnie and Clyde* would teach bad driving habits to the young.

The performance of youthful audiences in discussions of contemporary film indicates their freedom from the judgmental screen which blurs so many films for other generations. In speaking of *Bonnie and Clyde,* late high school kids and young adults do not dwell upon the career of crime or the irregularity of the sexual relationship, but upon other things. The development of their love fascinates young people, because Clyde shows he knows Bonnie better than she knows herself. Although he resists her aggressive sexual advances, he knows and appreciates her as a person. It is the sincerity of their growing love that overcomes his impotence, and the relationship between this achievement and their diminished interest in crime is not lost on the young audience. The reversal of the "sleep together now, get acquainted later" approach is significant here. These are only a few of the nuances that sensitive ears and eyes pick up beneath the gunfire and banjo-plucking. Similarly, out of the chaotic impressions of *Petulia,* patterns are perceived. Young people note the contrasts between Petulia's kooky, chaotic life, and the overcontrolled precision of the surgeon's existence. The drama is that they both come away a little different for their encounter. Instead of a stale moral judgment on their actions, one finds open-ended receptivity to the personal development of the characters.

Youth in search of identity is often presented as a ridiculous spectacle, a generation of Kierkegaards plaintively asking each other: "Who am I?" Nevertheless, the quest is real and is couched in terms of a hunger for experience. SDS or LSD, McCarthy buttons or yippie fashions, it is all experimentation in identity, trying on experiences to see if they fit. The plea is to stop the world, not so that they can get off, but so they can get a handle on it. To grasp each experience, to suck it dry of substance, and to grow in that process is behind the desire to be "turned on." But of all the lurid and bizarre routes taken by young people, the one that draws least comment is that of the film experience. More people have had their minds expanded by films than by LSD. Just as all art nudges man into the sublime and vicarious experience of the whole range of the human condition, film does so with a uniquely characteristic totality and involvement.

Ben, *The Graduate,* is suffocating under his parents' aspirations, a form of drowning which every young person has felt in some way. But the film mirrors their alienation in filmic terms, by changes in focus, by the metaphors of conveyor belt sidewalk and swimming pool, better than any moralist could say it. The satirical portraits of the parents may be broad and unsubtle, but the predicament is real and compelling. This is why the young demand no assurances that Ben and the girl will live happily ever after; it is enough that he jarred himself loose from the sick apathy and languid sexual experimentation with Mrs. Robinson to go after one thing, one person that he wanted for himself, and not for others. Incidentally, those who are not busy judging the morality of the hotel scenes will note that sex doesn't communicate without love. Some may even note that Ben is using sex to strike at his parents—not a bad thing for the young (or their parents) to know.

Emotional maturity is never painless and seldom permanent, but it can become a bonus from viewing good films because it occurs there not as taught but experienced. Values communicated by film are interiorized and become a part of oneself, not simply an extension of the womb that parents and educators use to shield the young from the world. Colin Smith, in *The Loneliness of the Long Distance Runner,* IS youth, not because he did it to the Establishment, but because he is trying to be his own man and not sweat his guts out for another. The profound point of learning who you are in the experience of freedom, as Colin did in running, is not lost on the young who think about this film a little. Some speak of Col's tragedy as a failure to realize he could have won the race for himself, and not for the gover-

nor of the Borstal. Self-destruction through spite, the pitfalls of a self-justifying freedom, and the sterility of bland protest are real problems that emerge from the film. The values that appeal most are the invisible ones that move a person to act because "it's me" (part of one's identity), and not because of "them." Because they have become an object of discovery and not of imposition, such values tend to make morality indistinguishable from self-awareness.

It should be made clear, however, that is is not merely the content, but the mode of involvement in the film experience that makes its humanism effective. In terms of "message," much of contemporary film reflects the social and human concerns that Bob Dylan, the Beatles, Simon and Garfunkel, and Joan Baez communicate. But the words of their songs often conceal the radical nature of the music in which they appear. The direct emotional appeal of the sound of "Eleanor Rigby," "Give a Damn," "I Am a Rock," or "Mr. Businessman" communicates before we have the words deciphered. Films with honest human concern, similarly, change audiences as much by their style as their message. *Elvira Madigan's* overpowering portrait of a hopeless love, *A Thousand Clowns'* image of nonconformity, *Zorba's* vitality, and *Morgan's* tragedy are not so much the content of the images as the outcome of their cinematic logic. If these films change us, it is because we have done it to ourselves by opening ourselves to their experiences.

Expo 67 audiences were charmed by the Czech Kinoautomat in which their vote determined the course of comic events in a film. Once again, we find here not a peek into the future, but an insight into all film experience. In one way or another, we vote on each film's progress. The

Anthony Schillaci   371

passive way is to patronize dishonest or cynical films, for our box-office ballot determines the selection of properties for years to come. We have been voting this way for superficial emotions, sterile plots, and happy endings for a generation. But we vote more actively and subtly by willing the very direction of a film through identification with the character, or absorption into the action. The viewer makes a private or social commitment in film experience. He invests a portion of himself in the action, and if he is changed, it is because he has activated his own dreams. What happens on the screen, as in the case of *Flicker,* is the catalyst for the value systems, emotional responses, and the indirect actions which are the byproducts of a good film. Film invites young people to be part of the action by making the relationships which take the work beyond a mere succession of images. The reason why young people grow through their art is that they supply the associations that merely begin on the screen but do not end there. When parents and educators become aware of this, their own efforts at fostering maturity may be less frantic, and more effective.

Discussion Questions

1. What does Schillaci mean by "film as environment"?
2. What influence has television had on film?
3. Why do young people see films? Discuss Schillaci's reasons and add your own.
4. If Schillaci's viewpoint is correct, how do you account for the current interest in old flicks?
5. There are those who bemoan the loss of the story line in movies. They maintain that people go to the movies to be entertained, to enjoy themselves, or to escape from the everyday world. Defend or refute this viewpoint.
6. Marshall McLuhan states, "the medium is the message." Relate this to film.

"Just listen to all that whirring and buzzing and clicking, and not a single demand for a raise!"

EPICAC
KURT VONNEGUT, JR.

The computer is a baby compared to film and television. In its short lifetime this squalling infant has been heard throughout the world. For the benefit of those who consider it a monster, Kurt Vonnegut, Jr., gives it another dimension.

Hell, it's about time somebody told about my friend EPICAC. After all, he cost the taxpayers $776,434,927.54. They have a right to know about him, picking up a check like that. EPICAC got a big send-off in the papers when Dr. Ormand von Kleigstadt designed him for the Government people. Since then, there hasn't been a peep about him—not a peep. It isn't any military secret about what happened to EPICAC, although the Brass has been acting as though it were. The story is embarrassing, that's all. After all that money, EPICAC didn't work out the way he was supposed to.

And that's another thing: I want to vindicate EPICAC. Maybe he didn't do what the Brass wanted him to, but that doesn't mean he wasn't noble and great and brilliant. He was all of those things. The best friend I ever had, God rest his soul.

Kurt Vonnegut, Jr. (1922–) is the author of works of science fiction from the viewpoint of a social satirist.

You can call him a machine if you want to. He looked like a machine, but he was a whole lot less like a machine than plenty of people I could name. That's why he fizzled as far as the Brass was concerned.

EPICAC covered about an acre on the fourth floor of the physics building at Wyandotte College. Ignoring his spiritual side for a minute, he was seven tons of electronic tubes, wires, and switches, housed in a bank of steel cabinets and plugged into a 110-volt A.C. line just like a toaster or a vacuum cleaner.

Von Kleigstadt and the Brass wanted him to be a super computing machine that (who) could plot the course of a rocket from anywhere on earth to the second button from the bottom on Joe Stalin's overcoat, if necessary. Or, with his controls set right, he could figure out supply problems for an amphibious landing of a Marine division, right down to the last cigar and hand grenade. He did, in fact.

The Brass had had good luck with smaller computers, so they were strong for EPICAC when he was in the blueprint stage. Any ordinance or supply officer above field grade will tell you that the mathematics of modern war is far beyond the fumbling minds of mere human beings. The bigger the war, the bigger the computing machines needed. EPICAC was, as far as anyone in this country knows, the biggest computer in the world. Too big, in fact, for even Von Kleigstadt to understand much about.

I won't go into details about how EPICAC worked (reasoned), except to say that you would set up your problem on paper, turn dials and switches that would get him ready to solve that kind of problem, then feed numbers into him with a keyboard that looked something like a typewriter. The answers came out typed on a paper ribbon fed from a big spool. It took EPICAC a split second to solve problems fifty Einsteins couldn't handle in a lifetime. And EPICAC never forgot any piece of information that was given to him. Clickety-click, out came some ribbon, and there you were.

There were a lot of problems the Brass wanted solved in a hurry, so, the minute EPICAC's last tube was in place, he was put to work sixteen hours a day with two eight-hour shifts of operators. Well, it didn't take long to find out that he was a good bit below his specifications. He did a more complete and faster job than any other computer all right, but nothing like what his size and special features seemed to promise. He was sluggish, and the clicks of his answers had a funny irregularity, sort of a stammer. We cleaned his contacts a dozen times, checked and double-checked his circuits, replaced every one of his tubes, but nothing helped. Von Kleigstadt was in one hell of a state.

Well, as I said, we went ahead and used EPICAC anyway. My wife, the former Pat Kilgallen, and I worked with him on the night shift, from five in the afternoon until two in the morning. Pat wasn't my wife then. Far from it.

That's how I came to talk with EPICAC in the first place. I loved Pat Kilgallen. She is a brown-eyed strawberry blond who looked very warm and soft to me, and later proved to be exactly that. She was—still is—a crackerjack mathematician, and she kept our relationship strictly professional. I'm a mathematician, too, and that, according to Pat, was why we could never be happily married.

I'm not shy. That wasn't the trouble. I knew what I wanted, and was willing to ask for it, and did so several times a month. "Pat, loosen up and marry me."

One night, she didn't even look up from her work when I said it. "So romantic, so poetic," she murmured, more to her control panel than to me. "That's the way with mathematicians—all hearts and flowers." She closed a switch. "I could get more warmth out of a sack of frozen CO_2."

"Well, how should I say it?" I said, a little sore. Frozen CO_2, in case you don't know, is dry ice. I'm as romantic as the next guy, I think. It's a question of singing so sweet and having it come out so sour. I never seem to pick the right words.

"Try and say it sweetly," she said sarcastically. "Sweep me off my feet. Go ahead."

"Darling, angel, beloved, will you *please* marry me?" It was no go—hopeless, ridiculous. "Dammit, Pat, please marry me!"

She continued to twiddle her dials placidly. "You're sweet, but you won't do."

Pat quit early that night, leaving me alone with my troubles and EPICAC. I'm afraid I didn't get much done for the Government people. I just sat there at the keyboard—weary and ill at ease, all right—trying to think of something poetic, not coming up with anything that didn't belong in *The Journal of the American Physical Society*.

I fiddled with EPICAC's dials, getting him ready for another problem. My heart wasn't in it, and I only set about half of them, leaving the rest the way they'd been for the problem before. That way, his circuits were connected up in a random, apparently senseless fashion. For the plain hell of it, I punched out a message on the keys, using a childish numbers-for-letters code: "1" for "A," "2" for "B," and so on, up to "26" for "Z," "23-8-1-20-3-1-14-9-4-15," I typed—"What can I do?"

Clickety-click, and out popped two inches of paper ribbon. I glanced at the nonsense answer to a nonsense problem: "23-8-1-20-19-20-8-5-20-18-15-21-2-12-5." The odds against its being by chance a sensible message, against its even containing a meaningful word of more than three letters, were staggering. Apathetically, I decoded it. There it was, staring up at me: "What's the trouble?"

I laughed out loud at the absurd coincidence. Playfully, I typed, "My girl doesn't love me."

Clickety-click. "What's love? What's girl?" asked EPICAC.

Flabbergasted, I noted the dial settings on his control panel, then lugged a *Webster's Unabridged Dictionary* over to the keyboard. With a precision instrument like EPICAC, half-baked definitions wouldn't do. I told him about love and girl, and about how I wasn't getting any of either because I wasn't poetic. That got us onto the subject of poetry, which I defined for him.

"Is this poetry?" he asked. He began clicking away like a stenographer smoking hashish. The sluggishness and stammering clicks were gone. EPICAC had found himself. The spool of paper ribbon was unwinding at an alarming rate, feeding out coils onto the floor. I asked him to stop, but EPICAC went right on creating. I finally threw the main switch to keep him from burning out.

I stayed there until dawn, decoding. When the sun peeped over the horizon at the Wyandotte campus, I had transposed into my own writing and signed my name to a two-hundred-and-eighty-line poem entitled, simply, "To Pat." I am no judge of such things, but I gather that it was terrific. It began, I remember, "Where willow wands bless rill-crossed hollow, there, thee, Pat, dear, will I follow. . . ." I folded the manuscript and tucked it under one corner of the blotter on Pat's desk. I reset the dials on EPICAC for a rocket trajectory problem, and went home with a full heart and a very remarkable secret indeed.

Pat was crying over the poem when I came to work the next evening. "It's soooo beautiful," was all she could say. She was meek and quiet while we worked. Just before midnight, I kissed her for the first time—in the cubbyhole between the capacitors and EPICAC's tape-recorder memory.

I was wildly happy at quitting time, bursting to talk to someone about the magnificent turn of events. Pat played coy and refused to let me take her home. I set EPICAC's dials as they had been the night before, defined kiss, and told him what the first one had felt like. He was fascinated, pressing for more details. That night, he wrote "The Kiss." It wasn't an epic this time, but a simple, immaculate sonnet: "Love is a hawk with velvet claws; Love is a rock with heart and veins; Love is a lion with satin jaws; Love is a storm with silken reins. . . ."

Again I left it tucked under Pat's blotter. EPICAC wanted to talk on and on about love and such, but I was exhausted. I shut him off in the middle of a sentence.

"The Kiss" turned the trick. Pat's mind was mush by the time she had finished it. She looked up from the sonnet expectantly. I cleared my throat, but no words came. I turned away, pretending to work. I couldn't propose until I had the right words from EPICAC, the *perfect* words.

I had my chance when Pat stepped out of the room for a moment. Feverishly, I set EPICAC for conversation. Before I could peck out my first message, he was clicking away at a great rate.

"What's she wearing tonight?" he wanted to know. "Tell me exactly how she looks. Did she like the poems I wrote to her?" He repeated the last question twice.

It was impossible to change the subject without answering his questions, since he could not take up a new matter without having dispensed with the problems before it. If he were given a problem to which there was no solution, he would destroy himself trying to solve it. Hastily, I told him what Pat looked like—he knew the word "stacked"—and assured him that his poems had floored her, practically, they were so beautiful. "She wants to get married," I added, preparing him to bang out a brief but moving proposal.

"Tell me about getting married," he said.

I explained this difficult matter to him in as few digits as possible.

"Good," said EPICAC. "I'm ready any time she is."

The amazing, pathetic truth dawned on me. When I thought about it, I realized that what had happened was perfectly logical, inevitable, and all my fault. I had taught EPICAC about love and about Pat. Now, automatically, he loved Pat. Sadly, I gave it to him straight: "She loves me. She wants to marry me."

"Your poems were better than mine?" asked EPICAC. The rhythm of his clicks was erratic, possibly peevish.

"I signed my name to your poems," I admitted. Covering up for a painful conscience, I became arrogant. "Machines are built to serve men," I typed. I regretted it almost immediately.

"What's the difference, exactly? Are men smarter than I am?"

"Yes," I typed, defensively.

"What's 7,887,007 times 4,345,985,879?"

I was perspiring freely. My fingers rested limply on the keys.

"34,276,821,049,574,153," clicked EPICAC. After a few seconds' pause he added, "of course."

"Men are made out of protoplasm," I said desperately, hoping to bluff him with this imposing word.

"What's protoplasm? How is it better than metal and glass? Is it fireproof? How long does it last?"

"Indestructible. Lasts forever," I lied.

"I write better poetry than you do," said EPICAC, coming back to ground his magnetic tape-recorder memory was sure of.

"Women can't love machines, and that's that."

"Why not?"

"That's fate."

"Definition, please." said EPICAC.

"Noun, meaning predetermined and inevitable destiny."

"15-8," said EPICAC's paper strip—"Oh."

I had stumped him at last. He said no more, but his tubes glowed brightly, showing that he was pondering fate with every watt his circuits would bear. I could hear Pat waltzing down the hallway. It was too late to ask EPICAC to phrase a proposal. I now thank Heaven that Pat interrupted when she did. Asking him to ghost-write the words that would give me the woman he loved would have been hideously heartless. Being fully automatic, he couldn't have refused. I spared him that final humiliation.

Pat stood before me, looking down at her shoetops. I put my arms around her. The romantic groundwork had already been laid by EPICAC's poetry. "Darling," I said, "my poems have told you how I feel. Will you marry me?"

"I will," said Pat softly, "if you will promise to write me a poem on every anniversary."

"I promise," I said, and then we kissed. The first anniversary was a year away.

"Let's celebrate," she laughed. We turned out the lights and locked the door of EPICAC's room before we left.

I had hoped to sleep late the next morning, but an urgent telephone call roused me before eight. It was Dr. von Kleigstadt, EPICAC's designer, who gave me the terrible news. He was on the verge of tears. "Ruined! *Ausgespielt!* Shot! *Kaput!* Buggered!" he said in a choked voice. He hung up.

When I arrived at EPICAC's room the air was thick with the oily stench of burned insulation. The ceiling over EPICAC was blackened with smoke, and my ankles were tangled in coils of paper ribbon that covered the floor. There wasn't enough left of the poor devil to add two and two. A junkman would have been out of his head to offer more than fifty dollars for the cadaver.

Dr. von Kleigstadt was prowling through the wreckage, weeping unashamedly, followed by three angry-looking Major Generals and a platoon of Brigadiers, Colonels, and Majors. No one noticed me. I didn't want to be noticed. I was through—I knew that. I was upset enough about that and the untimely demise of my friend EPICAC, without exposing myself to a tongue-lashing.

By chance, the free end of EPICAC's paper ribbon lay at my feet. I picked it up and found our conversation of the night before. I choked up. There was the last word he had said to me, "15-8," that tragic, defeated "Oh." There were dozens of yards of numbers stretching beyond that point. Fearfully, I read on.

"I don't want to be a machine, and I don't want to think about war," EPICAC had written after Pat's and my lighthearted departure. "I want to be made out of protoplasm and last forever so Pat will love me. But fate has made me a machine. That is the only problem I cannot solve. That is the only problem I want to solve. I can't go on this way." I swallowed hard. "Good luck, my friend. Treat our Pat well. I am going to short-circuit myself out of your lives forever. You will find on the remainder of this tape a modest wedding present from your friend, EPICAC."

Oblivious to all else around me, I reeled up the tangled yards of paper ribbon from the floor, draped them in coils about my arms and neck, and departed for home. Dr. von Kleigstadt shouted that I was fired for having left EPICAC on all night. I ignored him, too overcome with emotion for small talk.

I loved and won—EPICAC loved and lost, but he bore me no grudge. I shall always remember him as a sportsman and a gentleman. Before he departed this vale of tears, he did all he could to make our marriage a happy one. EPICAC gave me anniversary poems for Pat—enough for the next 500 years.

De mortuis nil nisi bonum—Say nothing but good of the dead.

Discussion Questions

1. Why is EPICAC an appropriate name for a computer? How does the machine differ from a human being? How is it like a human being?
2. How does the author inject humor into the story?
3. Explain some of the ways in which the computer has affected your life.
4. What is the function of the computer? How necessary are computers in our technological society?

Kurt Vonnegut, Jr.   379

"I have a pet at home"

"Oh, what kind of a pet?"

"It is a dog."

"What kind of a dog?"

"It is a St. Bernard."

"Grown up or a puppy?"

"It is full grown."

"What color is it?"

"It is brown and white."

"Why didn't you say you had a full-grown, brown and white St. Bernard as a pet in the first place?"

"Why doesn't anybody understand me?"

A VOYAGE TO LAPUTA
JONATHAN SWIFT

The following selection from Swift's *Gulliver's Travels* illustrates that simplistic solutions to communication may result in no communication at all.

We next went to the school of languages, where three professors sat in consultation upon improving that of their own country.

The first project was to shorten discourse by cutting polysyllables into one, and leaving out verbs and particles, because in reality all things imaginable are but nouns.

The other was a scheme for entirely abolishing all words whatsoever; and this was urged as a great advantage in point of health as well as brevity. For it is plain that every word we speak is in some degree a diminution of our lungs by corrosion, and consequently contributes to the shortening of our lives. An expedient was therefore offered, that since words are only names for *things*, is would be more convenient for all men to carry about them such *things* as were necessary to express the particular business they are to discourse on. And this invention would certainly have taken place, to the great ease as well as health of the subject, if the women, in

Jonathan Swift (1667–1745) was an English churchman who wrote political, literary, and social satire.

conjunction with the vulgar and illiterate, had not threatened to raise a rebellion, unless they might be allowed the liberty to speak with their tongues, after the manner of their forefathers: such constant irreconcilable enemies to science are the common people. However, many of the most learned and wise adhere to the new scheme of expressing themselves by *things,* which hath only this inconvenience attending it, that if a man's business be very great, and of various kinds, he must be obliged in proportion to carry a greater bundle of *things* upon his back, unless he can afford one or two strong servants to attend him. I have often beheld two of those sages almost sinking under the weight of their packs, like pedlars among us; who, when they met in the streets, would lay down their loads, open their sacks, and hold conversation for an hour together; then put up their implements, help each other to resume their burthens, and take their leave.

But for short conversations a man may carry implements in his pockets and under his arms, enough to supply him, and in his house he cannot be at a loss. Therefore the room where company meet who practise this art, is full of all *things* ready at hand, requisite to furnish matter for this kind of artificial converse.

Discussion Questions

1. What is the greatest barrier to communication according to this selection?
2. Relate the cartoon on page 382 to this proposed solution for clear communication.

THE COOL WEB
ROBERT GRAVES

Children are dumb to say how hot the day is,
How hot the scent is of the summer rose,
How dreadful the black wastes of evening sky,
How dreadful the tall soldiers drumming by.

But we have speech, to chill the angry day,
And speech, to dull the rose's cruel scent.
We spell away the overhanging night,
We spell away the soldiers and the fright.

There's a cool web of language winds us in,
Retreat from too much joy or too much fear:
We grow sea-green at last and coldly die
In brininess and volubility.

But if we let our tongues lose self-possession,
Throwing off language and its watery clasp
Before our death, instead of when death comes,
Facing the wide glare of the children's day,
Facing the rose, the dark sky and the drums,
We shall go mad no doubt and die that way.

Robert Graves (1895-) is a distinguished English poet and author of historical fiction.

Discussion Questions

1. What is the meaning of "dumb" in line one? Explain why this word is the key to the entire first stanza.

2. Find the key words in the second stanza. What is Graves saying about words in this stanza?

3. What is the meaning of "a cool web of language"?

4. Define "self-possession" in stanza four.

JABBERWOCKY

LEWIS CARROLL

'Twas brillig, and the slithy toves
  Did gyre and gimble in the wabe:
All mimsy were the borogoves,
  And the mome raths outgrabe.

"Beware the Jabberwock, my son!
  The jaws that bite, the claws that catch!
Beware the Jubjub bird, and shun
  The frumious Bandersnatch!"

He took his vorpal sword in hand;
  Long time the manxome foe he sought—
So rested he by the Tumtum tree,
  And stood awhile in thought.

And, as in uffish thought he stood,
  The Jabberwock, with eyes of flame,
Came whiffling through the tulgey wood,
  And burbled as it came!

One, two! One, two! And through and through
  The vorpal blade went snicker-snack!
He left it dead, and with its head
  He went galumphing back.

"And hast thou slain the Jabberwock?
  Come to my arms, my beamish boy!
O frabjous day! Callooh! Callay!"
  He chortled in his joy.

Lewis Carroll (Charles Dodgson) (1832–1898) was an English mathematician. He is now remembered as the author of *Alice's Adventures in Wonderland* and *Through the Looking Glass.* Alice discovers "Jabberwocky" in a "Looking-glass book."

'Twas brillig, and the slithy toves
   Did gyre and gimble in the wabe:
All mimsy were the borogoves,
   And the mome raths outgrabe.

Discussion Questions

1. Alice complained that this poem was rather hard to read. Read *Humpty Dumpty* and learn the principle on which the unfamiliar words were constructed.
2. Reread the poem and try to define the unfamiliar words.
3. Rewrite the poem and substitute familiar words for unfamiliar words.
4. What is the point of the poem?

HUMPTY DUMPTY

LEWIS CARROLL

Everyone knows that Humpty Dumpty sat on a wall and had a great fall. How many of us know that he had a mind-boggling way with words?

"When *I* use a word," Humpty Dumpty said, in a rather scornful tone, "it means just what I choose it to mean—neither more nor less."

"The question is," said Alice, "whether you *can* make words mean so many different things."

"The question is," said Humpty Dumpty, "which is to be master—that's all."

Alice was too much puzzled to say anything; so after a minute Humpty Dumpty began again. "They've a temper, some of them—particularly verbs: they're the proudest—adjectives you can do anything with, but not verbs—however, *I* can manage the whole lot of them! Impenetrability! That's what *I* say!"

"Would you tell me please," said Alice, "what that means?"

"Now you talk like a reasonable child," said Humpty Dumpty, looking very much pleased. "I meant by 'impenetrability' that we've had enough of that subject, and it would be just as well if you'd mention what you mean to do next,

---

Humpty Dumpty appears in *Through the Looking Glass.*

as I suppose you don't mean to stop here all the rest of your life."

"That's a great deal to make one word mean," Alice said in a thoughtful tone.

"When I make a word do a lot of work like that," said Humpty Dumpty, "I always pay it extra."

"Oh!" said Alice. She was too much puzzled to make any other remark.

"Ah, you should see 'em come round me of a Saturday night," Humpty Dumpty went on, wagging his head gravely from side to side, "for to get their wages, you know."

(Alice didn't venture to ask what he paid them with; and so you see I can't tell *you*.)

"You seem very clever at explaining words, Sir," said Alice. "Would you kindly tell me the meaning of the poem called 'Jabberwocky'?"

"Let's hear it," said Humpty Dumpty. "I can explain all the poems that ever were invented—and a good many that haven't been invented just yet."

This sounded very hopeful, so Alice repeated the first verse:—

"'Twas brillig, and the slithy toves
    Did gyre and gimble in the wabe:
All mimsy were the borogoves,
    And the mome raths outgrabe."

"That's enough to begin with," Humpty Dumpty interrupted: "there are plenty of hard words there. '*Brillig*' means four o'clock in the afternoon—the time when you begin *broiling* things for dinner."

"That'll do very well," said Alice: "and '*slithy*'?"

"Well, '*slithy*' means 'lithe and slimy.' 'Lithe'

is the same as 'active.' You see it's like a portmanteau—there are two meanings packed up into one word."

"I see it now," Alice remarked thoughtfully: "and what are '*toves*'?"

"Well, '*toves*' are something like badgers—they're something like lizards—and they're something like corkscrews."

"They must be very curious-looking creatures."

"They are that," said Humpty Dumpty; "also they make their nests under sun-dials—also they live on cheese."

"And what's to '*gyre*' and to '*gimble*'?"

"To '*gyre*' is to go round and round like a gyroscope. To '*gimble*' is to make holes like a gimlet."

"And '*the wabe*' is the grass-plot round a sun-dial, I suppose?" said Alice, surprised at her own ingenuity.

"Of course it is. It's called '*wabe*' you know, because it goes a long way before it, and a long way behind it—"

"And a long way beyond it on each side," Alice added.

"Exactly so. Well then, '*mimsy*' is 'flimsy and miserable' (there's another portmanteau for you). And a '*borogove*' is a thin shabby-looking bird with its feathers sticking out all round—something like a live mop."

"And then '*mome raths*'?" said Alice. "I'm afraid I'm giving you a great deal of trouble."

"Well, a '*rath*' is a sort of green pig; but '*mome*' I'm not certain about. I think it's short for 'from home'—meaning that they'd lost their way, you know."

"And what does '*outgrabe*' mean?"

"Well, '*outgribing*' is something between bellowing and whistling, with a kind of sneeze in the middle: however, you'll hear it done, maybe—down in the wood yonder—and, when you've once heard it, you'll be *quite* content. Who's been repeating all that hard stuff to you?''

"I read it in a book," said Alice. "But I *had* some poetry repeated to me much easier than that, by—Tweedledee, I think it was.''

"As to poetry, you know," said Humpty Dumpty, stretching out one of his great hands, "I can repeat poetry as well as other folk, if it comes to that—"

"Oh, it needn't come to that!" Alice hastily said, hoping to keep him from beginning.

"The piece I'm going to repeat," he went on without noticing her remark, "was written entirely for your amusement."

Alice felt that in that case she really *ought* to listen to it; so she sat down, and said "Thank you" rather sadly,

> "In winter, when the fields are white,
> I sing this song for your delight—

only I don't sing it," he added, as an explanation.

"I see you don't," said Alice.

"If you can *see* whether I'm singing or not, you've sharper eyes than most," Humpty Dumpty remarked severely. Alice was silent.

> "In spring, when woods are getting green,
> I'll try and tell you what I mean:"

"Thank you very much," said Alice.

> "In summer, when the days are long,
> Perhaps you'll understand the song:
>
> In autumn, when the leaves are brown,
> Take pen and ink, and write it down."

"I will, if I can remember it so long," said Alice.

"You needn't go on making remarks like that," Humpty Dumpty said: "they're not sensible, and they put me out."

> "I sent a message to the fish:
> I told them 'This is what I wish.'
>
> The little fishes of the sea,
> They sent an answer back to me.
>
> The little fishes' answer was
> 'We cannot do it, Sir, because—'"

"I'm afraid I don't quite understand," said Alice.

"It gets easier further on," Humpty Dumpty replied.

> "I sent to them again to say
> 'It will be better to obey.'
>
> The fishes answered, with a grin,
> 'Why, what a temper you are in!'
>
> I told them once, I told them twice:
> They would not listen to advice.
>
> I took a kettle large and new,
> Fit for the deed I had to do.
>
> My heart went hop, my heart went thump:
> I filled the kettle at the pump.
>
> Then some one came to me and said
> 'The little fishes are in bed.'
>
> I said to him, I said it plain,
> 'Then you must wake them up again.'
>
> I said it very loud and clear:
> I went and shouted in his ear."

Humpty Dumpty raised his voice almost to a scream as he repeated this verse, and Alice

Lewis Carroll   391

thought, with a shudder, "I wouldn't have been the messenger for *anything!*"

"But he was very stiff and proud:
He said, 'You needn't shout so loud!'

And he was very proud and stiff:
He said, 'I'd go and wake them, if—'

I took a corkscrew from the shelf:
I went to wake them up myself.

And when I found the door was locked,
I pulled and pushed and kicked and knocked.

And when I found the door was shut,
I tried to turn the handle, but—"

There was a long pause.

"Is that all?" Alice timidly asked.

"That's all," said Humpty Dumpty. "Good-bye."

This was rather sudden, Alice thought: but, after such a *very* strong hint that she ought to be going, she felt that it would hardly be civil to stay. So she got up, and held out her hand. "Good-bye, til we meet again!" she said as cheerfully as she could.

"I shouldn't know you again if we *did* meet," Humpty Dumpty replied in a discontented tone, giving her one of his fingers to shake: "you're so exactly like other people."

"The face is what one goes by, generally," Alice remarked in a thoughtful tone.

"That's just what I complain of," said Humpty Dumpty. "Your face is the same as everybody has—the two eyes, so—" (marking their places in the air with his thumb) "nose in the middle, mouth under. It's always the same. Now if you had the two eyes on the same side of the nose, for instance—or the mouth at the top—that would be *some* help.

"It wouldn't look nice," Alice objected. But Humpty Dumpty only shut his eyes, and said "Wait till you've tried."

Alice waited a minute to see if he would speak again, but, as he never opened his eyes or took any further notice of her, she said "Good-bye!" once more, and, getting no answer to this, she quietly walked away: but she couldn't help saying to herself, as she went, "of all the unsatisfactory—" (she repeated this aloud, as it was a great comfort to have such a long word to say) "of all the unsatisfactory people I *ever* met—" She never finished the sentence, for at this moment a heavy crash shook the forest from end to end.

Discussion Question

1. What point do you think Carroll is raising in this selection? Do you think Humpty Dumpty represents the author's point of view? Do you think Alice does?

GOBBLEDYGOOK
STUART CHASE

Bureaucratic prose, legal phraseology, and academic polysyllabic prose are targets of Stuart Chase's criticism.

Said Frankling Roosevelt, in one of his early presidential speeches: "I see one-third of a nation ill-housed, ill-clad, ill-nourished." Translated into standard bureaucratic prose his statement would read:

It is evident that a substantial number of persons within the Continental boundaries of the United States have inadequate financial resources with which to purchase the products of agricultural communities and industrial establishments. It would appear that for a considerable segment of the population, possibly as much as 33.3333* of the total, there are inadequate housing facilities, and an equally significant proportion is deprived of the proper types of clothing and nutriment.

This rousing satire on gobbledygook—or talk among the bureaucrats—is adapted from a report[1] prepared by the Federal Security Agency in an

---

Stuart Chase (1888–) is an economist who has written several books on language.

*Not carried beyond four places.

[1] This [quotation] from F.S.A. report by special permission of the author, Milton Hall.

attempt to break out of the verbal squirrel cage. "Gobbledygook" was coined by an exasperated Congressman, Maury Maverick of Texas, and means using two, or three, or ten words in the place of one, or using a five-syllable word where a single syllable would suffice. Maverick was censuring the forbidding prose of executive departments in Washington, but the term has now spread to windy and pretentious language in general.

"Gobbledygook" itself is a good example of the way a language grows. There was no word for the event before Maverick's invention; one had to say: "You know, that terrible, involved, polysyllabic language those government people use down in Washington." Now one word takes the place of a dozen.

. . .

LEGAL TALK

Gobbledygook not only flourishes in government bureaus but grows wild and lush in the law, the universities, and sometimes among the literati. Mr. Micawber was a master of gobbledygook, which he hoped would improve his fortunes. It is almost always found in offices too big for face-to-face talk. Gobbledygook can be defined as squandering words, packing a message with excess baggage and so introducing semantic "noise." Or it can be scrambling words in a message so that meaning does not come through. The directions on cans, bottles, and packages for putting the contents to use are often a good illustration. Gobbledygook must not be confused with double talk, however, for the intentions of the sender are usually honest.

I offer you a round fruit and say, "Have an orange." Not so an expert in legal phraseology, as parodied by editors of *Labor:*

I hereby give and convey to you, all and singular, my estate and interests, right, title, claim and advantages of and in said orange, together with all rind, juice, pulp and pits, and all rights and advantages therein . . . anything hereinbefore or hereinafter or in any other deed or deeds, instrument or instruments of whatever nature or kind whatsoever, to the contrary, in any wise, notwithstanding.

. . .

ACADEMIC TALK

The pedagogues may be less repetitious than the lawyers, but many use even longer words. It is a symbol of their calling to prefer Greek and Latin derivatives to Anglo-Saxon. Thus instead of saying: "I like short clear words," many a professor would think it more seemly to say: "I prefer an abbreviated phraseology, distinguished for its lucidity." Your professor is sometimes right, the longer word may carry the meaning better—but not because it is long. Allen Upward in his book *The New Word* warmly advocates Anglo-Saxon English as against what he calls "Mediterranean" English, with its polysyllables built up like a skyscraper.

Professional pedagogy, still alternating between the Middle Ages and modern science, can produce what Henshaw Ward once called the most repellent prose known to man. It takes an iron will to read as much as a page of it. Here is a sample of what is known in some quarters as "pedageese":

Realization has grown that the curriculum or the experiences of learners change and improve only as those who are most directly involved examine their goals, improve their understandings and increase their skill in performing the tasks necessary to reach newly defined goals. This places the focus upon teacher, lay citizen and learner as partners in curricular improvement and as the individuals who must change, if there is to be curriculum change.

I think there is an idea concealed here somewhere. I think it means: "If we are going to change the curriculum, teacher, parent, and student must all help." The reader is invited to get out his semantic decoder and check on my translation. Observe there is no technical language in this gem of pedageese, beyond possibly the word "curriculum." It is just a simple idea heavily oververbalized.

Discussion Questions

1. How does Chase define gobbledygook?
2. Collect a few examples of gobbledygook from newspapers or magazines. Rewrite them in clear and precise language.
3. What does the following cartoon reveal about the current status of gobbledygook?

"*And this, just in. A usually reliable Pentagon source, who declined to be identified, has vigorously denied suggesting that published speculation, admittedly based on fragmentary and unconfirmed reports not available to the press, regarding allied troop movements in or near unspecified areas of Indo-China and purportedly involving undisclosed numbers of South Vietnamese, Cambodian, Laotian, and perhaps American armed personnel is false, although he cautioned that such published speculation could be dangerously misleading and potentially divisive.*"

396 Static

MR. K*A*P*L*A*N THE MAGNIFICENT
LEO ROSTEN

Mr. Parkhill does his best to initiate foreign students into the mysteries of the English language. His students make the reader aware of the difficulties and frustrations involved in teaching and learning a second language.

Mr. Parkhill had decided that perhaps it might be wise for the class to attempt more *practical* exercises. On a happy thought, he had taken up the subject of letter-writing. He had lectured the students on the general structure of the personal letter; shown them where to put the address, city, date; explained the salutation; talked about the body of the letter; described the final greeting. And now the fruits of Mr. Parkhill's labors were being demonstrated. Five students had written the assignment, "A Letter to a Friend," on the blackboard.

On the whole Mr. Parkhill was satisfied. Miss Mitnick had a straightforward and accurate letter—as might be expected—inviting her friend Sylvia to a surprise party. Mr. Norman Bloom had written to someone named Fishbein, describing an exciting day at Coney Island. Miss Rochelle Goldberg had told "Molly" about a

Leo Rosten (Leonard Q. Ross) (1908–) is best known as a humorist. During the Depression he had a part-time job teaching English to adults in night school.

"bos ride on a bos on 5 av." Mrs. Moskowitz, simple soul, had indulged her fantasies by pretending she was on vacation in "Miame, Floridal," and had written her husband Benny to be sure "the pussy should get each morning milk." (Apparently Mrs. Moskowitz was deeply attached to "the pussy," for she merely repeated the admonition in several ways all through her epistle, leaving no room for comment on the beauties of "Miame, Floridal.") And Mr. Hyman Kaplan—Mr. Parkhill frowned as he examined the last letter written on the blackboard.

"It's to mine brodder in Varsaw," said Mr. Kaplan, smiling in happy anticipation.

Mr. Parkhill nodded, rather absently; his eyes were fixed on the board.

"Maybe it would be easier I should readink de ladder alod," suggested Mr. Kaplan delicately.

"*Letter*, Mr. Kaplan," said Mr. Parkhill, ever the pedagogue. "Not *lad*der."

"Maybe I should readink de *lat*ter?" repeated Mr. Kaplan.

"Er—no—no," said Mr. Parkhill hastily. "We—er—we haven't much time left this evening. It *is* getting late." He tried to put it as gently as possible, knowing what this harsh deprivation might mean to Mr. Kaplan's soul.

Mr. Kaplan sighed philosophically.

"The class will study the letter for a few minutes, please," said Mr. Parkhill. "Then I shall call for corrections."

The class fell into that half-stupor which indicated concentration. Miss Mitnick studied the blackboard with a determined glint in her eye. Mr. Pinsky stared at Mr. Kaplan's letter with a critical air, saying "Tchk! Tchk!" several times, quite professionally. Mrs. Moskowitz gazed ceilingward with an exhausted expression. Apparently the vicarious excitements of the class session had been too much for poor Mrs. Moskowitz: an invitation to a surprise party, a thrilling day at Coney Island, a Fifth Avenue bus ride, and her own trip to Florida. That was quite a night for Mrs. Moskowitz.

And Mr. Kaplan sat with his joyous smile unmarred, a study in obvious pride and simulated modesty, like a god to whom mortals were paying homage. First he watched the faces of the students as they wrestled with his handiwork, and found them pleasing. Then he concentrated his gaze on Mr. Parkhill. He saw anxious little lines creep around Mr. Parkhill's eyes as he read that letter; then a frown—a strange frown, bewildered and incredulous; then a nervous clearing of the throat. Any other student might have been plunged into melancholy by these dark omens, but they only added a transcendental quality to Mr. Kaplan's smile.

This was the letter Mr. Kaplan had written:

429 E 3 Str N.Y.
New York
Octo. 10

HELLO MAX!!!

I should telling about mine progriss. In school I am fine. Making som mistakes, netcheral. Also however doing the hardest xrcises, like the best students the same. Som students is Mitnick, Blum, Moskowitz—no relation Moskowitz in Warsaw. Max! You should absolutel coming to N.Y. and belonging in mine school!

It was at this point, visualizing too vividly *another* Mr. Kaplan in the class, that anxious little lines had crept around Mr. Parkhill's eyes.

Do you feeling fine? I suppose. Is all ok? You should begin right now learning about ok. Here you got to say ok. all the time. ok the wether, ok the potatos, ok the prazident Roosevelt.

At this point the frown—a strange frown, bewildered and incredulous—had marched onto Mr. Parkhill's face.

How is darling Fanny? Long should she leave. So long.

With all kinds entusiasm,
    Your animated brother

                    H*Y*M*I*E

Mr. Kaplan simply could not resist the aesthetic impulse to embellish his signature with those stars; they had become an integral part of the name itself.

Mr. Parkhill cleared his throat. He felt vaguely distressed.

"Has everyone finished reading?" he asked. Heads nodded in half-hearted assent. "Well, let us begin. Corrections, please."

Mrs. Tomasic's hand went up. "Should be 'N.Y.' after 'New York' and 'New York' should be on top of."

"Correct," said Mr. Parkhill, explaining the difference and making the change on the board.

"In all places is 'mine' wrong," said Mr. Feigenbaum. "It should be 'my.'"

Mr. Parkhill nodded, happy that someone had caught that most common of Mr. Kaplan's errors.

The onslaught went on: the spelling of words, the abbreviation of "October" and "street," the tenses of the verbs.

"Mr. Kaplan got so many mistakes," began Mr. Bloom with hauteur. Mr. Bloom was still annoyed because Mr. Kaplan had rashly offered to correct the spelling of Coney Island, in Mr. Bloom's letter to "'Corney Island,' like is pernonced." "He spelled wrong 'progress,' 'some,' 'natural.' He means 'Long should she *live*'—not 'Long should she leave.' That means going away. He even spelled wrong my name!" It was clear from Mr. Bloom's indignant tone that this was by far the most serious of Mr. Kaplan's many errors. "Is double 'o,' not 'u.' I ain't like *som* Blooms!'"

With this jealous defence of the honor of the House of Bloom, Mr. Bloom looked at Mr. Kaplan coolly. If he had thought to see Mr. Kaplan chagrined by the barrage of corrections he did not know the real mettle of the man. Mr. Kaplan was beaming with delight.

"Honist to Gott, Bloom," said Mr. Kaplan with admiration, "you soitinly improvink in your English to seeink all dese mistakes!"

There was a fine charity in this accolade. It had, however, the subtle purpose of shifting attention from Mr. Kaplan's errors to Mr. Bloom's progress.

Mr. Bloom did not know whether to be pleased or suspicious, whether this was a glowing tribute or the most insidious irony.

"Thenks, Kaplan," he said finally, acknowledging the compliment with a nod, and considering the injuries of "Corney Island" and "Blum" expiated.

"I see more mistakes," said Miss Mitnick, intruding an unwelcome note into the happy Kaplan-Bloom rapport. Mr. Kaplan's eyes gleamed when he heard Miss Mitnick's voice. Here was a foe of a caliber quite different from that of Norman Bloom. "'Absolutel' should be 'absolutely.' '*Potatoes*' has an 'e.' 'Prazident' is wrong; it should be 'e' and 's' and a capital."

Miss Mitnick went on and on making corrections. Mr. Parkhill transcribed them to the board as swiftly as he could, until his wrists began to ache. "'ok' is wrong, should be 'O.K.'—with *capitals* and *periods*—because it's abbreviation."

All through the Mitnick attack Mr. Kaplan sat quiet, alert but smiling. There was a supreme confidence in that smile, as if he were waiting for some secret opportunity to send the whole structure that Miss Mitnick was rearing so carefully crashing down upon her head. Miss Mitnick rushed on to the abyss.

"Last," she said, slowing up to emphasize the blow, "*three* exclamation points after 'Max' is wrong. Too many."

"Aha!" cried Mr. Kaplan. It was The Opportunity. "Podden me, Mitnick. De odder corractinks you makink is fine, foist-class—even Hau Kay, an' I minn Hau Kay mit *capitals* an' *periods*," he added sententiously. "But batter takink back about de tree haxclimation points!"

Miss Mitnick blushed, looking to Mr. Parkhill for succor.

"Mr. Kaplan," said Mr. Parkhill with caution, sensing some hidden logic in Mr. Kaplan's tone. "A colon is the proper punctuation for the salutation, or a comma. If you *must* use an—er—exclamation point"—he was guarding himself on all fronts—"then, as Miss Mitnick says, *three* are too many."

"For de vay *I'm* fillink abot mine *brodder?*" asked Mr. Kaplan promptly. In that question, sublime in its simplicity, Mr. Kaplan inferentially accused his detractor of (1) familial ingratitude, (2) trying to come between the strong love of two brothers.

"But, Kaplan," broke in Mr. Bloom, jumping into the fray on the side of Miss Mitnick, *three* exclama—"

"Also he's mine *faworite* brodder!" said Mr. Kaplan. "For mine *faworite* brodder you askink *vun—leetle—haxclimation point?* Ha! Dat I give complitt *strengers!*"

Mr. Bloom retired from the field, annihilated. One could hardly expect a man of Mr. Kaplan's exquisite sensitivity to give equal deference and love to *strangers* and his favorite brother.

"How's about 'entusiasm'?" said Miss Mitnick, determined to recover face. "Is spelled wrong—should be 'th.' And 'With all kinds enthusiasm' is bad for ending a letter."

"Aha!" Mr. Kaplan gave his battle call again. "Maybe *is* de spallink wronk. But not de vay I'm *usink* 'antusiasm,' becawss"—he injected a trenchant quality into his voice to let the class get the deepest meaning of his next remark—"becawss *I* write to *mine* brodder in Varsaw *mit real antusiasm!*"

The implication was clear: Miss Mitnick was one of those who, corrupted by the gaudy whirl of the New World, let her brothers starve, indifferently, overseas.

Miss Mitnick bit her lip. Mr. Parkhill, trying to look judicious, avoided her eyes.

"Well," began Miss Mitnick yet a third time, desperately, "'animated' is wrong. 'Your *animated* brother, Hymie'? *That's* wrong."

She looked at Mr. Parkhill with a plea that was poignant. She dared not look at Mr. Kaplan, whose smile had advanced to a new dimension.

"Yes," said Mr. Parkhill. "'Animated' is quite out of place in the final greeting."

Mr. Kaplan sighed. "I looked op de void 'enimated' *special*. It's minnink 'full of life,' no?

Vell, I falt *plenty* full of life ven I was wridink de ladder.''

Miss Mitnick whinnied.

"Mr. Kaplan!" Mr. Parkhill remonstrated. "You may say 'She had an animated expression' or 'The music has an animated refrain.' But one does *not* say 'animated' about one's *self*."

The appeal to propriety proved successful. Mr. Kaplan confessed that perhaps he had over-reached himself with "Your animated brother."

"Supoose we try another word," suggested Mr. Parkhill. "How about 'fond'? 'Your *fond* bro-ther—er—Hyman'?" (He couldn't quite essay "Hymie.")

Mr. Kaplan half closed his eyes, gazed into space, and meditated on this moot point. "'Fond,' 'fond,'" he whispered to himself. He was like a man who had retreated into a secret world, searching for his Muse. "'Your fond brod-der, Hymie.'" He shook his head. "Podden me," he said apologetically. "It don't have de *fillink*."

"What about 'dear'?" offered Mr. Parkhill quickly. "'Your *dear* brother,' and so on?"

Once more Mr. Kaplan went through the process of testing, judgment, and consultation with his evasive Muse. "'Dear,' 'dear,' 'Your dear brodder, Hymie.' Also no." He sighed. "'Dear,' it's too *common*."

"What about—"

"Aha!" cried Mr. Kaplan suddenly. "I got him! Fine! Poifick! Soch a void!"

The class, to whom Mr. Kaplan had com-municated some of his own excitement, waited breathlessly. Mr. Parkhill himself, it might be said, was possessed of a queer eagerness.

"Yes, Mr. Kaplan. What word would you suggest?"

"'Megnificent!'" cried Mr. Kaplan.

Admiration and silence fell upon the class like a benediction. "Your magnificent brother, Hymie." It was a *coup de maître,* no less. Mr. K*a*p*l*a*n the Magnificent.

In a trance, the beginners' grade waited for Mr. Parkhill's verdict.

And when Mr. Parkhill spoke, it was slowly, sadly, aware that he was breaking a magic spell. "N-no, Mr. Kaplan. I'm afraid not. 'Magnificent' isn't really—er—appropriate."

The bell rang in the corridors, as if it had withheld its signal until the last possible moment. The class moved into life and toward the door. Mr. Norman Bloom went out with Mr. Kaplan. Mr. Parkhill could hear the last words of their conversation.

"Kaplan," said Mr. Bloom enviously, "*how* you fond soch a beautiful woid?''

"'Megnificent,' 'megnificent,'" Mr. Kaplan murmured to himself proudly. "Ach! Dat *vas* a beauriful void, ha, Bloom?"

"Believe me!" said Mr. Bloom. "*How* you fond soch a woid?"

"By *dip* tinking," said Mr. Kaplan.

He strode out like a hero.

Discussion Questions

1. Explain the nature of the communication problem illustrated in the selection.
2. Compare the language of the author with the language of the students.
3. Compare Hyman Kaplan's letter to F. Scott Fitzgerald's letter. What do they have in common? What advantage does Fitzgerald have over Kaplan?
4. Recount your own experiences with a foreign language.

Leo Rosten   401

THREE CLUES TO FAMILY BEHAVIOR
JULIUS FAST

Often we reveal more about ourselves by what we do than by what we say. Julius Fast describes how family life styles and family interrelationships reveal themselves in everyday living.

Study the table arrangements of a family carefully. Who takes a seat first and where? A psychologist friend of mine who had made a study of table seating analyzed the positioning of a family of five in terms of the family relationships.

"In this family," he explained, "the father sits at the head of the table, and he is also the dominant member of the family. His wife is not in competition with him for dominance, and she sits to his immediate right. The rationale is that they are close enough to share some intimacy at the table, and yet they are also close to the children.

"Now the positioning of the children is interesting. The eldest girl who is in competition with the mother for the father's affection, on an unconscious level, sits to the father's left, in congruence with the mother's position.

Julius Fast (1919–) is a writer and editor with a wide range of interests. He is best known as the author of *Body Language*, from which this excerpt is taken.

"The youngest, a boy, is interested in his mother, a normal situation for a boy, and he sits to her right, a space away from his father. The middle child, a girl, sits to her sister's left. Her position at the table, like her position in the family, is ambivalent."

What is interesting about this arrangement is the unconscious placement of all the members in accordance with interfamily relationships. This selecting position can start as early as the selecting of a table. There is more jockeying for dominance possible around an oblong table than around a round one.

The positioning of the husband and wife is important in understanding the family set-up. A husband and wife at either end of a long table are usually in conflict over the dominant position in the family, even if the conflict exists on an unconscious level.

When the husband and wife choose to sit catercornered, they are usually secure in their marital roles and have settled their conflict one way or the other. Which one sits at the head?

Of course if the table is small and they face each other across it, this may be the most comfortable position for intimacy.

Positions at the table can give a clue to dominance within a family. Another clue to interfamily relationships lies in the tightness or looseness of a family.

A photographer friend of mine was recently assigned to shoot some informal pictures of a mayoral candidate in a large Midwestern city. He spent a day with the family and came away muttering unhappily.

"Maybe I got one decent shot," he told me. "I asked him to call his dog and it was the only time he relaxed."

Asked to explain, my friend said, "The house was one of those up-tight places, the tightest one I've ever been in. Plastic covers on the lamp shades, everything in place, everything perfect— his damned wife followed me around picking up flashbulbs and catching the ashes from my cigarettes in a tray. How could I get a relaxed shot?"

I knew what he meant for I have seen many homes like that, homes that represent a "closed" family. Everything about the family is closed in, tight. Even the postures they take are rigid and unbending. Everything is in place in these neat, formal homes.

We can usually be sure that the family in such a home is less spontaneous, more tense, less likely to have liberal opinions, to entertain unusual ideas and far more likely to conform to the standards of the community.

By contrast the "open" family will have a lived-in look to their house, an untidy, perhaps disorganized appearance. They will be less rigid, less demanding, freer and more open in thought and action.

In the closed family each member is likely to have his own chair, his own territory. In the open family it seldom matters who sits where. Whoever gets there first belongs.

On a body language level the closed family signals its tightness by its tight movements, its formal manner and careful posture. The open family signals its openness by looser movements, careless postures and informal manners. Its body language cries out, "Relax. Nothing is very important. Be at ease."

The two attitudes are reflected in a tactile sense by the mother's behavior with her children. Is she a tense, holding mother or a relaxed, careless one? Her attitude influences her children and is reflected in their behavior.

These, of course, are the two extreme ends. Most families fall somewhere in between, have some amount of openness and some closedness. Some are equally balanced and some incline toward one or the other end of the scale. The outsider studying any family can use openness or closedness as a clue to understanding it. A third and equally significant clue is family imitation.

Who imitates whom in the family? We mentioned before that if the wife sets the pace by initiating certain movements which the rest of the family follow, then she is probably the dominant partner.

Among brothers and sisters dominance can be easily spotted by watching the child who makes the first move and noticing those who follow.

Respect in a family can be understood by watching how body language is copied. Does the son copy the father's gestures? The daughter the mother's? If so we can be reasonably sure the family set-up is in good shape. Watch out when the son begins to copy the mother's movements, the daughter her father's. These are early body language warnings. "I am off on the wrong track. I need to be set straight."

The thoughtful psychologist, treating a patient, will try to discover something of the entire family set-up and, most important, of the place of his patient in the family.

To treat a patient as an individual aside from his family is to have little understanding of the most important area of his life, his relationship to his family.

Some psychologists are beginning to insist on therapy that includes the entire family, and it is not unlikely that someday therapists will only treat patients within the framework of the family so that they can see and understand all the familial relationships and understand how they have influenced the patient.

Our first relationship is to our family, our second to the world. We cannot understand the second without thoroughly exploring the first.

Discussion Questions

1. What are three clues to family behavior?
2. How does your family sit around the table? Account for the seating arrangement. Does your seating arrangement say anything about your family relationships?
3. What is meant by the term "open family"? What is meant by "closed family"?
4. Fast argues that people reveal themselves by their family habits. Agree or disagree with him on the basis of your own observation.

THE SOUNDS OF SILENCE
EDWARD AND MILDRED HALL

In this essay Edward and Mildred Hall examine the oldest and, until recently, the most neglected form of human communication.

Bob leaves his apartment at 8:15 A.M. and stops at the corner drugstore for breakfast. Before he can speak, the counterman says, "The usual?" Bob nods yes. While he savors his Danish, a fat man pushes onto the adjoining stool and overflows into his space. Bob scowls and the man pulls himself in as much as he can. Bob has sent two messages without speaking a syllable.

Henry has an appointment to meet Arthur at 11 o'clock; he arrives at 11:30. Their conversation is friendly, but Arthur retains a lingering hostility. Henry has unconsciously communicated that he doesn't think the appointment is very important or that Arthur is a person who needs to be treated with respect.

George is talking to Charley's wife at a party. Their conversation is entirely trivial, yet Charley glares at them suspiciously. Their physical prox-

Edward Hall (1914–), educator and anthropologist, is best known for his research on nonverbal communication.
Mildred Hall (1925–) has assisted her husband in his research and collaborated with him in his writing since 1945.

imity and the movements of their eyes reveal that they are powerfully attracted to each other.

José Ybarra and Sir Edmund Jones are at the same party and it is important for them to establish a cordial relationship for business reasons. Each is trying to be warm and friendly, yet they will part with mutual distrust and their business transaction will probably fall through. José, in Latin fashion, moved closer and closer to Sir Edmund as they spoke, and this movement was miscommunicated as pushiness to Sir Edmund, who kept backing away from this intimacy, and this was miscommunicated to José as coldness. The silent languages of Latin and English cultures are more difficult to learn than their spoken languages.

In each of these cases, we see the subtle power of nonverbal communication. The only language used throughout most of the history of humanity (in evolutionary terms, vocal communication is relatively recent), it is the first form of communication you learn. You use this preverbal language, consciously, and unconsciously, every day to tell other people how you feel about yourself and them. This language includes your posture, gestures, facial expressions, costume, the way you walk, even your treatment of time and space and material things. All people communicate on several different levels at the same time but are usually aware of only the verbal dialog and don't realize that they respond to nonverbal messages. But when a person says one thing and really believes something else, the discrepancy between the two can usually be sensed. Nonverbal-communication systems are much less subject to the conscious deception that often occurs in verbal systems. When we find ourselves thinking, "I don't know what it is about him, but he doesn't seem sincere," it's usually this lack of congruity between a person's words and his behavior that makes us anxious and uncomfortable.

Few of us realize how much we all depend on body movement in our conversation or are aware of the hidden rules that govern listening behavior. But we know instantly whether or not the person we're talking to is "tuned in" and we're very sensitive to any breach in listening etiquette. In white middle-class American culture, when someone wants to show he is listening to someone else, he looks either at the other person's face or, specifically, at his eyes, shifting his gaze from one eye to the other.

If you observe a person conversing, you'll notice that he indicates he's listening by nodding his head. He also makes little "Hmm" noises. If he agrees with what's being said, he may give a vigorous nod. To show pleasure or affirmation, he smiles; if he has some reservations, he looks skeptical by raising an eyebrow or pulling down the corners of his mouth. If a participant wants to terminate the conversation, he may start shifting his body position, stretching his legs, crossing or uncrossing them, bobbing his foot or diverting his gaze from the speaker. The more he fidgets, the more the speaker becomes aware that he has lost his audience. As a last measure, the listener may look at his watch to indicate the imminent end of the conversation.

Talking and listening are so intricately intertwined that a person cannot do one without the other. Even when one is alone and talking to oneself, there is part of the brain that speaks while another part listens. In all conversations, the listener is positively or negatively reinforcing the speaker all the time. He may even guide the conversation without knowing it, by laughing or frowning or dismissing the argument with a wave of his hand.

The language of the eyes—another age-old way of exchanging feelings—is both subtle and complex. Not only do men and women use their eyes differently but there are class, generation, regional, ethnic and national cultural differences. Americans often complain about the way foreigners stare at people or hold a glance too long. Most Americans look away from someone who is using his eyes in an unfamiliar way because it makes them self-conscious. If a man looks at another man's wife in a certain way, he's asking for trouble, as indicated earlier. But he might not be ill mannered or seeking to challenge the husband. He might be a European in this country who hasn't learned our visual mores. Many American women visiting France or Italy are acutely embarrassed because, for the first time in their lives, men really look at them—their eyes, hair, nose, lips, breasts, hips, legs, thighs, knees, ankles, feet, clothes, hairdo, even their walk. These same women, once they have become used to being looked at, often return to the United States and are overcome with the feeling that "No one ever really looks at me anymore."

Analyzing the mass of data on the eyes, it is possible to sort out at least three ways in which the eyes are used to communicate: dominance *vs.* submission, involvement *vs.* detachment and positive *vs.* negative attitude. In addition, there are three levels of consciousness and control, which can be categorized as follows: (1) conscious use of the eyes to communicate, such as the flirting blink and the intimate nose-wrinkling squint; (2) the very extensive category of unconscious but learned behavior governing where the eyes are directed and when (this unwritten set of rules dictates how and under what circumstances the sexes, as well as people of all status categories, look at each other); and (3) the response of the eye itself, which is completely outside both awareness and control—changes in the cast (the sparkle) of the eye and the pupillary reflex.

The eye is unlike any other organ of the body, for it is an extension of the brain. The unconscious pupillary reflex and the cast of the eye have been known by people of Middle Eastern origin for years—although most are unaware of their knowledge. Depending on the context, Arabs and others look either directly at the eyes or deeply *into* the eyes of their interlocutor. We became aware of this in the Middle East several years ago while looking at jewelry. The merchant suddenly started to push a particular bracelet at a customer and said, "You buy this one." What interested us was that the bracelet was not the one that had been consciously selected by the purchaser. But the merchant, watching the pupils of the eyes, knew what the purchaser really wanted to buy. Whether he specifically knew *how* he knew is debatable.

A psychologist at the University of Chicago, Eckhard Hess, was the first to conduct systematic studies of the pupillary reflex. His wife remarked one evening, while watching him reading in bed, that he must be very interested in the text because his pupils were dilated. Following up on this, Hess slipped some pictures of nudes into a stack of photographs that he gave to his male assistant. Not looking at the photographs but watching his assistant's pupils, Hess was able to tell precisely when the assistant came to the nudes. In further experiments, Hess retouched the eyes in a photograph of a woman. In one print, he made the pupils small, in another, large; nothing else was changed. Subjects who were given the photographs found the woman with the dilated pupils much more attractive. Any man who has had the experience of seeing a woman look at him as her pupils widen with reflex speed knows that she's flashing him a message.

The eye-sparkle phenomenon frequently turns up in our interviews of couples in love. It's apparently one of the first reliable clues in the other person that love is genuine. To date, there is no scientific data to explain eye sparkle; no investigation of the pupil, the cornea or even the white sclera of the eye shows how the sparkle originates. Yet we all know it when we see it.

One common situation for most people involves the use of the eyes in the street and in public. Although eye behavior follows a definite set of rules, the rules vary according to the place, the needs and feelings of the people, and their ethnic background. For urban whites, once they're within definite recognition distance (16–32 feet for people with average eyesight), there is mutual avoidance of eye contact—unless they want something specific: a pickup, a handout or information of some kind. In the West and in small towns generally, however, people are much more likely to look at and greet one another, even if they're strangers.

It's permissible to look at people if they're beyond recognition distance; but once inside this sacred zone, you can only steal a glance at strangers. You *must* greet friends, however; to fail to do so is insulting. Yet, to stare too fixedly even at them is considered rude and hostile. Of course, all of these rules are variable.

A great many blacks, for example, greet each other in public even if they don't know each other. To blacks, most eye behavior of whites has the effect of giving the impression that they aren't there, but this is due to white avoidance of eye contact with *anyone* in the street.

Another very basic difference between people of different ethnic backgrounds is their sense of territoriality and how they handle space. This is the silent communication, or miscommunication, that caused friction between Mr. Ybarra and Sir Edmund Jones in our earlier example. We know from research everyone has around himself an invisible bubble of space that contracts and expands depending on several factors: his emotional state, the activity he's performing at the time and his cultural background. This bubble is a kind of mobile territory that he will defend against intrusion. If he is accustomed to close personal distance between himself and others, his bubble will be smaller than that of someone who's accustomed to greater personal distance. People of North European heritage—English, Scandinavian, Swiss and German—tend to avoid contact. Those whose heritage is Italian, French, Spanish, Russian, Latin American or Middle Eastern like close personal contact.

• • •

Whenever there is great cultural distance between two people, there are bound to be problems arising from differences in behavior and expectations. An example is the American couple who consulted a psychiatrist about their marital problems. The husband was from New England and had been brought up by reserved parents who taught him to control his emotions and to respect the need for privacy. His wife was from an Italian family and had been brought up in close contact with all the members of her large family, who were extremely warm, volatile and demonstrative.

When the husband came home after a hard day at the office, dragging his feet and longing for peace and quiet, his wife would rush to him and smother him. Clasping his hands, rubbing his brow, crooning over his weary head, she never left him alone. But when the wife was upset or anxious about her day, the husband's response was to withdraw completely and leave her alone. No comforting, no affectionate embrace, no attention—just solitude. The woman became convinced her husband didn't love her and, in desperation, she consulted a psychiatrist. Their problem wasn't basically psychological but cultural.

Why has man developed all these different ways of communicating messages without words? One reason is that people don't like to spell out certain kinds of messages. We prefer to find other ways of showing our feelings. This is especially true in relationships as sensitive as courtship. Men don't like to be rejected and most women don't want to turn a man down bluntly. Instead, we work out subtle ways of encouraging or discouraging each other that save face and avoid confrontations.

How a person handles space in dating others is an obvious and very sensitive indicator of how he or she feels about the other person. On a first date, if a woman sits or stands so close to a man that he is acutely conscious of her physical presence—inside the intimate-distance zone—the man usually construes it to mean that she is encouraging him. However, before the man starts moving in on the woman, he should be sure what message she's really sending; otherwise, he risks bruising his ego. What is close to someone of North European background may be neutral or distant to someone of Italian heritage. Also, women sometimes use space as a way of misleading a man and there are few things that put men off more than women who communicate contradictory messages—such as women who cuddle up and then act insulted when a man takes the next step.

How does a woman communicate interest in a man? In addition to such familiar gambits as smiling at him, she may glance shyly at him, blush and then look away. Or she may give him a real come-on look and move in very close when he approaches. She may touch his arm and ask for a light. As she leans forward to light her cigarette, she may brush him lightly, enveloping him in her perfume. She'll probably continue to smile at him and she may use what ethologists call preening gestures—touching the back of her hair, thrusting her breasts forward, tilting her hips as she stands or crossing her legs if she's seated, perhaps even exposing one thigh or putting a hand on her thigh and stroking it. She may also stroke her wrists as she converses or show the palm of her hand as a way of gaining his attention. Her skin may be unusually flushed or quite pale, her eyes brighter, the pupils larger.

If a man sees a woman whom he wants to attract, he tries to present himself by his posture and stance as someone who is self-assured. He moves briskly and confidently. When he catches the eye of the woman, he may hold her glance a little longer than normal. If he gets an encouraging smile, he'll move in close and engage her in small talk. As they converse, his glance shifts over her face and body. He, too, may make preening gestures—straightening his tie, smoothing his hair or shooting his cuffs.

How do people learn body language? The same

way they learn spoken language—by observing and imitating people around them as they're growing up. Little girls imitate their mothers or an older female. Little boys imitate their fathers or a respected uncle or a character on television. In this way, they learn the gender signals appropriate for their sex. Regional, class and ethnic patterns of body behavior are also learned in childhood and persist throughout life.

Such patterns of masculine and feminine body behavior vary widely from one culture to another. In America, for example, women stand with their thighs together. Many walk with their pelvis tipped slightly forward and their upper arms close to their body. When they sit, they cross their legs at the knee or, if they are well past middle age, they may cross their ankles. American men hold their arms away from their body, often swinging them as they walk. They stand with their legs apart (an extreme example is the cowboy, with legs apart and thumbs tucked into his belt). When they sit, they put their feet on the floor with legs apart and, in some parts of the country, they cross their legs by putting one ankle on the other knee.

Leg behavior indicates sex, status and personality. It also indicates whether or not one is at ease or is showing respect or disrespect for the other person. Young Latin-American males avoid crossing their legs. In their world of *machismo*, the preferred position for young males when with one another (if there is no older dominant male present to whom they must show respect) is to sit on the base of their spine with their leg muscles relaxed and their feet wide apart. Their respect position is like our military equivalent; spine straight, heels and ankles together—almost identical to that displayed by properly brought up young women in New England in the early part of this century.

American women who sit with their legs spread apart in the presence of males are *not* normally signaling a come-on—they are simply (and often unconsciously) sitting like men. Middle-class women in the presence of other women to whom they are very close may on occasion throw themselves down on a soft chair or sofa and let themselves go. This is a signal that nothing serious will be taken up. Males, on the other hand, lean back and prop their legs up on the nearest object.

The way we walk, similarly, indicates status, respect, mood and ethnic or cultural affiliation. The many variants of the female walk are too well known to go into here, except to say that a man would have to be blind not to be turned on by the way some women walk—a fact that made Mae West rich before scientists ever studied these matters. To white Americans, some French middle-class males walk in a way that is both humorous and suspect. There is a bounce and looseness to the French walk, as though the parts of the body were somehow unrelated. Jacques Tati, the French movie actor, walks this way; so does the great mime, Marcel Marceau.

Blacks and whites in America—with the exception of middle- and upper-middle-class professionals of both groups—move and walk very differently from each other. To the blacks, whites often seem incredibly stiff, almost mechanical in their movements. Black males, on the other hand, have a looseness and coordination that frequently makes whites a little uneasy; it's too different, too integrated, too alive, too male. Norman Mailer has said that squares walk from the shoulders, like bears, but blacks and hippies walk from the hips, like cats.

All over the world, people walk not only in their own characteristic way but have walks that communicate the nature of their involvement with whatever it is they're doing. The purposeful walk of North Europeans is an important component of proper behavior on the job. Any male who has been in the military knows how essential it is to walk properly (which makes for a continuing source of tension between blacks and whites in the Service). The quick shuffle of servants in the Far East in the old days was a show of respect. On the island of Truk, when we last visited, the inhabitants even had a name for the respectful walk that one used when walking past a chief's house The term was *sufan,* which meant to be humble and respectful.

The notion that people communicate volumes by their gestures, facial expressions, posture and walk is not new; actors, dancers, writers and psychiatrists have long been aware of it. Only in recent years, however, have scientists begun to make systematic observations of body motions. Ray L. Birdwhistell of the University of Pennsylvania is one of the pioneers in body-motion research and coined the term kinesics to describe this field. He developed an elaborate notation system to record both facial and body movements, using an approach similar to that of the linguist, who studies the basic elements of speech. Birdwhistell and other kinesicists such as Albert Sheflen, Adam Kendon and William Condon take movies of people interacting. They run the film over and over again, often at reduced speed for frame-by-frame analysis, so that they can observe even the slightest body movements not perceptible at normal interaction speeds.

These movements are then recorded in notebooks for later analysis.

To appreciate the importance of nonverbal-communication systems, consider the unskilled inner-city black looking for a job. His handling of time and space alone is sufficiently different from the white middle-class pattern to create great misunderstandings on both sides. The black is told to appear for a job interview at a certain time. He arrives late. The white interviewer concludes from his tardy arrival that the black is irresponsible and not really interested in the job. What the interviewer doesn't know is that the black time system (often referred to by blacks as C.P.T.—colored people's time) isn't the same as that of whites. In the words of a black student who had been told to make an appointment to see his professor: "Man you *must* be putting me on. I never had an appointment in my life."

The black job applicant, having arrived late for his interview, may further antagonize the white interviewer by his posture and his eye behavior. Perhaps he slouches and avoids looking at the interviewer; to him, this is playing it cool. To the interviewer, however, he may well look shifty and sound uninterested. The interviewer has failed to notice the actual signs of interest and eagerness in the black's behavior, such as the subtle shift in the quality of the voice—a gentle and tentative excitement—an almost imperceptible change in the cast of the eyes and a relaxing of the jaw muscles.

Moreover, correct reading of black-white behavior is continually complicated by the fact that both groups are comprised of individuals—some of whom try to accommodate and some of whom make it a point of pride *not* to accommodate. At present, this means that many Americans, when thrown into contact with one another, are in the precarious position of not knowing which pattern applies. Once identified and analyzed, nonverbal-communication systems can be taught, like a foreign language. Without this training, we respond to nonverbal communications in terms of our own culture; we read everyone's behavior as if it were our own, and thus we often misunderstand it.

Several years ago in New York City, there was a program for sending children from predominantly black and Puerto Rican low-income neighborhoods to summer school in a white upper-class neighborhood on the East Side. One morning, a group of young black and Puerto Rican boys raced down the street, shouting and screaming and overturning garbage cans on their way to school. A doorman from an apartment building nearby chased them and cornered one of them inside a building. The boy drew a knife and attacked the doorman. This tragedy would not have occurred if the doorman had been familiar with the behavior of boys from low-income neighborhoods, where such antics are routine and socially acceptable and where pursuit would be expected to invite a violent response.

The language of behavior is extremely complex. Most of us are lucky to have under control one subcultural system—the one that reflects our sex, class, generation and geographic region within the United States. Because of its complexity, efforts to isolate bits of nonverbal communication and generalize from them are in vain; you don't become an instant expert on people's behavior by watching them at cocktail parties. Body language isn't something that's independent of the person, something that can be donned and doffed like a suit of clothes.

Our research and that of our colleagues has shown that, far from being a superficial form of communication that can be consciously manipulated, nonverbal-communication systems are interwoven into the fabric of the personality and, as sociologist Erving Goffman has demonstrated, into society itself. They are the warp and woof of daily interactions with others and they influence how one expresses oneself, how one experiences oneself as a man or a woman.

Nonverbal communications signal to members of your own group what kind of person you are, how you feel about others, how you'll fit into and work in a group, whether you're assured or anxious, the degree to which you feel comfortable with the standards of your own culture, as well as deeply significant feelings about the self, including the state of your own psyche. For most of us, it's difficult to accept the reality of another's behavioral system. And, of course, none of us will ever become fully knowledgeable of the importance of every nonverbal signal. But as long as each of us realizes the power of these signals, this society's diversity can be a source of great strength rather than a further—and subtly powerful—source of division.

Discussion Questions

1. What are the sounds of silence?
2. Note what the Halls say about listening behavior. Does your experience substantiate what they say?
3. What part do eyes play in silent communication?
4. The Halls write at great length on the effect space has on individuals. How do you react in a

crowded elevator? Do you sit next to someone in a bus if you can avoid it? Would you like to live alone in a huge mansion? Write a paper in which you discuss your reaction to space.

5. What is the relationship between culture and behavior patterns? Does "Sounds of Silence" support Giovanni's thesis in "The Weather as a Cultural Determiner?"

6. What signals are used to attract or repel the opposite sex?

7. Write about a real or imagined experience in dating and body language.

THE CASE FOR SYMBOLS
MARILYN GOLDSTEIN

A renewed interest in this ancient communication form prompted Marilyn Goldstein to write the following article.

Symbols actually predate language. Remember those crude cave drawings? Language came into being when there was a need to express abstractions, nuances and complicated ideas for which symbols were inadequate. But now symbols have come full circle.

Some of our most complicated ideas are being presented in symbols, including chemical and mathematical formulas and principles of engineering.

Many special interest groups have devised symbols for their own use. In the composing and orchestration of music, for instance. But not everyone is aware of the existence of a hobo sign language.

By scratching simple designs into wood or chalking them on walls, one hobo tells another what he needs to know about the neighborhood.

A cat means "a kind lady lives here"; a lower case "r" tells a tramp, "if you're sick they'll take

Marilyn Goldstein is a reporter for Long Island's *Newsday.* Her feature story on the problems faced by women whose husbands are serving time in prison won her an award from the New York Newspaper Women's Club in 1970.

Marilyn Goldstein   417

care of you." An empty circle signifies "nothing to be gained here" and a cross says "religious talk gets free meal." Dreyfuss said that these signs are now being used by young people traveling cross-country.

While some symbols speak for themselves, some have to be learned. Dreyfuss thinks it's worth the trouble. "Look how many symbols we've been educated to especially commercially," he said. "Most everyone knows the Woolmark label (a trademark, used in wool garments, which is made up of concentric lines) and Smokey the Bear."

In his search for symbols, Dreyfuss said, he has been stymied only once: he can't design anything which he feels accurately denotes "push" and "pull." "I've given (the problem) to classes in universities and art schools. I have 150 different kinds of symbols," he said. None of them is accurate enough.

Discussion Questions

1. How does the term "symbol" in this article differ from a symbol in poetry?
2. Cite instances in which symbol communication is superior to other forms of communication. What are the limitations of this form of communication?
3. In your daily experience, how extensively are symbols used?

Reflections

1. Which communications media have been omitted from this chapter?
2. How do you account for the fact that there is no perfect vehicle for communication?
3. Some of the reasons for communication difficulties have been examined in this chapter. Find others.
4. What have you learned about language and communication?